Spun Out

A BLACKTOP COWBOYS® NOVEL

LORELEI JAMES

JOVE
New York

A JOVE BOOK
Published by Berkley
An imprint of Penguin Random House LLC
penguinrandomhouse.com

Library of Congress Cataloging-in-Publication Data

Names: James, Lorelei, author.
Title: Spun out / Lorelei James.
Description: First Edition. | New York : Jove, 2019. | Series: A Blacktop Cowboys novel
Identifiers: LCCN 2019014056 | ISBN 9780399584138 (pbk.) |
ISBN 9780399584145 (ebook)
Subjects: | GSAFD: Love stories.
Classification: LCC PS3610.A4475 S68 2019 | DDC 813/.6—dc23
LC record available at https://lccn.loc.gov/2019014056

First Edition: November 2019

Printed in the United States of America
1 3 5 7 9 10 8 6 4 2

Cover art © Aleta Rafton
Cover design by Colleen Reinhart

Chapter One

"*I* quit."

No no no no no no no, not again.

Streeter Hale practically had to run after his babysitter as she hoofed it away from the house. "Please wait just a minute, Mrs. McCutcheon, I'm sure we can find a better way to deal with—"

That was all he got out before she whirled around so fast he nearly plowed into her.

"I'm done. That's it. I've tried. I've failed. Good luck finding a re-placement caregiver. You'll need it since I was your last option at the agency." Through gritted teeth she said, "That child . . ."

Don't you dare say it. I swear I will lose my shit if you call my daughter some-thing like the devil's spawn or a demon child.

"That child . . . what?" he said tersely.

"That child needs a firmer hand." She raised her chin and glared at him. "I have forty years of childcare experience. In addition to running a daycare and a preschool for twenty-five years, I have four children of my own and ten grandchildren. In those forty years I've never let a child best me. Never. Congratulations. Your five-year-old daughter did what so many others before her tried and failed to do: made me want to quit."

Streeter locked eyes with the older woman, who was a dead ringer for Mrs. Doubtfire. "Can I ask what Olivia did this time?"

"The fact you had to tack on 'this time' is the biggest indicator that there is a problem, Mr. Hale. It wasn't one action, although her drum solo on pots and pans was the final straw."

"I'm sorry."

She harrumphed. "*Olivia* should be apologizing, not you. Stop letting her use her mother's death as an excuse to misbehave—she's not the only child who's lost a parent. Besides, she's five years old, for crying out loud. She'll be starting kindergarten in the fall. The teacher won't put up with her tantrums or her backtalking or her manipulations. And you shouldn't either."

Why don't you tell me how you really feel?

But she wasn't the first person who'd told him that. With her being the sixth childcare provider who'd quit in the past eighteen months . . . he had to admit something had to change. "Thank you for your advice, Mrs. McCutcheon."

She sent him a look that said she didn't believe he'd take it. She shrugged and continued her escape.

Streeter took several deep breaths. Then he counted to ten slowly, six times, before he headed into his house.

The trailer was completely quiet, but the place was a total wreck.

He said, "Olivia. Come out here."

No response.

Louder, he said, "Now. I mean it."

The crocheted afghan on the back of the sofa cushion moved against the paneled wall and he watched his daughter crawl out from behind the tweed couch.

Kid was like a little mouse, squeezing into the tightest spaces.

Her super fine blond hair nearly stood on end from static electricity. His eyes narrowed on her clothing. Not what he'd dressed her in when he'd left the house two hours ago. She'd donned her one-piece mermaid swimsuit, pairing it with her *Frozen* Elsa leggings, the plaid satin Christmas skirt from last year and a beaded metal necklace. His heart stopped as he imagined that necklace getting caught in the loose threads on the back of the couch and choking her. Not to mention the fact she'd somehow gotten into his closet where he'd stashed her mother's costume jewelry—an area he'd warned her multiple times was off-limits.

Pick your battles. Do not give in to your fear by becoming angry and yelling.

That was hard as hell when his little spitfire looked at him defiantly and said, "What?"

"You know what." He pointed to the time-out chair. "Park it."

"But, Daddy—"

"Right now, Olivia Joyce."

Her blue eyes widened. He only pulled out her middle name when she was in deep shit. She dramatically flopped in the chair like a disgusted teen. Tough for a five-year-old to pull off, but she managed it.

"Tell me what happened with Mrs. McCutcheon today."

"She made me sit at the table and color." Her freckled nose wrinkled. "I told her I wanted to play the drums. She said no and when she went to the bathroom I got all the stuff out because she was in there a really really *really* long time."

"And?" he prompted again.

Her bare feet began to swing beneath the chair. "And when she finally came out, she told me to stop beatin' on the pans."

"Did you?"

She shook her head. "Then she tried to *make* me stop, but it's not my fault she tripped over my jump rope and fell down."

Streeter pinned her with a look. "Where was the jump rope, Olivia?"

"Umm . . . I tied it between a chair leg and the cupboard door handle."

"Like a booby trap?" he demanded.

She frowned. "A what?"

"A hidden trap."

"Well, yeah, 'cept it wasn't really hidden. I was just tryin' to keep her from comin' into the kitchen and stopping my drum practice."

He deeply regretted letting her watch that *Drumline* movie a few months back; she'd been obsessed with turning everything into a percussion instrument ever since. "Regardless. Who was in charge?"

"Mrs. McC."

"And if she told you no . . . what were you supposed to do?"

Olivia crossed her arms over her chest. "Listen to her and do what she says."

"And you didn't."

"It's *my* house, Daddy. Why won't she ever let me do what *I* want to do in my own house?"

"We've talked about this a hundred times, Olivia. You are *not* the adult. You are *not* in charge. *You* don't make the rules. You *follow* the rules set by the adults. *All* the rules. *All* the time."

"Even if the rules are dumb?" she countered.

"Yes." Streeter removed his cowboy hat and ran his hand through his sweaty hair. "And now I've had to take time off from work. So get your boots on, girlie, because we're leavin'."

"Mrs. McC isn't waitin' outside until you're done *setting me straight*?"

Good lord. The mouth and the brain on this girl. "No. She quit."

"Oh." Olivia slumped in the chair. "She smelled weird anyway."

His brain cautioned him not to ask, but his mouth was already moving. "What do you mean by *weird*?"

"She smelled mean."

"How do you know what mean smells like?"

"Because it smells like her."

Okay, then. "Get movin'. I don't wanna hear any complaints about you havin' a peanut butter sandwich for lunch again today."

"I'm comin' to work with you?"

Streeter stopped halfway to the kitchen and looked back at her. "Where else did you think you were gonna go?"

Olivia hopped off the chair. "To Aunt Jade's house."

"She just had baby Micah two months ago, sweetheart. She's busy with him and your cousin Amber."

"But I could help her!"

His sweet sister-in-law Jade was on the very short list of people who could handle Olivia on a regular basis. But he'd been careful not to overstep his bounds with his brother's wife, asking too much of her when it came to taking care of his daughter—even before Jade had two kids under age two.

"I would follow all the rules for her. I always do. Please, Daddy? I'll be good. I promise."

He had a lightbulb moment. "Is that what this has been about? You actin' up so Mrs. McC quits and you expecting that I'll let you stay with Jade instead?"

She looked guilty.

"Olivia, that ain't how things work. You know it. Now while I'm makin' your lunch, grab something to do in the truck 'cause you're gonna be in there a few hours."

"*Hours?*" she repeated with horror. "What am I s'posed to do for that long?"

"Bring your coloring stuff."

"Boring," she said with a sniff. "Can I play with your phone?"

"No." Maybe his smile was a little insincere when he said, "Or you could always practice your drumming on the dashboard."

∽

Later that night, while Olivia watched a movie, Streeter scoured Craigslist for potential daycare options. With Olivia signed up for a half a day at the Learning Center in Casper, and a full day at the upcoming Split

Rock Summer Day Camp, he only needed in-home daycare three days a week. Surely there had to be high school or college students looking for a part-time summer job. Without the agency fees tacked on he could afford to pay four bucks an hour more than the standard rate.

He followed link after link until his vision went blurry and his frustration mounted. As he was about to give up, he saw an ad for a babysitters' co-op, which appeared to be run by a woman and six of her female family members. He filled out the form, clicked send and crossed his fingers they'd get back to him soon.

Ten minutes later his phone rang. "Hello?"

"Mr. Hale?"

"Speakin'. Who's this?"

"Marianne Smolen. You sent an online inquiry to Helping Hands Daycare Co-op?"

"Wow. That's what I call a fast response."

"This is the only time of day I can deal with business. So before I get to your questions . . . can you give me some more family information?"

A ball of dread tightened in his gut. "Sure. What would you like to know?'

"You indicated that your daughter Olivia is five and you've been a single parent since she was six months old?"

"Yes. Her mother died when she was a baby." *Please don't ask specifics.*

"I'm sorry. As a single parent myself, I know how hard that is. Do you have other family members helping you out with her care?"

"Olivia spent one day a week with my sister-in-law until she had a baby two months ago. Olivia spends some weekends with her maternal grandparents. The rest of my workin' hours she's either with me or I have someone come in to take care of her."

"She's not new to a daycare situation."

"No. We tried the drop-off type a couple of times and it never worked out. In-home daycare is better for both of us."

"For this summer session you're only looking for part-time care?"

"Yeah. Olivia will be attending two different camps, so I'll only need daycare three other days during the week."

"Living in Muddy Gap is a bit of a drive for us, since we're based in Rawlins."

"I'm willin' to pay for travel time. But they'll need to be here by seven thirty a.m."

"Would you need a childcare provider with her own vehicle?"

Weird question. "Only to drive here. I'm not lookin' for someone to haul Olivia around, just someone to take care of her in her own home when I'm at work."

"Understood. To be clear, the reason we're called a co-op is I have six daycare workers in my employ. Because you'd be a part-time client, I can't guarantee a specific caregiver, but I believe that might serve your needs better given the other information you provided about Olivia."

"Okay."

"You have any questions for me?" she prompted.

"What are the ages of the caregivers you're considering for this position?"

"All teenagers, all out of high school and attending college, all with great referrals, which can be shared upon request." She paused. "I'll be blunt, Mr. Hale. This isn't the most economical option for any family. Are you sure you want to proceed?"

Streeter's cheeks flushed. He hated the assumption that he was dirt poor just because he was a ranch hand and lived in a trailer. "Yep. Do I need to pay a deposit?"

"We call it an application fee, which you can pay online." Papers shuffled in the background. "I'd like to send a caregiver one day this week. Wednesday at noon?"

"That'll work. Have her call my cell when she arrives at the Split Rock Resort and I'll meet her and show her where to go."

"Perfect. I'll email you an invoice with the pay link. And if anything changes, please contact us. We have a twenty-four-hour answering service."

"Will do."

She hung up.

Streeter stared at the phone for a moment. Then he said, "Huh. I guess when one door closes—"

"I always close the door, Daddy," Olivia interjected.

He glanced over at his daughter sprawled on the couch, wondering how much of his conversation she'd paid attention to. "Most of the time you do."

"Did I get a new babysitter?"

So she had been listening. "Yep. Someone will be here this week."

"Is she old like Mrs. McC?"

"Nope."

She rolled on to her stomach and looked at him. "I heard you tell 'em I don't got a mommy."

"That's something they need to know, squirt."

Olivia crossed, uncrossed and recrossed her ankles as she studied him.

He braced himself. Any change in her life triggered questions about her mother. He just hoped it didn't trigger her night terrors too.

"Can I ask you something, Daddy?"

"Sure."

"If I had my mommy would I still have a babysitter?"

How was he supposed to answer that? "Maybe."

She considered his response for a moment. "Gramma Deenie always tells me that my mommy loved me so so so much." Cross, uncross, recross. "But I think she's lyin'."

Jesus. "Why would you think that, Olivia?"

"Because Gramma cries every time she says it."

"Talkin' about your mom always makes your gramma sad."

"Maybe Gramma was sad because she knew my mommy didn't love me."

He took a deep breath in and let it out softly. The therapist told him to let these types of conversations run their course. Don't correct her. Don't change the subject. Ask her questions and listen to her answers. "You still haven't given me a reason why you think your mother didn't love you."

"Because if she really loved me then she wouldna died."

Streeter moved to sit beside her. He smoothed back her staticky hair. "Darlin' girl, we've talked about this. All the love in the world can't keep anyone from dyin'. My mama loved me and she died too."

She crawled onto his lap and rested her head on his shoulder—an odd reaction for her, and he held his breath. Several long minutes went by as she fiddled with the buttons on his shirt. "Do *you* think Mommy loved me?"

Such an innocent question shouldn't require him to take a couple of breaths before he answered. "Yeah, sweetheart, she did."

"You love Mommy, right?"

"I did." Thank god she was too young to pick up on the past tense.

"Gramma Deenie said I don't need another mommy as long as I've got her."

He kissed the top of her head. "Well, you needed another babysitter today after Mrs. McC quit."

"I hope this new one doesn't smell mean."

"Me too. Speaking of smellin' bad . . ." Then he sniffed her whole head like a pig searching for acorns. "Girl, you need a bath."

Olivia giggled and tried to wiggle away. "Daddy! That tickles!"

"You sure?"

"Yes!"

He kept doing it. She kept giggling.

This was what his child needed. Just him.

"Come on, in the tub with you." He grabbed her by the ankles and carried her into the bathroom, amid her happy shrieks and laughs.

Later, after he'd tucked her in, he returned to his email and saw Helping Hands had sent another document as well as a payment link.

A document that requested more details about his financial situation.

He couldn't blame them. They were covering their own asses to make sure a ranch hand earned enough to pay for a part-time private nanny.

Just to be ornery, he filled in the salary he'd earned at his last full-time job, when he'd been part owner at the Hale Ranch.

That seemed like a lifetime ago, although it'd only been four and a half years.

Back then, he'd had everything he ever thought he wanted. A stake in the family business, getting paid to do what he loved. A house nicer than the one he'd grown up in. A brand-new, beautiful, healthy baby girl. And most of all, he had Danica, the woman he'd loved for fifteen years, the woman he'd married, the woman he wanted by his side for the rest of their lives. He'd believed she was happy, they were happy.

That had turned out to be a lie.

After Danica's death, Streeter had been forced to go to part-time on the family ranch since his daughter required his full-time attention. After working with his dad and older brother Driscoll his entire life and doing more than his fair share of chores for most of those years, he assumed they'd understand his changed circumstances.

That had turned out to be a lie too.

They'd revised his pay from a salaried position to an hourly wage, claiming that he didn't "need" the money after Danica's life insurance policy paid out.

Streeter had never felt so completely abandoned, so he abandoned them and quit.

By the time Olivia was a year old, Streeter had moved an hour and a half away from the only home he'd ever known to work at the Split

Rock Ranch and Resort, job-sharing the ranch hand position with his younger brother, Tobin.

That turned out to be the best decision he'd ever made.

Not only had he and Tobin worked well together, his little brother had become his rock when he needed someone to lean on. When discussions about recouping his share of the Hale Ranch went south, Tobin had accompanied him to the lawyer's office. After their father and brother had grudgingly given Streeter one third of their herd and a cash buyout, Tobin offered his acreage as temporary grazing land.

The temporary solution had become a permanent operation. Streeter had used the payout money from Hale Ranch to purchase land adjoining his brother's. After they'd decided to go into the cattle business together—All Hale Livestock—they'd built a barn and corral halfway between Jade and Tobin's place and the area where Streeter had tentatively platted for a house.

Most days he was content working at the Split Rock part-time and living in a trailer on the property. He appreciated the flexibility in his hours and being part of a community that understood the real meaning of family first.

But some nights, he hated the loneliness of his life after Olivia went to bed, even when he knew it'd take a miracle for his single status to ever change.

Chapter Two

"Look at you, little Angel. Your name fits. So soft, sweet, cute and cuddly." Bailey smooched her niece's chubby cheek. "I could just eat you up, Angel cake."

"Good lord. You're almost as gooey with her as her daddy is," Harper complained with a smile.

Bailey rolled her eyes at her older sister as she nuzzled the red gold hair on the baby's head. "Oh, I think Daddy Bran would disagree."

"I'd disagree with what?" Bran said behind Bailey as he peered over her shoulder. "There's my darlin' Angel girl."

Angel smiled at him and cooed, squirming as if she wanted to leap into his arms.

"Obviously it's a mutual admiration," Harper said dryly.

"Can't help but adore the girl who is as sweet as her mama," Bran cooed back at his baby.

Bailey looked at Harper. "Tell him this is *my* baby time and he's not allowed to horn in."

"Hogging my girl again," Bran grumbled. Then he kissed the top of

Bailey's head. "I'm agreeing to this *only* because I gotta head to town and I'm happy you're here, brat."

Brat. Her brother-in-law's pet name for her. He claimed he called her that because she'd been in the army—aka a brat—almost the entire time he'd known her. But Bailey suspected the nickname initially started because she *had* been an eighteen-year-old brat when Bran had gotten involved with Harper. She cringed, thinking of the horrible way she'd treated her sweet sister who'd stepped up to raise her after their mother had skipped the country with a married man.

"I'm just happy to be welcome in your house, bro."

"Always. And you can stay here as long as you like, Sergeant Masterson."

Then he crossed over to Harper and cupped her face in his hands as he kissed her. He murmured something to her that had Harper wrapping herself around him and burying her face in his neck.

These two. Even after being married for years they were still so gone for each other. The first few times she'd witnessed such intimacy between them, she'd purposely looked away. But now Bailey watched them closely, wondering if she'd ever have that kind of deep connection with someone.

But these days, she was better off with a hookup that was brief and shallow.

The sound of a slamming door and rushed bootsteps ended Harper and Bran's private moment. Arguing preceded Tate and Jake, Bran and Harper's two oldest boys, as they burst into the kitchen, their little brother, Gage, dragging in behind them.

"I told you it wasn't gonna work, dumb butt," Tate snapped at Jake.

"At least I'm not too chicken to try something new," Jake retorted, tacking on "butthead" under his breath.

"I shouldn't hafta remind you boys there's no name-callin' in this house," Bran told them. "Now what's the ruckus about?"

While Jake jumped in to overexplain before his big brother could utter a single word, five-year-old Gage sidled up and got right in Angel's face. "Hiya, sissy."

Angel kicked her legs with pure baby happiness.

Bailey watched Gage's animated face as he talked to his baby sister. Gage had inherited his mother's sweetness and helpful nature, but in appearance the kid was his dad's mini-me with dark hair and piercing blue eyes. All of Harper and Bran's kids were born blond, yet none of them had the same hair color or eye color. Bailey, Harper and their older sister Liberty all had different physical attributes, but they'd chalked up the differences to the fact that they didn't have the same father. But all four of Harper's kids had the same dad and none of them looked alike either. Genetics were weird.

"You like babies, huh?" Gage prompted.

She smiled at him. "Yep. I snuggled you up when you were a baby too."

He furrowed his brow. "I don't remember that."

"I know. But I do and that's what's important." She picked off a long piece of grass that had stuck to his shirt. "Were you out playing in the weeds?"

"Uh-huh. Then they started fightin' and it wasn't no fun no more." He held out his index finger for Angel to grab onto. "At least she likes me."

"I like you too, G-man."

He flashed her a shy smile that just melted her.

So much for being the tough army sergeant.

"How about when Angel goes down for her nap you and I do something fun."

Gage's face turned hopeful. "Just the two of us?"

"Yes, sirree. But I'll warn you, no skydiving or bungee jumping. I've got a sore back today."

He giggled. "You're funny, Aunt Bailey. I like you bein' here."

"I like being here too."

Gage bounded off.

In the two weeks she'd been staying here, Bailey noticed that Gage spent a lot of time by himself. Not that he was ignored, but Tate and Jake were closer in age and were always together. And a three-month-old baby took most of Harper's attention, leaving Gage to entertain himself.

As the third child, Bailey knew how that felt. She remembered when she was Gage's age, she tried to find a quiet corner when Mom and her oldest sister, Liberty, raged at each other. Then after Liberty joined the army, Mom focused her attention on turning Harper into a beauty queen and Bailey was ignored. She never resented her sisters for being bold and beautiful, she resented her mom for not bothering to get to know her at any stage of her life.

Bran whistled loudly to break up the bickering. "Enough. Since I can't trust you two not to set the hayfield on fire with your rocket ship shenanigans, you're comin' into town with me."

"But I thought we were spendin' the day with Aunt Bailey," Tate said.

"Yeah, she promised she'd show us how to rappel out of the hayloft," Jake added.

Bailey felt both Harper and Bran's suspicious stares. "I said I'd do that *if* you two could keep from fighting for one entire day. So far, that hasn't happened." Little doubt in her mind that they couldn't uphold their end of the deal . . . oh, *ever*, so she wouldn't have to uphold hers.

After Harper handed Bran a list, she wandered over to where Bailey sat at the table and smiled at her now-snoozing daughter. "This kid can fall asleep through anything, thank god."

"She'll have to be resilient with three older brothers."

"I can put her in her crib," Harper offered.

Bailey shook her head and looked down at the babe's sweet face. "I like holding her."

"You're really good with kids, Bails."

"You sound surprised."

"Maybe I am. I mean, you never babysat or anything when you were old enough."

She sent her sister a sharp look. "What are you talking about? I started babysitting when I was twelve."

Harper blinked at her. "You did? Why don't I remember that?"

"Because you weren't there. You went away to school. I needed my own money since Mom spent hers on booze and slutty clothes. By the time I was fourteen I was staying overnight with people's kids at least one weekend night, maybe two." Bailey would've been stuck home alone anyway; she might as well be making money. "How do you think I ended up attending a private Christian high school?"

"Huh. I guess I never really thought about it. How did you?"

"My friend Amy introduced me to some families in her church. I made a good impression and they got the school to offer me a partial scholarship. I was excited until I talked to Mom . . ." *Until she laughed in my face.*

Shame bloomed whenever Bailey recalled the nasty words her mom had spewed out like poison that day.

If you think I'm gonna stay in this dirty little town, working a dirty job where everyone treats me like a dirty whore, while you strut around, acting holier-than-thou, kissing the tight asses of the family values set, think again. You want their Christian charity so bad, take it. But nothin' is free, daughter, and they'll have you on your knees one way or another.

"Bailey?" Harper said softly. "What haven't you told me?"

"Just that Mom never paid a dime for my tuition."

"How'd you pay the difference?"

"By babysitting. Right before Mom left, they raised the tuition and I couldn't earn enough to pay for it by myself. And I didn't want to change high schools my last two years, or seem pathetic, so I lied to you and said Mom covered the difference."

"So you let me believe that you were out partying with your friends, without a care in the world, when you didn't come home on the weekends during high school?"

She felt her cheeks heat. "You worked two jobs, Harper, and it still wasn't enough. Rather than ask you for more money, I earned some on my own."

Harper shook her head. "I thought I knew everything about you, Bails. Come to find out . . . I didn't know you at all. We were so determined to put up a front to everyone in town that we were all right after Mom skipped out on us that we kept up that same front with each other."

"That's why you were so shocked when I joined the army."

"I still blame Liberty," Harper retorted.

"She never suggested it, but I knew she loved army life. I couldn't think past getting as far away from Wyoming as soon as possible. I didn't want to go to U-Dub and take general classes and try and figure out what I could be when I grew up. Taking the Armed Services Vocational Aptitude Battery—ASVAB—gave me an idea of where my strengths were, and the military taught me to hone those skills." She looked at her sister. "The nomadic, hand-to-mouth way we grew up made me crave stability. In the army I didn't have to worry about housing or food or healthcare. All I had to worry about was learning to do my job better than everyone else so I could move up the ranks faster."

Harper sighed. "I've said it before, but you did the right thing for you. Still chaps my hide how you went about it, though."

She smiled at baby Angel, then at Harper. "It worked out well for you too, sis."

"No argument from me." She folded her arms on the table and leaned closer.

Bailey's gaze was immediately drawn to Harper's enormous boobs—even bigger than normal since she was still breastfeeding. "Since Bran isn't here to salivate and Angel cake here is snoozing and not looking for a snack, put those knockers away. Sheesh. I don't need to be reminded that I'm the only Masterson girl with tiny tits."

"Most days I'd trade ya. Especially now that I'm once again in the milk cow stage of my life."

Bailey reached for her hand. "That's why I'm here. To help you with your boys and get my baby fix." *Since I doubt I'll ever have a baby of my own.*

Harper squeezed her hand back. "I worry you'll be bored out here on the ranch all the time. Would you wanna mix it up and help out at the clothing store?"

"Doing what?"

"Filling in, mostly. Now that the boys are out of school for the summer, I'd like to spend more time at home." She sent Angel a soft smile. "I'm lucky to own my own business and I can take her to work with me. That said, I don't get a whole lot done while I'm there either."

"Either?" Bailey repeated.

Harper's chin quivered. "I feel like I'm failing as a mother and a business owner. Doing a half-assed job at both."

Whoa. Harper never swore unless under extreme duress. "I'm here in any capacity you need. I'll even put on a damn dress and convince your customers I know everything about fashion. But I draw the line at wearing heels on the job."

Harper laughed and wiped her eyes. "So noted."

Gage bounded over, inserting himself between them. "Are you ready to play yet, Aunt B?"

"Since Angel is still sleeping, why don't you and your mom play? I'm sure she'd love to have you all to herself for a little while."

He turned hopeful eyes on his mother. "Really? I've got the Legos all set up."

At first, Bailey worried Harper would refuse, citing the million things she always had to do. But as she looked at her son, her face softened and she ruffled his hair. "Lead the way, Lego master."

Halfway into the living room, Harper turned around. "If you're serious about helping out at the store, you can start tomorrow."

"Sounds good."

Chapter Three

*T*he next afternoon Bailey wandered through Wild West Clothiers, the western store Harper owned that was located in the main building of the Split Rock Ranch and Resort.

Harper's unique sense of style helped create a fun, funky space featuring new and vintage apparel, accessories, home décor and a vast array of "Made in Wyoming" items including candles, lotions and candy. While Bailey was proud of her sister's accomplishments, she couldn't help but wonder how Harper managed to do it all. Just being a ranch wife was a full-time job, not to mention raising four kids.

"This meeting shouldn't take long. Maybe an hour," Harper said from behind the counter.

"Will the boys be with you?"

She shook her head. "They'll be watching a movie with the other kids in the conference room."

Thank god for that. Jake, Tate and Gage were chasing each other around the store. Bailey caught a rack of scarves they'd plowed into before it knocked over a jewelry display. She looked over at Harper, hoping she'd rein in her unruly sons, but she didn't react beyond saying, "Settle down, boys. I mean it."

The boys didn't hear their mother, or if they did, they ignored her. Bailey ground her teeth. She loved her nephews, but after being around them, it was obvious they needed discipline. Not that she'd ever tell her sister and brother-in-law that . . . unless they asked.

"Okay, let's go. No running!" Harper said after all three kids tore out the door, knocking the cowbell off the door handle. She just sighed, re-attached it and followed after them.

Putting the situation out of her mind, Bailey returned to the counter and cracked open her laptop. A former colleague had recently launched a software company that specialized in military games, and he'd convinced her to design weapons and apparel for his upcoming phone app. With no customers or phone calls interrupting her, she managed twenty productive minutes.

She returned from refilling her coffee cup in the back room to see a small, pigtailed blond girl racing out the door. The candy rack was still wobbling and the bottom row was missing four packages of candy.

Son of a bitch.

Cursing, Bailey took off after the little thief.

Blondie ran at full speed, her pigtails bobbing, but her scrawny legs were no match for Bailey's years of PT.

At the end of the hallway, Bailey caught her by the arm and spun her around.

The girl screamed and dropped the candy, trying to jerk her arm from Bailey's firm grip. "Hey! Let go!"

"Not a chance. Where's your mom?"

"I don't have a mom! She's dead! Everybody knows that."

That shocked Bailey enough that she did let the girl go.

The girl took advantage of Bailey's distraction, abandoning her spoils and racing away.

The last thing Bailey saw before she scooped up the bags of candy was the little shoplifter zigzagging around the pillars in the main guest area of the resort.

And then the girl was gone.

What the hell? Where could she have disappeared to so fast?

Bailey didn't see her scaling the stairs to the guest rooms on the second floor. The bar and restaurant were closed, and she couldn't have escaped through the heavy wooden door marking the main entrance without Bailey hearing it shut.

As Bailey started toward the office, she heard a soft grunt behind her. She reversed course and saw the girl crawling out from underneath the couch.

"Seriously?"

When Blondie heard Bailey, she let out another scream even as she put on a burst of speed and raced down the opposite hallway.

A door at the end opened and she ran inside. But not before Bailey noticed who was holding the door for her.

Gage.

Bailey shouted her nephew's name and he stared at her in horror, allowing her enough time to reach the door before he slammed it in her face.

She entered the conference room and froze.

Kids were wreaking havoc all over the damn place.

Two conference tables had been turned on their sides, serving as shelter from the chunks of ice being whipped back and forth. A couple of kids were stacking chairs in a life-sized game of Jenga. Two others were jumping—or maybe dancing—on the couch. A cartoon blared in the background—a cartoon no one paid attention to.

Only Gage and the pigtailed blonde were even aware she'd entered the room.

Bailey marched over, grabbed the remote and hit the mute button. The silence finally caught the attention of the hooligans.

When she turned on the lights, they scattered like cockroaches.

Frantic whispering came from behind the tables, followed by a loud *"Shhh!"*

"Who's in charge here?" she demanded.

Silence.

No way would adults leave this many kids unattended.

"Jake, Tate and Gage Turner, front and center right now." She paused. "And the rest of you too or I'll call the police."

The closest table tipped over, the kids moved so fast.

Bailey scanned the group. Tate stood next to two boys his age. Jake stood between a boy and a girl his age. And Gage lined up next to a boy his age and one a little younger. Her eyes narrowed. "Where is the blond girl?"

Gage said, "She's scared of you because she said you yelled at her."

"I yelled at her because she stole four bags of candy from your mom's store." Bailey's gaze zipped down the line, from the three oldest boys, to the three kids in the middle, to the three youngest. "Now where is she?"

That was when Bailey heard someone beating on the door at the back of the room, a door with a chair jammed beneath the handle.

She stalked over, kicked the chair aside and opened the door.

A small redheaded girl barreled out past Bailey, screaming, "You guys are in so much trouble!"

Then mass chaos erupted.

Pushing, yelling, furniture being tipped over . . . it turned into a grade school version of WWE.

Bailey put her fingers in her mouth and let loose an ear-piercing whistle.

That got their attention.

"Line up." When no one moved, she added, *"Now."*

Her recruits had never lined up so fast. Even the little blond thief came out of hiding.

She pointed to the redheaded girl. "Your name and what happened."

"I'm Brianna. The grown-ups put me in charge—"

"Hold up. How old are you?"

"Almost thirteen."

"You just turned twelve, you liar," the boy next to Tate shouted.

This girl looked to be about eight, but she'd never been a good judge of ages. "Keep going, Brianna."

"So while the grown-ups have their stupid meeting and I went to look for cups, these brats locked me in the closet."

"That's because you were bein' a jerk," a boy Tate's age said hotly. "Mom said you have to be nice to us."

"Yeah," the boy standing next to Gage added. "You're so bossy."

"Because I'm the oldest, lamebrain. I'm supposed to be bossy."

"We're gonna tell Dad that you were callin' us names."

"And you were swearin' at us," the littlest boy piped in.

That got them all riled up and everyone started yelling.

Bailey whistled again. "Enough. You're all in trouble. But before anyone tattles, you'll work together to get this room in order." To Gage and the youngest boy she said, "Grab a bucket and start picking up ice." Next she addressed Tate and his cohorts. "Put the tables back the way you found them." Lastly she pointed to Jake and his buddies. "You three round up the chairs."

"But, why—"

"You can ask questions when you're done cleaning up."

"What in the devil is goin' on in here?" a deep voice said behind her.

Bailey spun around so fast she lost her balance. Strong hands latched onto her arms and she looked up.

The greenest eyes she'd ever seen gazed down on her. Before she took more than a cursory look at the man to see if the rest of him was as dreamy as his eyes, a body wiggled between them. Bailey caught a glimpse of blond pigtails before she heard a girlish cry of "Daddy!"

Immediately she took a step back.

"How come *she* doesn't have to help pick up?" Tate demanded, moving to accuse the candy-stealing kid, who was now hiding behind her dad.

"Yeah, she always gets special treatment," his buddy said behind him with disgust.

"It ain't fair," Jake complained.

"Because she scared me!" Blondie shouted, adding, "She was yellin' at me, chasin' me and she grabbed me," with a dramatic sob.

Oh, you lying little—

"Is that true?" the big bad daddy demanded of Bailey after putting a protective hand on Blondie's head.

Bailey met his glare with one of her own. "Yes, I chased her after she stole four bags of candy."

"From where?"

Harper walked in and stopped behind the man, taking in the room's wreckage. "What on earth happened?" Then she looked at Bailey. "Bailey? Why are you here?"

"Because you didn't warn me that apprehending preschool shoplifters was part of my job description."

"What job?" green-eyed Daddio asked.

More adults entered the room—Bailey recognized the first two as Renner and Tierney Jackson, the owners of the Split Rock that she'd met earlier today.

"Brianna, you were supposed to be watching them," Janie Lawson, the Split Rock's general manager, said to the oldest girl.

"It's not my fault, Aunt Janie! They locked me in the closet after I wouldn't let them go to the ice machine. And they did it anyhow." She gestured to the ice all over the floor.

Janie's eyes narrowed on the dark-haired boy standing next to Tate. "Tyler Lawson. Whose idea was it to have an ice fight?"

Silence.

Bailey could've told her the older boys wouldn't rat on one another. The younger kids, however . . .

The girl Jake's age stepped forward and addressed the couple. "Mom and Dad, I told them not to lock Brianna in the closet. I only went along with it because I didn't want to get pelted with ice."

"That's bull crap, Isabelle." Jake sneered at her. "You're the one who built the table forts!"

"Oh yeah? At least *I'm* not the one who sent the little kids to steal candy!" she shot back.

"That wasn't my idea," Jake said.

"Then whose was it? Dylan's?" They both spun on the third member of their gang.

Dylan shook his head. "It was Olivia's idea." He gestured to the girl still clinging to her dad. "She made Gage be a lookout."

Gage stepped forward and stuck out his chin. "Don't blame Olivia. It was my idea to get the candy. Wasn't stealin' if my mom owns the store, right?"

No way sweet little rule-following Gage had concocted the idea. Why was he protecting the candy thief?

"Then why didn't *you* go, huh?" Tate demanded.

"Because Olivia's the fastest runner. Me'n Rhett and Cody needed to stay here and make our *own* fort outta the chairs so we wouldn't have to share the candy since you wouldn't share the ice," Gage retorted.

"I'm bein' punked, right? My family put you up to this?" a new voice said from the doorway.

Bailey saw Janie, Tierney and Harper exchange an oh-shit look.

"Who are you?" Daddio demanded.

"I'm here to interview for the summer day camp counselor's job."

"How long have you been standing there?" Harper asked.

"Long enough." The young woman's eyes took in the scene before her. "Are these kids in the program?"

"It's not really a . . . program," Tierney explained. "It's just one day a week."

"Just one person handling all these kids?"

"Brianna would be your assistant."

"Brianna . . . the one they shut in the closet?" the young woman asked suspiciously.

"It wasn't my fault!" Brianna said, and pushed the boy next to her. "It was his."

"You deserved it!" he said and pushed her back.

"Stop fighting, it's annoying," the one called Isabelle said, trying to separate them.

"*You're* annoying." Tate sneered.

"Don't you talk to my sister like that," the youngest boy said, launching himself at Tate.

And once again, it was on.

As the parents rushed in to break up the fighting, the job applicant raised her hands in surrender. "I'm out. Workin' at my uncle's dairy farm isn't looking so bad right now."

"But you're—"

"Not nearly desperate enough to deal with this." She gestured to the kids. "They need a warden, not a camp counselor."

Then she was gone.

Renner bellowed, "Clean this up now!"

Kids scattered.

He turned and addressed his wife, Janie, Harper and green-eyed Daddio. "Now what? She was our only applicant. We're out of options and we're headin' into the busy season. While I'm glad we're a family-run business, there are times like this that there ain't enough family members to go around."

Bailey tried to edge away. This discussion had nothing to do with her. Plus, she'd left the store unattended and Harper hadn't noticed that yet.

"Don't you work with a company in Casper for Olivia's daycare?" Janie asked the green-eyed man.

"I did. But the last one quit on us."

"The last one? Meaning . . . ?"

Making sure his daughter was out of earshot, he sighed and adjusted his cowboy hat. "We've gone through every daycare provider in their employ."

"*All* of them?"

"Yeah. Essentially we've been blacklisted."

No surprise, Bailey thought, if the babysitters had to deal with the sassy-mouthed candy thief every day.

"What are we gonna do about a day camp for these kids?" Janie asked.

Day camp? These kids needed boot camp. At that thought Bailey couldn't stop the snorting laugh from escaping her mouth.

Then all sets of parental eyes zoomed to her.

Harper said, "What's so funny?"

"No offense, sis, you know I love my nephews, but they are hellions. And from what I saw today—and what you can clearly see happened in this room—*all* of these kids are out of control. They need boot camp rather than some artsy-fartsy day camp."

Green-eyed Daddio was in her face. "Exactly who are you to be tellin' us what you think our kids need?"

Bailey immediately snapped into her military posture. "I'm Sergeant Bailey Masterson, United States Army. And who, sir, are *you*?"

"Bailey, stand down." Harper sighed. "Streeter, this is my sister Bailey. She's on military sabbatical. Bailey, this is Streeter Hale. He's the Split Rock ranch foreman and Olivia's father."

"Olivia the candy snatcher." He opened his mouth to dispute that moniker, but Bailey held up her hand. "I saw her take the candy, dude."

"But you got the candy back."

"That's your takeaway from this?" She sidestepped him. "You know what? Not my concern. Now that you've all been apprised of the situation and I've recovered the stolen merchandise, I'm going back to work. Good luck with the day camp thing."

She left unsaid, *You're gonna need it.*

❧

An hour later Harper, Janie, Renner and Streeter showed up together at Wild West Clothiers.

As soon as Bailey finished with her customer, Renner closed the door and flipped over the Closed sign.

This couldn't be good.

"Can I help you with something? We're running a special on scarves."

Janie offered her a chipper smile. "We forgot to say thanks for dealing with our kids."

Bailey glanced at Harper, but her sister was busy studying her nails. "Where are the kids now?"

"Tierney is supervising their cleanup," Renner said, "so let's cut to the chase. How would you like to take over the kids' summer day camp?"

She laughed.

"We're serious."

"Why?"

Janie leaned on the counter, her face troubled. "Look, it sucks when someone points out that your kids are undisciplined and disrespectful. My boys are sweet and decent about seventy percent of the time. It's that other thirty percent that worries me and their father. So we're in agreement that you're the perfect candidate to work with them."

"Work with them . . . how?"

"Teaching them discipline and respect. You're military. You're perfect for this."

Bailey looked every one of them in the eyes—god, the hope she saw was hard to ignore—but she counted to twenty before she spoke. "When I suggested your kids needed boot camp, *I* wasn't volunteering to run it."

"Of course we wouldn't expect you to volunteer," Janie said. "We'd pay you."

"That's not the point I was trying to make."

"So this ain't about money?" Streeter said skeptically.

"I'm not in Wyoming to find work for the summer," she retorted. "I'm here to help my sister." *And to decide a few things about my future*—not that she was prepared to share that.

Harper moved behind the counter—moved in for the kill, most likely. "It'd be a huge help to me and Bran if we had one day out of the week that we weren't passing each other on the road as we're juggling childcare schedules. One day where we could just stay home knowing the boys had something fun and cool to do that is making them better-behaved humans." Then she pulled out the puppy-dog eyes. "I've watched you the past two weeks. I know you'd love a chance to whip Tate, Jake and Gage into shape. They want to be like you. You've heard them say that."

Oh, you suck, sis.

"In addition to your nephews, you'd have my boys, Tyler and Dylan, and their cousins Brianna, Cody and Jason—who were all there today."

Like that was supposed to be an incentive?

"Plus our two, Isabelle and Rhett, who could use a dose of discipline," Renner added.

Then Bailey's gaze connected with Streeter's.

The muscle in his strong jaw flexed before he spoke, as if the words were hard to get out. "I don't know if you're what Olivia needs, but I'm willin' to give it a shot."

She did a quick count in her head. "That's eleven kids versus one adult."

"Versus. You're so funny. Technically it's ten kids, since Brianna would be a helper," Janie said. "According to the state childcare rules you can have up to twelve kids supervised by one adult. And keep in mind it's only one day a week."

"What day?"

"Fridays."

"Who'd decide the curriculum?"

"Entirely up to you since you're the boot camp expert."

A million thoughts went through Bailey's head—few of them positive.

Renner leaned in. "What would it take to sweeten the deal, Sergeant? Unlimited horseback ridin'? Free meals? Complimentary drinks?"

"How about a quiet place to hear myself think?" she half muttered.

Shit. She shouldn't have said that out loud. She sent Harper a guilty look.

"My place is a madhouse. I get it. I didn't blame you for needing an escape last weekend. I know you're used to living alone, and I also know you didn't plan on being here for the whole summer. I understand that you'd need your own space, especially if you're also helping me out in the store."

"Well, getting you a place to think is an easy fix. There's an empty trailer I'd let you stay in if you're workin' for Harper."

She looked at Renner. "Seriously? Even if I'm very part-time?"

"Yep. Provided you agree to run the kids' boot camp. Housing is a perk for all Split Rock employees—even seasonal workers." He elbowed Streeter. "Ain't that right?"

It took Streeter a moment to respond. "Only if you're truly lookin' for a quiet place, because we don't put up with wild parties."

Bailey could've ignored Streeter's challenging—and totally fake—smile. Instead, she matched his insincere grin with one of her own. "Understood. And I don't need to worry that your daughter will be running around unattended disturbing your neighbors' quiet time and stealing candy?"

Those green eyes narrowed.

Harper clapped her hands. "It would be such a blessing not to have to be here at nine a.m. to open the store every day now that the boys are out of school and Penelope can't be here until noon."

It had been especially chaotic the past week in the Turner household. And maybe as much as Harper appreciated Bailey's help, having her sister living with them all summer would get tiresome for them too. "I have meetings in Casper and it *would* be easier not to have to drive an extra two hours back to the ranch each time," Bailey admitted.

"Good. Then it's decided," Janie said. "You'll start the boot camp next Friday. That'll give you time to come up with a plan and to get settled in your trailer. Swing by the office before you leave today and we'll get the paperwork sorted, okay?"

Bailey said, "Okay," despite her reservations.

After Renner, Janie and Streeter left, Harper faced her. "Did it seem like I was railroading you into that?"

"Maybe a little. I don't feel like I'll be as much help to you if I'm living here." She took a deep breath and blurted out, "Are you sick of me staying with you?"

Harper's eyes widened. "Goodness, no. Even if you're not in the house with us, I'll still get to see you and spend time with you for the rest of the summer, not just a couple of weeks. It's been easy for me to forget that you're young and single. You'd probably like to go out and do things and not get stuck hanging with an old married lady like me. This gives us both the best of both worlds."

"You're sure?"

"Positive. And just because you'll have a place here doesn't mean you can't crash with us whenever you want. In fact, I hope you'll still come and stay even after we get you settled."

"So you're not firing me as your temporary household help because I forgot to do the dishes last night?"

"You wish." She bumped her hip. "Besides, you always forgot to do the dishes, nothing new there. But now . . . I can send the boys home with Aunt Bailey for the night and have some *boom chicka wow wow* with my man."

Bailey rolled her eyes. "Nice try, but you heard that warning from green-eyed grumpy dude that I need to comply with the neighborhood watch. The hooligans hardly count as quiet."

"True."

"What's the deal with that guy and his kid anyway?"

"Streeter?" She paused. "I don't know him very well, to be honest."

"How long has he worked here?"

"At least three and a half years."

Split Rock was a microscopic community. How did Harper not know everything about him?

Before she could ask, Harper said, "Streeter used to job-share the ranch foreman position with his brother Tobin. But Tobin is working full-time in Casper, although he does help out sometimes. Bran and I know Tobin better than Streeter, but Streeter is a nice enough guy." Harper glanced up from digging in her purse. "Why all the questions?"

Because the man is hot as fire and that prickly façade is like catnip to me.

Bailey managed a shrug. "Just curious since we'll be neighbors and his daughter will be in boot camp. When I tried to catch her after she took the candy and asked where her mother was, she yelled that her mom was dead. Is that true?"

"Sadly, yes. She died when Olivia was just a baby. I don't know the particulars. But that's probably why he's super protective of his daughter even when she's a handful."

"That's probably *why* she's a handful," Bailey said.

"No doubt. I'd warn you to steer clear of him, but chances are he'll steer clear of you first. Streeter keeps to himself like no one I've ever met." She smirked. "Well, besides Bran. The Bran *before* he married me and we had a million kids."

Bailey laughed.

"Speaking of . . . I need to grab the boys and get home to feed my girl." Harper kissed her cheek. "After supper tonight we'll load you up with housewares for your new place since all of your things are in storage."

Chapter Four

Streeter hustled through his morning routine, hard as that was to do with Olivia along for the ride. He tidied up the trailer as she finished her lunch.

Today they were "interviewing" the new childcare provider. *Interviewing* being a loose term; as long as the woman hadn't been in jail she was as good as hired.

"Daddy?"

He glanced over at his daughter, sitting at the table with the stack of books they'd checked out of the Casper library. "Yeah, punkin?"

"What does 'w-a-r-l-o-c-k' mean?"

He hung up the umbrella he'd found under the couch and walked over to her. "Show me the book."

She flipped it to the front cover. *Which Witch Has the Switch?*

"I don't remember you picking that one."

"I liked the rhyme."

"Ah. Well, let's look up the word." He pulled out his phone, swiped to the dictionary app and loaded it. Then he handed her the phone. "Type it in."

Olivia used one finger to poke the keyboard. "Found it!" She passed the phone back to him.

"Warlock—a male witch. A wizard. A spellcaster." He glanced up at her. "Is that what you thought it meant?"

She shook her head. "I thought it was a kind of lock." She scowled. "That's dumb. A male witch should be a mitch or a mizard since a woman witch starts with a 'W.'"

The way her brain worked sometimes truly boggled his. "You have a point. Put your books away and wash up. We've gotta meet Meghan soon."

Her feet started swinging beneath her chair—a sign her thoughts were spinning.

"Something wrong?"

"What if I don't like her?"

"What if she becomes your favorite babysitter ever?" he countered.

"What if she locks me in my room?"

"What if she lets you play the drums as much as you want?"

Olivia blinked. "Really?"

He shrugged. "It's possible. So how about we focus on the good and not the bad."

She hopped off her chair. "Okay." Then she gave him a quick hug—an oddity for her. She wasn't prone to spontaneous affection unless she was in trouble.

Ten minutes later when they walked up to the main parking lot, Olivia didn't hold his hand. He was used to it now. But when she'd first started to walk and she'd systematically denied his help at every turn, he'd taken it as judgment on his parenting skills. Olivia's therapist had finally helped him understand that he wasn't the cause of her detachment disorder. All he could do was show her love and hope she learned how to form attachments by example. Other people—including Olivia's grandmother Deenie—took Olivia's aloofness as a personal affront. Deenie tried to force her affections on Olivia and vice versa, which always resulted in Olivia screaming in exhaustion and Deenie in tears. It'd only been in the past year that Olivia had relaxed her singular attachment to him, which gave Olivia some autonomy and him some freedom.

He just hoped this Meghan person could handle Olivia's indifference and her bouts of single-mindedness.

The Split Rock parking lot was mostly empty. A young woman with vivid pink hair exited a Honda and waited for them to come to her.

That awarded her some major points. Evidently she had read Olivia's personality profile.

Streeter offered his hand. "Meghan?"

"Yes. Nice to meet you, Mr. Hale." She shook his hand briefly. "And this must be Olivia."

"You've got pink hair," Olivia said in a reverent tone.

Meghan smiled. "For now. I might change it to a different color next month."

Olivia whirled on her dad. "Can I have pink hair too?"

Never. "We'll talk about it later." Then he addressed Meghan. "Follow the gravel road on the right down the hill until you reach a cluster of trailers. That's where we'll meet you."

Olivia skipped happily beside him as they returned to the employee quarters.

After talking with Meghan and seeing her interacting with Olivia, Streeter felt comfortable enough to leave them together for a few hours.

He drove over to the barn to deal with paperwork he'd been putting off. But when he walked into the office he shared with Ted, he saw his young ranch-foreman-in-training poring over the binders that held the supply purchase orders from years past, checking them against something on the computer screen.

Ted glanced up when he heard Streeter's bootsteps on the wood floor. He sent a nervous look to the open books and then to Streeter. "Hey, Street. Didn't expect to see you here this afternoon."

Obviously.

"Uh. What's up?"

"Maybe I oughta ask you the same question?" He pointed to the books strewn across the desk. "Searchin' for something in particular?"

"Actually . . . yeah." Ted scrubbed his hands over his face. "We're runnin' low on the Permectrin. I don't see that livestock insecticide has been ordered for two years."

"We haven't needed it." Streeter fought the urge to defend himself. "If you want me to order it, just leave me a note, Ted."

He shook his head. "I need to know where to find the information so when it becomes my job, I'll have an idea where to look. You ain't always gonna be around to hold my hand."

"Give a guy a chance to move up and the next thing ya know, *boom*— he's muscling you outta the way."

Ted blushed. "Not true."

"Just givin' you shit, kid. And I did the same thing when I started here. Except I had to ask my little brother to decipher his damn filing system. He had a great time messin' with me, but I probably deserved it."

"Tobin is awesome. You're lucky you two get along so well. Me'n my older brother can't hardly be in the same town without mixing it up."

"Why? You guys keepin' grudges from when you were kids?"

He shrugged. "He's lazy. I recognized it early on, but my dad didn't. Soon as we graduated me'n my best buddy Zack moved to Denver. We knew after we both finished trade school that we wouldn't return to our hometown. My brother was pissed. He thought I'd come back and work even harder on the ranch to prove I'd been educated." Ted shook his head. "Crazy bastard."

"Sounds like my older brother." He clapped Ted on the shoulder. "At least you were smarter to get out of that type of situation sooner than I did. How's Zack handling the pressure of bein' assistant chef?"

"He loves it. He's learning a ton. Us working opposite schedules sucks. Seems we hardly ever see each other."

Streeter envied Ted and Zack's friendship. They lived together, worked together, spent their free time together. He'd never had a buddy he could rely on like that.

"So what are you doin' here?" Ted asked.

"Killin' time." Yeah, it was pathetic he didn't have anywhere else to go. "Thought I'd recheck supplies and update the work schedule."

"Don't hardly seem fair to you that I get most weekends off."

"You'll work your fair share of them when you're the boss." Streeter pointed at the computer. "You about finished?"

"Sure." He closed his files and stood. "Pete asked if one of us could take the backup mower to the repair shop. He already called Moody so he's aware of the problem, and he loaded the mower onto the trailer. Since I gotta go to Rawlins anyway, you want me to handle it?"

"That'd be great."

As Ted reshelved the binders, he said, "Heard we're getting a new neighbor today. Harper's sister Bailey, who's been workin' at WWC."

Streeter's body tightened at the mere mention of the sergeant.

"Have you met her?"

"Yeah. She'll be runnin' the day camp. She's warned us it'll be a kid's boot camp."

"I don't doubt that. She's got that back-off vibe down." Ted turned and grinned. "She reminds me of you, Street."

"Piss off, pup."

He laughed. "See? A match made in heaven."

Streeter fiddled with the mouse, rolling it over the mouse pad. It occurred to him that Ted was a good-looking guy. A nice guy too. "Bailey doesn't seem much older than you. Maybe you'd be her perfect match." He paused. "Any plans on askin' her out?" Streeter glanced up to see an odd look cross Ted's face.

"Nah. She ain't my type. What did Olivia think of her?"

"Ask me after the first day of camp."

"Will do." Ted snagged a notebook off his desk. "See ya tomorrow."

"Later."

After Ted closed the door, Streeter flipped on the beat-up boom box that still functioned as a radio. Most people listened to music on their phones, but he rarely had the luxury of popping in a pair of ear-buds and tuning out the world—either at work or at home. He preferred the radio, ads and all. Having music always playing in the background kept him from going crazy after Danica died. It'd seemed to soothe Olivia too.

Humming along to Dwight Yoakam's song "Little Sister," he got to work.

The timer on his phone went off and he noticed he'd worked for three hours without a break. He'd accomplished more than enough for one day. After locking up, he drove his truck to the other side of the resort. Might seem silly that he drove instead of walked, but he often had to go directly from the Split Rock Ranch to his brother's place. He spent enough time in the fresh air that he didn't need to hoof it back and forth between his trailer and the barn a few times a day.

Streeter parked his truck behind his SUV. Just as he was about to get out, a silver Toyota Highlander sped past, kicking up dust. The taillights flashed as the driver hit the brakes. Then the driver's-side door opened and Sergeant Bailey Masterson hopped out, dark glossy brown hair atop her head in a high ponytail, mirrored shades covering her eyes.

The next thing he noticed were her legs. Her bare, muscular legs that seemed a mile long in those frayed and faded Daisy Dukes. She wore an army green tank top with *ARMY STRONG* emblazoned across the front and no bra.

Mercy. The musculature in her arms and shoulders indicated strength that he found as sexy as the curves of her hips. The sassy ser-geant was a potent package.

After opening the hatch on her SUV, she leaned forward to grab something out of the back. That maneuver gave him a front row seat to the nicest ass he'd ever seen.

Streeter groaned. He couldn't tear his eyes away from her backside, especially when it wiggled and jiggled as she tugged an enormous laundry basket.

Maybe you should offer to help *her instead of helpin' yourself to an eyeful of her ass.*

Playing fetch and carry would be the neighborly thing to do . . .

Not if it's in the guise of doin' her.

She disappeared around the corner.

How the hell had she seen where she was going over that enormous pile of bedding? The woman was gonna fall and bust her very fine ass, and that'd be a damn cryin' shame.

Streeter jumped out of his truck and followed her, half expecting to see her sprawled on the wooden walkway, but she'd set the load down in front of the trailer on the opposite end of his.

She unlocked the door, picked up the basket and went inside.

He doubled back to her SUV and grabbed the two biggest suitcases. She hadn't emerged from her trailer yet, so he said, "Knock, knock," as he walked through the door. "Where do you want these?"

"Set them down anywhere."

He put them next to the recliner and looked at her.

"You didn't have to do that, but thank you."

"Let's get the rest of it unloaded." He reached her car before she caught up to him.

"I've got this," she said tersely, practically hip-checking him out of the way.

"Good lord, woman. Me lendin' a hand ain't a judgment on your ability to do it yourself." He sidestepped her, opening the rear passenger door to pick up the cooler wedged in the back seat. Damn thing was heavy. He shot her a look. "Whatcha got in here? Beer?"

"No." Bailey flashed him a fake smile. "Grenades."

Jesus. He turned and headed toward her trailer.

And like he expected, the little spitfire was right on his heels.

She'd lugged a big crate filled with pans and other household items, which she half dropped on the floor.

Which she had to bend over to reach.

Which put that perfect heart-shaped backside of hers directly in front of him.

He couldn't have looked away if he'd wanted to.

When she straightened up and spun around, he made sure his focus was on her face, but somehow it got stuck on her equally sexy mouth.

"Look, Skeeter—"

That redneck name had his annoyed gaze snapping up to hers. "My name isn't Skeeter, *Barley*, as you well know." He fucking hated being called Skeeter. *Hated* it. And it happened far more often than he liked.

She laughed. "Barley. Good one."

And Streeter couldn't think of another thing to say. He wasn't a witty guy. He'd never done much flirting. Before she realized that he was nearly paralyzed by social interaction, he wheeled around and hoofed it back to her car. Two smallish suitcases, a box of food, a crate of books and a laptop bag piled onto another crate of computer equipment was what remained. He stacked the food on top of the books and passed her on the walkway.

She muttered something about him being lucky he hadn't stacked anything on her computer equipment.

Her prickly, I-can-do-it-myself attitude amused him, and he smiled despite himself.

After he set the box and crate on the floor, he took a moment to look around. The only difference between this space and his was his big-screen TV. The only room he'd "decorated" was Olivia's bedroom. Besides the artwork hanging on the fridge and pinned to the bulletin board, their home looked much like this: impersonal as a cheap hotel. Like they'd just moved in—not that they'd lived there for three and a half years.

Streeter had left every physical reminder of their old life behind. Bad juju surrounded those things. He'd kept the photos—although someone else had packed them up and he hadn't looked at them since shoving them in storage—and Danica's jewelry, the quilts and afghans his mother and grandmother had made, and a few family heirlooms he'd set aside for Olivia.

Bailey breezed in carrying both suitcases. "Your girlfriend and your daughter are looking for you."

"Girlfriend?"

"Yeah, you know, the hot little thing with the pink hair prancing around here."

The only hot little thing I've seen prancing around here is you, baby.

He frowned at that inappropriate thought. "That's Meghan, Olivia's babysitter. Which means she's young enough to be my *kid*, not my damn girlfriend."

She smirked.

This woman poked every one of his buttons. He had to leave now before he started poking back. Without saying a word, he walked past her and into the sunshine.

"Daddy!" Olivia shouted from the opposite end of the walkway.

As he started toward her, he heard Bailey yell, "You're welcome!" from inside her trailer.

Unbelievable. She oughta be thanking him.

All thoughts of his troublesome new neighbor vanished when he saw the happy look on his daughter's face.

He placed his hand on Olivia's head after she'd run to him. Then he said, "Everything go all right?" to Meghan.

"Everything went fine. We had a great time. I can't guarantee that I'll be Olivia's regular caretaker, but I'll be here at least once a week."

"Sounds good."

Olivia insisted on walking Meghan to her car. After she drove off,

Olivia rested her weight against him. "Daddy, can we go to McDonald's for supper?"

He caught a glimpse of Bailey's very fine ass as she rooted around in her back seat for something.

Getting away from here—and her—for a few hours had him herding Olivia to his SUV. "Sounds like a great idea."

Chapter Five

On a boring Sunday afternoon at WWC, Bailey decided to work on her camp curriculum since camp started in five days.

Thirty minutes had passed and all she'd accomplished was drawing clouds on the notebook in front of her.

How was she supposed to occupy ten kids for ten hours a day?

Break it down. Start with what you know.

Food. Give the kids half an hour for breakfast, an hour for lunch, and two fifteen-minute snack breaks. Presto. Two hours accounted for.

Which left her with eight hours to fill.

If she really meant to treat it like a boot camp, she'd have to use military terms for everything.

A morning roll call—insist on campers using "yes, ma'am" and "no, sir" to her and one another, which would teach them respect. They'd revisit the camp rules and review the daily schedule. She'd need to set up an area for makeshift lockers, which would be subject to inspection during this time.

PT would follow roll call—wouldn't hurt the kids to run; they chased each other all over the place anyway. Then they'd receive morning assignments, team-building tasks like picking up trash or helping around the resort, followed by morning snacks. A prelunch skills class would be anything from archery practice to running an obstacle course.

In the afternoon they could watch training films—aka movies—for a quiet time. She'd make them responsible for setting up their own bedrolls. Then late-afternoon PT. Following afternoon snacks, they'd have craft time. Not the usual kind. The older kids could create dioramas, build models of bridges and buildings with toothpicks and Popsicle sticks. The younger kids could make masks and work on a ghillie suit or color maps of the world.

Lastly they'd clean up and be dismissed.

Boom. Ten hours filled.

As she recopied her ideas, it allowed her to be excited for this odd venture after seeing the camp in terms she understood.

Her phone rang. Caller ID read: LIBERTY.

Bailey answered, "Heya. I'm putting you on speaker."

"If this is an attempt to keep me from swearing, you're fucked, Sergeant."

Bailey laughed. "Good to hear from you, although I'm surprised since it's probably the middle of the night over there. Where are you?"

"At a military base in Germany. And it's midnight here. Devin and the band are still signing autographs and talking to their fans."

"What are you doing?"

"Drinking the free booze and waiting to jump my man when he's done."

"Nikki is tucked in for the night?"

"Finally. That kid goes until she drops. Goddamned Energizer bunny. Just like her dad."

"Suck it up, soldier. You're the one who married an internationally famous country music superstar and then bore him the golden child. And if she can sing? Dude. You could quit your job."

"Fuck off. No way am I quitting. I got a promotion before I started this tour."

Bailey stopped doodling. "Another promotion?"

"Yep. Senior security advisor to A-list clients."

"Congrats, Lib! That's huge!"

"Thanks. I almost didn't take the position."

Please don't say because Devin didn't want you to. "Why not?"

"It means more hours at the office every week. Time away from Devin and Nikki."

"But you're still in Denver. Nikki is three. She has zero concept of time. Plus, you have an awesome nanny."

"True." The sound of glassware tinkling echoed from the background. "Now that I'm one of the big bosses, I've been thinking."

"About?"

"Convincing you to come to work for me now that your gig is up in the army."

Bailey switched the phone off speaker. "Uh, Lib, that bit of information is still on the down-low."

Silence stretched.

"You haven't told anyone yet?"

That I failed my FFD evaluation? Uh, no.

"Bails?"

"Nope."

"But—"

"I don't want Harper to think I'm here only because I didn't have anywhere else to go, okay?"

A heavy sigh. "All right. That I do understand."

"I'll know when the time is right to tell her. And trust me, she doesn't need another damn thing on her plate right now."

"How is she doing?"

"She's been honest with me about feeling overwhelmed. When she's at home she wants to be at work and vice versa. From what I've seen, Angel is a good baby. She sleeps, she eats on schedule, she's not fussy, she'll let anyone hold her. With this being their fourth kid, Harper doesn't insist on doing everything baby related, but Angel does come to work with her most days."

"I imagine it'd be hard for even a great dad like Bran to check cattle with an infant in a car seat," Liberty mused.

"Not that he hasn't tried. Bran is so head over heels for his baby girl it's ridiculous." Bailey smiled. "It's sweet. But at the same time, Tate and Jake take advantage of their parents' distraction over the new baby. Gage gets left out and then he acts out to get attention. They're wilder than ever. Bran has the boys-will-be-boys attitude, so unless they're constantly entertained, they're making their own entertainment. They're not bad kids, they're just . . ."

"Ranch kids," Liberty inserted.

Bailey sighed. "How can that be an excuse?"

"I don't know. We weren't ranch kids. Without sounding stupid, being raised on a ranch means they're a different kind of kid. When Devin tells me some of the stuff he and his buddies used to do, I'm like . . . we're never letting Nikki spend time at the Turner Ranch without us being right there."

"Smart. But I might've done a not-so-smart thing."

"What did you do?"

She paced around the edge of the counter. "Oh, last week I informed the parents who own this place, as well as parents who work here, that all their kids are hellions in need of discipline."

"Christ, Bails, you didn't."

"Yes, I did. So guess who's in charge of the Split Rock boot camp starting on Friday?"

Liberty laughed so hard that Bailey made ten laps around the store before she stopped. "Damn, girl, talk about going balls to the wall."

"It's only one day a week. And three of the ten kids are my nephews, so I've convinced myself that I'll have at least a thirty percent success rate."

"Please take videos," she begged. "I wanna see Sergeant Masterson forcing kids to do push-ups and pull-ups or they're denied their ration of Pudding Pops."

Her sister busted a gut again.

Coolly, Bailey said, "Are you done yet?"

"Yeah. But in all seriousness, you'll do great."

"Thanks." At least she had one vote of confidence. "The other perk of employment at the Split Rock is they assigned me a trailer at the complex."

Liberty went quiet.

"What?"

"Are you sure being by yourself is a good idea?"

"I won't be by myself all the time. I have neighbors."

Streeter's handsome face came to mind, but she shoved that possibility aside. He'd avoided any interaction with her since he'd helped her move in.

"Don't take this wrong, but are you sure you can handle all of this?"

"I guess we'll see if I hold up or if I end up in a straitjacket talking to myself."

"Don't be flip," Liberty warned. "I have a legitimate reason to worry."

"I know." And her big sister had no idea how much she hated that.

"Are you taking your meds regularly? No issues getting refills?"

"Yes, *Mom*, do you need proof that I set a damn timer every day so I don't forget?"

It's only because she cares about you.

"Sorry." Bailey took a couple of breaths. "Yes, I'm taking them. And last week, I started attending my mandatory appointments in Casper."

"That medical records transfer happened fast for the government."

"It's almost like they want me out of uniform."

"Bailey."

"Anyway, just for shits and giggles when I'm in Casper, I'll be taking tests, figuring out what 'real world' job my military experience qualifies me for. And I expect my suspicions to be confirmed that inventory record keeping is the same regardless if it's for AR-15s or boxes of tissue paper, which is what I've been doing the last two years."

"Which is why you need to come to Denver and work for me. You've got experience securing munitions and have computer know-how."

"Is 'know-how' a technical term in the security biz?" she said with a snicker.

"Piss off, smart-ass. How about . . . your mad genius computer skills are in high demand in the private sector?"

"Better. It almost sounds like I have actual, usable skills when you put it that way."

"You do. Plus, the cherry on top of living in the Mile-High City is the VA here is *ah*-mazing."

"I don't doubt that." She sighed again. "Know what really sucks? It doesn't matter if I stay here or move to Denver. Either way I'm sponging off one of my sisters."

"Bails. I wouldn't see it that way and I doubt Harper does either."

"But I do." Bailey rang the cowbell on the door. "Sorry, sis, I have a customer and I have to go. Love you, kiss Nikki and Dev from me. We'll talk soon." She hung up.

She didn't have the energy to think about her future, so she forced herself to do as her counselor suggested and focused on the present.

⤚⤳

The next morning Bailey finished typing her camp list and sent it as an email to all the parents. Then she cleared a space in the back for the benches and lockers for her campers.

The cowbell rang and Bailey returned up front to see Penelope, Harper's full-time employee, rush in, all apologies. "Sorry I'm late."

"Traffic was a bitch?" Bailey said drolly.

"I might've hit a tumbleweed on my way here." Penelope skirted the counter and disappeared into the back room.

Bailey followed her, taking in Penelope's outfit: red stilettos, a red and black plaid A-line skirt, a sleeveless black silk shirt with a Peter Pan collar. Penelope dressed as if she worked in a clothing boutique—a feat Bailey had yet to master. She fought the urge to straighten the cuffs on her white capris or readjust the sleeves of her polka-dotted cold-shoulder blouse, silently lamenting that her life had been so much easier in uniform.

Penelope sent her a look over her shoulder. "Why is there an open space on the wall where the clothing racks were?"

"That's where the lockers for the kids' boot camp will go."

"What boot camp?"

After Bailey explained, Penelope put her hands together in a prayer-like manner and said, "Please, please, *please* consider letting my daughter Jessamyn participate."

"How old is she?"

"Six going on sixteen," she said wryly, "which means boot camp would be perfect."

Another girl would balance the group out genderwise. "If you're interested, talk to Janie. She's handling the payments and scheduling."

"I definitely will during my break today. Thank you."

After tackling the list Harper had left, and crossing off the items they'd completed, Bailey noticed that Penelope seemed tense. "Is there a problem I missed or something I did wrong? Because you don't seem happy we're nearly done with the list."

"I'm not happy." Penelope's dark brown eyes narrowed at her. "And I'll tell you why if I'm talking to Bailey my coworker and not Bailey my boss's sister."

Hard not to outwardly bristle but Bailey managed. "I'll admit that's a fine line for me to straddle, but I'll try."

That answer seemed to satisfy her. "When I came to work here two years ago this was a thriving business. Harper had two full-time employees in the summer, plus a part-timer who only handled the online store. Some days there were three of us working and we still had customers waiting to be helped. Resort guests loved this place and spent a ton of money here. Plus, we had loyal shoppers from all over the state. The online store was nearly its own entity."

"And?"

Penelope gestured to the store. "And how many customers have you had today?"

"None, but it's a Monday."

"But the resort is fully booked. We should've had at least one guest pop in, even if they were only looking for a quick candy fix." She pointed to the computer. "Were there any sales this weekend from the online store?"

Only two and it'd taken Bailey less than ten minutes to pull the inventory and package it for shipping. "Online sales have been sluggish—"

"For months," she inserted. "If we're being brutally honest, sales have been in steady decline for a year. Ever since . . ."

Harper found out she was pregnant.

Penelope saw the moment it clicked for Bailey. "Now you understand why I haven't mentioned this to her."

Bailey raised an eyebrow. "And you think *I* oughta bring it up since I'm her sister?"

"Yes." She sighed. "No. I don't know. I don't have access to WWC's profit-and-loss statement, but I don't need to see it to know this place is losing money because Harper's mind isn't on her business—even when she's here."

"No shit."

"Before you fry my hair with that glare, hear me out. I love this job. From day one Harper has accommodated my strange schedule—trust me, not everyone understands the issues with being a single parent. Then add in the screwed-up situation with my ex and the court order requiring me to live in Rawlins . . ." She took a breath. "When I was looking for work, fast-food places wouldn't hire me. I never imagined I'd land my dream job in a retail clothing store when I applied here. I'm telling you this because I'm worried about being let go, since I heard that you're living at the Split Rock now."

"I'm not here for you to train me as your replacement, Penelope. But when I realized how much Harper was struggling, I decided to stay for the summer and help her in any way I can."

"Even if that means she'll decide to close the store?"

"Yes." Bailey held up her hand. "Not that we've discussed that option, but I'm being up-front with you that if it comes down to it, I'll suggest it as a possibility. Harper's well-being is what I care about."

They stared at one another for a few more seconds before Penelope gave her a brittle smile. "I can't say I'm thrilled with your answer, but I understand."

For some reason Bailey felt compelled to ask, "Meaning you'd do the same thing for your sister?"

Penelope barked out a harsh laugh. "God, no. I'd let my sister twist in the wind—just like she did to me."

Wow. Okay.

"Not all families are close and supportive, Bailey. Count yourself lucky that yours is."

"I do."

"Good. Now that I'm up to speed, there's no reason for us both to be here today."

"You're right. I'm headed out to the ranch for the rest of the day. Text me if you need anything."

"Will do."

⟡

Eight hours later Bailey returned to the Split Rock. She'd kept the radio off for the drive and enjoyed the silence, keeping the windows rolled down so she could breathe in the pine-scented breeze.

It'd been a trying day in the Turner household. Bailey arrived to hear Angel crying—a state she'd been in for almost twenty-four hours, according to her parents. Harper hadn't gotten any sleep and she and Bran were bickering about whether to take the baby to the doctor.

Talk about uncomfortable, listening to her normally sweet sister snapping at her beloved husband and witnessing Bran stomping off.

Then Harper was so agitated she wouldn't let Bailey take the baby from her.

Bailey watched helplessly as Harper paced and patted Angel's back, cooing to her and trying to shush her. After Angel expelled a burp that'd make a frat boy proud, she quit wailing.

Bran returned with the baby carrier. He took Angel and gently placed her in the carrier against his chest. In a dangerously soft voice he said, "Haul that cute butt upstairs and get some sleep, Mama. I got this. And Aunt Bailey is gonna take the boys into town and get them outfitted for boot camp. Ain't that right, brat?"

She said, "Absolutely," without hesitation. "I'm guessing it'll take all afternoon."

"Perfect plan." Bran made a shooing motion at his wife. "Every second you stand there worryin' is time you coulda spent napping."

"Bran—"

"We got this. Now go on."

"I know. I just wanted to say I love you."

"Back atcha, babe."

Harper blew them both a kiss and disappeared up the stairs.

Bran snagged his wallet off the counter, pulled out a wad of bills and handed them to Bailey. "The boys are relatively clean. Buy 'em camp clothes, take 'em to a movie, feed 'em a couple of times . . . hell, I don't care how you entertain them, but if you could kill at least six hours, I'd appreciate it."

Six hours? Crap. She was thinking like . . . four. Max.

If you can't make it through six hours with three kids, what makes you think you'll survive ten hours with a dozen kids?

Stupid voice of reason.

"Of course. I'll bring back supper for you guys too."

Her nephews were mostly good during their daylong break from home and hearth. They seemed excited for camp.

Bailey only stayed long enough at the Turner Ranch to drop off the pizza and the boys and gauge her sister's state of mind. Harper did appear rested and she had hugs, kisses and smiles for her sons.

As she trudged to her trailer, she decided first she'd indulge in a long shower, then she'd don her pajamas and pour a big rum and Coke. It'd been a helluva day and the week had just started.

The trailer had gotten stuffy. After opening the windows, she propped her bare feet on the coffee table. With a cold beverage in her hand and her head settled into a fluffy pillow, she felt relaxed for the first time since she'd rolled out of bed this morning.

At first she dismissed the tinny-sounding whack-whack-whack, assuming it was an echo coming from the main lodge.

But it happened again, with more strikes in a row. Louder thwacks. Closer smacks. Her head had finally stopped pounding so she knew it wasn't literally all in her mind.

Then a deep, teeth-jarring thud began to accompany the metallic whacks in a steady, annoying rhythm . . . almost as if someone was playing the drums outside her window.

She had no choice but to check it out.

Bailey's trailer was at the end of a wooden plank walkway. There weren't any streetlights, which was how she nearly stumbled over the little person.

A little person who'd arranged two big plastic pails and three different-sized pans around her in a semicircle. In one hand she had a plastic mallet from a kids' toy and in the other she had a soup ladle. She was beating on her makeshift drums with such concentration that she hadn't noticed Bailey looming behind her.

Why weren't any of their other neighbors bothered by all the noise?

The blond terror continued to do her imitation of Animal from the

Muppets in complete oblivion until Bailey said, "Olivia," sharply during a break in the rhythm.

The girl screamed. The "drumsticks" flew out of her hands and the soup ladle hit Bailey on the chin. Then Olivia was up, hurdling away from her drum set and booking it down the walkway.

They reached the Hales' trailer at the same time green-eyed Daddio burst out the door. "Olivia!"

She tried to sidestep her father, but he clamped onto her shoulder. "What in the devil is goin' on? I heard you scream."

"Because she scared me again!"

Streeter shot Bailey a confused look before he focused on his daughter. "Why were you outside?"

Olivia started to wail, but he wasn't having any of it. He crouched down so they were face-to-face. "Stop. Answer the question."

"You said I couldn't practice my drumming in the house anymore, so I went outside. Then she came up behind me and scared me. That's when I screamed and ran and she chased me."

Bailey started to defend her actions, but a dark look from those hard eyes of his kept her mouth closed.

"Are you supposed to go out of the house without permission?" he demanded.

Olivia shook her head.

"But you did. Not only that, you were banned from drumming."

"But, Daddy—"

"Not your turn to talk. It's mine." He stood. "Not another word until I ask you a direct question." Then he faced Bailey and those angry eyes searched her face, his gaze zeroed in on her chin. "Did she do that?"

"Her soup ladle drumstick flew up when I startled her."

That strong, sexy jaw tightened and he turned away to address his daughter. "See that mark on her chin? You did that."

"I didn't mean to!"

"How many rules did you break tonight?"

"Umm . . . two?"

"Wrong." He held up four fingers. "One: you snuck outside. Two: you took a toy that I'd put on the time-out shelf. Three: you played the stolen toy outside and bothered our neighbor." He paused. "Now you tell me the fourth rule."

She appeared to be thinking hard before she blurted out, "I hurt somebody."

"Through your careless, dangerous and selfish actions."

Bailey had the conflicting need to assure Olivia she wasn't hurt and to commend Streeter for pointing it out. It was hard to keep quiet, but she managed.

"You know what's next," he said to his teary-eyed daughter.

Olivia stepped forward. "I'm sorry I hurt you because of my careless, dangerous and selfish actions."

She couldn't tell if the kid was being sincere, but she had to take it at face value. "Apology accepted."

He gave Olivia a little shove. "Go pick up your drum stuff."

She raced off.

Streeter ran his hand through his hair. "I can't even take a shower without worryin' she's up to something." His gaze hooked hers. "I'm really sorry about all of this."

"I can see that."

"It won't happen again. The outdoor drumming, I mean."

Bailey raised an eyebrow.

"Yeah, I wouldn't believe me either." He sighed. "Only one way to ensure that I keep my word. Would you go along with it?"

"With what?"

Olivia returned, dragging a pan-filled bucket in each hand.

"Since you disturbed Miss Masterson's quiet time, Olivia, she'll decide when to give your drums back to you."

"Hey, that's not—"

"Up for debate. Go inside."

"But . . ."

"Now. And without slammin' the door," he added.

He picked up the buckets and stepped around Bailey, giving her no choice but to follow his long-legged strides.

She was too annoyed to speak until they reached her trailer. "What the hell was that? Your daughter already acts like I'm the big bad. Me having her drums—"

"Will likely make her act more pleasantly toward you, since she loves these goddamned things so much." His grin was both smug and sly.

Her mouth dropped open.

"Surprised I have a few practical parenting tricks up my sleeve?"

"No, I'm shocked that you actually smiled at me."

Streeter cocked his head. "And I've yet to see an answering smile in return."

Bailey harrumphed, mostly because that damn sexy smile affected her far more than she'd like to admit. "Not happening tonight, bud. Catch me on a day that hasn't seemed a week long."

"I've had one of those myself."

"During your epically long day did you happen to check your email?"

"Not yet. Why?"

"I sent camp requirements."

"I'll look at them after Olivia's in bed."

"Good." She pointed to the pails. "I don't want them cluttering up my house."

"Ain't like you don't have room."

"How would you know that?"

He lifted both brows. "I helped you haul stuff in, remember?"

Bailey had few belongings and most everything she'd brought belonged to Harper. "Maybe I unloaded the rest of my stuff this weekend. Maybe the place is full. Maybe I've got a grand piano in the living room."

"You'd have to be a damn magician to get it in there." Then he gifted her with that sly smile again. "But if you did manage that . . . now when you get tired of playin' the piano, you can switch to the drums." Then he handed her the pails.

He did have a sense of humor. "How long do you want me to keep these?"

"For as long as you want."

Her eyes narrowed. "Tired of drum concerts?"

"Like you wouldn't believe." He stared at her. Opened his mouth. Closed it.

"What?"

"Nothin'." He turned and walked off without another word.

That was the second time he'd done that.

Apparently Olivia came by her unsociable behavior naturally.

Just to be ornery, she yelled, "And a good night to you too, Mr. Hale," before she stormed inside and slammed the door.

Chapter Six

$\mathcal{S}$treeter returned home to find Olivia in bed.

He leaned in the doorway and listened to her reading to her rag doll. They'd read that story so many times she had it memorized.

Olivia peered over the top of the book at him. "I'm sorry, Daddy."

The immediate burst of love for his girl turned his anger and fear into frustration. Somehow he had to make her understand the seriousness of what she'd done.

Crossing over, he perched on the edge of her bed. "Olivia, you need to really listen to me, okay?"

"Okay."

"Our house rules are for your safety. After I heard you scream and saw you weren't in the house, it scared me."

"It did?"

"Yeah. It's not safe for you to be runnin' around outside by yourself, and you bein' in the dark by yourself is ten times more dangerous. You could get hurt. Or someone could see you alone and try to take you. That happens all the time."

Her eyes went round with fear. "It does?"

"We know our neighbors, but the guests staying at the lodge change every day. We don't know any of 'em. What if a guest saw you and decided they wanted a little girl? They could pick you up, put you in their car, drive away and I'd never see you again." He paused and took her hand. "Do you understand why I was scared when I realized you weren't where you were supposed to be?"

She nodded.

"I don't make rules to keep you from havin' fun. I make rules to keep you safe. And I have to be able to trust you. I have to know that you won't forget or think it doesn't matter, because it does. You are the most important thing in the world to me, Olivia."

She threw herself at him, making apologies and promises even as she sobbed.

Hopefully he'd finally gotten through to her. He stayed in her room until she quit asking questions and fell asleep.

Streeter returned to the kitchen and grabbed the bottle of Jameson from the top cupboard. After he poured himself a shot over ice, he flopped on the couch.

One sip, one heavy sigh later he felt the silence closing in on him. He hated this time of day, when he was alone without distractions. When he had time to think. Time to realize that loneliness was the only other constant companion in his life besides his daughter.

A self-imposed loneliness, his therapist had told him.

Streeter hadn't bothered to argue that point.

And the reality was: he didn't see that changing any time soon. He focused his energy on his daughter and his job, plus reserving a small amount for his brother and his family. There wasn't anything left. Nothing for friends. Nothing for a woman.

For some reason Bailey Masterson popped into his head. Maybe because she wasn't like any other woman he'd ever met.

Or maybe because he'd seen that she was *all* curvy woman in her tiny tank top and tight booty shorts. Whenever they crossed paths she carried herself as if dressed in full body armor. But tonight with her hair floating around her freckled face and barefoot, she'd seemed softer.

Softer. Right. She'd throw him on his ass if she knew he'd used the word *soft* to describe her in any way.

Speaking of the sergeant, he'd better check his email. He picked up his phone and scrolled to his mail app. Hers was the only new email.

Guardians:

Please read the following information about SRBC12 (Split Rock Boot Camp, 12 for the number of recruits).

For simplicity, the recruits will address me as Sergeant B.

Your recruit will need to arrive at camp on Fridays with these items:

Breakfast each day
Lunch each day
2 snacks each day (NO CANDY)
Sunscreen
A bedroll—sleeping bag or blanket
Canteen—or a water bottle with a carabiner
A long-sleeved jacket with a hood

In addition, the recruit must wear the SRBC12 uniform, which consists of ONE of each of the following items:

Khaki or camo shorts OR khaki or camo pants
A PLAIN short-sleeved army green or tan T-shirt
Hiking boots or shoes suited for outdoor athletics
A ball cap, preferably tan

The recruits will each be assigned a locker on their first day. They may choose to leave the required items in their lockers at the end of the training day. Items that are NOT on this list are NOT allowed at any time. Specifically candy, gum, cell phones, handheld video games, earbuds, fidget spinners. NO EXCEPTIONS. Infractions could result in expulsion from the program.

Thank you in advance for your cooperation. Please bring the signed registration form, medical form, and liability waiver. See you Friday at 0700 at WWC.

Streeter couldn't help but groan. He wasn't sure if this boot camp would be good for Olivia or an absolute disaster.

One thing was for certain, Sergeant Bailey Masterson took her job very seriously.

Sounds like you.

Well, they'd get along great, then.

He printed the forms and started filling them out. On the last section of the medical form, in the subsection marked ADDITIONAL COMMENTS, he read the last two questions twice.

Has your child ever been diagnosed with Autism Spectrum Disorder (ASD)?

Does your child have any emotional triggers that result in abnormal behavior? If yes, please list cause and effect.

Streeter scrubbed his hands over his face. How was he supposed to answer without writing a damn book about Olivia's short history that'd have Bailey gawking at his daughter—and him—differently? Before camp even started?

Not happening.

The ASD question . . . he wrote *NO*.

Olivia was a high-functioning child. She'd *passed*, for lack of a better term, the precursor checklist for an autism diagnosis, but she hadn't gotten off scot-free. She'd been diagnosed with a dissociative disorder, which still required weekly appointments with a child psychologist. Olivia had made progress, and he held on to hope that would continue.

In the meantime, he enrolled her at a private academic institute that kept her mind stimulated—at least three hours a day, once a week. And the report from the babysitter on rotation this week had been short of glowing. One benefit of Olivia's detachment? She hadn't asked why pink-haired Meghan hadn't been around.

He stacked the papers on the counter.

Lights off, door locked, kiddo checked on, he crawled into bed and waited for the sweet oblivion of sleep.

&cen;

Friday morning, the first day of boot camp didn't start out great.

Olivia was used to choosing her own clothing—in some shade of purple or pink—and balked at wearing a tan T-shirt and "boy" pants.

He compromised, allowing her to pack her pink raincoat, because the required color for that hadn't been spelled out. He also used pink hair ties because she only owned ones in a pastel shade.

With Olivia's backpack loaded and her new hiking boots on, Streeter walked his daughter up to the Split Rock Lodge. He could've spent the time going over the camp rules one more time, but the morning was pretty—sunshine, bright blue skies, a slight chill in the air—and he opted to enjoy their rare quiet time.

Olivia hadn't asked a million questions. She hadn't let him carry her backpack either. As they approached the side door, she said, "Daddy?"

"What's up, buttercup?"

She didn't crack a smile. "If I hate this camp, can I quit?"

"You won't hate it. Your friends are here. It's only one day a week. And it'll help you learn to listen and follow the rules since you start school at the end of the summer."

"I already know how to follow the rules. I just don't like 'em."

Hard not to laugh at that.

She kicked at a dandelion.

"Something else on your mind?"

"I don't think she likes me."

"Who?"

"Sergeant B."

"What makes you think that?"

"She hasn't given me back my drums."

He fought a smile. It wasn't for lack of trying. Every morning Olivia marched up to Bailey's door and politely asked for the return of her drum set. Every morning, as he waited at the end of the walkway, Bailey said no. "I'm thinkin' if you prove to her that you can listen and follow the camp rules, she'll see you're ready to be responsible with your drums again."

Her wrinkled nose indicated her skepticism.

He bent down and kissed it. "The day will fly by. I'll be back before you know it."

In the back room of Wild West Clothiers he helped Olivia put her things in her "locker"—a milk crate with her name on it.

"If you'll stand in front of your lockers," Sergeant B said, "I'll take roll call."

Streeter joined the other parents, all women—not a surprise, he was used to being the lone male at many parental functions—who were clustered along the back wall.

Only one locker hadn't been claimed.

He watched Bailey's face when Penelope sailed in, dragging her daughter behind her.

Great. Last year when Penelope discovered he was a single parent, she'd insisted on setting up a playdate between Olivia and her daughter Jessamyn. Only, it'd felt too much like a *date* date between them. Then Jessamyn turned out to be bratty—Olivia's words—and she'd informed him she'd never play with Jessamyn again.

Sergeant B marched over to the parental group. Her military bearing, her army fatigues, her stance broadcasted *woman in charge* and damn if he didn't have the urge to stand up straighter.

"With all of you working at the Split Rock in some capacity, I'm asking that you please respect what I'm trying to accomplish and don't 'drop by' to see how your child is faring. If there's an issue, you will get a full report at the end of the day. See you at seventeen hundred."

Talk about a dismissal. No one argued with her or asked for additional information. And none of the kids raced over for last good-byes either.

He walked back to the employees' compound, climbed in his truck and drove over to Tobin's place. This back-and-forth stuff was getting old. Maybe it was time to break ground on their house. A house with a yard. A house away from strangers. A house where he wouldn't freak out if Olivia went outside unsupervised.

Who the hell was he kidding? He'd never let her out of his sight on the ranch either.

Streeter spent the morning checking cattle and dealing with ranch business before he returned to the Split Rock. He and Ted scoured the backwater sections of the ranch searching for a couple of heifers and their calves that'd disappeared. The terrain required horses instead of four-wheelers, so by the time he'd dealt with brushing down his horse and putting away his tack, he was ten minutes late to pick up Olivia.

All the other kids were already gone.

He'd been racked in the family jewels enough times that he automatically turned his hips when she ran at him. "Hey, girlie." He bent to kiss the top of her head and it crunched beneath his lips. "What's in your hair?"

"I hafta tell you something but you can't get mad 'cause I already got demerits from Sergeant B" came out in a rush.

"Demerits for what?"

"Usin' the glue without permission."

"You put glue in your hair?" Christ. She was five. She knew better than that.

"No, Daddy, we were makin' masks and the glue kinda got everywhere." His gaze caught Sergeant B's. "Where were you?"

"A very brief bathroom break."

Before he could ask how many times the kids had been left alone, Olivia piped in with, "And Sergeant B got a demerit for leaving her post!"

"Who gave Sergeant B a demerit?"

"She gave it to herself! And when we had to do push-ups as our DA, she did them too. Twice as many as we did."

Olivia looked positively gleeful. After getting in trouble?

Streeter glanced over at the drill sergeant. "What's a DA?"

"Disciplinary action. It teaches consequences for breaking a rule." She shrugged. "I learned the hard way not to leave them unattended for even five minutes. It showed them no one is above the rules. Not even me."

He was about to give her props . . . when he noticed archery equipment propped in the corner. Not plastic bows, but real carbon-fiber bows. And the arrows weren't a kid's suction-cup type, but actual arrows with metal tips. "I hope you're not turnin' the recruits loose with those," he said half-jokingly.

"Don't be ridiculous. They were fully supervised. I only set up two targets during archery skills. I oversaw every shot from every kid."

In three strides, Streeter loomed over her. "You let these kids shoot real arrows today?"

"Those arrows have practice tips. Which are used for archery practice. It's not like I loaded them with broadhead tips."

"You are missin' the point, Sergeant," he half growled. "I didn't sign my kid up for some dangerous—"

"Yes, you did. Would you like to see the release form that you signed, Mr. Hale?" she said sweetly.

Dammit. "What are your qualifications?"

"Maybe you should've asked that *before* you signed her up."

"None of the other parents have an issue with you teachin' military-level archery on the first day of camp?"

"You could've asked them that yourself, had you been on time to pick Olivia up today."

His cheeks heated.

She smiled at his discomfort. "And it's not military level. The bows and arrows belong to Brianna Lawson and Isabelle Jackson. Both girls are currently part of an archery club, and their parents agreed to let them be team leaders on that skill."

Son of a bitch. "Why didn't you tell us—"

"Daddy? What's wrong?"

Everything. Streeter forced himself to step back. "Nothin'."

"Did Sergeant B tell you how good I did at archery today?"

Smarmy Sergeant B lifted a brow.

"Uh, we—"

"Hadn't gotten to that part yet," the sergeant finished. "Why don't you tell him the exciting news yourself, recruit?"

Olivia did a little bounce. "I got a merit for bein' the best archer in my group!"

"That's great, sweetheart."

"You don't sound very excited," she complained.

The sergeant's comments rankled. Why was he the bad guy for worrying about his daughter's safety?

Let it go. She had fun. Earning a merit and a demerit officially makes this day a wash.

He set his hand on Olivia's shoulder. "Time to go." He got them out of there before he said something he'd regret.

Halfway down the hill, Streeter realized that was the third time he'd skipped saying good-bye to her.

Once they cleared the privacy fence separating the employees' quarters from the lodge grounds, Olivia said, "Gramma?"

"There's my little princess."

This was the perfect capper to his day—dealing with his former mother-in-law an hour early.

Streeter looked at his watch. "You weren't supposed to be here until six, Deenie."

"I couldn't wait to see my girl." She frowned at Olivia's outfit and gingerly touched her head. "What's this?"

"Glue."

"Glue? How on earth did that happen?"

"A craft accident at her day camp. I figured she'd have time to shower before you showed up."

Deenie sent him a tight smile. "It's not like I haven't bathed her before." She winked at Olivia. "Guess this means you'll have a bubble bath in Gramma's big garden tub first thing."

"Yay!"

"She's not packed either," he pointed out.

She sighed. "Honestly, Streeter, you know she has her own bedroom and her own clothes at my house."

"I'm well aware of that. You feedin' her supper too?"

"Of course."

"I already know what I want, Gramma. Macaroni and hot dogs and cupcakes with pink frosting and gummy worms on top!"

"I've already got it all laid out."

Guess he'd be dining alone on the macaroni and hot dog supper he'd planned for him and Olivia. He started toward the parking lot. "I'll grab her car seat."

"Is that really necessary? I mean . . . she *is* five."

He whirled around. "The car seat goes or she stays. Your choice."

"Fine. I just think you're being a little overprotective."

Maybe if you'd been a little more overprotective with your own daughter, she wouldn't be dead.

Sometimes he couldn't keep from playing the blame game. He immediately felt guilty for it, especially since he knew Deenie's thoughts had traveled that same path about him.

He sucked it up and said nothing. He transferred the car seat from his SUV to hers. Then he crouched down and took Olivia's hands. "I love you, girlie."

"I love you too, Daddy."

"Be good for Gramma. And remember our house rules apply at her house too." Then he buckled her in and shut the door.

Across the car roof he caught Deenie's eye. "Grandpa Steve is takin' her for a little while tomorrow?"

"So he says."

"I'd better hear from both of you as soon as you figure it out, Deenie. Your problem with him and vice versa ain't my problem or Olivia's. The moment it becomes a problem . . . these weekend visitations end. Understand?"

She sniffed. "Yes, Streeter, you've made that abundantly clear."

"Good. Call me if you need anything."

He watched his heart drive away until she turned the corner and he couldn't see her waving anymore.

For most people weekends flew by. For him, they never seemed to end.

Chapter Seven

"Stay at this end of the pool, Gage. I mean it. If I see you inch even your baby toe past the elephant slide, we're packing up."

"But there's nobody here to play with," he complained.

"You've got me." Bailey whipped off her bathing suit cover-up and tossed it on a lounge chair. "C'mere and get your sunscreen on."

After thoroughly coating his skin—including the tips of his ears—she grabbed the plastic ball and the doughnut-shaped floaty. "You're up first, sport. Try to get the ball in the hole before the jets come on."

It was fun having the Split Rock pool to themselves. They made up crazy games, went down the slide backward. She even let him hang like a monkey on the end of the diving board as she swam around him pretending to be a shark.

After an hour she forced him to take a break from the sun and they lounged under a big beach umbrella.

She'd known their private pool time wouldn't last, but she was surprised to see Streeter and Olivia Hale passing through the gate.

She didn't think green-eyed Daddio could swim with that stick up his ass.

Not nice, Sergeant.

But true, nonetheless.

Things were still tense between them. The first day at camp had gone well for her . . . until the last hour. In the five minutes Bailey had taken to use the bathroom, she'd come back to see that Olivia had up-ended a gallon-sized bottle of glue for the mask-making craft, showing Rhett, Gage and Cody how to make molds—by slapping glue-soaked strips of newspaper on their faces and heads. Although it'd been hard enough to scrub off, it could've been worse.

Streeter hadn't gotten upset about that. He'd blown a gasket when he'd seen the kids' archery supplies. Immediately demanding answers about her teaching qualifications, safety measures, safety precautions, until she'd suggested he discuss it with Renner and Janie since it'd been their idea.

And she hadn't seen him since.

Bailey assumed they'd been out of town, because Olivia hadn't knocked on her door all weekend, asking whether she could have her drums back, a habit she'd gotten into every morning.

Gage started bouncing on the lounger as soon as he noticed Olivia. "Can I play with her? Please?"

"Finish your snack."

"But . . ."

Bailey leaned in. "Gage, honey, let Olivia have time with her dad first. If we're still here after that then you can ask if she wants to play."

"But she's waving at me!"

"Not the same thing as waving you over to her, bud. So wave back."

He grumbled and slurped his juice box really loud.

Bailey adjusted her lounge chair and tilted the umbrella to put them completely in the shade. Too much sun caused her extra problems. She glanced up in time to see Streeter taking off his T-shirt. When he faced her, lucky thing she wore sunglasses because her eyes nearly bugged out of her head.

Green-eyed Daddio was supposed to have a "dad" body—slumped

posture, flabby arms, a soft middle, hairy in all the wrong places, pasty white skin and sporting ugly Bermuda shorts—not broad shoulders, a firm chest, muscled biceps, a flat abdomen and the perfect amount of dark hair arrowing down his torso and disappearing into sexy board shorts.

Holy shit.

She groaned.

"What's wrong, Aunt B?"

"My throat's dry. Hand me a juice box, would you?"

To keep Gage engaged during their pool break, she let him play games on her phone. She turned her head, hoping she looked as if she were napping, when in reality, she couldn't keep her eyes off Streeter's banging body.

When he turned around and she got a gander at his muscled back and tight ass, she groaned again.

Gage handed her another juice box without saying a word.

But Bailey noticed while she had her focus on Streeter that *his* focus was one hundred percent on Olivia. He was teaching her to swim in the deep water, trying to allay her fears while building her enthusiasm. He had an abundance of patience with her, even when she became frustrated. He understood when she'd had enough and they retreated to the shallow end to frolic. When Streeter laughed, Bailey couldn't help but smile because he truly looked relaxed and happy.

A few minutes later, Olivia bounded over. "Can Gage play with me, Sergeant B?"

"It's okay with your dad?"

"Uh-huh."

"All right." Gage jumped up and she snagged him by the arm. "But first you need another coat of sunscreen."

He knew better than to argue.

When Bailey stood, she noticed that Streeter had moved the red rope with the plastic disks closer to the slide. "Good plan." She plopped down next to him on the cement. "I never would've thought of that."

"I have to be very literal with Olivia on rules or she'll find a way around them."

"You don't have to tell me that."

Silence passed as they watched the kids playing.

She stared ahead but she felt Streeter's eyes on her. "What?"

"I'm surprised you're down here. I thought you'd lounge in your deck chair."

"Gage is in the water, I'm in the water. I'd never take a chance with my nephew's safety," she said tersely.

Streeter held up his hands. "Sorry, that came out wrong. It's just . . . I can't trust Olivia's aunt on land with her, say nothin' of the water."

Bailey brushed a bug off her leg. "I know my limits. I'd never take all three boys swimming at one time in a place with no lifeguard. I don't know that even my sister has tried that." She took a chance on continuing the conversation. "Olivia's aunt . . . meaning your sister?"

He shook his head. "Her mother's sister."

Interesting that he didn't say his *wife's* sister.

After that, Streeter didn't utter a peep and Bailey wondered if he was this closed off around everyone or just with her.

Then he said, "I have two brothers, no sisters."

"Older? Younger?"

"One of each."

She grinned. "Ah. The middle child. Are you the peacemaker in your family?"

"Nope. I'm the clichéd forgotten one." He sat up. "Olivia. No running."

"That goes for you too, Gage," she warned.

Silence stretched between them again and it drove Bailey crazy. How was she supposed to get to know hot-bodied Daddio if he wouldn't talk to her?

Maybe that's the point, dumb-ass.

So naturally, she pushed the point. "I'm the youngest and Gage is the youngest so that's why I seem to have a special bond with him."

"But he's not the youngest anymore."

"That's why it's hard for him. He's been the baby his whole life, and now he's not. Things might've been different if they'd had another boy, but a baby girl . . . he's getting lost in the shuffle. And as the forgotten youngest, I know how that feels."

A minute or so passed before he spoke.

"I imagine my younger brother would agree with you. My older brother and I were thick as thieves and mostly ignored him growin' up. It's only been the past few years he and I have gotten close."

"What changed?"

Streeter's entire demeanor turned so rigid she could've used his body as a surfboard. But she didn't apologize. Like it or not, they were in each other's lives as neighbors, and as parent and teacher. Maybe if they got past his barrier they could actually be friendly.

When Streeter shifted as if he intended to stand up, Bailey set her hand on his leg. "Stay and talk to me."

"Why does it matter to you?"

"Because I don't know anything about you or your family, and I wasn't trying to chase you off by asking anything personal."

He snorted derisively. "You really expect me to believe that the damn gossipmongers haven't gleefully shared the tale of poor Olivia and Streeter Hale?"

Bailey removed her hand from his muscular thigh and shoved her sunglasses on top of her head. "If by 'gossipmongers' you mean my sister and brother-in-law . . . no, they haven't told me anything about your family because I haven't asked them. I hope you have more faith in your employers than to believe *they'd* gossip about an employee's personal life to another employee if I'd asked them—not that I'd do that. So I'm asking you, Streeter, to tell me what changed in your life that allowed you to get close to your younger brother. That's it."

His eyes searched her face so intently she wondered if he'd counted her freckles. But whatever he saw took the starch out of his spine. "Sorry. Habit."

She didn't look away when she said, "Apology accepted."

He offered his hand. "Truce?"

When Bailey shook his hand she noticed it engulfed hers completely. "Truce."

Olivia shrieked.

They both turned to see Gage aiming a water tube at her. Bailey tensed, waiting for Streeter to tell Gage to knock it off. But he just said, "Olivia. Stop screaming."

"But it's cold!"

"You want to get out?"

"No!"

"Then stop screaming." He sighed. "Never knew that little girls screamed so much."

Bailey laughed. "I never knew that little boys hit each other so much."

Streeter smiled at her.

Oh, damn, damn, damn. Not fair. The corners of his eyes crinkled when he smiled like that.

He turned away to watch his daughter, giving Bailey time to lower her shades and splash some cold water on herself.

A few minutes passed and Streeter tensed up again, but he didn't clam up. "My life changed when Olivia's mother died. Olivia was six months old and I went from bein' a full-time rancher to a full-time parent. At the time I was ranching with my dad and older brother. They made it so miserable that I quit after they accused me of not pullin' my weight."

"That's awful."

He shrugged. "Come to find out they're awful guys. My job skills were limited to ranching and I was lucky enough to land this job. The irony is, I started out job-sharing with my little brother."

"Why is that ironic?"

"Because me'n our older brother and dad cut him out of our family ranching business. I realized what we'd done to him was all kinds of wrong when I was standin' on the wrong side of the fence, so to speak. Anyway, he's a better man than me. He had no issue with us workin' together, knowing I had to put Olivia first. Then when his position in Casper went to full-time, Renner kept me on. Now my brother is my closest friend and I don't know how I would've made it through the last four years if not for him and his wife."

Bailey forced herself to be satisfied that he'd opened up and bit back the million other questions she had. "I'm glad for you. The irony in my situation is that I had to join the army and move away from my sister to get closer to her."

"Your older sister too?"

"Liberty is twelve years older than me. She moved out when I was six. But since we were both in the army, we now have that common thread. I'm happy after she retired she settled in Denver so she and Harper get to see each other more often."

She felt him studying her before he refocused on Olivia. "What about you? Are you done with army life?"

"Yes . . . and no."

"That cleared things up." Streeter splashed her. "Try again."

Bailey laughed and splashed him back. "I'm on sabbatical for the summer."

"Ain't that unusual for you to be on sabbatical for so long?"

Most people didn't pick up on that. "Technically, I had a bunch of leave saved up and I took it. Without sounding pathetic . . . I had nowhere else to go. Traveling alone on vacation sucks. After talking to Harper, I got the feeling she could use extra help with her kids and the store. So my intentions of hanging around and burning a couple of weeks of vacation has turned into me being here the entire summer. And running a day camp."

"Do you feel we railroaded you into takin' on the kids' camp?"

"Maybe a little. But it was also a good excuse."

"An excuse for what?"

Bailey wasn't used to talking about family matters. But she'd demanded honesty from him so he deserved the truth from her. "To help Harper any way I can."

"I don't follow."

"My sister is overwhelmed with being a mother to four kids, a rancher's wife and a business owner. She jokes about it, but she's not been herself. Bran knows her better than anyone and I'm not sure he knows how to help her either." She briefly pressed her lips tighter, biting back her confession that she understood how sadness could spiral you deeper into that vortex of darkness and hopelessness. "Depression is one of those things that no one talks about, especially when someone appears to have it all. So I'll be here to bolster her, to help her wherever, whenever and however she needs me until she's ready to tackle the decisions weighing on her."

Streeter abruptly stood. "Olivia, it's time to go."

Bailey did a double take. What the hell? He was leaving right in the middle of a conversation? That was ruder than his usual habit of walking away without saying good-bye when he tired of talking to her.

He'd stepped up his . . . *and we're done* game.

Screw that.

No, screw him.

"You're starting to burn, Sergeant."

Sergeant. They were back to that now.

"Oh, I think you've burned me plenty of times now, Mr. Hale."

Ignoring his proffered hand, she rolled to her feet and walked over to Gage. "Hey, bud, you ready for another game of shark attack?"

His blue eyes lit up. "Can Olivia play too?"

"Nope. It's just us. So climb on, monkey boy." Bailey picked him up and spun him around piggyback style, and they waded into the deeper water.

When she turned around at the diving board, she saw that Olivia and her grumpy father were gone.

She should be thinking *good riddance, whatever, I tried.* But she just felt sad. She'd put herself out there, like her therapist had suggested, and she'd failed . . . which just circled back to why she didn't "put herself out there" to begin with. She was dealing with enough personal failures; she didn't need his continual rejection on top of it.

Chapter Eight

"Daddy, where we goin'?"

"To Uncle Tobin and Aunt Jade's for supper."

"Oh. I forgot."

Streeter looked at Olivia in the rearview mirror. "Where'd you think we were goin'?"

"To town so I could buy my own bow and arrow."

"We'll see if you're still interested in archery after this week's camp, okay?"

She returned her gaze out the window. Then she added, "Sergeant B said she's gonna let us have BB guns next time."

Not if he had anything to say about it.

But that's the problem, isn't it? You don't know what to say to the sexy spitfire sergeant.

Streeter couldn't remember the last time anyone had pushed him to talk. It'd surprised him that she didn't know the gruesome details about how Olivia's mother had died. Maybe she already knew, but he opted to believe she'd truly been interested in his relationships with his brothers. Which had opened the door for her to talk about her sisters, specifically her worries over Harper's stress levels with a new baby.

And he'd panicked. He'd cut her off and run before she could do the unthinkable and ask him how Olivia's mom had dealt with postpartum depression. Because he couldn't really answer the way he wanted: *Well, my wife didn't talk about her depression and told me everything was fine—a lie I believed right up until the minute I found her body.*

Even in his own head he knew he sounded clinical and bitter describing the event in those terms, but his therapist assured him that addressing it without euphemisms would allow him to move past it.

He'd moved past some things, others not so much.

Yet, Streeter understood that no one could fault him for not trying to meet new people, because he'd be back to square one: explaining what had caused him to be a single parent and a widower at such a young age.

He turned down the long driveway and parked in front of the funky house Tobin and Jade had inherited from Jade's grandmother. Streeter and Olivia both loved it here. This place had become home to them.

Tobin paced on the porch with his two-month-old son cradled in his arms. He opened the childproof gate that kept their energetic two-year-old daughter, Amber, corralled. "Get in here quick because I don't have the energy to chase her down again."

Streeter laughed.

Olivia immediately led Amber to the opposite end of the porch and they settled amid a pile of toys.

"Good to see you, T." Streeter held up a six-pack of hard cider. "Here's our contribution to supper."

"That's perfect. Ask Jade if she wants one when you go inside to grab the opener." Tobin gently jiggled the baby. "This is the first time Micah has slept all damn day."

"Rough, man. I'll be right back." Streeter didn't let the screen door slam when he entered the house. He turned the corner into the kitchen and saw his sister-in-law chopping carrots like a professional chef.

She was also crying.

What to do? Should he go away?

Put his arms around her?

He sucked at this.

Or maybe you could just stand here paralyzed at the thought of talking to a petite woman who you consider your sister.

Fuck that. He started toward her. "Knock knock."

Jade glanced up and wiped her face on her sleeve. "Hey, Street."

"Smells good in here."

"Don't get too excited. It's pasta. I'm behind on making the sauce because our son wouldn't let me put him down all day."

"Tobin mentioned that you might be needing an adult beverage."

"God, yes please."

Streeter plucked the magnetic bottle opener off the fridge and popped the tops on the cider. He and Jade clinked bottles before they each took a sip.

Jade sighed. "That's what I needed. Thank you." She gestured with the knife. "Now off with you so I can finish my sauce."

He peered in the saucepan. "You put carrots in your red sauce?"

"It's an extra serving of vegetables for my husband and daughter that I don't have to nag them to eat, so don't tattle on me."

"I wouldn't dream of it." Streeter snagged the bottles and returned outside.

Tobin lounged on the porch swing with Micah tucked close to his body.

After Streeter handed over the cider, he lowered himself into a wicker chair.

"So what's new?"

"Nothin' much." *Except I'm attracted to a sexy drill sergeant with a body that sends dirty thoughts straight to my dick and I'm such a moron I don't even know how to talk to her about normal stuff.* "How about you?"

"Workin' and changing diapers."

He swallowed a long drink of crisp, cold cider.

"Ain't we the exciting pair?" Tobin said.

"No one's ever used 'exciting' to describe me, bro."

Olivia hopped up and rested her hands on Streeter's thigh. "Something exciting happened to *me*, Uncle Tobin."

He grinned at her. "I'm all ears, darlin'."

"We got to use bows and arrows at boot camp! And Sergeant B says I'm a natural."

"That *is* exciting."

"Uh-huh. I even hit the target more than Tate did, and he's *nine*."

Tobin whistled softly. "You're a real Katniss Everdeen."

Olivia frowned. "Who's that?"

"A reference that's a little over her head, Uncle Tobin." Streeter smoothed Olivia's hair back. They'd rushed from the pool and he'd forgotten to comb out the tangles—an oversight he'd pay for after her bath tonight. "It's a book you'll read when you're older."

"I can read now!"

"I know you can. In fact, why don't you read to Amber? She loves that."

"Okay." Olivia skipped away.

Tobin lowered his voice. "How's she doin'?"

"She hasn't chased off either of her new babysitters. She barely threw a tantrum when she came back from Gramma Deenie's. I only got one incident report from her camp counselor." He sipped his cider. "And she hasn't had night terrors for an entire week."

"That's progress, right?"

"Yep."

"Deenie's still insisting on weekly visits?"

"Uh-huh. And Steve too."

"But doesn't Olivia act up more after she's been with her grandma and grandpa?"

Streeter picked at the label on his bottle. "Not as much as she used to, but what am I supposed to do about it?" He glanced over his shoulder to make sure she wasn't listening. "Olivia is all they have of Danica. It sucks that Deenie and Steve divorced after Danica died, but I can't deny either of them time with her."

"But one of them takin' her for an overnight visit ain't givin' you the break you deserve when they have to call you to find out why she's cryin' and upset."

"She turns into a dictator because they each spoil her rotten tryin' to outdo the other. Then they're surprised when they try to tell her no and she doesn't listen. On the plus side, they've finally grasped that because her level of attachment is minimal, she doesn't hold grudges." He rubbed the furrow between his brow, trying to stave off the headache from thinking about his former in-laws. "Deenie stopped givin' her unlimited sweets, which curbed some of the behavior issues, despite Deenie arguing with me that too much sugar is just an old wives' tale. They still buy her anything she wants, but at least the things they buy her have to stay at their houses. I call that a win."

Tobin sighed. "I don't know how you do it, man."

Streeter shrugged. "I don't have a choice. I love her. The people who loved her mother need to love her too and I have to let them."

"Fine. Be all altruistic and shit. But Friday night, after she gets picked up by Gramma Deenie, you'n me are havin' a beer at the Buckeye."

"I doubt Jade would be happy about you ditching your family to buy me a beer."

"I haven't forgotten that you're my family too, Street."

Streeter looked away.

Jade breezed out, set two more ciders on the table and hugged Streeter from behind. "I think you boys having a brew at the Buckeye is a marvelous idea since I know you'd both rather be drinking beer than cider." She kissed his cheek and whispered, "Tobin needs adult time with someone other than me." Then she crossed over, laid a steamy kiss on her husband and plucked their son from his arms. "Little dude is down for the count. Supper will be ready in ten."

"Thanks, babe."

The girls were being too quiet, giving Streeter an excuse to see what they were doing. They were so engrossed in flipping through books they didn't notice him, so he sauntered over to lean on the porch pillar.

"She's fine," Tobin said.

Streeter frowned at him. "I know. I just checked on her."

"Not Olivia. Jade." Tobin stood and moved next to Streeter. "I know you watch her."

This kind of talk made him so goddamned uncomfortable, but he couldn't deny it. "You sure she's fine? She was cryin' in the kitchen when I walked in."

"She always cries when she's chopping onions."

But it was carrots stuck on the tip of his tongue.

"You worry. I get it. I get why you've kept an eagle eye on her after Amber was born and now after Micah." He gulped his cider. "I ain't gonna lie. She's had a couple of meltdowns. Then again, so have I."

Streeter managed a smile.

"But I'll tell you that it's *because* of you that Jade and I talk it out. All of it. There's no stone left unturned in our lives—good, bad or ugly."

"I'm relieved to hear that."

"She's goin' back to work next week."

"Where? At the Split Rock?"

He shook his head. "Teaching summer violin lessons. Just three hours a day, three days a week to start."

"Who's watchin' the kids?"

"Me, one day. Grandma Garnet and the Mud Lilies the other two." Tobin held up his hand. "They'll have strict parameters. But they've raised ten kids between them, so I'm fine with it. Like Garnet said . . . ain't like we're expecting them to do calculus with Amber and infant aerobics with Micah. They'll love up on them while they're little and cute and can't talk back."

"Sounds like Garnet."

"She's been on her best behavior. She didn't want to add to Jade's pregnancy stress."

"You guys are really lucky to have so many people lookin' out for both of you and your kids."

Tobin cocked his head. "This is the most you've ever talked about this kinda stuff."

"Been on my mind. I still suck at talkin' about it but at least I didn't freeze up with you like I did earlier today."

Why had he said that? Now he sensed Tobin's curiosity.

"Who else you been talkin' to?"

Streeter said nothing.

"Maybe I oughta ask who's been tryin' to talk to *you*?"

"Harper's sister, Bailey."

Tobin nodded. "I heard she was in town. Anyway, go on."

"Ain't much to 'go on' about. Before she could ask me more questions, I panicked and bailed." He'd bailed on Bailey. He'd find that funny if it hadn't been at his own expense. "Forget I said anything."

"Huh-uh. Bailey's in the army. Is she the one Olivia called Sergeant B?"

"That'd be her."

"What's she like?"

Tempting.

Streeter cleared his throat. "She's sassy. For bein' like five foot nothin', she is large and in charge."

"At the kid's boot/day camp thing?"

"And everywhere else I've run into her."

"You been hangin' out someplace besides the Split Rock, bro?"

"That's what I'm tryin' to tell you. Bailey is livin' at the Split Rock."

Tobin's expression went from shock to delight. "That's great."

"No, it's not great, it's messin' with my head."

"Meaning what?"

"Meaning I see her every day." Even if she didn't see him.

"You do live and work at the same place, so that's not so unusual."

"Wrong. I wouldn't have to see her every day, except that she has Olivia's drum set so I have to accompany Olivia when she marches down there every morning to ask for it back."

Tobin frowned. "I thought you told me that you took Olivia's drums away?"

Streeter explained what'd happened.

His brother busted a gut laughing. "You didn't think that one through, did you?"

"Shut it." He lowered his voice. "Then today I saw her in a damn swimsuit at the pool. She plopped down and started talkin' to me like we were old friends."

"And?"

"And it's been so goddamned long since I've been that close to a half-naked woman that I froze up and tried not to stare at her body like some old pervert."

"Dude. First of all, if she struck up a conversation with you, did you ever think she might be interested in you?"

Streeter blinked at his brother like he'd lost his marbles. "We were the only ones at the pool. Wasn't like she had anyone else to talk to."

"But if she was interested?"

"She's Olivia's teacher."

"So?"

"So it's pointless to talk about because I ran off when the conversation hit too close to home. Now I hafta come up with an apology for bolting on her, but she gets me so flustered that I can barely talk to her—"

"Hey, guys," Jade called out through the screen door, "time to eat."

Tobin got in his face. "Don't think you were saved by the dinner bell, Street. We ain't done with this convo."

But it turned out they were done talking for the night.

After supper Jade offered to bathe Olivia with Amber, saving him from dealing with her snarly hair, so he cleaned up the kitchen and did the dishes. Then he read the girls a couple of books so Jade could shower.

While that was going on, Tobin dealt with Micah. Even after Tobin fed and changed him, the baby continued to cry and fuss.

Streeter remembered dealing with an unhappy baby and how it seemed ten times worse when he had an audience judging his parenting skills, so he and Olivia headed home.

He'd hoped she'd fall asleep in the car, but the girl was wired. And she asked questions that even Google couldn't answer.

If dinosaurs were the biggest animals, what scared them?

Who got to pick the names for all colors? What if blue should really be called orange?

Why do people skip rocks across the lake?

She asked him what he'd do if he saw a magical fairy in the forest (his answer to leave it be earned him a heavy sigh) and then she gave an explicit explanation of what she'd do: learn how to do its magic and become the queen of the world.

It was good to have goals.

By the time he'd unbuckled her from her car seat, she was asleep. Then she nestled her head on his shoulder as he carried her toward their trailer.

He loved these quiet times with her because they were becoming rare. Pretty soon she'd be too big to carry, or worse . . . she wouldn't want to be carried.

That would break his heart.

He'd stopped to dig his keys out of his pocket when he heard a door close. He glanced down the walkway to see Bailey leaving her trailer with a duffel bag.

Was she headed to the gym this late?

Maybe she'd gotten a booty call.

No surprise she'd have no trouble finding a hookup.

Knock it off, perv.

Bailey paused when she reached him. "Do you need help?"

"Nah, I got it. But thanks." He turned the key in the lock before looking at her again. "You're out late." Way to sound accusatory.

"I missed my workout this morning." She gave him a once-over. "You're out late yourself."

"We had supper with my brother and his family. That's why we left the pool, uh . . . like we did."

She cocked her head. "Really? You *suddenly* remembered you had dinner plans during the middle of our conversation?"

They studied each other for a moment.

Somehow he found the guts to say, "No."

"Okay. That's progress. Tell me . . . did I say something to offend you?"

"Nope. I just . . ." *Don't know how to act around you.*

"You just . . . what? My friendliness annoyed you because you have enough friends?"

"God, no. That's not it. Not even close."

"Then what?"

He leaned in. "This right here is *what* it is. Surely you've noticed I'm no good at small talk." He shifted Olivia higher. "I ain't so hot at big talk either."

She laughed softly. "I know you're not trying to be funny, but—"

"But you're laughin' at me."

"Not *at* you, Streeter. I'm laughing because usually I'm the one who's awkward."

"I doubt that."

"You've probably noticed that I tend to come on strong."

"You? Nah."

She laughed again. "Maybe you're just out of practice with small talk."

"Yeah, well, cattle ain't much on talkin' back."

"See? You *are* funny."

Her grin widened and he saw she had a tiny dimple on the right side of her smile. How hadn't he noticed that sexy little divot before now?

When she continued to smile without speaking, he said, "What?"

"Nothing. I just like seeing you like this."

"Like what? Fumblin' my words like a tongue-tied fool?"

"No, I like that you're not trying to get away from me."

He blinked at her and kept his mouth shut.

"Plus, you're cute when you're flustered."

Cute? "Jesus. No one has called me 'cute' since junior high."

"Then maybe it's past time you heard it. You're very cute, Streeter Hale, and I'm crushing on you big-time."

His jaw might've hit the top of Olivia's head when it dropped.

"I'm not good at small talk either. I'm more a cut-to-the-chase kinda chick."

"Good to know."

She bumped him with her hip as she walked past. "Sweet dreams, cutie. See ya around."

❧

The following night Streeter had just finished watching the fourth episode of the third season of *Portlandia*—such a weird fuckin' show but he'd gotten sucked into binge-watching it—when he heard a whack-whack-whack outside.

He hit mute and listened.

Another two rounds of it started and stopped.

Then he heard voices.

He pulled his T-shirt over his head and shoved his feet into his boots before he sailed out the door.

That was when Streeter saw Bailey beating something—a shoe?—against the post at the end of the walkway. He started toward her, not stealthily, but he doubted she could hear him over her cursing.

"Stupid-fucking-Wyoming-mud-fucking-everywhere-cheapassmotherfucking-shoes-burn-them-starting-with-these-goddamned-busted-shoelaces—"

"Bailey?"

Her head snapped up. She wiped her sweaty brow with the back of her forearm and said, "Oh. Hey, Streeter," like he hadn't caught her beating the fuck out of her shoe.

His eyes narrowed on her. She had the left shoe on, a sock on her right foot and the right shoe in her hand. Her shorts and T-shirt were plastered to her body. Her legs, arms and face were splattered with mud. And was that more mud running down the side of her shin, or blood? He stormed closer. "What happened to you? Are you all right?"

"I'm pissed off. I went for a run and the laces on this shoe"—Bailey held up the offending shoe—"fucking unraveled and broke. Broke! Like they'd been pre-nicked with scissors and it unraveled like it'd been run through a cocksucking shredder. Cheap-assed things. And of course it happened when I was three fucking miles from here. So my choices were to do a walking shuffle combo or to take the shoe off and walk with one bare foot on the gravel road or in the muddy grass. I tried both options, which both sucked ass by the way. I fell down twice in the goddamned mud . . . which again, what the fuck is wrong with me because I'd somehow forgotten that this place was named Muddy Gap for a reason." She took a breath. "I'm just so fucking mad that I thought if I could beat this shoe to pieces I'd feel better."

"Do you?"

"A little." She blinked at him. "What are you doing out here?"

"I heard 'whack whack whack' and thought maybe you'd taken up Olivia's drums, so I came out to listen."

Bailey gave him the crooked smile that just did it for him. "Sorry to disappoint you."

"You didn't mention the other option besides shuffling home. You could've called"—*me*—"someone to come get you."

"I didn't have my phone."

"What?"

She gestured to her tiny orange running shorts and her skintight yellow T-shirt. "Does it look like I have any pockets? Besides, who would I have called? I don't have any friends here. So that leaves Harper. And she'd have to drive thirty minutes to come and find me at eleven at night? Everybody around here is in bed before that."

"I'm not," he pointed out.

"But Olivia is. And you would've had to wake her and put her in the car and go looking for me and don't pretend you would've been happy about it."

Streeter ran his hand through his hair. "I'm not happy that you went runnin' by yourself, after ten o'clock at night, in a remote area, on a moonless night, without your phone."

"Yeah, but—"

"That is dangerous, Bailey, and you know it. For christsake, we have mountain lions and coyotes around here. Not to mention the human predators who see a hot little thing out runnin' alone late at night, they could just overpower you and toss you in their car—"

"I can throw a two-hundred-and-fifty-pound man on his ass, so I'm not exactly some helpless damsel, Streeter," she said crossly. "And if you think I am, why don't you—"

"Come at me, *bruh*?"

His sarcastic response surprised her.

"Is that really where you wanna go with this?" he demanded when she stayed silent. "Toss off something flip when I tell you I'm worried about you?"

"That's the tack *you're* gonna take after you called me a hot little thing?"

Streeter leaned closer. "I shoulda called you a reckless, *stubborn* hot little thing."

She rolled her eyes at him. "Calling me a 'little' anything is insulting."

"Yeah? Well you called me 'cute' last night, so I guess we're even. Cute. Christ. Makes me sound like a damn chipmunk."

"You *are* chattering at me like an angry chipmunk, Streeter."

He was. God. What was wrong with him? He started to back away, an apology forming in his mouth, when she jumped in front of him, stopping his retreat.

"Ah-ah-ah, buddy. You're *not* bailing on me again because I will chase you down."

His eyebrow winged up. "You think you can catch me when you're wearin' one shoe with defective laces and a muddy sock?"

"Dude." She gestured to his clothing. "You have no room to talk about what *I'm* wearing when you're half-dressed and prancing around in shitkickers. Bold fashion choice. I kinda hate that it works on you."

Once again he blushed around this woman.

"Anyway, what I meant to say is . . . you do have a point about me acting reckless." She sighed. "The walls of the trailer were closing in on me and the treadmills at the fitness center were full, so I took off because I needed to run. After my shoelace broke, I felt like an idiot, limping through the dark. I spooked myself because I realized I could've been a late-night snack for some wild critter. Or I could've fallen down and gotten hurt worse than this and no one would've known where I was." She ducked her head. "And then to be truly morbid, I wondered if anyone would even notice I was gone."

"I would've noticed."

"You mean *Olivia* would've noticed when she showed up tomorrow morning to ask me to give back her drums."

"No, I would've noticed. I pay attention to hot little things like you far more than I'm comfortable admitting."

She blinked at him.

He crouched down to escape her questioning eyes. "Dammit, this is blood."

"It's just a scratch."

"I need to see it in the light. Come inside."

"I'm not gonna drag mud into your house. I'll be fine. If it were serious it'd probably hurt and it doesn't."

He stared her down. "Pain is not a gauge to determine the extent of the injury. You could've cut it so deep it's become numb."

"Streeter. Don't, please."

"Don't what?"

"I . . . can't . . ."

Something in her tone clawed at him. "Talk to me."

"I can't stand the sight of blood. I get woozy and want to throw up, and I don't want you to see me like that," she said in a rush.

It took every bit of his will to remain there, through the flashback of finding Danica's body. Blood everywhere. She'd slashed her wrists before she used the gun to make sure she didn't fail in taking her own life.

"I'm sorry," Bailey said, yanking him back from that horrendous memory.

"Me too, sweetheart, 'cause I'm gonna hafta insist on seein' to that cut now." He tipped her chin up to peer into her eyes. "I can't let you go and take the chance you'll pass out in the shower with no one around to help you in case you hit your head." He swept his thumb across her dimple. "Even if you let me help you, I still think you're a badass, Sergeant."

She stared at him and those pretty hazel eyes shimmered with embarrassment. "Fine. But just to keep things fair, you have to tell me something that freaks you out."

You.

When he hesitated to answer, she supplied, "You're afraid of clowns, aren't you?"

He grinned. "I think maybe you're projecting."

"Then tell me."

"Fine. Chain saws have freaked me out since I was a kid. Even now I refuse to use one."

"So you've never seen the movie . . . ?"

Streeter shuddered. "Never. Now march, soldier, so I can get you fixed up."

He held the screen door open for her. Once inside, he pointed to the counter. "Hop up."

She didn't argue.

He washed his hands and wet two paper towels. With his left hand on her knee, he gently swabbed away the mud. He saw the mark was more of a scrape than a cut.

"What's the verdict?"

"More mud than blood."

"Told ya."

He chuckled. "Couldn't resist, could you?"

"Nope."

He grabbed the first-aid kit from under the sink. "Antibacterial spray or gel?"

"Gel."

Streeter took his time dabbing gel on the tiny scrape on Bailey's very smooth, very muscular leg.

"You're good at this whole patching-up thing, Hale."

"Comes with the territory of havin' a kid who sees life as an obstacle course." He couldn't drag this out any longer without seeming like a perv. "And lucky you, I have a wide selection of bandages."

"Wonder Woman?"

"Of course." He dug through the kit until he found the small bandage and pressed it on. "Done."

"Thanks for the TLC."

He bit back a snort and fussed with the first-aid kit.

"But you forgot something." She leaned closer. "Aren't you gonna offer to kiss it and make it better?" she said in a husky voice that stirred his cock.

"First time I kiss you ain't gonna be on your leg." The words just slipped out of his mouth.

Silence.

What the fuck had possessed him to say that all cocky-like? As if sexy stuff dripped from his lips all the damn time. Christ. He couldn't even look at her now.

Bailey slid off the counter. She paused behind him.

Streeter didn't turn around.

"That's something I'm looking forward to." She squeezed his biceps. "It's late. I'll see myself out."

Then she was gone.

Chapter Nine

Olivia Hale was nothing if not persistent.

She'd knocked on Bailey's door Monday, Tuesday and Wednesday mornings at seven a.m., asking politely if she could have her drum set back.

Every morning Bailey replied she'd think about it.

So Bailey found herself disappointed on Thursday morning when there'd been no sign of her little neighbor. At seven thirty she grabbed her gym bag and headed to the fitness center. An hour of cardio and weight training cleared her head, although she'd probably hit the gym again for some stretching. Staying in shape and trying to eat right allowed her to feel some measure of control.

But her day hadn't played out well at all. She and Harper had their first fight of the summer.

In the past, they could barely get through two days without sniping at each other. This time they'd lasted a month. Bailey's hopes that her older sister would value her opinion were dashed when Harper refused to even discuss the issue.

Then she'd given Bailey the day off. Which had only amounted to two hours, but still, it was the principle of the thing.

While she picked up supplies for boot camp, her old friend Amy called. They'd been trying to get together for two weeks and Amy finally had a free Friday night since her ex-husband had the kids for the weekend. After making plans to meet, Bailey decided she needed new duds to wear out and about in the greater Muddy Gap area. The irony that she worked in a clothing store and ended up buying a couple of outfits in Casper wasn't lost on her.

She didn't return to the Split Rock until after dusk. The first thing she noticed after exiting the car was the glow of a campfire. She followed the sounds of laughter to the common area at the end of the last trailer and saw Pete and Bobbie, the married caretakers, on one side of the fire pit, and Olivia and Streeter on the other side.

Bobbie noticed her first. "Bailey! Pull up a chair. There's plenty of room."

"Thanks. Let me ditch my bags and grab a beer." Her gaze moved between Bobbie and Pete. "You guys interested?"

"Sure, we'll both have one," Pete said, "since I know you don't drink them weird-flavored kinds."

Then Bailey looked at Streeter. His dark blond hair had taken on a golden glow from the fire, turning it reddish gold. Normally he kept that thick hair hidden beneath a ball cap or a cowboy hat, which also allowed his face to remain half-shadowed. But tonight, without that usual armor, he looked younger. More relaxed. Approachable.

It also helped that he wasn't exuding those back-off vibes. "How about you, Streeter? Care for a beer?"

"That'd be great."

"Olivia? Would you like a juice box?"

"Yes, please. And you can have one of my hot dogs," Olivia offered. She held out a stick that had a black chunk on the end that might've been meat at one time.

"Thanks, but I already ate."

"Then you could bring us some marshmallows."

"Olivia. Is that the polite way to ask?" Streeter said sharply.

She sighed. "Sorry. Daddy said we had s'mores stuff but all we got is graham crackers. Do you have any marshmallows?"

"I'll check to see what I have."

"Yay! Oh, and we don't got chocolate either."

Bailey laughed. "Not much of a s'mores party, is it?"

"That's what *I* said!" Olivia hopped up. "I'll help you."

Streeter scooped her up and popped her back on his lap. "You've been enough help."

Inside her trailer, Bailey tossed her bags on the couch and made a beeline for the bathroom.

Great. She looked like hell. She adjusted her ponytail, smoothing back the flyaway strands, and quickly swept powder across the shiny spots on her face. She reached for her lipstick but changed her mind. Too obvious.

She snagged the beer, a juice box, a bag of marshmallows and her stash of Reese's peanut butter cups and sailed out the door.

"That was fast," Pete said.

Bailey smiled as she passed around cans. "I've been looking forward to a beer all day."

"You weren't working in the clothing store today," Bobbie pointed out.

"I did for a little while this morning. Then I had errands in Casper." She selected the seat beside Streeter, telling herself it'd be better than sitting across from him and staring at his handsome mug in the firelight.

Olivia scooted closer to eye the bag of marshmallows.

"Give her a minute before you start naggin' her for them, okay?" Streeter said to his daughter.

She released a heavy sigh.

Silence stretched, not in an uncomfortable way.

Finally, Bailey said, "This is really nice."

Pete nodded. "We used to have real wood for a campfire, but it's so windy Renner worried about stray sparks carrying over into the woods, so he put in this gas fire pit." He grinned. "Now no one has to haul wood either."

"It's been a long time since I sat in front of a fire on purpose. When I was overseas, seeing smoke wasn't a good sign."

"How many times were you over there?"

"In the sandboxes? Three. Each time nine-month stretches." She took a drink of beer. "Not as much time as some in my company."

"Well, it's good you're on leave. I know Harper is happy for your help."

That was up for debate after today.

Bailey changed the subject. "This might be a random question, but who else lives in these trailers? I hear doors and cars but I only ever see the four of you."

"Ted, who works with me at Jackson Cattle Company, lives here. His roommate, Zack, is the assistant chef up at the lodge," Streeter said.

"I doubt you've seen Zack since he doesn't finish up at the lodge until after eleven most nights," Pete added. "The trailer down from theirs is empty."

"Marta is in charge of housekeeping Monday through Friday, and she goes home to Rock Springs for the weekend. She's in the trailer next to ours, and she's the early-to-bed, early-to-rise type," Bobbie said. "We're glad to have a new, friendly face here. Been a while."

"Although I'm sure you were hopin' for neighbors your own age," Pete added.

Bailey shrugged. "Bein' military, I've learned to adapt wherever I am."

"How old are you, if you don't mind me asking?" Bobbie said.

"I'm thirty. I left Muddy Gap when I was eighteen." She tipped her head back and studied the stars. "Never thought I'd be back here for any length of time, to be honest." *Never wanted to come back* hung in the air, unspoken.

"This is our last season as the Split Rock caretakers," Pete said. "We're packing up during Christmas break."

"Why? Don't you like it?"

"We love it here, but Renner rotates workers. He says it's better to have a firm end date so everyone can make plans goin' forward."

"How long have you worked here?"

"Two years." He pointed at Streeter. "They've been here the longest."

Bailey looked at him. "How long have you guys lived here?"

"Three and a half years. I'm not a seasonal worker. But I'm not full-time either. It's complicated."

A heavy sigh sounded and Olivia demanded, "Is it time to roast marshmallows yet?"

Streeter chuckled. "Go ahead."

Olivia rustled in a bag next to her chair and brought over a package of graham crackers. "You can have the first one, Sergeant B."

Almost without thinking Bailey brushed a staticky strand of Olivia's hair behind her ear. "When we're not at camp you can call me Bailey."

"Really?"

"Yep."

"Kinda like we're friends?" Olivia said skeptically.

"Sure."

A sly look crossed her face. "My *friend* would give my drums back."

She laughed at the kid's audacity. "Nice try. I expected you to come this morning and ask for them."

"I kinda forgot 'cause Daddy was crabby. He yelled at me and everything."

"Olivia."

Bailey ignored Streeter's protest and leaned in to admit, "My sister yelled at me too, today."

Olivia scrutinized her face. "Didja cry?"

"Nope. Did you?"

She hung her head. "Uh-huh."

"Sometimes crying is the only way to let people know you're upset." She tipped Olivia's chin up. "Everybody cries. It's no big deal, okay?"

"Okay."

"Now that we're friends, I'm gonna share my secret family recipe for peanut butter s'mores."

"I'm good at keepin' secrets," Olivia confided.

Bailey felt green-eyed Daddio watching her interaction with his daughter. It surprised her that he didn't get in the middle of it. "Good." She threaded two marshmallows onto the stick. "Here you go."

Olivia turned toward the fire, brandishing the stick, almost smacking her father in the face with it.

"Ah-ah-ah. We do it together." Streeter kept her in the circle of his arms as they held the stick over the flame.

"Don't turn them into black blobs," Bailey warned.

"But I like 'em burned," Olivia said.

"Really?" She unwrapped the peanut butter cups and balanced them on the crackers. "I like mine soft but not gooey."

"Guess that's a matter of opinion," Streeter said.

Her eyes met Streeter's. "You don't agree?"

"Nope. The best part is seein' how hot you can get 'em, then bein' rewarded with a sweet, sticky center."

Lucky thing she had a good grip on the plate; she might've knocked it into the dirt when her knees went weak. Was he . . . flirting with her?

He offered her a quick grin and refocused on charring the marshmallow.

With the way her face flamed—not from just the fire pit—she nervously knocked back a big swig of beer.

Bobbie said, "Looks like that one's done, Olivia."

She moved it out of the fire and directed it to Bailey.

"Hold on to it until I get the top ready. Good. Okay, now take the stick out." She handed Olivia the plate. "Voilà. One peanut butter s'more."

"Use both hands," her dad warned.

He held the plate as Olivia brought the treat to her mouth and took a big bite. Her eyes widened and she tried to speak until her dad said, "Chew with your mouth closed."

As soon as she finished, she took another huge bite.

Bailey forced herself to look at Pete and Bobbie. "You guys want one?"

"Nah. Time for us to be headin' in." Pete stood and pulled his wife to her feet. "Bobbie's already got a sweet treat lined up for me before bedtime, doncha?"

Bailey's gaze connected with Streeter's and they smirked at each other.

Then Bobbie whapped Pete on the biceps. "It was supposed to be a surprise, snoopy man."

Neither Bailey nor Streeter could hide their grins.

When Bobbie realized how their conversation had sounded, she flapped her hand at them. "Oh pooh, you two. Me'n Pete are too old for them kinda shenanigans on a Thursday night. New ice cream is what's got him excited."

As she watched the older couple walk away, she muttered, "I hope I'm never too old for them kinda shenanigans on any night."

"I ain't had them kinda shenanigans for a long time."

Startled by his comment, her gaze hooked his. "Me either."

Please ask me to get into some dirty shenanigans with you.

"Can I have another one?" Olivia asked her dad, interrupting the moment.

He glanced down at her and wiped a smudge of chocolate off her chin. "We'll share. I didn't even get a bite."

"I don't like to share."

"I know that, girlie, which is exactly why you *are* gonna share with me."

After charring another marshmallow, he slapped it on the peanut butter cup and waited as Bailey added the top layer.

Those gorgeous green eyes widened after he tried a bite. "That is tasty."

"It's even better if you don't ruin the marshmallow," she teased.

Bailey stared into the fire, wondering if she should make her excuses and head back to her trailer. Then all of the day's events kept racing through her mind and she lost track of how long she sat there brooding, watching the flames, until she realized neither Olivia nor Streeter had spoken for a while. She glanced up and saw Olivia sprawled across Streeter's lap, so sound asleep her mouth hung open.

When she caught his eye, she mouthed, *I'll go,* and started to get up.

But Streeter reached out and set his hand on her leg. "Stay. Please," he said in a relatively normal tone of voice.

"You sure?" She tipped her head at Olivia, who hadn't moved. "Don't you want to put her in bed?"

"Nah. She's crashed. She'll sleep through anything. Besides. It's a nice night." He paused. "It's, ah, nice sittin' out here with you."

She smiled because he was so damn cute. Especially when she realized he hadn't moved his hand from her leg.

Her stomach did somersaults.

"Did you go for a run tonight?" he asked.

"After the stern warning you gave me the other night? No. But I probably should do something to get rid of this pent-up aggression."

"I know something that'll help."

Her gaze clashed with his.

His smirk indicated he'd recognized the mindless-sweaty-sex idea that'd flitted through her eyes. But he merely said, "For right now I was thinkin' more along the lines of you talkin' about it."

"Streeter Hale. Are you actually volunteering to listen to me?"

"I reckon I am." He squeezed her knee and let go. "Just don't expect good counsel, because I don't take my own advice half the damn time."

"Is this where I mention that my counselor had no advice to offer me today either?"

"You see a counselor?"

She nodded and quickly tacked on, "It's an army thing," so he wouldn't ask specifics.

"Sure." If he didn't believe her, he hid it well. "When you were talkin' to Olivia, it sounded like you and Harper had words today."

"We did. Bad words. Mean words. Words that were totally uncalled-for."

He shifted and Olivia turned her head and snuggled into his chest. "At the pool, you mentioned something about her havin' to make 'hard decisions.' Is that what brought about the fight?"

"More or less. She argued every point I made. Then she told me to leave. I spent the rest of the day fuming, thinking, *I oughta just pack up and really leave. Then she'd think twice about tossing out someone who was only trying to help her.* But I realized, that was exactly what Harper expected me to do, because the younger me would've blown a gasket and bailed on her. So I'm gonna stick around to spite her stubborn ass and do the I-told-you-so dance when she admits I was right and she was wrong." She sighed. "Mature, huh?"

"Well, there are them days when you work with family when 'neener neener' is the least offensive thing said."

She smiled. "Somehow, I don't see you saying 'neener neener,' Streeter."

"I did on those days it was harder takin' the high road." He shifted Olivia again. "Were the words about her kids?"

"No. About her store." Bailey kept her focus on the fire. "I've been careful not to overstep my bounds when it comes to WWC. It's been her baby since before she had kids. But that doesn't change the fact she's ignoring certain problems. She takes issue when anyone brings it up."

"Anyone . . . meaning who?"

"Me." She drained her beer. "Penelope."

He snorted. "I'd take issue if Penelope tried to tell me anything too."

She knocked her knee into his. "You might not like her, but she is right. Except she wasn't dumb enough to bring it up with Harper."

"Instead she got you to do it."

"Yep. I'm back to being the know-nothing little sister, who's babysitting the store until Harper gets her shit together." She sent him a panicked look after she remembered Olivia was right there. "Sorry."

"No worries. The kid is a power sleeper." He sent her sprawled form a soft smile. "When me'n Tobin started workin' together, I acted the same way. I'm older than him, I know how things oughta be better than him. And it wasn't the way he'd been doin' things."

"Who won?"

"No one. That's the point."

"How'd he *get* to the point that he didn't want to punch you in the face every day?"

Streeter chuckled. "You'll hafta ask him. For me . . . I had to realize he wasn't tryin' to one-up me. As kids we competed for everything. The winner was better, faster, smarter, all that stuff. I had to let go of seein' him as someone I had to teach and accept that I could learn a lot from him."

"Did it take a while for you to get into that mind-set?"

"Longer than it should have."

"Maybe I should just let it go. I'm only here until the end of the summer. Maybe the fact she's willing to fight with me means she knows changes have to be made."

"Has the end of the summer always been your timeline for leavin'?"

"Roughly."

They were each lost in their own thoughts.

Bailey listened to the wind in the pine trees. But it wasn't loud enough to mask the chirping crickets. Tilting her head back, she stargazed. Until she joined the army she hadn't spent much time out in nature. Now that her time in the service was over, she doubted she'd turn into one of those camping, hiking, outdoor enthusiasts.

But the more time she spent out of uniform, the less confident she was about who she was.

"Can I ask you something?" Streeter asked softly.

"Sure." Her gaze challenged his. "As long as you're aware that I'm a tit-for-tat kinda chick."

"Meaning you'll expect me to answer something in return."

"Yep."

He smiled. "Guess that's fair."

"Ask your question."

"Did you really hate livin' here in Wyoming so much that you joined the army?"

Not what she'd expected. "Yes."

"Why?"

Bailey leaned forward and held her hands in front of the fire. "Muddy Gap isn't home for me. It's just another place that my mom dragged us in her search for a man to take care of her. The guy she'd hooked up with—I don't even remember his name now—lasted about six months, then we were on our own again. Then she decided that Harper was pretty and talented enough to enter beauty pageants so that became her focus."

"How old were you?"

"Twelve when we moved here. They did the pageant thing long enough for Harper to get a few scholarships, and she went off to community college." She wiped her sweaty hands on her jeans, dragging her palms up and down her thighs. "Mom only noticed me if I was in her way. She was busy sleeping with guys for rent money or food or booze or whatever struck her fancy."

"Jesus, Bailey."

"It gets better. She ran off with a married guy when I was sixteen. She managed to give Harper a heads-up before she vanished, and Harper came back here to take care of me." She snorted. "As if I hadn't been taking care of myself for four years. And to be honest, I resented her. She was everything I wasn't: gorgeous, sweet, and everyone loved her. Everyone praised her for giving up her dream to raise me." She continued to rub her palms on her jeans. "Truth was, I did need someone to keep a roof over my head—god knows babysitting didn't pay enough for food and rent and tuition. But Harper immediately started working two jobs and it was exactly the same situation I'd been in with Mom. My sister didn't see me as a person. She saw me as a responsibility, then she saw me as a chance to get out of this crappy place too." She paused to breathe. "She never asked me what I wanted to do after I graduated from high school. Harper assumed I wouldn't know. She made plans for us, not realizing I'd already made plans for myself. I know that sounds so freakin' selfish. Everyone thought I was such a brat for—"

A rough hand enclosed hers, stopping her agitated movement.

Bailey's startled gaze zoomed to his.

"Don't say that. Doesn't matter how it looked to people outside your family. It's your life experience and it shaped you. You feel how you feel."

"Are you speaking from your life experiences?"

"Yeah."

The fierce look in his eyes cut her deep. Without thinking, she brought his hand up and rested it against her face. "Sometime will you tell me about what shaped you?"

He frowned. "Sometime? Not now?"

Oh, sweet man, you're not ready for that yet. "Of course not now. This conversation is all about me, so please refocus."

Her lighter tone chased the worry from his face—as she'd intended, and Streeter actually laughed. "I like you, Bailey Masterson."

"You like me. I think you're cute. We're holding hands . . ." She sighed dramatically. "Is this now a mutual crush?"

"Appears so."

"What happens next?"

"I guess I ask if you'll go out with me sometime."

"Sometime? Not now?" she teased.

He gestured to his sleeping child. "Be a little awkward to have you both sittin' on my lap, doncha think?"

"Stupid voice of reason."

"It's a gift."

"Or a curse." Bailey kept hold of his hand. "Why haven't you grilled me about my boot camp plans for tomorrow?"

"Because I was enjoying a conversation between us that wasn't about my daughter." He angled his wrist and stroked his knuckles down her jawline. "You push me out of my comfort zone. Half the time I wanna run away from you—"

"Ah, dude? You run away from me *all* the time, not just half of the time."

He continued lazily caressing her face. "You're ruining the moment."

"Sorry. What do you want to do with me the other half of the time you're not running away from me?"

"Be brave enough to stay."

There went the butterflies in her belly again.

Olivia squirmed.

Streeter released Bailey's hand and bent his head closer to his daughter's when she mumbled.

Realizing their alone time had come to an end, Bailey stood and skirted the fire pit to turn it off. She gathered up the trash and chucked it in the garbage. By the time she'd shoved the marshmallows and chocolate into a plastic grocery bag, Streeter was standing there, watching her.

The sweet, chivalrous man wouldn't go inside his trailer until she was safely locked inside hers.

She said, "Thanks for listening to me tonight," as she walked backward down the walkway.

"Anytime."

"See you in the morning."

"Good night, Bailey."

She could totally swoon every time he uttered her name in that husky tone. "Night, Streeter."

Chapter Ten

$\mathcal{S}$treeter paused inside the entryway to Buckeye Joe's, needing a moment to get his bearings. He hadn't expected the bar to be so full this early on a Friday night. His gaze swept over the crowd as he searched for his brother.

All he had to do was follow the sound of laughter and he found Tobin. His brother was one of those guys who knew everyone, and everyone liked him.

Streeter had a twinge of envy that he'd never been that guy—with a ton of friends and a favorite local hangout. Although he hadn't been a hermit during his married years, his friends were "couple" friends. And those friendships faded damn fast when he wasn't part of a couple.

He felt awkward as a single man. He hated the term *widower* and refused to use it as an explanation of his marital status. Then again, he'd kept himself so isolated from social situations like these the past four and a half years that he needn't have worried about being labeled.

Tobin gave Streeter the nod that indicated he'd seen him, so Streeter sauntered over to an open spot at the bar to wait for him.

A brunette bartender offered him a smile. "Be with you in a jiff, son."

"No problem."

By the time she returned, Tobin had sidled up and clapped him on the back. "Told ya the first round is on me, bro. Sherry, two Coors, please."

"You've got it. How's that new baby boy doin'?"

Tobin grinned at her. "Kid's growin' like crazy." He whipped out his phone. "Take a look."

She leaned over the bar. "Such a cutie. Got his mama's smile."

"And he's got his mama's sweet disposition too."

"How's your darlin' daughter?"

"Great. Amber hasn't showed any jealousy yet."

"You're a lucky man." She set the bottles on the bar top. "Start a tab?"

"That'd be great, Sherry."

Tobin led the way to a table that wasn't deep enough in the corner for Streeter's taste. After they'd settled in, Tobin held his bottle up for a toast. "Thanks for meetin' me."

Streeter tapped his bottle to his brother's. "It's a cause for celebration that you've seen me twice in one week."

"Yeah, 'cause most weeks I see you more than twice."

"Ha."

"Olivia is with Gramma Deenie?"

"Yeah. There's some family deal in Cheyenne this weekend, so Olivia won't be back until Sunday night."

"That's trusting of you."

He shrugged. "Deenie had talked it up to Olivia and she was lookin' forward to it. Be a dick move to change my mind." He sipped his beer. "Besides, I got a lot of stuff to catch up on this weekend."

"So that's what you're gonna do when you have a kid-free weekend, Street? Work?"

"Yep."

"That's it?"

"What else would I do?"

"You're seriously gonna make me spell it out?" Tobin rested his forearms on the table. "It has three letters."

Streeter scowled. "Not everything has to do with sex."

Tobin snickered. "While that statement is blatantly untrue, I was referring to the word 'fun.' F-U-N. The fact that word didn't come to mind just proves how much fun is missin' in your life. When was the last time you had any fun?"

Christ. He couldn't even remember.

Yes, you do. Maybe it wasn't Tobin's idea of fun, but you liked sitting by the fire and talking to Bailey last night.

"Aha! You do have something fun in mind." He lowered his voice. "Tell me it involves a certain new neighbor of yours."

Do not blush.

"Street. Come on, don't pull that strong, silent type with me."

Streeter drained his beer. "I need stronger truth serum than this watered-down horse piss."

"You got it." Tobin motioned to the bartender.

Within moments she sauntered over with four shots and two more beers, which she dropped off without saying a word.

"How'd you do that?" Streeter demanded.

"I've been a regular here for years. Done my share of listening to my buddies' tales of woe. Conversations about women require whiskey—at least two shots." Tobin picked up a shot glass. "Here's your serum; after this I want the truth from you."

Streeter held up his glass and muttered, "Bossy much?" before he downed it.

"Okay. Lay it out for me so I can help."

"No offense, but there is no help for me. I have no game, T. None."

Tobin frowned. "That's bein' hard on yourself, ain't it?"

He shrugged.

"But you like her."

"Yeah. Bailey is this mix of scrappy and sweet, funny and introspective, bossy and kind, all wrapped up in a sexy little package."

"And that's bad?"

"For me? Yeah. Because I don't have anything to offer her."

"Street. Man. You're gonna hafta spell it out for me because I'm not following you."

"I'm almost thirty-seven years old. How am I supposed to tell her that I've only kissed two women in my life? And the only woman I ever had sex with was Danica?"

Tobin didn't bother to hide his shock. "Why is this the first time you've ever talked about this?"

He snorted. "Like I'm gonna bring it up with my little brother, who's always been some kind of ladies' man."

"Jesus, Streeter. It's not about notches on a damn bedpost. It's about the fact you're hurtin' and hidin' and you haven't said a goddamned thing to me about it in four years. How am I supposed to help you when you're so secretive?"

"Because I'm embarrassed, okay?" He messed with his empty shot glass. "I've had nothin' but time to think about relationships and secrets. I mean, I always thought I made Danica happy in bed. But I thought I made her happy out of bed too, so clearly I don't have a fuckin' clue. I haven't been ready to bring my failings as a man into the light. I don't know that I ever will be."

"I hate that you feel this way. I ain't bein' a dick when I ask how long it's been since you've seen your counselor?"

"A couple of months. Why?"

"Maybe a visit is in order. Maybe she could shed light on why you feel unworthy of happiness."

Streeter's eyebrows nearly disappeared into his hairline. "Excuse me?"

"Hear me out." Tobin downed his shot. "I know you haven't been carryin' a torch for Danica, like you lost your one true love and soul mate. You're a good man. You're a good father. You work hard. Those are the kind of qualities that most women look for. Anything else you think you need to be? That's a skill you can learn."

"Skill. Like bedroom skill?"

"Yep. So let's get down to brass tacks." He cocked his head. "You feel like you're the 'fake it 'til you make it' kinda guy or the 'teach me to please you' kinda guy when it comes to sex?"

"What the ever-lovin' fuck has gotten into you?"

"Honestly?"

"No, I want you to fuckin' lie to me, Tobin." He slammed the second shot. "Get to whatever point you're tryin' to make."

"Fine." All amusement disappeared from his brother's face. "I hate what Danica did. I hate how Dad and Driscoll treated you afterward. But I am really grateful that forced a change in your life and you moved here. I'd given up hope that I'd ever have a close relationship with any member of my family. I've watched you adapt to everything that's been thrown at you and I'm damn proud of you. Jade and I feel humbled that you credit us with helpin' with your healing process."

"But?"

"There's no 'but.' This is an 'and' conversation. And I swore I wouldn't ever push you into this type of conversation . . . until it came up. Now it has, so here goes."

Streeter wished he had another shot of whiskey; he made do with gulping down a mouthful of beer.

"Bailey is the first woman you've talked about. She's the first woman you've admitted bein' attracted to. So you need to put aside your fears and take her on a damn date, bro."

Tobin raised his hand, stopping Streeter's protest, so his brother didn't have a clue that he'd already asked her on a date.

"I get you weren't ready before. Now you don't have an excuse. Olivia's with her grandparents at least one weekend night. Every. Weekend. You have the time. You've found a woman. So find your balls, Street, and do it."

He's right. Isn't that what your counselor told you too? You'll know when you're ready.

"Fine. Fuck." He exhaled. "What if—"

"She says no?" Tobin inserted. "You're more worried she's gonna say yes. Here's the tough love. Either you take her out, or I'll set the Mud Lilies on the hunt for your first post-Danica date. They've wanted to play matchmaker for you for years but Jade has held them off."

He sent his brother a death glare. "You wouldn't."

"I will with absolute fuckin' glee. You've got one week, bro, or I'm bringing in the big guns. Literally. Them ladies have an arsenal and you can bet they'd use them to scare up some interesting date options for you."

"You're such an asshole."

"And you're such a chickenshit," Tobin shot back.

They stared at each other for several long moments.

Tobin broke the silence first. "Ain't we a shining example of brotherly love?"

"And the height of maturity."

"If only Dad and Driscoll could see us now. They'd be so damn proud we're carryin' on the family tradition of threats and name callin'."

Streeter laughed. "Shut it. I hate that I can't stay mad at you, T."

He shrugged. "Few can."

"Now can we talk about something else?"

"Like what?"

Anything. "Like I'm ready to choose a house design."

"Why now?"

"Olivia starts school in the fall. Ted is ready to take on more responsibilities at the Split Rock. It's time for me to transition out of the daily operations."

"I hear ya. Have you mentioned it to Renner?"

Streeter shook his head. "Somehow I think he already knows. Anyway, once I settle on a house style, I wanna break ground as soon as possible."

Tobin pointed at Streeter's phone. "Still got access to the blueprints Holt sent you?"

"Yeah." He clicked on an icon and waited for it to load. "The files are huge, so these aren't high-res."

"I left my glasses in my office, so I can't see details anyway."

They bent their heads together and studied every option. Then when Sherry swung by to check on them, Tobin asked her for scratch paper. While Streeter sketched out revisions, Tobin talked about his bioengineering job. Then the conversation changed yet again to building herd diversity when they turned the bulls out next month.

The next time Streeter reached for his beer, he realized it'd gotten warm. A glance at his phone indicated more than an hour and a half had passed. He got up to use the bathroom and as he walked through the bar, he saw Bailey and another woman sitting at a table around the corner.

His heart started racing even as his feet stopped moving.

Right at that moment, Bailey looked up and their eyes met.

She did a double take, and then a sly, sexy smile bloomed on her face.

What did he do?

Gave her a hat tip and booked it back to the table.

A *hat tip*, for christsake.

Tobin looked at him oddly when Streeter flopped down, scooted his chair in and hunched over the table. "What's wrong with you?"

"She's here."

"Who?"

"Her." He downed the last of his warm beer. "Bailey."

"Really? Didja talk to her?"

"No."

"Didja at least let her know that you saw her?"

"Sorta. I gave her a hat tip."

Tobin flipped Streeter's hat up, and he barely caught it before it sailed to the floor.

"What the fuck was that for?" he demanded as he resituated his Stetson.

"For bein' a flamin' idiot with a fuckin' *hat* tip. Jesus." Then Tobin lifted his gaze to something behind Streeter.

Not something; someone.

Two hands slapped on the table, forcing Streeter's attention to the owner of those hands.

"Fancy meeting you here, Streeter."

"Uh, hey, Bailey."

"Were you seriously trying to hide from me just now?"

"No."

"Oh, so you were running from me again. I thought we'd gotten past that."

"We have."

"Really? Then why did I see the ass end of you instead of you coming over and saying hello?"

Streeter straightened up and squared his shoulders. "Because I saw you were with someone and I didn't want to be rude and interrupt a private conversation." *Unlike some people* was heavily implied.

"Bullshit."

Tobin snickered and Bailey focused her attention on him. "And you are?"

"Tobin Hale." He offered his hand. "Streeter's younger, more socially adjusted brother. You must be Bailey."

"Yes, I am. It's nice to meet you, Tobin."

"Likewise. I've heard a lot about you."

Shut it, Tobin.

"From who?"

"Streeter. And Olivia." He paused. "You're Harper's little sister, right?"

Streeter saw Bailey's smile dim a little. "Yes."

"I've known her for years."

"As you can see, we look nothing alike. She got all the looks and the charm in our family."

"Huh. That sounds familiar. Streeter got all the looks and the charm in our family too."

Bailey laughed. "What *is* it about those middle children that turns them into attention hogs?"

"Beats me. That's why I married an only child." Tobin pointed to the chair next to Streeter. "We'd love to have you join us, wouldn't we, Street?"

"Sure." Tobin kicked him under the table; apparently he hadn't answered enthusiastically enough. "I'd really like that."

"I don't want to be rude and interrupt a private conversation," she said with a smirk.

"All right, I was a dick for not sayin' hello to you before. I'm sorry." Streeter pulled out the chair next to him. "Park it, Sergeant."

"I need to let my friend know where I went."

"She's welcome to join us too," Tobin offered.

"Thanks, but she's leaving. Her ex was supposed to have their kids this weekend but he got called into a work emergency."

"But you're comin' back?" Streeter asked.

"Yep. And you're buying the first round, cowboy."

With that, she sauntered off.

As soon as she was out of earshot, Tobin said, "I'm headin' out."

"Like that won't be obvious."

Tobin leaned across the table. "It's obvious she likes you, dumb-ass. It's obvious you've spent time with her since the last time we talked. Take this opportunity and run with it—not away from it. You have a kid-free weekend. She's a sexy woman. Anything can happen. Be open to it, okay?"

"Fine. I'll be my charming damn self."

"That's what I wanted to hear." He stood and clapped Streeter on the shoulder. "Keep me posted."

"Tell Jade hey and kiss those kids from Uncle Street."

"Will do."

Sherry the bartender/cocktail waitress arrived back at the table the same time as Bailey. "What can I get you two?"

"I'll have a Bud Light," Bailey said, taking the chair Tobin had vacated.

"Make it two."

"You got it."

As soon as Sherry left, Bailey folded her arms on the table. "I didn't chase your brother off, did I?"

"Nope. He was getting ready to leave anyway. What about your friend?"

"Gone. When she suggested a girls' night out . . . I'll admit this wasn't where I thought we'd end up."

"You're not a fan of this place?"

Her eyes narrowed. "Do you come here often?"

"Rarely. It ain't exactly kid-friendly."

When Bailey gave him that sweet crooked grin, all he could think about was feeling those lips against his as he kissed her.

"Speaking of . . . where is Olivia?"

His jaw dropped. "Shit. I knew I forgot something at home."

"Very funny."

"She's with her grandma." He didn't tack on that she'd be gone all weekend, because it was too blatant.

Sherry dropped off the beers.

Streeter reached for his wallet, but Sherry's hand on his shoulder stopped him. "Tobin said to tell you he's got it covered."

"Thanks." He dropped a ten-dollar bill on her tray anyway. As soon as Sherry left, his gaze snagged Bailey's. He held up his beer for a toast. "I'm glad we ran into each other tonight."

She touched her bottle to his. "Same."

They drank and a lull settled between them.

Streeter would've been content to watch her pretty face all damn night, but that was kinda creepy, so he said, "You avoided answering the question."

"Which one?"

"If you're at Buckeye Joe's on a regular basis."

"First time since I came back. I wasn't sure I'd be welcome in here at all."

"I'd think havin' a hot little thing like you hangin' out in the bar would be good for business."

She rolled her eyes. "Still with the 'hot little thing'?"

"Well, you are all that."

"I'd tell you that you moved from cute to charming, but you'd get an ego, so you're stuck at 'cutie,' cowboy."

"I'll take it. So, tell me why you weren't sure if you'd be welcome in here?"

"Remember when I told you my mom ran off with the married owner of a local bar? See the woman with the short brown hair running the register? Her husband is the man Mom skipped town with."

"Shit."

"Yeah."

Streeter frowned. "But Harper and Bran come in here, so she must've gotten over it."

"But Harper doesn't look like Mom." Bailey sipped her beer. "I do. So I've got that goin' for me."

"Hey." He reached across the table and took her hand. "I didn't get a chance to talk to you after camp today. Seemed like you and Bran were havin' a serious talk. Is everything all right?"

"He was grilling me on what I'd done to poor Harper yesterday . . ." Bailey threaded her fingers through Streeter's. "She didn't come in to the store today and she was supposed to close, since Penelope opened. Bran came to get the boys and asked if I'd stay late. I said no because I had plans. Then he reminded me that Harper had closed last night for me, which pissed me off because she made me leave." She ducked her head. "I kept my cool and reminded him that I was there to help out, and I'd done my part by working ten hours with the boot camp kids. I also suggested he initiate a conversation with his wife about whether her apathy about WWC was causing the drastic change in revenue or vice versa."

"I take it Bran didn't like that answer?"

She shook her head. "He had to ask Tierney to watch the store since it was advertised as being open until seven o'clock and the lodge is full tonight. So that was the long answer to your question. The short answer . . . no, everything is not all right."

"I'd hoped things were better for you today." He set his beer aside and put his fingers under her chin, forcing her to meet his gaze. "I'm sorry you're havin' a rough go with your sister."

"Thanks."

He stroked the edge of her jaw with the backs of his knuckles.

"You're staring at me."

"Because I really like the look of you."

"Is that why you're touching me like—"

"Like I've thought about you every damn day since we were at the pool?"

She gave him a slow, sexy blink. "That long, huh?"

"Yep."

Staring into her eyes as he touched her seemed too intimate, so he dropped his gaze to her mouth.

Christ, that was worse because now all he could think about was kissing her.

Her full lips curled into a sexy smile.

His gaze moved back up to her eyes. "You smirking at me?"

"Yep."

"Why?"

"Because I was wondering if you were ever gonna make a move on me."

"Is that what this is?"

"I think so. But your next move will let me know for sure."

"Which move is that?"

"Asking me to dance."

Emboldened, Streeter outlined her bottom lip with the pad of his thumb. "Will you dance with me, Bailey?"

Her tongue darted out and she licked his thumb before she said, "I'd love to."

Somehow he scooted back quickly without knocking his chair over or releasing Bailey's hand. He towed her to the dance floor, noticing there were only two other couples dancing to the tunes pouring out of the sound system, but he wouldn't have cared if they were the only ones out there. He spun her into his arms, keeping their clasped hands together and placing his right hand on the small of her back.

She took the hint they weren't about to two-step and slipped her arm around his waist, ignoring the "respectable distance" he'd had beaten into his head at school dances, bringing her body closer to his.

Streeter couldn't name the song or the artist, couldn't tell if this was a song meant for fast dancing or slow, because as soon as he and Bailey were body to body, they fell into a rhythm entirely their own.

After a few minutes, she said, "You're a really good dancer."

"Thanks, you ain't so bad yourself."

"Just following your lead. I rarely feel compelled to dance when I go to a club."

"What do you do?"

"Listen to the music. Drink. People watch." She paused. "How about you?"

"Mostly dancin' around the house with Olivia these days. Last time I danced with a woman over the age of five was at Tobin and Jade's wedding a few years back. Most of that was two-steppin' with the Mud Lilies. Them old gals wore me out."

"Harper talks about them but I don't think I've met any of them."

"You'd remember if you had, trust me."

They didn't speak for a while and a different song came on. A slower one.

Bailey rested her cheek against his chest and sighed. "Why do you have to smell so good too?"

"Too?"

"You look good and you move good. You should smell like cowshit or something so you're not so damn perfect."

Perfect? Never heard that word to describe him before.

He had no idea how to respond to that so he didn't.

She sighed again. "I overstepped, didn't I?"

"No, I'm just in shock, to be honest."

"Why?"

"Not used to compliments, say nothin' of a compliment from a sexy-as-fuck woman who leaves me tongue-tied if I'm not yellin' at her."

She smiled against his chest. "Sexy as fuck, huh? Now there's a compliment and a step up from 'hot little thing.'"

"You're also sassy, sweet, bossy, ballsy, funny, honest and exasperating. But you're still a hot little thing too."

"You don't seem so tongue-tied now," she murmured.

"I am. I'm not good at this."

She tipped her head back to look at him. "Streeter—"

"Lemme say this before I lose my nerve, okay?"

"Okay." She resituated herself, twining her arms around his neck and nestling her face into his neck.

He moved his hands to her hips and took a moment to appreciate her soft curves. "I've been alone since my wife died four and a half years ago, focused on raising Olivia. I've not gone on one date. No hookups, no fuck-buddy-type relationships. Not because I'm still in love with

Danica, I just haven't been interested in any woman . . . until I met you. Hell, I haven't even kissed a woman since I've been single."

He lowered his mouth to her ear and whispered, "See, I met Danica when we were sixteen. Married her when we were twenty. She was the first and the last woman I asked out. The first and only woman I've had sex with. So I'm about as experienced as a teenage boy when it comes to this. That's hard to admit when you're a thirty-six-year-old man."

"Why?"

"Fear. Bein' this honest with you scares me, Bailey. Because even before I unloaded my baggage on you just now, I couldn't believe that a woman like you would be interested in a guy like me."

"A woman like me?" she repeated.

"Sexy, sassy, sweet . . . bossy, ballsy and beautiful."

"You're wrong. I'm very interested in a man like you."

"A man like me?" he repeated.

"Brooding, bossy, buff . . . hot, humble and handsome."

He chuckled. "Well, we've got bossy in common."

"Mmm-hmm." She softly kissed his neck, damn near sending his body into convulsions from the eroticism of that simple show of affection.

"Since you've come this far with the honesty, Streeter, I need to know if part of my attraction is you knowing I'm not sticking around here. We can get involved . . . but not too involved."

Streeter nudged her head up to peer into her eyes. "Maybe. Is that an issue for you?"

"No. But *can* you do casual? Because that's all I can offer you."

I don't have a freakin' clue. "I'm willin' to give it a shot."

She kissed his chin. "Okay, then."

Gripping his hand, Bailey led him through the Friday night crowd and out the front door. She turned left, heading into the shadow of the building.

Even in the near-dark he could see she was breathing hard and her pulse jumped in her throat. He knew that mad dash out of the bar hadn't left her breathless; he'd done that to her.

No fucking pressure.

"Bailey?"

Her fists were clenched by her sides. "Your move, cutie."

Streeter did something he'd never done: took off his cowboy hat and tossed it on the ground. He didn't want anything getting in the way.

Curling his fingers around her fists, he squeezed them, then moved his hands up, over her wrists and forearms, stopping to sweep his thumbs across the bend in her elbows. Then continuing upward, caressing her muscled biceps and gliding over her shoulders and neck. Stopping to cradle her beautiful—but wary—face in his hands.

He brought his mouth down to hers with more confidence than he felt. His heart hammered and he fought the urge to lick his lips before he pressed them to hers.

Goddamn. Her lips were soft. Sweet. Slightly parted, granting him access to a deeper kiss whenever he wanted.

And he wanted, all right. He wanted her crazy, messy, hungry kisses.

But he took his time, teasing his lips across hers with gentle consideration. He kissed the corners of her smile, nibbling on her lower lip and darting his tongue across that plump flesh for a tiny taste, gratified when he felt her quick intake of breath.

Then he moved in and deepened the kiss.

His worry about his rusty make-out skills vanished at the first touch of his tongue to hers.

Bailey molded her body against his as he tasted her. Switching it up from a fierce mating of tongues to a flirty exchange of soft smooches. Holding her head in place, his thumbs caressing her cheekbones as he tilted his head, kissing her from every angle.

Streeter felt her hands clutching the fabric of his shirt, using it to anchor herself, and a primitive need rolled through him. A need unlike anything he'd ever experienced.

He slid his hands into her hair and broke the kiss, trailing his mouth down her neck until she shivered and released a husky moan. After he pressed his lips to the hollow of her throat, he feathered kisses back up her neck until he reached her ear. He whispered, "I want more of that."

"I do too." She kissed his chin and released his shirt before she stepped back, forcing him to drop his hands. "But this is as far as it goes tonight."

"Why?"

Bailey shoved her hands in her back pockets. "Look, I want you to think about what it'll mean for us to get involved. Even if it's just sexual, it'll require full communication on everything from when we can have smexy time, because you do have a daughter, to dealing with our individual desires and limits. I'm not trying to be clinical or cynical, but this is a much bigger step for you than it is for me. Us fucking each other stupid outside of Buckeye Joe's would be hot as hell, but it'd probably lead to regrets. And I refuse to feel guilty about sex."

He raised both eyebrows. "You sayin' *I'd* have regrets?"

"I'm saying I don't know if you would, and frankly, I don't think you know either." She paused and her gaze searched his face. "Am I wrong?"

"No." Feeling a little foolish for jumping the gun, he reached down for his hat and ran his hand through his hair before he settled it on his head. "Will you go out on a date with me tomorrow night?"

She smiled. "I'd love that. Text me and we'll set up a time."

"Great." Streeter placed his hands on her ass, directly over hers still jammed in her back pockets, immobilizing her and tugging her closer just to see if she'd surrender control.

She did.

Then she tipped her head back to look at him.

Even in the darkness he saw her eyes flare with heat.

He lowered his mouth to her ear and whispered, "Tilt your head to the left, hot stuff. If you're gonna be with me, you gotta learn how to kiss me when I'm wearin' my hat."

This time when he kissed her, he kept it sweet. Swallowed her groans of frustration that he didn't turn this kiss into the frenzied mouth fuck she wanted. This had to be enough for both of them tonight.

Streeter released her and stared into her eyes. "Need to go back in and get your stuff before I walk you to your car?"

Bailey shook her head. "I'm good to go." She reached out and ran the tips of her fingers across his lips. "Good night, Streeter."

"Night, Bailey."

He watched as she climbed into her SUV and drove away.

Now he was too wired to go home. Chances were good if he returned to the Split Rock right now he wouldn't have the willpower not to knock on her door.

Good thing Walmart was open twenty-four hours.

He hopped in his truck and headed for Casper.

Chapter Eleven

$\mathcal{O}$kay.

A date.

A normal, regular date. With a normal, regular guy.

Except he wasn't like any other guys Bailey had ever met.

Besides the fact he was Daddy to a five-year-old.

Besides the fact he was a widower.

Besides the fact he was hot as fuck.

Besides the fact he wasn't aware he was hot as fuck.

Besides the fact that oblivious hot-as-fuck Daddio hadn't been fucked for a very fucking long time.

Hey. No pressure.

Oh, and no pressure that he'd only had sex with one woman in his thirty-six years.

The woman he'd been married to for a dozen years . . . before she died.

Yeah. This was light-years away from a normal date.

Bailey locked up Wild West Clothiers and exited out the side entrance, using the cut-across to get to the employee compound.

She waved to Bobbie and Pete, who were making final evening rounds on the ATV.

Before she went home to prepare for her date, she stopped at her car and grabbed the box of condoms she'd purchased after last night's make-out session with Streeter.

Her belly did a little flip, remembering how quickly Streeter had gotten his kissing skills back up to speed. She hadn't ever been kissed with such thoughtful deliberation. With such barely controlled greed. Add in his admission that he wanted to learn how to please her and she'd just about jumped him in the parking lot.

She'd gotten lost in those kinds of thoughts as she backtracked to her place. But before she reached it, she heard a rhythmic thumping coming from Ted and Zack's trailer. Specifically from the bedroom at the back of the trailer, which was situated right across from her bedroom. She glanced up and saw their bedroom windows were open.

Weird. They kept their place buttoned up, preferring to keep their window air conditioner running night and day.

And when she heard a very masculine groan, followed by, "Fuck me harder, Ted. I need to come now. My break's nearly over," Bailey understood why they kept the windows shut.

She also understood why the two young men were content in each other's company.

Good for them that they'd found love or hot fucking or whatever. But since they'd kept their relationship secret, she oughta give them a sign that keeping their windows closed would maintain that privacy.

Even though she wasn't ready to see him yet, she marched over to Streeter's trailer and banged loudly on the door.

Sure enough, all audible activity in the Ted and Zack secret sex show stopped immediately.

Bailey knocked again. Louder. She added on, "Streeter, I know you're in there," for good measure.

Locks tumbled and the door opened to reveal a shirtless Streeter, brandishing a washcloth in his left hand. "Bailey? I thought we agreed on seven o'clock."

Good lord, would you look at those damn abs?

The only way they could've been more appealing was if he'd just stepped out of the shower and tiny drops of water rolled between those firm pillows of glistening flesh. And then more drops followed the happy trail of dark blond hair into the white towel wrapped around his hips. A towel that was dangerously close to dropping to the floor. Or combusting, given the deep cut of muscle that disappeared into his jeans—his body was hot enough that it could happen.

"Bailey?"

"Oh. Yeah. Right. Six-pack. Seven o'clock, whatever."

Warm fingers curled around the bottom of her jaw and tilted her chin up.

Damn. The view of his rugged face was just as droolworthy as his belly.

Amusement danced in his sexy green eyes. "You do realize you said 'six-pack' and not 'six o'clock'?"

"I did?"

"And hot stuff, this is the first time you've looked me in the eyes since I opened the door."

"Well, you shouldn't go around half-dressed, flashing those abs at people. They're distracting."

Streeter raised an eyebrow. "*You* knocked on *my* door."

"So I did. Should I be sorry?"

"No. I'm happy to see you, even if you're seein' more of me than I intended." He stepped back. "Come in and I'll finish getting dressed."

"You don't need to do that on my account" slipped out.

He chuckled.

As soon as she stepped inside and he shut the door, she went toe-to-toe with him. "I feel we need to be totally, one hundred percent, brutally honest with each other."

Some of the amusement in his eyes dimmed. "What's on your mind?"

"You. And me. Naked."

He waited.

"We've gotten to know each other over the past couple of weeks to realize we like each other. Last night we acted on our mutual attraction with that superhot make-out session. I don't want to waste the limited amount of time we've got alone together suffering through a dinner we probably won't taste, in a public place where neither of us wants to be, when we're both wondering if we'll end up in bed after the dessert course, when it's obvious that's where this is headed. So let's cut out the boring middle and get right to the explosive ending."

"You're serious."

"Completely and utterly serious."

His face showed his suspicion. "This ain't some kind of test?"

"A test? Like to see if I eat dessert first?"

"What?"

Oh, and lookit whose eyes zeroed in on her groin with her eat-dessert-first comment.

They both seemed to realize that the train had already veered off the track.

She managed a quick "Explain the test thing."

"Like you have a dating rule where I have to prove I'm a gentleman and tell you I don't want to fuck you stupid on the first date, so you think my intentions are honorable or some shit, and that's when you tell me I passed the test. Because I'll admit right now, I'm about to fail that motherfucker with flying colors."

Bailey's brain got stuck on *fuck you stupid*. Could she be so lucky that he had all that going on *and* he was a dirty talker in bed?

"Are you even listenin' to me?"

Her gaze winged back to his. "Uh. No. Everything you said after *fuck you stupid* became white noise."

"So your 'eat dessert first' philosophy truly sums this up."

"Yes. I'm a sure thing." Dammit. "I meant dessert is a sure thing if it's the first course. Or the only course."

Streeter stepped back and dropped the washcloth at her feet.

"Does that mean what I think it means?"

"That I'm throwin' in the towel? Yep. You wanna do this now, I wanna do this now, so baby, we're doin' this now."

Then they came at each other so fast it was a wonder they didn't knock their damn teeth out.

Between voracious kisses, Streeter muttered, "Off. Get your clothes off. I need to touch you."

Their fingers got tangled as they both tried to undo her buttons.

Streeter trapped her face in his hands. "You strip and I'll do this."

And he kissed her with such raw hunger that she nearly tore her blouse off, screw the buttons. Then she reached behind her and unhooked her bra, baring herself to him.

Immediately he slid his hands down her neck and over her chest to palm her tits.

She was mesmerized by how thoroughly his rough-skinned hands searched for her trigger points—not the obvious ones. First kneading and stroking her whole breasts, then working her nipples, pulling and pinching, until he'd learned which ones made her arch into his touch, which ones caused her to gasp. And as he figured out that after a hard pinch to her nipples, she craved a lighter caress to soothe the sting, he kept up the ebb and flow of their kiss.

Until the moment he ripped his mouth free and bent her backward over his arm to feast on her tits.

"Streeter."

He said, "Mmm?" as he tongued her nipple.

"You're breaking my back, dude."

That brought him upright. "Sorry."

"Take me to bed. Unless we're doing this right here on the living room floor?"

"No, bossy. I do have some class."

"Me too." Bailey snatched the box of condoms out of her purse.

"An entire box?"

"That oughta get us through tonight." She sashayed down the hallway, heading straight to his bedroom at the back of the trailer.

When Streeter paused in the doorway, he said, "Bailey? What're you doin'?"

"Checking to make sure the windows are closed."

"Why?"

You don't wanna know. "Maybe I'm a screamer."

"If you're tryin' to get me more riled up, it's workin'." Streeter pointed to her pants. "Off."

She shimmied her capris down to her ankles, trying to be sexy as she did it. The way his eyes flared with heat indicated she'd achieved sexy with the removal of her panties. Go her!

"Now you."

He undid the top button on the waistband of his jeans and eased the zipper down. His "date" jeans were baggier than the Wranglers he wore every day on the job, so she caught a quick glimpse of his boxers after he shed them. Then he stood naked before her and she couldn't look anywhere except at his dick.

His truly magnificent dick in all its long, thick, circumcised glory.

Had she mentioned long?

Had she mentioned thick?

"You're starin' at it."

"So?"

"So, you're givin' me a complex."

Bailey managed to tear her gaze away from the one-eyed monster and look into his eyes. "Here's a hint, cowboy. You know you've got a big dick. Let me admire it." She paused. "Please tell me you've got lube."

"Yes, I've got lube."

"You sound testy."

"I am. This ain't goin' the way I thought it would."

She sauntered forward. "You're naked. I'm naked. We're in your bedroom. We've got a box of condoms, lube and the whole night ahead of us. How is this *not* going in the right direction?"

He jammed a hand into his hair. "I'm nervous. I thought we'd be kissin' and then the next image in my head is of us rollin' around nekkid in bed."

"You skipped a few crucial steps in that fantasy. The reality is I've gotta be prepared to take that bad boy or it's gonna hurt." She smoothed her palms over his pecs. "You grab the lube. I'll open a condom and we'll meet on the bed. Deal?"

"Deal."

She turned away, but he pulled her back against his body with one hand on her belly and one arm braced across her chest.

"Wait."

Please don't change your mind.

Then she felt his lips gliding back and forth across her hair. "Be patient with me."

His rapid exhales tickled her ear, causing her skin to tingle from that spot straight to her core. "Do you want to stop?" she said a little breathlessly.

"Fuck no."

"Then grab the lube and we'll get to the rolling-around-naked part."

Thankfully he couldn't see how much her hands shook as she opened the box of condoms. She was nervous too.

When she faced the bed, she noticed Streeter's eyes on her butt. "You're staring at it."

"So?"

"So, it's giving me a complex."

"Here's a hint, hot stuff. You know you've got a damn fine ass. Let me admire it." He smirked. "That lube is gonna come in handy, ain't it."

"Omigod, no, you are not fucking me in the ass at least until our third date."

"Damn, dating rules do exist." He cocked his head. "I wanna take a bite outta that cute butt of yours, though."

"And then what would you do?"

"Bite the other side."

Bailey walked across the mattress on her knees. "And then?"

"Then I'd rub my face all over it, so we're cheek to cheek in a whole new way."

"Cheeky man." She ran her fingertips down his jawline from one side to the other. "You shaved for our date. I like that."

"I'd like you to put the condom on me. Now."

Any momentum they'd lost blasted through them as she rolled the condom on.

And on.

His hand covered hers as he slammed his mouth down on hers.

God. She loved his mix of raw sexuality and innocence. She let go of his dick and grabbed onto his shoulders, pressing their bodies together.

The heat between them increased with every kiss. Every touch.

Streeter had a hold of her hair, limiting her movement, which was . . . wow. Way sexier than she'd imagined it'd be. When he broke their kiss to whisper, "Spread your legs for me," her heart raced faster, her blood seemed to run hotter and her need ran deeper.

His growl of satisfaction rumbled in her ear when he touched her pussy and found her wet. Really wet.

He urged her onto her back as he remained on his knees.

"So fucking sexy." Streeter squirted lube into his hand and coated his cock. Another dollop covered his fingers and he kept his slumberous gaze focused on hers as he slipped those digits inside her. Once. Twice. Three times.

"You wet enough to take me?"

"Yes, but keep the lube handy."

There was no hiding his emotions in those beautifully expressive green eyes as he planted his left hand above her shoulder and rolled his pelvis up, dragging his cock over her mound.

She groaned. "Do that like a hundred more times."

"You're way more optimistic than I am about how long this is gonna last." He pushed into her slowly. Watching her face like there would be a test later about exactly when pleasure overtook her pain.

It'd been so long since she'd felt that stretching burn—and never like this—as he inched his way inside.

"Streeter."

He stopped.

She felt his legs shaking. Watched the sweat building on his hairline. Saw him clenching his jaw when he forced out a terse "What?"

"Kiss me." Bailey twined her arms around his neck. "Please."

"I can concentrate on fucking you or kissing you, but not both at the same time yet, so pick one."

She bit her cheek to keep from laughing. "Definitely fucking."

"Thank god." He snapped his hips and he was all in.

The weight of him was the perfect amount of pressure on her clit. And if he stayed like that, she might embarrass herself and come at the first hard thrust.

"Tell me what'll get you off."

"Rock forward. Oh god, yes, just like that. So close."

"Already?"

"Yes! And no goddamned judgment when you just admitted you were ready to blow too. Please just . . ."

Streeter laid his hands on the insides of her thighs and pushed them flat to the mattress, pinning her like a butterfly. Then he started to move.

That one adjustment was all she needed. She unraveled immediately. Arching hard, swearing a streak of gibberish, then unable to make a single sound as she held her breath through every throbbing pulse.

It. Was. Fantastic.

A dozen fast jabs later, she looked up as Streeter closed his eyes and groaned.

She felt every pulse of his cock and clamped her inner muscles to the rhythm of his release.

Sex-drunk, he pitched forward and buried his face in the crook of her neck.

A heavy sigh later and he started nibbling her jawline. Then her earlobe. He kissed a path to her mouth, bestowing soft smooches and tiny sugar bites, pausing only to whisper praises into her neck and promises into her ear.

Their soul kisses started out slow but didn't remain that way for long. When she felt him harden inside her again, and that white-hot spark of need ignited between them, she clamped her hands on his ass and held on.

⤴

Bailey wasn't sure how long they'd lain in his bed, indulging in afterplay after the second time. But at some point, they both fell asleep.

"Streeter?"

"Yeah."

"I need food. I'm starving."

On cue, her stomach rumbled.

She kissed his shoulder and rolled to the opposite side of the bed. "I'll cook since it was my idea to have dessert first." She found her panties and one of Streeter's T-shirts, which hung to her knees but was still better than putting on pants.

She wandered into the kitchen and peered into the fridge. Of course it was fully stocked. She took out the eggs, a package of sharp cheddar cheese and a gallon of milk.

When Streeter appeared, his hair adorably messy, wearing just his boxers, she bit back a sigh. He really was too good to be true. "So, cutie, I've decided on scrambled eggs with cheese and tomatoes."

"Sounds good. I'll make the toast. The pan you'll need is in the oven." He paused. "I've got bacon in the freezer."

"That'll take too long." That was sort of a half-truth. Bacon didn't agree with her so she usually avoided it.

The meal came together pretty fast.

After the first bite, Streeter set his fork down. "Thank you for cookin'."

"Thank you for fucking me stupid."

He smiled. "Totally my pleasure."

He was quiet too long after he finished eating.

Bailey touched his forearm and he jumped.

"Shit. Sorry. Lost in thought."

"About?" *Please don't say guilt.*

His troubled eyes met hers. "Why a beautiful, sexy, funny woman like you isn't married or in a relationship."

Maybe if she talked about her past he'd talk about his. "I've been in relationships, even a couple of serious ones. But I knew they wouldn't last."

"How?"

"They were based on convenience or the taboo nature of screwing around when we weren't supposed to be during deployment. My last relationship was with a guy in my company. It ended two years ago. He ended it, in case you were curious."

"I am. Why'd he break it off?"

Bailey snagged the piece of crust on her plate and proceeded to shred it into crumbs. "Logan said I wasn't what he wanted anymore. That stung. I mean, it would've been easier if he'd cheated on me. Then I could blame his new squeeze for the breakup. But when someone you care about says to your face, 'Babe, it's not me, it *is* you,' that's a personal blow to the core of who I am. Or who I was. That changed me. Not because I couldn't live without him, but because I could. I'd wasted a few years with a guy . . ." *Who ran at the first sign of trouble.* But she couldn't admit that. She cleared her throat. "With a guy who had a standard that I couldn't live up to."

"His loss"—Streeter leaned over and easily lifted her out of the chair and onto his lap—"is my gain."

"Just as long as you're aware that I'm only about the sex."

He frowned.

"If that's a problem, let's get it out there now."

"No, actually that's better for me. Then I won't feel guilty about spending my off-hours with Olivia."

She pressed her forehead to his. "See? That wasn't so hard."

"Surprisingly . . . no. But since this kick-started my libido, I can't wait to hear you knockin' on my door after Olivia's in bed." His gaze bored into hers. "It's gotta be here during the week. I can't leave her alone."

"I'd never ask you to do that."

They stayed like that for a while. Breathing the same air as Streeter trailed his fingers up and down her leg.

Finally he said, "After I told you I'm fine with just sex, I'm gonna ask you not to leave. It's only nine o'clock. Hang out with me."

"Streeter Hale. Are you asking if I wanna Netflix and chill with you?"

"Yeah."

Dear lord. Was the man . . . blushing?

Oh, Bailey, how are you gonna keep yourself from falling for him?

She'd think about that later. Much later.

"I don't care what we start watching first, but I wanna end our night with some porn." She kissed the muscle flexing in his jaw. "Don't tell me you don't watch it."

"Of course I watch it, but not out here where my kid could

catch me with my dick in my hand. Them kinda movies I watch in my bedroom."

"I'm in."

"But I'm gonna be honest. I don't wanna watch porn with you. I wanna do the things I've seen in porn with you."

"Even better."

Chapter Twelve

*I*t'd been so long since Streeter had a warm female body in bed next to him that he couldn't sleep.

Rather than risk waking Bailey, he carefully turned on his side, facing away from her.

He swore to himself he wouldn't overthink this.

But how was he supposed to focus on anything besides reliving the best sex he'd ever had?

And what did he do with the guilt that it'd never been like that between him and his wife?

Had that been his fault? Or hers?

After she'd died, he'd spent countless nights staring at the ceiling, missing her, hating her, hating himself for missing her and hating her.

During her pregnancy she'd curled into a protective ball around their child and he'd rubbed her aching lower back. Then he'd kissed her belly and marveled at the life that grew inside her.

He'd believed she'd felt that same sense of awe. But maybe her silence hadn't been because of wonder. Maybe she'd gone quiet because of dread.

Had he known something was troubling her after Olivia's birth? No.

Danica hadn't wanted to breastfeed. Not a big deal, a lot of women didn't. Streeter got up when Olivia started crying. Danica had become so used to him taking the late-night feedings that after a few weeks she didn't move when Olivia squawked on the baby monitor.

When he'd come home from a hard day on the family ranch, Danica had been all smiles, happy to see him. Yet looking back, he remembered almost every night he'd walked into the house he'd heard Olivia crying. Danica assured him "she'd just started that" because she'd set the baby down so she could fix supper.

Streeter had no reason to think Danica hadn't been telling the truth.

Even the couple of times he'd shown up midday and found Danica in her pajamas, snoozing away in their bed while Olivia wailed from her crib, his wife had a logical and tearful explanation. She'd only stretched out for a moment after she'd put Olivia down for her nap and she was just so tired from the demands of a baby that she'd fallen into an exhausted sleep.

All signs he should've noticed that something hadn't been right.

But his angry side chimed in that those were things his wife should've talked to him about. There was no way he ever would've told her she had nothin' to be depressed about when she finally had the baby they'd been trying for, for so long.

So his missing her had quickly turned into resenting her.

Resenting her had turned into hating her.

And the hating had turned everything about her, about their marriage, about their life into a void where nothing had ever been as it seemed.

Even now he feared he'd stay stuck in the past, in his own inadequacies.

A gentle touch skimmed the ball of his shoulder and down the outside of his arm. "I know you're not asleep."

"Did I wake you?"

"It's fine." She paused. "Do you want me to go?"

Did he?

He cleared his throat. "I . . . don't know."

"If I stay, we need to talk about her."

"I know."

A beat passed. "Would it be easier if you stay on your side like that so you don't have to look at me when you're talking?"

There wasn't a hint of anger or pity or reproach in Bailey's tone. And what kind of fucking saint did that make her for not running the fuck out of here? She didn't need this heavy stuff. She'd told him she'd just wanted sex. He should ask her to go. For her own good.

But he didn't.

He couldn't.

He'd tell her the truth, even if she chose to run from it and from him.

Well, that'd be tit for tat since he'd been running from this himself.

Streeter rolled over and faced her.

She blinked those beautiful hazel eyes at him.

"God, you're so pretty," he murmured as he touched her cheek. "If I were a smooth talker I'd say I couldn't sleep because I'd be afraid when I woke up that all of this was just a dream."

"Then I'm glad you're not a smooth talker. Because I'd rather have the truth."

"C'mere." He stretched out on his back and tucked her against his side, shoving the pillow under his head.

Bailey squirmed around until she got comfortable, twining her legs with his, making sure there wasn't any space between his body and hers.

He idly twirled a hank of her hair around his finger. "Once I get goin' on this, just let me ramble without any questions until I'm ready, okay?"

She kissed his pectoral. "Got it."

How . . . where . . . was he even supposed to start with this?

Find out what she knows.

"First I gotta ask how much you know about my history and Olivia's mother. Even if you heard it thirdhand, I wanna know."

"I haven't asked anyone about you, and no one from the Split Rock has come up and warned me off you, because I'm pretty sure no one would put us together as a couple."

"How wrong they were, huh?" He kissed the top of her head. "That was the hottest sex of my life, Bailey."

"It was right up there for me too." She wiggled against him, still searching for the perfect spot. "So I know that you married your high school sweetheart. I figure you were mostly happily married since you were together for years. You had a child together and she died. From the way you don't talk about how she died, it was probably a car accident rather than a medical condition like cancer."

"Or she committed suicide."

Bailey's body went rigid.

"The shock of sayin' that has worn off for me, although as you know, I don't talk about it at all if I can help it."

"Does Olivia know how she died?"

"No. I'll tell her, of course, when she's older, before someone else does. But there's part of me that thinks she already knows." He paused and swallowed hard. "That she remembers."

Bailey opened her mouth against his chest and then closed it again.

"When Olivia was six months old, Danica killed herself in Olivia's bedroom. She slashed her wrists first, but she also had a shotgun and pulled the trigger. That's what I came home to. Her dead and Olivia screamin' in her crib. And she must've done it right after I went to work." He kept twirling Bailey's hair. "All I could see beyond the blood was my beautiful baby who'd screamed so much she'd gone hoarse. When I called 911, the call center told me to stay put, not to do anything, until law enforcement showed up. But I could see that she'd been goddamned neglected all day, and I wasn't gonna let Olivia go hungry while we waited. I sat on the floor with the front door wide open, as I fed her the first bottle she'd had in probably nine hours.

"Not a lot of calls like that in to our county, so the deputy and ambulance got there pretty quick. First thing the deputy did was check my call log to see who else I'd been in touch with because at that point, I was a suspect. I listened as the deputy called my dad and my brother to verify that I'd been at work with them all day. Took about an hour for a crime scene unit to arrive and another half an hour for them to determine I hadn't killed my wife. Oh, and since a minor child was the only witness, and had been endangered by her own mother, social services was called to the scene too.

"The social worker went into Olivia's room and packed up a bunch of her clothes, diapers, blankets and stuff. She went upstairs with me and helped me bathe Olivia and get her dressed in clothes that weren't covered in blood. Danica's body was gone by the time we returned downstairs. Then I gave the deputy Danica's parents' contact info because I couldn't handle telling them. I threw some of my own stuff in a bag, tossed in formula and bottles and left. Checked into a motel. But I'll bet I didn't sleep more than two hours in three days and Olivia wouldn't let me out of her sight."

His chest was damp—he'd expected Bailey's tears and for some reason, instead of annoying him, that helped him keep talking.

"The weeks that followed were mostly a blur. The funeral, dealing with Danica's grief-stricken parents and sister. We were all in shock. None of us had seen it comin'. And because of that, ugly words were exchanged all around. I never went back to the house. Danica's best friend went in and boxed up all the pictures and baby items, a couple of heirlooms that'd been passed down from our families and some of Danica's things that Olivia might want someday. But the rest of it? I had it hauled off. It was either that or throw a fuckin' match inside the house and watch the place burn.

"I couldn't go anywhere in my hometown without invoking pity and questions. My fucked-up life was the topic of speculation and gossip. Olivia became a tragic figure. At six months old. But I muddled through for a while. My daughter had become so attached to me I couldn't work.

I couldn't stand to be around people, especially Danica's family because they looked to me for answers that I didn't have." He paused, wishing he'd grabbed a glass of water. "Then everything went down with my dad and brother that I already told you about. Also during that time it came to light that over the years Danica worked for the state, she'd quadrupled the amount of her life insurance. I had no fuckin' idea she'd done that. And it pissed me off because the last time she increased the payout was four years *before* we had Olivia. I couldn't help but think . . . did she know she was gonna off herself eventually? Had Danica always had bouts of depression and I just hadn't seen it? Or had postpartum depression brought on suicidal thoughts?

"All questions I'll be stuck wondering about the rest of my life with no possibility for answers. When I questioned the insurance company about the policy changes, they indicated that fertility problems were the reason Danica gave for increasing the life coverage level—she wanted to make sure that I or we—me and a baby—would be taken care of if anything went wrong during a procedure. So yeah, I had no issues getting the insurance company to pay the goddamned guilt money from my dead wife. But no amount of money would ever make our lives easier. Especially not after . . ."

Bailey pressed a kiss above his heart and dug her fingers into his chest, as if she were trying to hold his heart inside.

God. This woman soothed him with her unspoken sweetness. He hadn't realized how much he'd needed it.

He soldiered on. "Olivia has had a fuckton of psychological issues. Extreme separation anxiety, night terrors, short attention span. I started takin' her to a psychologist who specializes in childhood trauma when Olivia was just a year old. And because she's been subjected to so goddamned many psychological tests, they told me early on she is intellectually gifted. What the hell was I supposed to do with that? I'm a damn rancher. I didn't go to college. So her childhood has been anything but normal; it's been a day-by-day thing for both of us. The kid started readin' her board books at age three. At first the docs believed she might be high-functioning on the autism spectrum. But they called in some specialist from Denver Children's Hospital and he observed her for almost two weeks. He diagnosed her with a detachment disorder. He even wrote a medical paper on her and got it published."

"What does a detachment disorder mean exactly?"

"In all likelihood Danica never bonded with our daughter. After talkin' to me about what I saw between Danica and Olivia those first six months, they believe Danica ignored Olivia completely. Let her cry in her crib all day. Never picked her up to change her. Didn't hold her even to feed her, but propped a bottle up on a pillow so she wouldn't have to touch her. That's when I realized I'd done all the bottle makin' and bathing. I got up with her at night. On the weekends when Danica's parents weren't there, I took care of our baby because Danica was exhausted. The docs suspected Danica suffered from extreme postpartum depression, and maybe that was why she did what she did. When the psychology specialist and his colleagues started interviewing us about Danica's past behavior, no one—not me, her parents, her friends, her coworkers—could recall a time when Danica had shown signs of depression. What the docs refused to confirm for me was whether Danica's detachment was a safety mechanism to keep herself from hurtin' our baby.

"So the only person Olivia has attached herself to is me. To be blunt, she doesn't give a damn about anyone else. Not her grandparents, not her preschool pals, not any of her babysitters. At this point in her development she can't form attachments because I fill all the roles she needs in her life or some shit. It's an issue that might change as she gets older, but no one knows. But there's no doubt in my mind that her mother's detachment is the sole cause of it. With each new thing I learned about how that indifference affected Olivia, I blamed Danica. I have to live with the question of whether I ever knew her at all."

After a while, when his heart rate turned to normal, Bailey said, "Thank you for telling me."

"It ain't a pretty part of my life, Bailey. But you deserve to know why I'm this way."

"What way?"

"A cynical dick."

She snorted. "You're not as much of one as you think. And being in bed with you has upped your status from cutie to holy-fuck-smokin'-hot *because* of your dick."

He managed a smile. "I'm amazed that you saw anything in me worth pursuing, because with few exceptions I've been a shell of a man the past four and a half years."

"Can I ask my questions now?"

"Yeah."

"What attracted you to Danica in the first place?"

Christ. Did he even remember? "She was pretty but she wasn't obsessed with her looks like other girls her age were. She turned me down the first three times I asked her out, but she was nice about it, so I figured she might say yes if I kept askin'. Eventually she did agree to one date. From that point on, we were a couple. I liked that she wasn't a drama queen, or a mean girl. Plus she liked to mess around, and to a sixteen-year-old boy that made her damn near perfect."

"I know she was the only one you'd ever been with, so was your sex life with her okay?"

"I had nothin' to compare it to. So if you mean did we have 'rip off the sheets and fuck like animals' sex . . . only a couple of times. There wasn't much adventure. I guess maybe no drama meant no passion either. Then when we found out about the fertility problems, sex was pretty scripted."

"How long did you try to have a baby?"

"Six years. She never had any miscarriages, she just couldn't get pregnant until she finally did."

"Normal pregnancy?"

"Picture-perfect. She didn't care about bein' with me sexually, after

Olivia was born. Maybe that shoulda been a sign, but I was exhausted too during that time. I worked a ten-hour day on the ranch and came home and took care of Olivia. When I was in bed and the baby was asleep all I wanted to do was sleep too."

"Does Olivia look like her?"

"Short answer? No. The longer answer circles back to that idea that I'm a dick, because after what we went through I'm really fuckin' relieved she doesn't resemble her mother in looks or temperament."

Bailey was quiet so long he knew he'd said something wrong. Or maybe he'd been too honest.

Ya think? Maybe the fact you're dissecting the sex life you had with your wife with your new lover is what's wrong, dumb-ass.

His entire body flamed with embarrassment.

"My, my, you certainly got warm all of a sudden, cowboy."

"Yeah. I could use a drink." He shifted until she moved enough for him to sit on the edge of the bed. He found his boxers and pulled them on.

"You don't have to put those on, on my account," she said with a purr.

"Habit. Not used to walkin' around nekkid when a kid's in the house." He stood. "You need anything while I'm up?"

She shook her head.

"Okay. Be right back."

Except he didn't go right back.

He downed a glass of water. Washed his face and his hands in cold water to try to cool himself down. Stared out the front kitchen window into the nothingness beyond.

Streeter wondered if he'd made a mistake opening himself up. He had no experience with casual sex, but he wanted to change that. For as long as Bailey was here, he wanted to gorge himself on hot sex with her. But he also wanted to hang out. Eat together. Watch TV. Maybe she didn't want that. Maybe she was putting her clothes back on right now.

Maybe you oughta quit bein' such a chickenshit and go ask her what she wants.

He wheeled around and Bailey was right there. Naked except for the shirt he'd draped over the ironing board, the shirt he'd intended to wear on their date earlier tonight.

A shirt that looked a hundred times better on her, with her sweet tits playing peekaboo with the lapels and the shirttail brushing across the tops of her thighs.

With her hair sleep tousled, her lips puffy from kissing him and her eyes dancing with mischief, he couldn't believe she was here with him.

"It's not easy to get lost in a trailer, but somehow you managed." She sauntered forward. "Or maybe you were hoping I'd get the hint and leave?"

"Not at all. I'm standin' here watchin' you walkin' toward me and wondering how I got so lucky that you're here at all, to say nothin' of you bein' here mostly nekkid."

"Hmm. I thought maybe you were out here thinking too much."

"That too."

Bailey moved in and flattened her palms on his chest. Then she tipped her head back and studied him.

"What?"

"I'll say my piece and you can take it or leave it, okay?"

Streeter just nodded.

"If I have my way? We'll be fucking a lot. But only if we're fully honest with each other in what we want. You need to be able to talk specifics to me without embarrassment." She blinked those sexy eyes at him. "Maybe tomorrow you'll want a hand job while we're sitting on the couch. Maybe you'll want to fuck me hard and fast against the door without any foreplay. Maybe you just want to cuddle. Whatever strikes your mood, I'm in. Don't think I'm not interested in doing it or trying it because *she* didn't. This is your chance to reclaim your sexuality."

"And what about you?"

She winked. "Oh, I have no issues telling you exactly how I want to be fucked."

Streeter curled his hands around her face, getting lost in this singular pleasure of just kissing her. Sucking on her lips and tongue. Nibbling on the edges of her smile. Swallowing her husky moans. Fucking *reveling* in the way she arched into him, rubbed against his body, wanted him.

His heart raced as sexual need crowded out everything else. He kissed a path to her ear. "Bailey."

"Oh god, your voice is pure sex."

"And your mouth is my wet dream." He licked the shell of her ear. "Which is why I wanna feel it." He grabbed her hand and placed it on his erection. "Here."

He felt her smile against his cheek. "Polite, but dirty. I like it."

Then she dropped to her knees. Keeping her focus on him, she inched his boxers down to his feet. "Next time don't bother with these when it's just us."

At the first touch of her soft, damp lips to the crown of his cock, he sucked in a breath.

Holy shitballs. That was like . . . a million times more intense than he remembered. He glanced down to see her looking up at him with heated eyes and a coy smile.

"Gonna tease me until I beg, ain't ya," he muttered huskily.

"No," she said as she licked the head like a lollipop. "Your eyes are already begging me. I will warn you to hold on to the counter, though."

He placed his hands behind him and his eyes crossed when he felt the hot rush of lips and tongue and teeth. He allowed a grunt of satisfaction when she began to work him over.

Little whips of her tongue around the head that tightened his balls.

Followed by an iron grip at the base of his cock and quick jerks as her lips met her fist in the middle of his shaft.

No way could he last. It'd been too damn long and it'd never been this good.

Warm, wet, steady movement with her hand had him bumping his hips forward.

God, yes.

"That. Right there. Don't stop."

She released a humming noise that shot straight up his dick like a damn rocket. His entire body seemed to be throbbing, keeping rhythm with the pull and glide of her mouth.

Streeter held his breath when that tingle in his tailbone started. He had no chance to warn her the end was near. He had no desire to move lest this amazing sensation would somehow end.

Then he lost it as he started to come. Head back, hips pumping, air billowing in and out of his lungs with each suctioning pull of that crazy talented mouth of hers.

White light exploded behind his lids and his entire being went supernova.

His body returned to the atmosphere, although his legs were still quaking. Streeter managed to peel his eyes open and peer down at the dark head moving across the top of his thigh as she planted kisses there.

He reached out with a shaking hand and touched her cheek.

Bailey glanced up at him and smiled. "Hey."

What was he supposed to say? She'd swallowed. Wasn't like he'd given her a choice. "Uh, sorry I didn't warn you I was about to . . . I sorta lost my head."

"Good. That's what I was going for."

He traced her lips, all soft and shiny from the friction of his cock. "Truth time. I've never—"

"Had a blow job?" she inserted with shock.

"Never one as good as that," he muttered, and then wished he could take it back. "You swallowing. That was a first for me."

"You okay with that?"

"Very okay. Very, very, very, perfectly okay with it."

She chuckled. "Awesome. Because I really really really like sucking your cock. It gets me hot."

Streeter pulled her to her feet and covered her mouth with his. He needed to know how he tasted on her. Danica never wanted to kiss him after he'd gone down on her either.

But Bailey moaned and wrapped her arms around his neck, canting her head, allowing him to take the kiss deeper.

Fuck. This woman . . . He cupped her breasts and thumbed her nipples. Next time he'd have these sweet tits in his mouth as he fucked her with her on his lap. A dark sound of need rumbled from his mouth to hers, causing her to pull back.

"What?"

"I wanna return the favor." Feeling shy, he ducked his head and nipped her chin.

"I want that too." She slid her arms down to frame his face in her hands. "But I'm gonna make you use your words, Street. You need to look me in the eyes and tell me what you plan to do to me. Every dirty, delicious thing." Her gaze dipped to his mouth. "Go on."

He'd never been verbal in bed—either in expressing his needs or workin' dirty talk. Danica hadn't liked it and he'd just felt foolish the time he'd tried it. But Bailey, beautiful, sexy, bold Bailey demanded that from him.

"What do I want to do to you?" His voice was suspiciously close to a whisper. "I wanna lay you on my bed and follow every one of these curves as I'm spreading your legs wide open. When I see how wet you are for me, that's when I sorta lose my head and belly-crawl across the mattress to get to you and bury my face in your pussy. Licking up your sweetness, filling my mouth with your taste, savoring the rush of wetness as I start to use my tongue. You're grindin' against my face and moanin' so I don't drag it out. I wanna watch you come undone. I *need* to know that I can do it for you. And as I'm feelin' your blood pulsing beneath my lips, I suck on your—"

Bailey pressed her fingers over his lips. "Now show me."

He could've kissed her all the way back to his bedroom.

Instead, he clamped his hands on her ass, picked her up and threw her over his shoulder in a fireman's hold and *ran* all the way back to his bedroom.

Her husky laughter vibrating against his ass might've been one of the best moments in his life.

After gently laying her on the bed, he crawled on his knees toward her. He pushed aside the shirttails that were blocking his view.

"Do you want me to take it off?" she said.

"Nope. When I'm done makin' you come, I'm gonna wipe my mouth on the inside of that shirt, so when I wear it tomorrow, I'll have a reminder of how hot and wet I can make you."

Her eyes darkened.

Streeter smiled and devoured her.

She bucked against his mouth, yanked his hair and came so fast, so hard, he started all over again almost as soon as she finished, just to make sure he could get it right twice in a row.

He did.

By that time his dick was raring for another round.

Bailey reached for the condoms first. She kissed him with such druggingly sweet kisses as she rolled it on, he damn near felt dizzy. Then she straddled his lap, her knees tight against his hips, and fit his cock inside her in one quick glide.

He murmured, "Perfect," and lavished attention on her nipples and her chest, collarbones, neck and throat.

She groaned. "God. I love your cock."

He smiled against the upper swell of her left breast. "It's yours anytime."

Then she moved on him slowly, her hands on his shoulders, or in his hair, or one arm wrapped around his neck.

Even though she was doing all of the work, his skin beaded with sweat, which just added another layer of pleasure. Slick skin sliding on skin as they fed each other openmouthed kisses. The rise and fall of their breathing, in tandem, in opposition as chests touched with each inhalation. That first time was hot as fire with her. But it was lust-fueled fucking.

This, to be a total fucking cliché, was making love.

Bailey rested her forehead to his. "I need more direct pressure."

"What can I do?"

"Lie back."

As soon as Streeter's head hit the mattress, Bailey attacked his neck with hard kisses and soft bites as she slid forward, grinding her clit into him with each backward glide.

He clamped his hands on her ass and moved with her, against her, whispering, "Come on, baby, that's it. Take it however you want it."

She released a whimpering cry and her pussy started to contract around his cock. Each hard pulse pulled him closer to the edge.

Don't move. Don't change.

The pulses slowed and stopped.

After the last one, she sighed and snuggled into him.

He nuzzled the top of her head. "Bailey. Hold on."

Then he rolled them until she was on her back, arching beneath him as he drove into her.

His thrusts were faster, but not rough enough to keep them from kissing. But when he'd reached the end point, he tore his mouth free, closed his eyes and let loose a long groan.

Goddamn. There were those white lights and bright lights again as he came in a hot rush.

His focus to the real world returned in slow increments and he angled his head to get to Bailey's mouth. The way she kissed him, like she couldn't get enough, moved him in ways he couldn't put into words.

Yet.

He pushed up onto his arms, taking his weight from her. "Will you stay with me the rest of the night?"

"Yes."

After he ditched the condom, he crawled back in bed and spooned her.

"Streeter?"

"Hmm?"

"I haven't been with anyone for two years. Not since Logan. I've had a battery of medical tests and I can show you that I'm free and clear of sexually transmitted diseases."

"I'm pretty sure my right hand hasn't contracted anything in the past few years."

She snickered. "Also, I have an implant in my arm to prevent pregnancy." She exhaled. "Can we skip the condoms? I want to feel all of you with no barriers between us."

"You have birth control in your arm?" he said skeptically.

"Yes. You can feel it. Give me your hand." She took his fingers and pressed them on the inside of her right arm, above the crease of her elbow.

He felt a bump. "Whoa. That's kinda freaky. Does it hurt?"

"Not really. I've had it in for almost two years and it's effective for five years."

"Ain't gonna hurt my feelin's to skip the condoms."

"Good." She snuggled her ass back into his groin. "Wake me up if you have a dirty dream and we'll act out all the good parts."

Apparently they'd talked and fucked themselves into exhaustion. After that they fell asleep.

Chapter Thirteen

*B*een a long time since Bailey had dealt with a morning-after situation.

She'd expected Streeter to get up at the crack of nothing, but he was still sawing logs at seven a.m. She couldn't lie there any longer so she slipped out of bed, found her clothes and escaped to the bathroom.

A glance at herself in the mirror had her blushing and feeling a bit cocky. She looked well and truly fucked. But her hair . . . damn. A bit of water tamed it and she borrowed mouthwash rather than using Streeter's toothbrush.

Needing coffee, she headed into the kitchen and started a pot, impressed that he had decent taste in dark roast.

Then she pawed through his cupboards, finding Pop-Tarts, sugary cereal and oatmeal.

Oatmeal it is.

She poured water in the pan and pulled out the toaster. Found fruit and nuts and chopped them together.

Streeter wandered into the kitchen in just his boxers—lucky her—and sent her a shy smile. "Mornin', hot stuff."

"Mornin', cutie."

"Got a cup of coffee yet?"

"Nope. It just finished brewing."

He poured two mugs and handed one to her. "Need cream or sugar?"

"Black is fine, thanks."

He leaned against the counter, watching her. "Am I supposed to be doin' that?"

Bailey looked at him. "Doing what? Cooking?"

"Yeah. I'm not exactly up on morning-after behavior. And you cooked for us last night too."

As she poured the oats into the boiling water, she said, "Maybe I should've asked if you minded if I cooked breakfast."

He moved in behind her and pressed his lips to the back of her head. "I'm grateful. Usually I just have coffee. And I don't usually sleep in this late." Another soft kiss. "Not used to that much physical activity."

"You don't look any worse for wear."

"I feel amazing."

Bailey stirred the oats. She sensed something was on his mind. "Cat got your tongue, cowboy?"

He made a growling noise. "Your pussy liked my tongue well enough last night that maybe I'm havin' a hard time usin' it to talk today."

"You won't hear me complain about your oral skills."

"I guess maybe that's my question. How was I—"

"In comparison to the last guy I was with?"

He sighed. "Sounds stupid, me askin' you that, doesn't it?"

"No, I asked you about Danica; it makes sense you'd want to know about my last sexual relationship too." She scraped the oatmeal down the edges of the pan. "Logan was great in bed, or lousy—depending on his mood. Notice I said *his* mood, not mine. Sex was a cure-all for him. I didn't realize that until after he broke up with me."

"What attracted you to him?"

She shrugged. "We were deployed together. We went from being friends to being lovers. The sneaking-around aspect appealed to both of us, but we stayed together for a while after we returned stateside."

"The loneliness is the hardest part after they're gone, isn't it?" he asked softly.

"For me? No. I've been alone most of my life, so the fact he moved on wasn't a huge shocker to me, because I've gotten used to it." In desperate need of a subject change, she said, "What do you do on Sundays?"

"Work, since I miss hours during the week to be with Olivia. I only check cattle once on Sunday unless it's calving season, and we're past that."

"Is Olivia with her grandparents every weekend?"

"Most of 'em. That didn't become a regular thing until about six months ago. She could only be with one or the other for a few hours and then she'd had enough. Neither her grandma nor her grandpa can handle her when she's like that. Hell, I have a hard time dealin' with her."

She glopped a spoonful of oatmeal into both bowls, then sprinkled on the fruit-and-nut mixture. "Shoot. I forgot to drop the toast."

"This is plenty. Thank you."

"What time will Olivia be back today?"

"Around suppertime."

"She's gone from Friday night until Sunday night?"

"Usually she's back by noon on Sunday, but Deenie had some family thing to take her to. She spent yesterday with her grandpa."

"They have separate visitation with her?"

He nodded and swallowed a bite. "About a year after Danica died, her parents got divorced. They split time with Olivia for now. But I never know how long anything is gonna stick with her. But if I didn't set up the time with them, she'd never see them because she wouldn't ask."

Bailey sat across from him at the small table. "One of the more awkward things to deal with in a morning-after situation is whether there'll be more."

Streeter set down his spoon. "Honesty between us, right?"

She nodded, wondering if he was about to send her packing.

"I'd like more than just morning-afters with you. I'd like to spend time with you during the week, if you're not busy in the evenings."

That was a happy surprise, but she needed clarification. "Meaning I show up after Olivia has gone to bed?"

He frowned. "I guess if that works better for you. But I was thinkin' more that you could hang out with both of us some nights."

"So you're okay with Olivia knowing we're seeing each other?"

"Yeah. Aren't you?"

"I'm good with that as long as you understand if we're alone together, I can't promise to keep my hands off you."

He lifted a brow. "Why would you think I'd want you to keep those greedy hands of yours off me?"

"Because of your young daughter."

"You worried she'll interrupt us when we're getting down and dirty?"

"Maybe. I'm also worried she'll wonder why I'm here."

"Not to be blunt, but Olivia won't care. She won't get attached to you, Bailey."

But will you *get attached to me?*

The unspoken question lingered between them.

He curled his hand over her forearm. "We've admitted we like each other. You've reminded me you're not sticking around. I wanna spend time with you. Naked. Clothed. In the evenings, afternoons, weekends . . . whenever it fits our schedules, for as long as you're here, for as long as we both want that."

Her conscience was screaming at her to buck up and walk away—for Streeter's good.

It was easy to ignore everything when she looked into his gorgeous eyes and realized she'd already gotten attached to him. "Okay."

He stood up and kissed her. Lazy, teasing kisses that were sweet and needy enough to cause an aching feeling in her chest.

"What are your plans for today?"

"I have to open WWC at nine. Then close down at three. That's the only compromise Harper was willing to make with Janie and Renner when they asked her to be open on Sundays during the summer."

"That's right, WWC isn't open on Sundays during the rest of the year. How much business is there on a Sunday?"

"I sold two packages of candy and a magnet last week."

"Not enough to pay your wages, I reckon."

Harper wasn't paying her. It wasn't as if she hadn't offered. But Bailey felt she was finally able to pay back the debt she owed to her sister from years ago.

"After that I'll probably work out."

"I work out on Sundays too. Weird that we haven't run into each other before." He smirked. "Maybe we oughta work out together. You could give me a demonstration of your self-defense moves."

She cocked an eyebrow at him. "You wouldn't mind me throwing you on your ass?"

"Nope, because I like that you're strong and confident. It's a huge turn-on. Hell, I'd probably be sporting wood the entire time you were in beatdown mode."

Laughing, she returned the coffeepot to the warmer and put away the breakfast supplies. Without a word Streeter got up and scraped and rinsed the dishes.

Bailey had a moment of déjà vu. As if they'd done this together before. Or maybe it was a premonition of wishful thinking; she hoped this would be the first of many times they'd do it together.

She turned to tell him good-bye, and Streeter was right there, pulling her into his arms, holding her tight and kissing her deeply. Whatever hesitancy he'd had about his make-out skills had disappeared. And he already seemed to know when she needed mind-scrambling passion or sweetness.

Or something like this—the perfect mixture of both.

You are in over your head with this man after one night together.

Streeter not-so-casually asked, "I will see you later, right?"

Rather than playing it cool, she nuzzled his neck and kissed the hollow of his throat. "Absolutely."

∓

Bailey showered at her trailer, touching the tender spots on her body, reassuring herself the soreness was from the sexual acrobatics she hadn't had in a long damn time.

After fixing a "superfood" smoothie for later, she walked up to the Split Rock.

Not a single customer came through the door the first hour, which allowed her to get her boot camp planned out for Friday.

Harper had sent a text to make sure Bailey was opening the store, which annoyed her. She'd not missed a day or even been late one time—more than she could say for the store's owner. Things weren't getting worse between her and Harper, but they couldn't stay the same either. And if Bailey had to make the first move to smooth everything over, she would.

The day dragged on. At two thirty, half an hour before the store closed, five women strolled in. These customers were an interesting bunch—they all appeared to be over seventy and given their outlandish clothes, maybe they were headed to a costume party.

She greeted them with a smile. "Ladies. How may I help you today?"

"Got any of them concealed-carry purses?" a stout woman dressed head to toe in camo asked. Literally head to toe—both her hat and her combat boots were jungle-print camouflage.

"No, I don't believe I've ever seen one in stock. But I'm sure we could order one for you."

"You don't need one of those, Pearl, since your concealed-carry permit expired," a gray-haired woman wearing a garish orange-and-fuchsia muumuu pointed out.

"Shut it, Maybelle," the lady in camo retorted. "Maybe I wanted to gift it to someone."

"You two are drivin' me bonkers," a slender woman decked out in an electric blue catsuit and matching disco headband complained. "We're supposed to be checking out Harper's little sister."

Bailey froze. "Excuse me?"

A redhead, stylishly dressed in pin-striped capris and a black lace top with a white scarf tied jauntily around her neck, stepped forward. "Hello . . . Bailey, isn't it?"

She nodded.

"You probably don't remember us, but we were at Harper and Bran's wedding. We're friends of your sister."

"She used to do our nails," interjected a tiny sprite with a cloud of cotton candy pink hair sporting a lime green sequined shirt and silver lamé leggings. "And give us advice."

"Who are you?" Bailey asked, even when she suspected she knew the answer.

"Around these parts, we're known as the Mud Lilies," Camo Lady said. "I'm Pearl."

They introduced themselves one by one—and her brain assigned descriptive words so she could remember their names.

Postulating Pearl.

Muumuu Maybelle.

Tiny Tilda.

Garish Garnet.

Va-va-voom Vivien.

"So you're here to see Harper?" Bailey finally asked, cutting through arguments between Garnet and Maybelle.

"No, we're here to see if you'd help us host a surprise party for your sister."

"What's the occasion?" Her birthday wasn't for a few months.

"We don't wanna make it specific," Garnet said. "That girl has thrown baby showers, and bridal showers, and birthday parties for tons of people in the community. She's hosted luncheons and run raffles and bake sales. It's time we show her our appreciation for all she's done."

And Bailey wondered if these ladies, who'd known her sister for years, had figured out that Harper had been struggling since Angel's birth.

"Don't you think that's a great idea?" Tilda said, adding an excited handclap.

No. "When are you planning to do this?"

"Oh, it'll take a couple of weeks to get everything in place. Invites sent out. Party favors and decorations ordered, and games chosen."

"Where is this taking place?"

"Right here. At the Split Rock," Garnet said.

Vivien shook her finger in Garnet's face. "Don't assume Renner and Janie will be on board after that time you fired a gun in the lodge."

"That was years ago," she scoffed.

"Plus, we're shareholders," Pearl said indignantly. "They *have* to give us fair use of the facility whenever we want."

Bailey's brain had gotten stuck on the phrase *fired a gun.* "Was there a reason for discharging a weapon?"

"Me'n Vivien had a duel over a man," Miss Maybelle inserted.

"And as Pearl says, Vivien brought a sword to a gunfight," Tilda confided.

"Ancient history," Miss Maybelle and Vivien said simultaneously.

Hoo boy.

"We wondered if since you've been in the army and are familiar with matters of stealth, you could take care of the subterfuge aspect." Pearl leaned on the counter. "I've got military ties. My dad was in WWII. He swore he joined up to fight so his children wouldn't have to. He nipped my military career in the bud before it ever began. Which is why I consider myself to be an amateur military strategist."

How was she supposed to respond to that? "Ah, it's good to have hobbies."

"They've come in useful. Mind if I call you by your rank?"

"My boot camp recruits call me Sergeant B."

"Excellent. So Sergeant B, we were hoping you'd have some ideas on how to get Harper to the party without her knowing it's a bash for her. See, we're thinking that we could have a fake robbery and you could 'save' her and sneak her out of the store and into the dining hall. That'd be a helluva surprise."

Especially if Harper started screaming and peed her pants with fear; her sister would never forgive her.

"*No one* thinks that cockamamie idea is good except for you," Garnet retorted.

"It's not like any of *you* have come up with something better."

And then it was on.

Bailey suspected they wouldn't notice if she snuck out.

Just as she was about to remind them that the store closed at three, Streeter strolled in.

"What in the world is goin' on in here? I heard you bickerin' clear down at the end of the hallway."

All the Mud Lilies turned to him and followed his progress as he moved from the doorway to behind the counter.

He loomed over Bailey. "You all right?"

She couldn't stop herself from smiling at him. "Why wouldn't I be?"

"These ladies come on strong."

"If I can handle a two-star general screaming in my face about a missing supply order, I can handle"—*Don't say cranky busybodies*—"a few loud suggestions."

"Streeter Hale," Maybelle said. "What are you doing in here?"

Maybe it hadn't occurred to him how it might seem odd, barreling in to rescue her. He sent the woman a look. "Well, Miz Maybelle, bein' as I work at the Split Rock and I heard a commotion, I decided to check it out."

"It is nice to see you out and about," Vivien said.

"Yeah, Tobin told me that you actually went out to the Buckeye with him the other night. Sorry I missed that. We're always lookin' for new drinkin' buddies." Garnet gave Bailey the side-eye.

Streeter grinned at Bailey and she nearly melted. "Fair warning, Sergeant. Rumor is no one makes it past these ladies' initiation shot."

"Oh pooh." Tilda flapped her hand. "Buncha lightweights."

"Remember when we used to be surrounded by all them ranching cowboys? Hank and Abe. Kyle. Renner. Fletch. Eli. Ike. Hugh. Tobin. Holt. Devin, if he was in town." Pearl sighed heavily. "No new possible recruits have moved here—except for you—which ain't a surprise, but it ain't fun for us, neither."

"You lookin' for a new man friend, Pearl?" he asked with a straight face.

"Negative, Hale."

"How about you, Streeter?" Maybelle asked.

Please don't ask if he's looking for a new female friend because the man will surely blush.

"I ain't lookin' for a new man friend either," he said with a wink. "But the next time Tobin and I grab a beer, we'll give the Mud Lilies a call."

Five happy faces beamed at him.

And Streeter claimed he wasn't a charmer.

He pointedly looked at the clock. "Sorry to hurry you along, but it's closin' time for WWC. And I told Sergeant B I'd help her do some stuff in the back room for boot camp."

Oh, and Streeter was a smooth liar too.

"Of course we wouldn't want to keep you two from doing that all-important 'stuff' together," Vivien said slyly. "Come on, Lilies."

"But . . . what about this surprise party you mentioned throwing for Harper? Where did we end up with that?"

"Don't worry, honey. It'll all work out." Tilda patted her hand. "And Bernice, who runs the Beauty Barn, said to tell you she'll offer a fifteen percent discount if you come in for a restyle."

Wait. Was that a hint that she needed a new hairstyle?

Streeter ushered them out. He flipped the sign and locked the door.

But he kept his hands pressed to the glass and didn't turn around immediately, giving her a nice long look at that fantastic cowboy ass encased in faded Wranglers. His shoulders heaved and she couldn't tell if he was laughing.

"Streeter? You okay?"

"Fuck no."

Bailey skirted the counter in an instant. "What's wrong?"

He whirled around and slowly lifted his head.

When her gaze caught his beneath the brim of his hat, she froze. His green eyes blazed with sexual heat, more intense than she'd ever seen from him.

"From the moment you touched me last night, I haven't been able to think about anything else except your hands on me. Your mouth on me. Your body on mine."

Her heart started to race. "Is that why you're here?"

"I'm here because I can't go another goddamned hour without knowin' if it's the same for you."

"The same . . . meaning if I'm reliving every moment of us rolling around naked? If I press my hand to my mouth as if I can still feel your lips there? Then yes, it's the same for me."

He made the sexiest growling noise. "Remember last night when you told me to tell you what I want?"

"Yes." Was he even aware that he'd started stalking her? She took two steps back.

"I'm here to tell you what I want, Bailey."

"What's that?"

"I want to fuck you. Hard and fast." Streeter closed the distance between them. "Now."

"Now?"

"Right fuckin' now." He leaned in until their lips almost touched. "That thing that I said I needed to help you with? Is me getting another taste of you." His mouth crashed down on hers.

Oh yes please. I'll give you a double helping of me any time you want.

This man had no idea of the power he wielded with those demanding, gruff words.

His kiss was hungry. Raw. He yanked his hat off and tossed it on the counter. Then his hands were on her ass, lifting her off the floor as he carried her into the back room.

She levered herself up until she could wrap her legs around his waist.

Streeter dodged the table and chairs and didn't stop until he'd pressed her back against a wall. Then his mouth slid down her chin and he planted frantic, damp kisses on her throat. "Christ, woman. You smell so damn good." He buried his face in the curve of her neck and inhaled. "Like sugar and flowers. Makes me hard as fuck."

Bailey groaned, loving the way his words rumbled against her skin, especially the feel of the sexy scrape of his teeth and how he soothed the sting with little sucking kisses.

He kept grinding his hips into her. Up and down. Side to side. Testing which way made her arch harder. Which way made her break the kiss and beg.

Against her throat he panted, "No condoms, right?"

"Right."

"You wet enough to take me?"

"I've been wet since you flipped the damn Closed sign over on the door."

"Get these pants off." He set her on her feet and shuffled back three steps.

Bailey kicked her shoes away. Then she peeled her leggings off and stood before him in her black lace panties. As she hooked her fingers into the waistband, he uttered a gruff "Wait."

He untucked his shirt—the white shirt she'd had on earlier—and unbuckled his belt. Down went his zipper. Out came his cock. He stroked it as he moved in to crowd her against the wall. "Your eyes, baby, tell me everything I wanna know."

"What's that?"

"That I ain't gonna take the time to take my boots off. That I'm gonna drop my jeans, pull off those sexy panties and fuck you against that wall until you scream."

If she hadn't been wet enough before, she sure was now.

She said, "Do it," and ditched her panties.

His jeans fell to his knees. Then his hands were on her ass, hoisting her up.

Bailey reached between them, guiding the head of his cock to her opening, tilting her pelvis as he slammed home.

Streeter pressed his face into the curve of her neck and groaned, "I need to build up my stamina, but you feel so goddamned good that this ain't gonna last long."

Gripping his hair, she jerked his head back, forcing his eyes to meet hers. "Then kiss me while you fuck me. It'll improve your multitasking skills."

"Always lookin' for the silver lining, ain't ya." He captured her mouth in a slow seductive kiss—which was diametrically opposed to the purposefully hard strokes of his cock.

And he hadn't been kidding about being quick on the trigger.

She'd just gotten into the rhythm of his breath and body, feeling herself starting to respond, when he ripped his mouth free from hers.

He was a beautiful sight with his neck arched, his eyes squeezed shut, his full lips parted. She even loved that his big hands were kneading her ass cheeks to the same fast pulses of his cock as it emptied inside her.

But she fought her disappointment it was over.

And really . . . how could she complain when he had warned her it'd be fast?

Plus, she'd never say anything that would dampen this emergence of his newfound sexuality.

Before she could tell him it was all right that she hadn't come, Streeter pulled out of her and returned her feet to the floor.

The clank of his belt buckle was her only warning before he dropped to his knees, spread her pussy open with his thumbs and began to eat her out.

The man didn't care that he'd just come inside her. He fucked her with his mouth until she came with a loud gasping groan.

Then he did it again, with his fingers *and* his mouth.

Holy fucking shit. That might've been a record for her too, being that quick on the trigger.

Twice.

When the blood roaring in her head had abated, she glanced down at him, still on his knees and peppering soft kisses over her mound and across her thighs.

Looking up at her, he grinned. "Not quite a scream, but good enough for me."

Bailey released the death grip she'd had on his hair. "That was . . ."

Streeter rolled to his feet and soul-kissed her with such raw passion she was grateful for the wall behind her.

He kissed a path to her ear. "I like the way we taste together."

"Me too."

His pants started buzzing. "That's my phone. Hang on."

While he answered the call, she slipped the bottom half of her clothes on.

Streeter had the phone balanced between his jaw and shoulder as he zipped up his pants and buckled his belt. "No, Deenie, that's fine. I'll meet you there in an hour. Yeah. Bye."

"Is everything all right?"

He shoved his phone in his back pocket before he tucked in his shirt. "I gotta pick Olivia up early."

Perfect timing. "I should be heading out to Harper and Bran's anyway."

"Will I see you later?"

"Text me."

After another long kiss, he left.

◦◦

Bailey exited her SUV at the Turner Ranch and saw that Bran had all three boys in the enclosed cab of the tractor, doing ranch stuff, but to her it looked like he was just driving in circles. After a quick wave, she sought out Harper, taking advantage of the fact they wouldn't be interrupted for a little while.

She found Harper sitting on the covered swing on the back deck.

At least she thought it was her sister.

Harper had pulled her messy blond hair into a high ponytail, and her shirt was off, leaving both breasts exposed. Her bare feet peeked out from beneath Christmas-themed pajama bottoms and Angel—looking decidedly milk-drunk—slept soundly on the cushion beside her.

Harper held up her hand when she saw Bailey. "Better not come closer if the sight of my nipples is gonna bother you because I'm not putting that goddamned bra back on. My nipples are chafed and I'm airing them out."

Okay.

"Bare titties don't bother me. Need anything before I sit down?"

"Yeah. A gin and tonic."

Was her sister serious right now?

"And use the Bombay gin. It's behind the cheap stuff in the liquor cabinet. Oh. And lots of limes."

She'd take that as a yes, Harper was serious.

Bailey mixed two drinks and added a pitcher of ice water to the tray before she returned outside.

She handed Harper a drink, took one for herself and eased onto the swing, trying not to wake the baby.

They clinked their glasses together, muttered cheers and drank.

"All right, Bails, out with it. Why are you here?"

Bailey briefly put her head on Harper's shoulder. "I hate fighting with you."

"Samesies, brat."

"I'm sorry."

"Me too."

And that was it. They were back to normal.

Harper kept them swinging. "Can I ask you something?"

"Sure."

"Does the name 'Angel' sound like a stripper's name?"

Talk about a random question. "I dunno. Maybe. Why?"

"Bran overruled me on her name. I wanted to call her April. He said that was stupid since she was born in February."

"I sort of agree with Bran, sis."

"So I said, what about Avril?"

"Lemme guess . . . the smart-ass man started singing 'Sk8er Boi.'"

"If you can call that off-tune warbling singing." She sniffed. "I swear to god the man only wanted to name her that so he could call her 'Angel baby.'"

Bailey hid her smile behind her glass. "That is awful damn cute."

"I remember when he used to call *me* 'Angel baby.'"

"Then I can see your point." She swirled the ice cubes in her glass. "Is everything all right between you and the fly-tyin' super dad?"

"As right as it can be with four kids constantly underfoot and sexy time limited to a quickie after the baby goes to sleep or before the boys wake up." She sighed. "I miss spontaneous sex. I miss the tease and the surprise and being loud. I miss my sexy husband taking his sweet time to do dirty things to me." Harper sent Bailey a sideways look. "TMI?"

"Nope."

"And I'm tired of my nipples hurting and feeling like a one-person dairy buffet."

"So quit nursing. That won't make you a horrible mother." That title would belong to their mother—not that Bailey needed to remind her sister of the crap Mommy Whorest had pulled in the past. Not that she could use that secret moniker for their mother around her sister. "Admit that something's gotta give, since you're out here in broad daylight on a Sunday with your knockers blowing in the breeze."

Harper laughed. "I hate that you showed up looking so fit and healthy."

Oh, if you only knew how untrue that is.

"I'd trade my monster jugs and mom body for yours in a freakin' heartbeat."

"No, you wouldn't. Your body is a well-oiled machine. Popping out four kiddos with no problems. You're still sexy, sassy and secure in who you are. I envy you for that." She paused. "On second thought, let's trade."

"I love how you can build me up, sis, when I need it the most. Thank you."

"You're welcome. As long as I'm on a roll with advice, I think you oughta surprise Bran with the spontaneous sex you've been missing."

"Please give me a very detailed plan on how to make that happen, complete with bullet points," she said dryly.

"I'll come out tomorrow and watch all four kids and you take my shift at WWC. After Penelope arrives, go to my trailer and call Bran. Tell him you've got three hours of absolute alone time and you're horny as fuck."

She cocked her head. "That might actually work."

"Get your fetish wear out. Then snap a shot of your snatch and send it to him."

"Snap a shot of my snatch?" She giggled. "Or maybe a candid of my cooter?"

"Or a pic of your pussy."

"Or a vignette of my vag?"

Bailey laughed. "We definitely need to day-drink more often."

"Amen to that." Harper laid her head on Bailey's shoulder. "I'm glad you're here. On so many levels, Bails. I was really mad at you for pointing out all of the issues with WCC last week."

"I know."

"I was hoping you hadn't noticed them. Then I wouldn't have to make any changes. But I have to because I know it—*I*—can't go on this way."

She made an affirmative noise.

"Things change. People change. Goals change. When I was first with Bran, I wanted to prove I was savvy enough to run my own business. I did that. I loved it. I still loved it after we had Tate. And after Jake. I loved working away from home less after Gage. And even before Angel was born, I'd started to resent the time WCC took me away from my boys. I didn't care nearly as much about success and staying up on fashion trends. It showed in the inventory. Then the lack of unique items showed in the sales receipts. The Split Rock has undergone some changes too, and I kept waiting for Renner and Janie to tell me they wanted to go in a different direction with the space. Especially after Renner dissolved Jackson Stock Contracting. That, more than anything, proved to me that everyone's goals have to adapt as their lives change." She paused. "So yeah, I wanna close the store."

Bailey immediately sensed Harper's relief that she'd admitted it out loud. "Does Bran know?"

"He's suggested, more than once, that I just turn the store over to you. And FYI—you can blame Liberty for spilling the beans to us that you're getting out of the army, or you're already out, or whatever."

She tamped down her anger and casually asked, "When did that come about?"

"Right before you got here. Liberty suggested you were floundering and maybe I could give you some purpose by having you get involved with the store."

"That sneaky bitch."

"Yeah. She also warned me she was trying to get you to come to work for her in Denver, so I shouldn't get too attached to the idea of you sticking around here."

Their big sister had played them both, suggesting to Bailey that *Harper* was floundering and needed help with the kids and the store. Liberty hadn't done it out of spite, and she hadn't given Harper the whole truth—thank god—but Bailey was still gonna kick her ass the next time she saw her.

"Here's the thing," Harper continued. "The summer schedule is set. Doing a switchover of retail spaces at the Split Rock would be a nightmare. So I've decided in the next week I'll meet with Renner and Janie and let them know I'm closing the store after Labor Day. I'll give Penelope two weeks' notice because I've no doubt she'll land on her feet. That way I'll still get to have you around the rest of the summer."

"I'm down."

"Good."

"It won't be a problem if I have to close the store and deal with army outprocessing stuff in Casper?"

"Nope. Just give me a heads-up."

"Cool."

"You've heard the Harper saga, so tell me what's new with you?"

"Well, as of last night I'm fucking Streeter Hale."

Harper choked on her drink. "Seriously?"

"Yep. He's hot, I like him and he knows it's temporary. All the requirements for a dirty summer fling."

"So much for my assumption he'd stay away from you."

"He tried." Bailey smirked. "And failed. It'd be best if you kept this on the down-low."

"I'm certain Angel won't say a word."

When loud noises from the boisterous boys drifted from the driveway, Bailey stood and grabbed the tray. "I'll head them off while you hide those hooters."

Chapter Fourteen

*J*esus, Street, pay attention!"

Tobin's shout brought Streeter out of his daydreaming.

Was it daydreaming if he was reliving last night's reality of fucking until they were both hot, sweaty and exhausted?

"Goddammit, catch her before she gets to the brush!" Tobin shouted.

Streeter focused on the heifer running away from her calf. Damn thing was a terrible mother; she hadn't wanted anything to do with that baby since the moment it'd slipped out of her body. It wasn't unusual in the cattle business, especially with first-time mothers.

The fact that maternal disconnect happened with humans too hadn't been a comfort to him.

He twirled his rope and let it fly, catching the heifer's rear leg the same time Tobin caught hold of a front leg. Thankfully they'd snared her before she got entangled in the brush in the one section they hadn't cleared out yet.

Streeter clicked at his horse and Pepper backed up slowly, allowing him to pull the rope taut. After quickly tying it off, he dismounted and walked to the heifer, now lying on the ground between the two horses.

"Even distracted you're a better heeler than I am," Tobin complained.

"You still got the skills, though . . . for a college boy."

Tobin shoved him and Streeter laughed. They stopped in front of the ornery heifer.

"So what the hell do we do with her?"

"Sell her or butcher her."

"I vote for steaks."

"Me too. I'll call the processing plant in the mornin'. For now, let's take her back and put her in the holding pen."

"You do that," Streeter said. "I'll do a head count and make sure we don't have any more stragglers." He untied the rope, let it hit the ground and galloped off to the new grazing area.

Tobin shut the gate behind him and dealt with moving the heifer.

Their herd wasn't big—fifty cow/calf pairs—so taking a head count went fairly fast. Some things his dad had ingrained in him—like taking stock of the livestock with every move to greener pastures—were actually practical.

An hour later he'd finished brushing down his horse and dealing with his tack when Tobin appeared. With a beer.

Bit early, but having one beer wouldn't hurt. "We celebrating something?" he asked his brother.

"You tell me. You're mooning around, your damn head in the clouds, not payin' full attention. So I take it things are good with Bailey?"

Streeter shrugged.

"Come on, man."

He meant to hedge, but "I can't keep my goddamned hands off her" came out instead.

Tobin grinned. "I'm glad to hear that."

"Even when it's ruining my concentration? I was thinkin' about last night and all the things I want to do to her tonight when I dropped the ball while we were movin' cattle."

"No biggie, Street. Everyone has off days. Especially after a particularly awesome night."

"Problem is, all my nights are awesome with her and this ain't the first time I've dropped the ball at work this week."

Tobin's beer stopped halfway to his mouth. "Hold on. Are you tellin' me you're banging her every night?"

"No." He scowled. "Give me a little credit for mixing things up. Sometimes it's in the mornin', sometimes in the afternoon. Sometimes it's all three."

When Tobin didn't say anything, Streeter looked at him.

"What?"

"You went from not havin' sex for almost five years to havin' sex a couple of times a day?"

"Yeah. So?"

"So you're an animal."

"That's what I'm afraid of. That wantin' her that much ain't normal." He swigged his beer. "I have nothin' to compare this to."

"Bailey is initiating sexy times too?"

"Yep. So this has gotta be lust, right?"

"Lust as opposed to what?"

Streeter groaned. "I don't fuckin' know. This is all new to me." He took another drink to keep from asking his brother how he'd stop himself from falling for her. Then he said, "Doesn't matter. She ain't stickin' around here."

"I don't know what to say, except to tell you to enjoy it while it lasts."

"Oh, I plan on it."

They were quiet for a while. Finally Tobin said, "Does Olivia know what's goin' on with you two?"

"Yeah. Bailey stays over some nights, but she's always gone when Olivia gets up. Her choice, by the way."

"Who else knows you two are seein' each other?"

He scratched his chin. "Maybe Pete and Bobbie, the caretakers. Probably Harper. Ted and Renner haven't said nothin' to me."

"So no one has caught you guys goin' at it in the supply closet?" Tobin teased.

That was when he remembered. Dammit. The Mud Lilies showing up at WWC the first weekend he and Bailey had gotten together.

"You're quiet, bro. That ain't good. What happened?"

"If Garnet and her buddies suspected me and Bailey were together, wouldn't they've said something?"

"The Mud Lilies saw you two boning?"

"No. But they were there a week or so ago when I stopped in to the clothing store to see Bailey and it might've been obvious that I wasn't there just to talk."

"Well, they either missed the signs, or they're keepin' the info to themselves to use later when they want something from one of you. Never underestimate them gals," Tobin warned.

A shout sounded behind them and they both turned. Amber was running across the yard toward him, Jade following with Micah strapped into a baby carrier on her chest.

"Sometimes I look at them and can't believe this is my life. I wanted this for more years than is probably healthy to admit."

"It's sappy to say that you deserve it, but you do."

"I still feel that powerful lust for my wife, but it's deepened and changed. After bein' married to Danica for so long I'm sure you understand—better than I do—those changes do happen."

No, Streeter didn't understand. He and Danica hadn't questioned an intense physical connection because it hadn't been there. He'd wondered if that lack of all-consuming passion had stemmed from them meeting so young and only being intimate with each other. He'd never woken up in the middle of the night with the physical need for her clawing at him. And if he had, Danica would've told him to go back to sleep from his wet dream.

As those thoughts bounced around in his head, he didn't feel guilty for them. That had been the reality of his life with Danica. He hadn't known—maybe he hadn't believed—that an intimate relationship could be different.

Thank heaven he'd taken a chance on opening up to Bailey so she could show him what he'd been missing.

Tobin tossed his daughter up in the air, laughing as Amber giggled and shrieked with happiness.

Jade ambled into view, wearing her usual joyous smile. "Hey, Street."

"You're lookin' good. How's the little man treatin' you?"

"Which little man?"

"Hey, tiger, you'd better take that back," Tobin said.

She laughed. "Micah is settling into a schedule."

"Lucky you."

"You know it. So when are you bringing Sergeant B out for a family dinner? Olivia talks about her incessantly."

Streeter frowned. "When did you talk to Olivia?"

"I started calling her when she told me about the landline in the trailer and asked if I'd call her to make sure it worked. It does."

Of course his curious daughter would circumvent his edict for her to *leave the phone alone* and who better to rope into helping her figure out the answers to her questions than her sweet aunt Jade. "Does she call you?"

"No." She paused and patted her son's butt when he began to fuss. "Olivia hasn't mentioned our chats?" Then she groaned. "Of course she hasn't. She doesn't miss us like we miss her."

"She misses you in her own way, Jade."

"She has told me she misses her drums," Jade said wryly. "I can't believe she hasn't gotten them back yet."

"It ain't for lack of tryin'." Last week he'd accompanied Olivia to Bailey's door every morning, hiding a smirk that she'd only rolled out of his bed an hour before. "Would you be up for havin' her overnight during the week? I'd like to take Bailey out, just the two of us."

"Of course, she's welcome anytime."

"Speakin' of . . . I'd best get home."

"See ya tomorrow," Tobin shouted as Streeter crossed the corral to climb into his pickup.

Before heading home, he stopped by the construction site to see if they'd made progress on the house.

The basement had been dug. Concrete forms were laid out, which hopefully meant the footings were about to be poured. Standing on the gravel pathway, he tried to imagine living here. Looking at this view for the next forty years. He hadn't brought Olivia here yet since the idea of a new home was an abstract concept to her. Once the frame started to go up, maybe it'd seem real to him too.

He pulled into his spot at the Split Rock employee compound, noticing Bailey's SUV. Hopefully he'd see her tonight after she finished working at WCC.

Olivia was pacing the walkway, apparently anxious to see him because she raced over for a hug. "Daddy! I missed you. I thought you'd never get here."

He kissed the top of her head. "I missed you too, sweet girl."

"Can we go to the pool?"

"Lemme talk to Asa first."

Asa—the most recent babysitter in rotation—gave Olivia a glowing report. His daughter had adjusted better than he'd hoped to the daily change-up in her daycare providers.

As soon as Asa left, Streeter said, "Let's get our suits on."

He might've been concerned that the Split Rock Resort wasn't doing well at seeing the pool area completely empty, but he knew the lodge had been booked all summer. After coating Olivia with sunscreen, he caught her in the deep end when she jumped in.

Her fearlessness required a constant balancing act, finding the line between encouraging her and cautioning her. He let her paddle around in her unicorn float as he floated beside her on a boogie board.

"Daddy? Can just Gage come to the pool with us again sometime?"

"Why don't you ask Bailey?" He looked at her when he realized she'd qualified the statement. "Just Gage? Not his brothers?"

She scowled. "They're mean to him. They called him a big stupid baby."

"During camp?"

"Uh-huh. And when I said I was gonna tell Sergeant B? Tate said it made Gage even more of a baby if his *girlfriend* was tattling for him."

Jesus. Boys were stupid. "What did you do?"

"Nothin'. Then it was snack time."

Ah. Never underestimate the power of pudding cups to end a dispute.

Just as they were about to leave, Tierney showed up with Isabelle and Rhett, so he agreed to stay another half an hour so the kids could play.

Tierney plopped down beside him just like Bailey had done. "Looks like we're the only ones here again. I'm starting to wonder if making the pool more family friendly was a bad financial decision. It seems fewer guests use it now than before."

"They know it's here. I think the guests would rather try their hand at rough stock and trail rides for a more Western experience."

"You're probably right. We've tried to adapt, changing things up to make this a place people want to come back to."

"You're thinkin' of adding on?"

Tierney shook her head. "It's almost more than we can handle now. We're looking at ways to work smarter, not harder. We've been a two-meal-a-day facility. But we've gotten complaints there's no lunch service, so that's an avenue we're considering. At least during the busy season."

"It ain't my business, but isn't staffing an issue?"

"Always. Right after this place opened Renner and I had a huge fight about the fact he'd advertised that a spa was coming soon. But he didn't have the dedicated space or the staff for it. To this day when guests ask about a spa, Renner calls me a dream killer."

Streeter laughed.

"Mom!" Isabelle screeched. "Make him stop!"

"Rhett. Quit splashing your sister or I'm putting you in time-out."

"But she started it!"

"Did not!"

"Did too!"

"Isabelle really did start it," Olivia said.

"Tattletale," Isabelle retorted to Olivia. "Of course you'd take the brat's side."

"Isabelle Jackson. We don't call names. Apologize."

"Sorry, O-liv-i-a."

Tierney pointed at her daughter. "Out of the pool for ten minutes. It'll give you time to think of offering a sincere apology to your brother too." She sighed. "Next time Renner gets pool duty."

"You're lucky you have the option."

"Sorry. Ignore me. Sometimes I talk before I think."

He shrugged. "It's my own fault. I could let one of the babysitters bring Olivia to the pool, but I haven't hit that trust point yet."

"Bailey!" Olivia shouted. "Are you gonna come swimmin' with us?"

Streeter turned and noticed Bailey by the fence.

"Maybe next time."

"Can you bring Gage too?"

Bailey laughed. "Of course."

With the late-afternoon sun shining on her dark hair and the genuine smile she aimed at his daughter . . . he realized in the weeks since they'd become lovers, she'd become the beacon that chased away his darkness. The feeling of fullness—of lightness—in his chest proved this was more than just lust between them.

"Tierney, can you keep an eye on Olivia for a second?"

"No problem."

Streeter stood and walked to where Bailey waited for him, her eyes absolutely devouring him. "Hey."

"Hey yourself, cutie." She gave him a very thorough once-over. "I love seeing you half-naked. But I prefer you fully naked."

"You tryin' to get me hard?"

"Always."

"You done for the day?"

"Yes. I'm gonna shower, eat and crash." She poked him in the chest. "Somebody fucked me stupid last night."

"Is that a complaint?"

"Never. I'm hoping for a repeat."

"Then please come over."

"Okay." She licked her lips. "Damn you, and this banging body. Now I'll be thinking about all the dirty things I want to do to it when I'm alone in the shower."

He leaned closer. "If you decide to prime the pump, you can reenact the shower scene for me later, baby."

Bailey's gaze dropped to his crotch. "Better jump in and cool that bad boy off before sitting down next to your boss's *wife*."

He groaned.

Peering around his arm, she said, "Nice seeing you, Tierney," before she sashayed off.

She just had to wiggle that biteable ass at him, which didn't help his current situation at all. He strode to the deep end of the pool and jumped in.

Cold water did the trick.

He toweled off and looked over to see Tierney grinning at him.

"You and Sergeant B, huh?"

Streeter didn't know if he was supposed to keep this thing with Bailey under wraps.

Maybe that's something you oughta find out.

"I'm happy for you, Streeter. For both of you. I like her."

He smiled back. "I like her too." Then he motioned to his daughter. "Time to go. Say good-bye to Rhett and Isabelle."

In the past, Olivia might've thrown a fit because she wasn't ready to leave. But she gathered her things, said her good-byes and waited by the gate for him.

Maybe boot camp had done her some good.

             ᔑ

Bailey didn't show up until after Olivia had been in bed for an hour.

She climbed on his lap, feeding him long, slow kisses. Digging her fingers into his scalp when his mouth wandered down her neck.

When she started to grind on him, he stood, his hands gripping her ass as he carried her into his bedroom.

After he locked the door and turned around, he expected to find her naked with that wicked dirty smile curling her lips, but she was standing by the bed.

"You all right?"

Bailey slid her palms over his pecs. "I will be once I get my hands on you. All over you." She stood on her tiptoes and pressed a kiss to his Adam's apple. "Strip, cowboy, and lie facedown."

He yanked his T-shirt over his head and shoved his athletic shorts to the carpet.

"I love that you go commando now."

"Anything that makes you happy, darlin'." Streeter glanced over his shoulder after he stretched out on the bed. "You getting nekkid too?"

"It's our natural state together." She straddled his thighs and spread her body over his—her belly curved over his ass, her tits pressed into his back, the side of her face against his neck.

"It doesn't only have to be that."

She lifted her head and looked at him. "Meaning what?"

"Meaning . . . we never went out on that date we talked about. We always get nekkid. Which ain't a complaint. But I'd still like to take you to dinner. Or to a show. Or anything out and about. Just the two of us."

"I'd like that." She brushed her lips across the fine hairs on the back of his neck, sending gooseflesh rippling across his skin. "I'd like that a lot."

When she rested against him, her arms layered on top of his, he realized she was waiting for something.

"We haven't defined this. Maybe that's my fault since I've never had to do that before. But I want people to know we're together. Like today at the pool. I wanted to kiss you so damn bad, but I wasn't sure that's what you wanted."

"You're the one with the kiddo, Streeter. We haven't hidden the fact we're spending time together, but you haven't kissed me in front of her either. Olivia should be the first to know."

He'd never had anyone so attuned to him on every level that mattered. "So tomorrow I'll lay one on ya, baby. But you oughta know that Tobin knows we've been seein' each other because I needed advice."

"On?"

"Sex." He rushed to explain. "I needed a pep talk before we got together because tellin' you about my lack of experience scared the crap outta me. And after we've been together I needed to know whether havin' this much incredible sex is normal."

"It's our normal, Street, and that's all that matters." Bailey peppered soft kisses across his shoulders. "You've become quite the sexpert in the past few weeks. You turn me inside out, upside down with just a look from those bedroom eyes of yours. And if I haven't said enough times before now . . . it's never been like this with anyone but you."

Then stay. Let's see where this can go for the long haul.

"So let me show you," she whispered in his ear, sending gooseflesh rippling down his spine. "Let me worship your body tonight."

"If you insist."

She sank her teeth into the nape of his neck.

Instantly he arched into her and went hard as a fucking fencepost.

"Mmm. This is gonna be some fun."

Torturous fun.

First she licked and sucked on the back of his neck as her fingers mapped the muscles in his arms, from the balls of his shoulders to the backs of his hands. Not quite a massage, but the pleasure of her touch was far from relaxing as she worked her mouth and the tips of her fingers and the long fall of her silken hair across his sensitized skin.

Then she followed his spine with her tongue, stopping at the top of the crack of his ass and brushing butterfly kisses over the dimples above his butt cheeks.

His entire body quaked.

And the response of the sexy, wicked temptress who was his lover? She laughed.

Goddamn, he was so crazy about her.

She nuzzled his cheeks and moved to scrape her nails down the backs of his thighs and calves. Then she'd treat his legs to long, tender sweeping caresses that caused the hair on his legs to nearly stand straight up. He'd never had this kind of rapt attention to his body. Now he didn't know how he'd ever lived without this intimacy, the give-and-take of power in the form of a simple touch.

Bailey avoided touching his feet, but she kissed his ankles.

Holy hell, how had he not known the thin flesh covering his ankle bones was an erogenous zone? He groaned and rolled his hips and basically had an orgasm without actually coming.

Before he'd realized she'd moved, he felt her teeth on his right ass cheek and then a powerful sucking on that spot as she gave him a hickey. And she gifted him with the same mark on his left side.

Pulling his feet closer together, she dragged her hard nipples up the length of his legs, where she'd brought every nerve ending to life, so he felt every breath, every soft sweep of her tongue. Every openmouthed kiss as she took her sweet time literally worshipping his body from his heels to the nape of his neck.

Streeter was a sweating, shaking, needy goddamned mess by the time those skilled lips touched his ear. "Streeter."

"Uh."

"Baby. I'm so fucking wet"—she licked his ear and he actually whimpered—"and so hot for you that I hafta rub one out right now." Another flick of her tongue behind his ear. "Say yes."

"Fuck yes. Anything you want."

She emitted a soft purr that vibrated straight down to his balls.

A moment later, she shifted her lower body and he felt the warm, wet press of her pussy to the upper swell of his right ass cheek.

Christ. She hadn't been kidding about being wet.

He turned his head and saw Bailey bracing herself on her arms, one strong leg stretched out over his lower back, her right knee next to his hip, which allowed her to rock her pelvis and grind on him.

Their eyes met.

Reaching back, he pushed her silken hair over her shoulder. "I want to watch."

She nodded and began to move again.

Chin up. Eyes closed. Back arched. Skin damp. Breathing hard. Rolling her hips and expelling a soft moan every time her clit got direct friction. She was a fucking goddess. Beautiful. Free. Kinky. Sweet. Determined. Vulnerable. Sexy.

And mine. Completely fucking mine and no other man will ever see her like this.

Her eyes flew open, almost as if she'd heard him.

Streeter let her see his possessiveness.

She rode him faster and in that moment Streeter knew exactly what she needed.

He tightened his ass cheeks. "There you go. Work it. I feel it. Take it, baby, it's right there."

"Yes, yes." Bailey gasped and threw her head back.

He felt the contractions of her orgasm against his skin. Each hard pulse. And it was a good thing he'd clenched his butt cheeks or he would've been coming right along with her.

Streeter couldn't take his eyes off her.

When she came back from that subspace where nothing existed but pleasure, a place she'd taken him to many times, their gazes met again.

"That was the hottest thing I've ever seen."

Her lips formed a smile. "Yeah?"

"Oh yeah."

"And just think . . . we're only getting started." She backed up on her hands and knees. Keeping their eyes locked, she lowered herself down and licked the smear of her juices from his skin.

Correction. *That* might've been the hottest thing he'd ever seen.

Next thing he knew, Bailey had flipped him on his back and she was sharing her taste with him in a seductive soul kiss that sucked breath and reason right out of his body.

"Mmm. Back side down, front side to go." She glided her lips across his. "You ready?"

Fuck no. "Uh. Yeah."

The delicious torture began again.

But on the front side, she left more love bites on him, marking his pecs, his ribs, his hips and the middle of his quads. He had no idea why he loved seeing her purplish red marks on his skin.

Maybe because you groan loudly every single time she sets that sucking mouth in motion.

Bailey touched him everywhere—except his cock.

When she tongued the crease of his thigh, letting her hair drift over his groin, he said, "Stop. I can't take any more unless you want me to come in your hair."

Again, that devilish twinkle in her eyes appeared. "Another time, perhaps."

She grabbed the lube from his bedside drawer and squirted a thick line of it from his cockhead to his balls.

He sucked in a breath at the jarring sensation of cold against hot.

After planting her right hand by his head, she curled the fingers of her left hand around his cock in a tight fist. "I'm gonna jack you slowly.

So slowly you might think I'll never let you come. But when you get off is up to you."

"What's the catch, hot stuff?"

"I want to look in your eyes as you come. I want to see what you feel when you let go."

"Can I touch you?"

She shook her head. "But you can kiss me up until the very end."

"Bring it on," he said huskily and took her mouth in a ravenous kiss.

Bailey stayed true to her word. She moved her hand with deliberate sensuality. Twice she let her longest finger slip down between his balls and press against his asshole. Then the little minx smiled against his lips. "You like ass play. One of these days I'm gonna stroke you there as I blow you."

He nipped her bottom lip. Hard. "You play with my ass, baby, you know I'm gonna want to be in yours."

"Might be something we'll have to work up to, given the size of this bad boy."

Streeter let her build him to the tipping point and then back off. But by the third time his control had started to crack. "Bailey. I need—"

Those pretty hazel eyes were locked onto his. "Don't look away."

She jacked him with speed and force that left him gasping.

In the eternity between when his balls drew up and he started to come, a universe of trust opened up between them.

And he'd never come so hard in his life.

Even as he fought for breath, she stroked him, gently bringing him back down.

Sated, cock spent, emotionally and physically drained, he slumped back in the pillows.

But Bailey only retreated far enough to lap up the spots of come that had cooled on his skin before she kissed him.

He loved that she wanted them to know each other's taste in every way imaginable.

She rested her forehead to his. "Thank you."

"I oughta be thankin' you." He twined his fingers in her hair that'd created a curtain around their faces. "Tonight was amazing. *You're* amazing."

"Back atcha." She pushed back and stood. "I've gotta go."

"I wish you could stay."

But she had her clothes on and was already at the door. "Later days, cutie."

Chapter Fifteen

⎯⎯⎯⎯⎯⎯

*T*wo days later Streeter's cell phone rang at four a.m.

Never a good sign.

He fumbled for it on the nightstand, mumbling, "Hello?"

Bailey sat up next to him, wondering who he was talking to.

"How'd they find out?" Pause. "Very good thing." Pause. "Yeah, I'll be there in twenty."

He hung up.

"What's going on?"

"Our cattle got out. Tobin's neighbor's kid nearly hit a calf on his way home from the bar. So I gotta go help him round them up." He flipped back the covers and turned to drop his feet on the floor. "Sorry. I hafta wake Olivia but you're welcome to stay."

"If I'm staying, you might as well let her sleep."

He gave her an odd look. "You don't mind?"

"Do you trust me with her?"

"Of course I do."

"Then go."

"I have no idea how long this will take. What time do you work?"

"Not until eight." She yawned. "Don't you have a babysitter coming?"

"She won't be here until after eight thirty today."

She shrugged. "I can stay with her until then and open the store late. No biggie."

"You're sure?"

"Positive." She pulled the covers back over herself and stretched out in the middle of his king-sized bed. "Go. So I can go back to sleep."

She vaguely remembered him kissing her forehead before she drifted off again.

Shrieking woke her.

And for a moment she thought it might've come from her.

Then she heard it again.

Shit. Olivia.

Her heart raced nearly as fast as her feet.

She burst into Olivia's bedroom and found her sitting straight up in bed. Her eyes were unfocused—or scarier yet, focused completely on something in the corner of the room. The darkest corner.

Bailey was almost afraid to look in case it was a terrifying presence. But when she peered over the edge of the dresser, nothing was there.

And still Olivia shrieked.

These night terrors were something Streeter had mentioned but she had no idea how to deal with it.

Yes, you do. It's an extreme version of a panic attack.

As she debated on whether she was supposed to try to wake her up or if that would make it worse, Olivia's entire body trembled like she'd gone into convulsions.

Bailey grabbed her shoulders and shook her. "Olivia. Wake up. You're having a bad dream."

Olivia stopped shaking.

Had she heard her?

"Olivia. Honey. It's okay. Come on, girlie. Wake up."

Then those eyes, so eerily like her father's and yet . . . not, swung toward Bailey. "Where's my daddy?"

"At the ranch with Uncle Tobin."

"I want my daddy."

"I know you do, sweetheart, but he's not here."

"I want my daddy *now*."

"He'll be back real soon."

She started to cry. "But he *is* comin' back?"

Oh, sweet girl. "Yes, honey, he is. I promise."

She whispered, "Okay," in such a broken voice that all Bailey wanted was to gather this broken child in her arms, hold her and chase her demons away.

But when Bailey reached for her, Olivia shrank back. Then she curled into a ball between the headboard and the wall.

Trying to hide.

Still crying.

Still breaking Bailey's goddamned heart.

Bailey couldn't leave her like this. She crawled on the bed next to her, making sure not to touch her as she pressed her back against the headboard.

A few moments passed before Bailey said, "Do you want to talk about it?"

"NO!"

Okay, then.

But she understood. She hated when people pushed her to talk. So she stayed quiet in the hellish silence of a child's tears.

Olivia's cries quieted. Her snuffles tapered off.

A whispered "I don't remember" floated to her, the tone more bewildered than frightened.

That was progress.

Still, Bailey didn't jump right in with questions.

"He always asks about what scared me in my sleep, and I don't remember."

"Who asks?"

"My daddy."

"He asks because he worries about you."

A few beats passed. "Sometimes he cries too."

I imagine he cries more often than you know.

This poor, damaged family.

"It makes him sad."

"What makes him sad?"

"That I wake up scared. And I can't remember why I was scared. I just am."

"My sister Liberty had bad nights."

Olivia was quiet so long, Bailey thought she'd gone too far. But Olivia finally said, "When she was a little girl?"

"No, honey. Since she's been a big girl."

"Oh."

"And she never wants to talk about them either. So it's okay that you don't."

The bed jiggled as Olivia left her safe little corner.

Bailey held her breath as Olivia curled up next to her. Not touching her, but closer than she had been.

"I wanna know when my daddy comes home."

"I'll wake you up. I promise."

Olivia didn't ask her to stay, but she didn't tell her to go.

So Bailey stayed.

Despite her concern she wouldn't fall back asleep, apparently she did. She woke to a little finger jabbing her in the side.

"Okay. I'm awake."

Olivia blinked her big blue eyes at her.

"What?"

"Can I please have my drums back today?"

Such a cheeky little thing. "No, but I'll tell you what. How about if we go to my house and you can play your drums while I'm making us breakfast?"

Olivia hopped to her feet and started jumping on the bed. "Yay!"

That was where Streeter found them an hour later, Bailey sitting at the table, working on her laptop while Olivia entertained her with a postbreakfast drum concert.

"Daddy! Look what Bailey showed me." Olivia took two metal pan lids and slammed them together over and over. "See? They're cymbals. Isn't that so cool?"

"And loud." Streeter looked at Bailey. "Very loud."

"It could be worse. I could've given her metal trash can lids." She smiled at him over the rim of her coffee cup. "You're welcome."

❧

Bailey didn't get a chance to talk to Streeter about the night terrors until later that evening.

After Olivia had gone to bed, they'd snuggled into the couch to watch *Modern Family* and Bailey said, "Does Olivia have nightmares often?"

"She hasn't had night terrors for a few weeks. I hoped she'd finally outgrown them."

"Does her counselor say that's a possibility?"

"Yeah."

"Are they related to her mother's suicide?"

Streeter shifted away from her and reached for his glass of ice water. "We're not sure. Olivia never remembers specifics. I guess that's not unusual. The clinic has talked about hypnotizing her when she's older, when she has more life skills to verbalize what she's seein', but that's no guarantee either. It's something I'll have to play by ear when the time comes." He brought her hand to his mouth and kissed her knuckles. "Thank you for stayin' with her and not panicking."

"Oh, I panicked plenty. Especially at first when it was dark and I worried there might actually be someone—or something—in her room."

He groaned. "It's scary as fuck, isn't it? Seein' her terrified eyes as she's starin' at nothin'. The first time I let her stay alone overnight at her Gramma Deenie's, she had an 'episode.'" Streeter made air quotes. "That's what Deenie calls them. Anyway, Deenie called me, freaked-out, and I had to go get Olivia in the middle of the night. That part didn't bother me. But when Deenie said Olivia was seein' the ghost of her mother, I lost my shit. Why would she say that to a three-year-old?"

Her mouth fell open. "No. She did not."

"Yes, she did. Tellin' Olivia that her mommy was always watchin' over her like a ghost in a corner. I ended the sleepovers as soon as I heard that. And after Deenie told me she'd been going to a medium to try to communicate with Danica's spirit."

Bailey couldn't keep the horror from her face.

"I don't believe in that stuff. And during that time, I was still really bitter about everything. I told Deenie if I would've come in contact with Danica's spirit, I'd tell her to fuck off and stay away. She wasn't there for us when she was alive; she sure didn't get to hang around after she was dead." He looked away. "You can imagine how well that went over."

"Streeter. I'm sorry."

"Deenie's not the same. None of us are. But she . . . can't move on. She's lookin' for answers she'll never find. It's exhausting bein' around her, and that's why Steve left her. I don't know if the quest gives her a purpose or what. Steve said that Deenie won't ever accept the fact Danica chose to end her own life. For a few really ugly months, she insinuated I'd killed her. Even if I hadn't pulled the trigger, I'd somehow neglected her, or belittled her or mentally abused her to the point she didn't care to live like that any longer. And the brutal way she'd done it was to punish me. That scenario would've been better, in Deenie's mind anyway, than the reality that she didn't know her daughter at all."

This was all way more than she could handle. Her head pounded. Her body ached. Her soul was battered. A sluggish sense of shame settled over her. Bailey knew she needed to get out of here, without it seeming like she was running away . . . even when she totally was.

"Well, you should get a medal for being forced to deal with your former mother-in-law on a regular basis." Bailey stood.

Streeter gave her a once-over. "Where you goin'? You've been here like an hour."

"I need my beauty sleep. And I get no sleep around you, Mr. Sex Machine." Resting her palms on the back of the couch, she tilted forward to kiss him. "Tomorrow is camp. Maybe this is blowing the surprise, but Renner agreed for a trail ride for the recruits. And you, Mr. Hale, will be one of the trail masters."

"You're takin' a dozen kids out on horseback?"

"Nope. *We're* taking a dozen kids out on horseback." She smooched the frown line that formed between his eyebrows. "Don't stay up too late."

"You implying I need my beauty sleep too?" he teased.

"No. I love that that beautiful soul of yours is finally awake. Don't ever let it sleep so long again."

He studied her with eyes that were both soft and filled with concern. "Are you okay?"

Not even close. "I'm tired if I'm babbling like this. See you in the morning."

Bailey made it back to her trailer before the shakes started.

Stress was a major red flag and she'd had her fill of it today.

She took her pills, found her soothing waves soundtrack and plugged in her earbuds. If she could just make it through tomorrow, she could hole up until this went away.

Chapter Sixteen

"Why did you approve the campers to have a trail ride?" Streeter asked Renner the next morning.

Renner shrugged and kept lining saddles up on the fence. "Some of the horses haven't been exercised as much as they need."

"Bullshit. Ted and Zack took them all out last weekend."

"Maybe I wanted to see how the kids act around Sergeant B."

"Why? Don't you feel like Isabelle and Rhett are getting anything out of boot camp?"

"They are behavin' better. I wanna learn her ways so after camp is over and she's gone I can still crack the whip on 'em when needed."

Streeter piled saddle blankets next to the saddles.

"No comment, Street? Really?"

He looked at Renner. "About what?"

"About Bailey's postcamp plans."

"How would I know?"

"Buddy, not only is my wife a financial whiz, but she is a hopeless romantic. She couldn't wait to tell me that she'd seen you and Bailey flirtin' at the pool."

Streeter groaned.

Which caused Renner to laugh. "Nothin' stays a secret around here for long."

"It's not a secret, it's just complicated."

"Because of Olivia?"

"Partly." He realized his boss was leaning against the fence as if settling in for a chat. "Also because she's leavin'. I'm tryin' to go with the flow."

"How's that workin' out for you?"

"Not worth a damn."

Renner laughed. "I've been there. Tobin has too. The reason you got this job was because he was movin' on. The right woman came into his life and he's still here. Happier than ever." He paused. "It can happen to you too. And I don't know anyone who deserves a shot at that more than you."

"I appreciate the pep talk. But it's different for Bailey and me. Uncle Sam decides when and where she moves."

"I get it. But don't tell Tierney. It'll crush her heart if she doesn't think there's a chance the two of you will ride off into the sunset together."

"If we keep goin' this damn slow getting ready for the trail ride, we won't be *done* until sunset."

Renner tossed him a lead rope. "Speak for yourself. I'm ready."

Then the kids came down the hill, racing, yelling, acting like Vikings ready to pillage the area.

A shrill whistle caught the kids' attention.

Sergeant B clapped twice and said, "Charlie formation against the fence, recruits."

Then the kids were lined up by height—from tallest to shortest.

When she marched toward him wearing camo pants, a tight tan T-shirt and spit-shined combat boots, the only thing missing from this live fantasy image was a riding crop. He could almost hear the slap, slap, slap of it against her palm as she walked closer to him.

You are a perverted motherfucker.

"Good morning, Mr. Hale."

"Good morning, Sergeant B."

"Are we ready to ride, sir?"

"Not quite. Ted and Pete will be here shortly to help saddle the horses."

"I don't need help saddlin' a horse," Tate scoffed.

"Me neither," Jake chimed in.

Then all of the kids, with the exception of Jessamyn, Gage, Rhett and Olivia, also declared they didn't need help. The fact that Tate, Jake, Tyler, Dylan, Jason, Brianna and Isabelle had their own saddles pretty much backed up that statement.

Bailey hung back and let the guys get the kids situated. Then she mounted up, riding tandem with Gage. Pete rode with Cody, Ted rode with Jessamyn, Renner rode with Rhett and Streeter rode with Olivia.

Streeter, raised a ranch kid, had never considered wearing a helmet when he climbed on a horse. But that was the first thing that jumped into his head when Olivia settled in front of him.

None of the other kids wore helmets.

That'd be her argument one day, but until that day, he was in charge. Next time she got on a horse, she'd be wearing a helmet.

Pete took the lead of their merry little band.

Streeter had been assigned the rear, as had Bailey.

When Rhett realized he and his dad were the second in line, he turned around and said, "Hah! I'm ahead of you, Isabelle!"

"Rhett Jackson, you just earned half a demerit for taunting," Sergeant B informed him. "From here on out, any horseplay will result in double demerits. Understood?"

A chorus of "Sir, yes, sir!" rang out.

"Proceed, Trail Master Pete."

Horseplay. Over the kids' heads but he thought it was funny. He caught her gaze and grinned.

She allowed a tiny smile.

They'd started out early enough that the day hadn't turned hot—a perfect morning for a trail ride. Brilliant blue sky overhead. No mud beneath the horses' plodding hooves. Beautiful bluffs and crimson-colored cliffs surrounding them. Every once in a while, he'd hear the jangle of spurs and the creak of a saddle. The cry of a bird and the snort of a horse. All things he took for granted every day, but the look of wonder on Bailey's face—the woman who couldn't wait to leave here—let him see this rugged country through fresh eyes.

Maybe instead of banging her into oblivion on the weekends, you could show her your world. Take her to check cattle. Show her your land. Share your life with her, not just your bed.

Why hadn't he thought of that before?

Olivia didn't provide a steady stream of chatter—odd for her. Or maybe boot camp had instilled in her the desire to listen, as well as the rest of the kids, because they weren't saying much either.

After an hour of riding, they reached the small stream that raged in the spring and was only a trickle in the summer. The horses drank and they reversed course, returning the way they came.

They'd almost reached the Split Rock when he noticed Jason Lawson and Tate Turner conspiring. Then they kicked their horses into motion, directing them to the outside of the main group of riders and racing ahead.

Not to be left in the dust, Isabelle Jackson raced off, with Jake Turner close on her horse's hooves.

But Dylan Lawson surprised them all by spurring his horse to gallop and reaching the corral before anyone else.

Streeter looked over at Sergeant B and he knew those kids were in a fuckton of trouble. Especially after he heard her say, "Goddamned ranch kids."

Odd.

But she didn't say a word as the kids brushed the horses down and returned the tack to the fence. Only when they finished did she say, "Bravo formation, recruits."

The kids scrambled to get into place. This lineup grouped the kids together by ages. Brianna on one end, Rhett on the opposite end.

Sergeant B walked the line of kids slowly, briefly stopping in front of each of the perpetrators of the horse race, before moving on. But she didn't say a word, she just kept walking the line as if she had all the time in the world.

If it made him nervous, he couldn't imagine what the kids were feeling. But they'd brought it on themselves by disobeying their leader. He considered himself lucky that Olivia had been riding with him, or she would've been in the thick of it.

Renner stood on his left side, Ted on his right. Pete had taken off to help up at the lodge. His boss leaned over and muttered, "This oughta be interestin'."

Bailey stopped in front of the middle of the line, every inch a soldier at rest. "No horseplay means no horseplay. Which is why I set that rule from the start. Most of you are familiar with riding horses, but you weren't familiar with *these* horses. When you broke rank, you put every one of us in danger. Those of you who ignored a direct order, step forward."

Isabelle, Jason, Tate, Jake and Dylan stepped up.

"Four demerits each."

They looked at one another as if that weren't so bad.

Then Sergeant B said, "Drop and give me ten push-ups."

"Right here in the dirt?" Isabel said with horror.

"Yep. And for questioning my order, Recruit Jackson, you've just added three more push-ups for everyone. The next complaint will result in these push-ups being moved to the pasture."

Not a word of complaint emerged.

"Drop and give me thirteen. And I'd better hear you counting."

"Sir, yes, sir!"

The kids turned the punishment into a competition—good thing they weren't expected to maintain good form.

As soon as they finished, Sergeant B said, "Now give me thirteen sit-ups."

Not a single kid complained about that either. When his gaze moved to Olivia and the line of kids not in trouble, he was pleased that their attention was rapt on their fellow recruits—not on causing more trouble since Sergeant B trusted them to behave.

"Good. On your feet."

Sergeant B turned and said, "Mr. Jackson, could you please come forward?"

Renner sauntered up next to her.

"Sir, how many shovels do you have?"

He said, "Five," without missing a beat.

"Lucky for us. I'm certain with a pack of trail horses there's horse dung that needs to be picked up."

"Yes, ma'am."

She gestured to the five perpetrators. "Demerits are worth ten minutes of DA—disciplinary action. So you've got these recruits to shovel horse dung for the next forty minutes. And fortunately for you, they will follow your orders in complete silence. If any of them talk, feel free to add more time to their DA."

"Understood, Sergeant B." Renner looked at Ted. "Grab the shovels and pitchforks out of the toolshed."

Ted grinned and said, "Yes, sir."

Bailey said, "Mr. Jackson, could you also round up some extra towels from housekeeping?"

"Sure. May I ask what for?"

"The recruits who didn't break rank will be learning warfare tactics with squirt guns and water pistols. I'm thinking they'll probably get a little wet."

"*They* get to have water fights when we're stuck picking up horse crap?" Tate demanded. "That ain't fair."

She got right in his face. "That outburst just earned your team another demerit, Recruit Turner." She looked at the group. "Anyone else?"

Silence.

Streeter had to turn away and pretend to adjust his chaps so he wouldn't laugh.

"I'll call the GM and have the towels ready," Renner offered.

"Thank you. I'll be back in an hour." She whistled and clapped twice as she moved to stand at the front of the line. "Alpha formation, recruits."

Of course she was the alpha.

Renner leaned in. "Buddy, your woman is something else. Tierney is gonna have a big ol' girl crush on her after I tell her how she handled these kids today."

"I've got a big ol' crush on Sergeant B myself."

⤳

Streeter was ten minutes late picking up Olivia at WWC that afternoon.

Bailey looked exhausted. Ten hours of constant interaction and disciplining these kids had taken a toll on her. For the first time he wondered if she was getting paid enough to do this.

"You're pushing your luck, Mr. Hale, showing up late. I've given out a lot of demerits today."

Olivia was loading her backpack, not paying attention to them, so he leaned closer and whispered, "I'll take any demerits you can dish out as long as you use a riding crop."

"That might be fun."

She hadn't said that with any enthusiasm.

"You okay, Sarge?"

She shook her head. "I'm not used to riding a horse. So I'm sore. It was a stressful day and I'm feeling that too."

"There's an easy fix for that." He tucked a flyaway piece of hair behind her ear. "I'll take care of you tonight. Hot bath, cold beer, deep massage, epically long orgasms; the works."

"About that." She glanced over his shoulder. "I'm spending the weekend at Harper and Bran's."

"All weekend?"

"Yeah."

Well, that sucked. "You're not workin' at WWC?"

"Nope. I swapped shifts with Penelope."

That seemed odd she hadn't mentioned it before now. "When will you be back?"

"Sunday night. Maybe Monday morning. We'll see how I feel."

Feel? That was really odd. "Okay." He curled his hand around the side of her face. Holy crap, her skin was hot. Had she gotten sunburned today? He scrutinized her. She looked paler than normal. Her eyes were dull too. "Baby, you're burnin' up."

"I'm fine." She took a step back. "It's just hot in here." Then she purposely—dismissively—pointed at her watch. "Deenie's gonna be here soon, so you'd better get going."

"Give me a kiss before I go."

Bailey's gaze moved to Olivia.

"Ain't like she hasn't seen us kissin' before."

She rested her hands on his chest and stood on her toes to peck him on the mouth. "Have a good weekend, Street. I'll miss you like crazy."

What in the devil was going on with her?

"Daddy?"

When he turned around after he'd helped his daughter, Bailey was gone.

Streeter had time to consider her behavior during his quiet weekend alone. They never did anything together besides fuck, watch TV and sleep. They hadn't done any of the date-type things that normal couples probably did. He definitely hadn't romanced her at all.

Maybe that was what she needed.

Then that was what he'd do.

Flowers, candlelit dinner, the whole shebang.

Chapter Seventeen

*D*ate night.

Why Streeter insisted on a date on a Tuesday night, instead of Friday night, made zero sense until he loaded Olivia and her overnight bag in his SUV.

Then they were on the road to his brother and sister-in-law's house.

The silence in the car drove her batty. Olivia had fallen asleep in her car seat almost before they left the Split Rock. And for some reason, Streeter didn't have the radio on—who didn't listen to music in their car?—which left her with first-date jitters bouncing around in her brain like a rogue pinball.

Bailey had met Streeter's brother and he seemed like a nice enough guy. His wife, Jade, was probably very lovely as well. These people had been Streeter's lifeline during the worst time of his life, so she wanted them to like her. She wanted them to understand she could make Streeter happy in whatever time they had together. But she didn't want to answer questions about whether she planned to stick around for the long haul. Because if she admitted that no, she wasn't staying in Wyoming, then they'd suspect that she'd leave Streeter brokenhearted, given his nearly virginal experience with relationships, and dislike her on principle.

Streeter's hand squeezed her thigh. "Why so quiet?"

Rather than admit her fears, she sighed. "I haven't been on a date for a while. I have concerns about your date-night expectations, Mr. Hale."

Those sexy lips quirked with amusement. "Such as . . . what, Sergeant B?"

"Such as . . . I'm not much of a drinker."

"There goes my plan to get you drunk and see if you'll shed your britches along with your inhibitions." He paused. "Oh, right, you ain't got any inhibitions."

She fought a smile. "I can be prim and proper."

"God, I hope to never see that."

"This is where we're back to date-night expectations. I am not the type of woman who'll put out on the first date."

Streeter leaned over and kissed her bare shoulder. He whispered, "Then it's a lucky thing we got the hot fucking out of the way before the date, huh?"

Damn him for reminding her that she had no willpower when he wore his ranch foreman duds—chaps, spurs, dusty jeans and well-worn boots, his hat shadowing half his face, the cuffs of his plaid western-cut shirt rolled up, exposing those ropy forearms.

He'd casually strolled in while she was at work and looked around. Seeing that no customers were in the store, he flipped over the Closed sign and ambled toward her. The chink-chink-chink of his spurs as he stalked her were the sexiest sounds of foreplay she'd ever heard.

But still, she tried to show some restraint. Not tackling him to the floor the minute she got a whiff of him—sweat, laundry soap, fresh dirt and the great outdoors—counted . . . right?

He moved forward; she moved back.

"Streeter. You can't just come in here and expect—"

"Oh, sweet darlin', I can, and I surely will, fulfill your expectations and then some."

Goddamn him and this new cockiness that was entirely justified.

"If I want you on your knees, you know you'd drop to the floor in front of me right now."

Chink-chink-chink echoed to her with his every bootstep.

"If I want a taste of your sweet cunt, you'll scramble onto the counter without hesitation and pull your skirt up for me."

Chink-chink-chink and they were past the counter and in the back room.

"But, baby, that ain't how I need it from you." He reached into his back pocket and dangled a pair of leather gloves between them. "Fresh off the rack. Never been worn. I need to break them in, and I know just how to do it."

She managed to croak out, "How?"

"I'm more of the show than the tell type." He pulled a glove onto his right hand with his teeth and then did the same sexy maneuver with the left glove.

Holy fuck. That was sexy enough to make her clit throb.

Streeter crooked his finger at her.

And in the next instant she was toe-to-toe with him.

He placed his left palm over her voice box, wrapping his fingers around her throat and sweeping his thumb across her chin.

The scent of new leather, the scent of him, the rough edges of the glove on her skin . . . talk about potent. Bailey was completely in his thrall.

"You haven't gotten to kiss me when I'm wearin' my hat recently, so I'm gonna hold this pretty face where I want it while we practice."

"Streeter—"

He tilted his head and began kissing her in the patient, precise way he wanted, keeping to his word of restricting her movement.

She let go and let him lead.

He broke the kiss long enough to whisper, "Put your hands on my hips," against her mouth.

Grateful for something to hold on to, she hooked her index fingers into the belt loops of his jeans and felt the smooth leather of his chaps brushing her knuckles.

Cool air drifted under her skirt as Streeter trailed his gloved hand up the inside of her thigh. The elastic in her panties gave way when he yanked them aside so he could slip his leather-clad finger inside her.

Bailey whimpered because she was already wet enough to take it.

He immediately added a second finger and thrust them in and out, growling in her mouth when he heard the squelching noises her body made as he finger-fucked her.

It was heady stuff, how much the sights, sounds, tastes and scents of sex affected him, and she'd gloried in his every discovery of what turned him on.

His kisses turned a little sloppy when he swept his thumb across her clit to the exact same rhythm as the slow stroking of his left thumb on the blood pumping through her carotid artery in her throat.

The tingling white noise started in her head much sooner than she'd anticipated, but her poor brain was on sensory overload. Giving him control of her body proved just how much she trusted him with every aspect of her pleasure. Her orgasm blasted her from all sides. She felt the pulsing throb in her lips, on her tongue, hardening her nipples, and the squeeze and release of her inner muscles around his stroking fingers even as her clit pulsed beneath his thumb.

She was panting against his throat when she came back to herself.

And as soon as Streeter felt her slump against him, he eased his fingers out of her and spun her around to face the wall, swearing a blue streak as he fumbled to get his jeans open while wearing new, stiff gloves.

Bailey didn't offer to help him; instead she flattened her palms against the wall and braced herself for the hot, hard fucking that would follow.

Not only had he proven he could convince her to fuck anytime and anyplace, he'd made her come again wearing that damn glove. Spreading her pussy lips open with those leather-covered fingers. Pounding into her with such force that the rough-edged seam on the glove abraded her clit with each thrust of his hips. She'd had to sink her teeth into his biceps to keep from screaming as she tipped over the edge of pleasure laced with pain.

And after he'd come in a series of grunts and groans, he slowed to gentle, almost soothing pumps of his pelvis, his mouth homing in on her neck as he destroyed her with sweet kisses. "You okay?" he murmured in her hair.

"Sex-drunk again," she managed through her dry throat.

"Same. Lord, woman. You are such an addiction."

He hadn't said sex was the addiction; she was the addiction.

That thought made her body—and soul—tingle more than any orgasm.

He moved his right hand and held it in front of her face. The leather was darker on the first two fingers, half of the palm, and the thumb pad, clear down to the ball of his hand.

She stifled a groan. She'd—her body had done that? "Sorry."

"Don't be. Now the leather conditioning is complete."

A sharp nip on her shoulder brought her back to the present. She looked over at Streeter, still smirking at her.

"I spent all afternoon thinkin' about our lunch break too."

"Cocky much? I wasn't thinking about it."

"I know what you look like when you're hot and bothered, Bailey, and it sure ain't the scenery that's makin' your skin flushed and your nipples hard."

"You are a dirty, dirty man, Mr. Hale, with a one-track mind."

"That's the nicest thing you've ever said to me, Sergeant."

Streeter slowed and turned onto a long driveway that ended at a big farmhouse, painted Dr. Seuss style. He parked, stole a kiss and jostled

Olivia. "Hey, girlie. Time to wake up. We're at Uncle Tobin and Aunt Jade's house."

Olivia yawned. "Okay."

Bailey waited while he extracted Olivia from her five-point-buckle-system car seat. Olivia hopped down, snagged her backpack and happily skipped up the steps, barging into the house without knocking.

"She tends to make herself at home."

"I see that." Bailey also saw that Olivia had breezed right past the two adults standing on the top of the steps without stopping to say hello.

Maybe she had to use the bathroom really bad.

Tobin smiled at her as she ascended the steps with Streeter's hand on the small of her back, guiding her. "Nice to see you again, Bailey. This is my wife, Jade."

A trim woman with glossy black hair, topaz eyes and a beautiful smile offered her hand. "It's so nice to finally meet you."

"Same."

"Streeter has told me absolutely nothing about you. Olivia, however, has suggested that you might secretly be Wonder Woman."

Bailey laughed. "Subversive flattery tactics to get her drum set back, I'm sure."

"I believe you also met my grandma. She's one of the Mud Lilies."

She tried to remember if any of the ladies had mentioned Jade. Looking at her, she couldn't decide which one it would be.

"Garnet. I call her GG," Jade said helpfully.

"Ah. Garnet of the blue disco jumpsuit."

Jade touched her nose.

"I'll admit they kind of ambushed me."

"Let me guess. They had some crazy story about why they were there, and bickered among themselves and then when they left, you were wondering ... WTF just happened?"

She blinked at Jade. "That's exactly how it played out."

"What reason did they give for grilling you?"

"They were planning a surprise party for Harper."

Jade rolled her eyes. "That is much lamer than their usual harebrained schemes. I'm guessing that someone"—she pointed at Tobin—"spilled the beans that you and Streeter were dancing at Buckeye Joe's."

Tobin blushed. "Hey, I was sleep deprived and GG was bein' really sweet, askin' about Streeter, so I might've let something slip."

A little person zoomed out of the shadows and ran squarely into Streeter's legs. He bent down and picked the child up, propping her on his hip. "This stealthy creature is my niece, Amber. Amber, say hi to Bailey."

"Hi, Bailey." She laid her pigtailed head on Streeter's shoulder. "I wanna come wif you, Unca Street."

"Another day, squirt. But I am leavin' your cousin Olivia here for a sleepover."

"K. I go find her." She squirmed to be let down. But as soon as Streeter set her down, she headed for the enormous pile of toys in the corner of the porch.

"Two-year-olds have such a short attention span," Jade said.

"She's only two? I thought she was four with how well she speaks." She sighed. "I'm a terrible judge of kids' ages, though."

"Me too!" Jade said. "When Tobin and I first got together, we ran into a friend of his who was babysitting her niece. I thought the girl was really articulate for being like . . . five. I felt like an idiot when her mom told me her daughter was eight."

"You wouldn't happen to be talking about Brianna Lawson?"

"Yes. How did you know?"

"She's my 'assistant' at boot camp. I couldn't believe it when she told me that she's twelve. She's so—"

"Small for her age," they finished at the same time.

Jade grinned. "Glad it's not just me."

"Listen to you two. Acting as if you're both six feet tall, instead of your small statures of what . . . five foot two?"

Streeter snickered at his brother's comment.

Bailey looked at Jade. "Maybe we oughta let these two big, blustering cowboys go on a date and you and me can stay here and play with the kiddos." She leaned in and looked at the wide-eyed baby cradled in Tobin's arms. "What's this one's name?"

"Micah."

"Hey, Micah." She stroked his cheek. "Bet you and my Angel baby niece will be schoolmates."

He cooed at her.

"Lookit you, already charming the ladies like the men in your family."

He cooed again.

"Oh lord, you're tempting me. I haven't had my baby fix in days."

Then Bailey felt the weight of the silence and all of them staring at her. She met Jade's gaze first. "Sorry."

"You're welcome to pop in and get your baby fix anytime, Bailey."

"Don't be surprised if I take you up on that."

The screen door slammed. Olivia pushed her way between Jade and Tobin. She scowled at her dad. "I thought you were leavin'."

"Maybe if you keep bein' mouthy we'll all just turn around and go home."

She sighed and watched the toe of her shoe as she rolled her foot back and forth.

Streeter waited for her apology.

Neither Tobin nor Jade said a word.

Olivia looked at her dad. "Sorry. I wanna stay."

"Then what do you gotta do?"

"Promise I won't be mouthy no more."

"Good. Now c'mere and gimme a hug."

Olivia pressed her cheek into his stomach as her arms circled his waist.

"And what else?"

"I promise not to throw a fit."

"And what else?"

"I promise I'll follow the rules."

"Which rules?" he prompted.

"*All* of the rules."

"Okay. Have fun and I'll see you in the mornin'."

"Bye, Daddy." She raced over to where her cousin played.

Streeter sent Bailey a look, as if she might be upset that Olivia had failed to say good-bye to her. Then she noticed Tobin and Jade looking at her the same way.

"That's how she is," she said softly, as if she needed to explain Olivia's behavior. "I'd be really suspicious if she acted differently."

"True. Have a fun date," Tobin said. "Good seein' you again, Bailey. We hope to see more of you."

"Yes, we'll have you all over for dinner soon," Jade added.

Streeter took her hand as they walked to the car. He even opened the door for her. She said, "Gentlemanly date behavior, Mr. Hale."

"It's about the only gentlemanly thing about me, Sergeant."

After he got behind the wheel, she said, "Shouldn't we leave Olivia's car seat with them just in case?"

His handsome face softened. "They've got an extra one from when Jade used to watch Olivia. But I'm glad you recognize the importance of her safety. Olivia's grandmother accuses me of bein' overprotective."

"Better to be overprotective than filled with regret."

He kissed her. "Come on, baby. Let's get this hot date started."

⤦⤦

Apparently Streeter had been listening to her during TV talk or pillow talk. He took her to a sushi place instead of a steak joint.

She leaned across the table. "You sure this is where you want to eat?"

"Wouldn't be my first choice, but I figure if I'm gonna try it, I'm in good hands with you since you can tell me what some of this stuff is."

"You don't hate fish, do you?"

"My experience with it is pretty much limited to frozen fish sticks and the crappies my dad and brother used to catch."

"You calling fish *crappy* isn't exactly filling me with confidence that you'll like anything I'll choose, Streeter."

He laughed. "Crappies are a type of fish."

"Oh."

"If you paid more attention to the amazing flies your brother-in-law Bran crafts, you might know that."

"I don't want Bran to think I'm fishing for compliments."

Streeter groaned. "Damn, do I love your puns."

The waitress took their order and returned with two bottles of Sapporo beer.

They clinked their bottles together. "Cheers."

"Happy date night."

"You've met all of my family that I'm willing to claim; is there a chance I'll get to meet your sister Liberty?"

"I don't know. Devin is on the last leg of a yearlong world tour. Whenever they're back in Denver they tend to be homebodies. Even driving to Muddy Gap is more traveling, which they're thoroughly sick of." She sipped her beer. "I'm a pussycat compared to my ball-busting sister."

"You said she and Devin have a daughter?"

"Nikki. She's three. And that girl would give Olivia a run for who's more stubborn." She shook her head. "Liberty was on assignment for two weeks right before this tour started. She came home and discovered that Devin hadn't combed Nikki's hair at *all*. Nikki had her daddy snowed that pulling the snarls out hurt her poor little head."

Streeter snickered.

"So Nikki practically had dreads, her hair was so matted. Which pissed off my sister because manipulation doesn't fly with her, especially when it's from her own daughter. She gave Devin and Nikki an

218 ∽ **LORELEI JAMES**

ultimatum: either Devin combed out every snarl and learned not to pull Nikki's hair, or they'd go to the salon and get all of Nikki's hair cut off. Bear in mind that Nikki has beautiful dark blond hair that falls in damn ringlets around her cherubic face."

"What happened?"

"Devin convinced Liberty to let his stylist detangle the precious one's hair. Except Ravenna is this sassy black woman who doesn't take any shit from anyone. Not her country music superstar boss or his precocious child. She combed the snarls out, but she made Devin sit and watch and gave Nikki running commentary about how lucky she is to have hair." Bailey laughed. "Normally, I'd think . . . the kid is three? How can she understand about combing her hair? But like I said, Nikki is smart and resourceful, not to mention the only child of parents with polar opposite parenting approaches. She takes full advantage."

"I shudder to think what kinda trouble Olivia and Nikki could get into."

"Me too."

The waitstaff delivered their order, beautifully arranged on Japanese serving platters, garnished with flowers crafted from fruits and vegetables.

Streeter leaned over and inspected each variety, poking at the seaweed edges with one chopstick. "Tell me what this is."

She listed the rolls she'd ordered by main ingredient first, and then pointed out the dipping sauces, the wasabi and the sides of pickled ginger, cucumber and radish.

"This looks too pretty to eat. If I were a foodie, or on social media, I'd take pictures and post them online to show that I'm hip. But I'm not up on any of that stuff so I'll just eat 'em."

Bailey had selected a dragon roll, a California roll, a spider roll and a rainbow roll. "I planned to ask if you'd accept my Facebook friend request now that we're fucking like bunnies."

He choked on his beer. "Jesus, Bailey."

"But you're not listed on social media anywhere." She looked at him. "Because of Danica?"

"Now? Yeah. I never did the whole Facebook thing. After her suicide I went to her page, thinkin' maybe I'd find something that was a clue as to why she did it. But she never really posted on there either. Her Twitter account was all retweets. No Instagram account. If I'm not on any social media, no one can tag me. It's a simple buffer, and I know that'll change when Olivia grows up, but for now . . ."

She hated that he'd had to comb through Facebook and Twitter for any glimpse into why his wife had killed herself. And with the shitshow that was Twitter, she couldn't imagine how cruel people might've been. She said, "Smart move."

"What about you? I see you on your phone a lot."

"I review strategy and first-person-shooter games for a buddy who started designing them while he was still in the military. He sold the first three apps but now he's developing his own and other people's with his new company, so he retains the rights. He sends me mock-ups for gear and weaponry add-ons. He thinks since I'm a chick and a soldier I'll have a better idea of what female customers want in their battle rattle." She snorted. "Definitely not goddamned pink shit like he'd originally designed." She glanced up and saw Streeter's jaw hanging open. "What?"

"How didn't I know this about you?"

"Well, lots of people don't like violent video games, especially ones where skill with firearms is the focus of winning." She poked at the pink pickled ginger with her chopsticks. "And given your history, I didn't want to bring it up."

He remained quiet.

"I've seen your Netflix recommendations, Streeter. No true-crime dramas, no women-in-peril-type shows, no police procedurals, and no horror. You watch comedies. The occasional musical. Kids' shows. How was I supposed to slip it into conversation that when the store isn't busy, or when I'm home, I get paid as a consultant to figure out how to make futuristic weapons more appealing to female consumers, so they'll look cool online when they're blowing away their competition?"

Her lungs tightened because she was holding her breath. Forgetting to breathe . . . first sign of a panic attack.

Please. Not here, not now.

Bailey scooted out of the booth with a mumbled "Excuse me" and booked it to the bathroom before he could stop her.

She locked herself in a stall and sat on the toilet, flattening her palms on the metal walls and pushing against them, in an attempt to turn her focus outward. No head-between-her-knees for her. No, she had to treat her panic like a movable force. Like lifting weights. Or doing a handstand in yoga. Giving her body the power, not the panic.

Once she felt calmer, she exited the stall, washed her hands in cold water and dampened a paper towel to press against the back of her neck. She had no idea how much time had passed. The first lesson she'd learned in dealing with these panic attacks was each one was different. It was more important to get control of the panic than to put a time on how much or little time it took for it to be over.

Bailey wasn't surprised to see Streeter leaning against the wall across from the restrooms, waiting for her.

Before she said a word, his hands were framing her face. "Are you all right?"

Not really. She cleared her throat. "I'm fine. Bad-tasting piece of sushi."

"Bailey. Don't."

She closed her eyes and leaned against him. Just for a moment. "What I do hurts you." *If you knew who I am, what I've done, you wouldn't be here with me now because it wouldn't merely hurt you; it'd devastate you.*

"Baby. Look at me."

Like he gave her a choice when he tipped her head back. She opened her eyes.

"It doesn't hurt me. It surprised me, that's all." He pressed a soft kiss to her lips. "I won't download the app, but you can talk about your work with me."

"You sure?"

"Yep. But you do realize what's good for the goose is good for the gander. I'm gonna be tellin' you all sorts of stuff you never wanted to know about cows and bulls."

She smiled.

"There's that beautiful smile from my beautiful girl."

When Streeter kissed her this time, it wasn't a sweet peck. He packed it with the heat and passion she'd come to expect from the man who acted on his lust and affection without hesitation.

"Streeter?"

He ended the kiss and faced the interrupter. But not before he slid his arm around Bailey's waist and pulled her closer.

"Hello, Deenie."

The woman gave her a once-over. Then she said, "Who is this?" to Streeter.

No one talked over her or as if she weren't there. "I'm Sergeant Bailey Masterson. Who are you?"

"Deenie Joyce. Streeter's wife's mother."

"Oh, you're Danica's mother," Bailey corrected her. "Since technically, Streeter is a widower."

"Where's my granddaughter?" she demanded of Streeter. "Did you leave her alone at the table so you could make out by the bathroom?"

"*My* daughter is with my family tonight."

"How long has this been going on?" She paused to narrow her eyes and look down her nose at them. "Is she why you've finally allowed me to spend weekends with my only grandchild? So you had free time to cruise the bars and find a—"

"Not another word, Deenie. My life is not your concern."

"It is if it affects my daughter's child."

"Olivia is *my* child."

His arm tightened around her back, and Bailey sensed his struggle to keep this conversation from deteriorating further.

"Yes, as you so gleefully point that out at every opportunity, don't you? Tell you what, Streeter. I'll let you have as much time as you want with *your* daughter." She stepped back. "You can forget about me taking care of her every weekend so you can screw around without a care in the world."

Streeter inhaled and exhaled before he spoke. "That is your choice, Deenie. I believe it's the wrong one, but I ain't gonna argue with you." He took Bailey's hand and led her around the woman, who was still fuming.

They had to stop at the hostess stand to pay the check.

Bailey felt Deenie's glare burning into the back of her neck, but she refused to turn around. As much as she'd wanted to defend Streeter and demand why he should be expected to live a miserable existence that her daughter's actions had caused . . . she kept quiet. She had no permanence in his life. And she doubted this had been the first time he'd battled with his former mother-in-law.

Outside in the parking lot, the night air was warm, but she shivered nonetheless.

Streeter noticed. He rubbed his hands up and down her arms. "Cold?"

"A little. I'm sorry I forgot a jacket."

"I'm sorry this date sucked."

"It's not your fault."

"But it is." He kissed her forehead and opened her car door.

She looked at the brooding set to his jaw and the distance in his eyes. "Streeter. Are you okay?"

"I'm fine."

When they were five miles out of Rawlins and Streeter hadn't said another word, she knew he'd be so lost in his own thoughts during the rest of the drive that he wouldn't notice the silence between them.

But she did.

She turned on the radio, flipping past a Kanye song and an Eagles tune, stopping when she heard the Wright Brothers Band singing "Fine Is Just Another 4-Letter Word."

How apt.

Streeter didn't even notice when the announcer cued up Devin Mc-Clain's newest song, "Richest Man in Town," nor did he notice when she softly sang along.

He parked in his spot and turned the car off. Without looking at her, he said, "I don't know if I have the right to ask, given the shitshow I subjected you to, but can I stay with you tonight?"

Say no. Say you're tired. Say you need to spend time on the weapons apparel app.

But when she opened her mouth, "Of course" tumbled out instead.

Chapter Eighteen

〜❧〜

$\mathcal{S}$treeter had Bailey pinned against the wall of his shower.

Naked, wet and squirming against the wall as he slowly pumped his cock into her.

"Streeter. Please."

"Please what?" he demanded, scraping his teeth across the slope of her shoulder, then sucking the water droplets from her skin.

She shivered.

She moaned.

He fucking loved how she responded to him. Every. Single. Time.

In the weeks they'd been together, he'd become better acquainted with her body than with his own. He'd earned every kiss, every sigh, every bite mark, every nail gouge, every sting of sweat dripping into his eyes as he learned how to be the lover she craved.

He attended to his daily studies religiously.

The rewards of being an eager pupil were the stuff wet dreams were made of.

Like this.

Her clawing, ripping need as he took her ass.

He'd never done that particular act—Danica had outright refused. She'd recoiled at the idea of ass play of any kind.

Not Bailey.

She'd reveled in initiating him into the pleasures of anal sex.

And what a fucking rush it was, from the extra time and care he used preparing her, to the mind-blowing sensation of slowly pushing into that unbelievably tight channel as he drove in hard and pulled all the way out.

Weeks of nearly daily fucking had given him the stamina and sexual confidence he'd lacked.

She'd given him that confidence.

And she'd benefited from his stamina.

Win-win all around.

Her cries echoed louder than the water pouring over them, loud enough to drown out the buzzing of the small vibrator resting against her clit. She couldn't come from anal penetration alone, so he'd found a way to make her come.

"Don't . . . please . . . don't change. Move just like that," she panted, her fingers clutching his hair so tightly his scalp stung.

"I got you, darlin'. You're almost there." He pressed his mouth next to her ear. "Even when I'm buried in your ass, I can feel your sweet pussy contracting when you come. It's the sexiest thing ever, baby. Give it to me." Then he sank his teeth into the magic spot below her jaw and she absolutely unraveled.

She whimpered as her clit pulsed and her pussy clenched, stopping movement entirely to feel the full force of her orgasm.

As soon as the tension in her body eased, she rested her forehead on his shoulder with a heavy sigh of satisfaction and said, "Ready."

Streeter hammered into her without pause. Plunging deeper, straining his neck, his abs, his ass cheeks tightened to get to that point . . . and motherfuck, there it was. White-hot pleasure that rolled through him like a blast furnace.

He'd gone completely nonverbal, grunting and groaning as his dick jerked and pulsed against those viselike walls; his vision had gone hazy and he tried to stay upright.

After the last heated burst of come released, he lost his balance. When he tried to catch himself, his hips moved and his cock slipped out in one fast jerk.

Bailey shouted, "Ow, goddammit, that hurt!"

"Sorry."

Four rapid knocks sounded on the door.

They both froze. They'd gotten so used to having the place to themselves on the weekend that they'd gotten carried away.

"Daddy?"

Shit. Fuck. "Uh, yeah?"

"Is Bailey in there with you?"

His gaze met Bailey's—her eyes were round with shock. She mouthed, "Answer her."

"Yes, she's in here."

"Why?"

Shit. Fuck. "I'm helpin' her wash her hair. It's kind of a mess."

Bailey slapped his ass hard and hissed, "Seriously?"

A brief pause outside the door and then Olivia said, "I'm hungry."

"I'll be right out."

"Okay."

Before Bailey could chew his ass, he kissed her. Then he whispered, "Ain't really a lie. I fucked your hair up pretty good this morning when you blew me."

That earned him another slap on the ass.

Totally worth it, though.

✎

Olivia was finishing her bowl of Frosted Flakes when Bailey entered the kitchen.

And for once, Olivia didn't ignore her. She scrutinized her.

Bailey sent a *WTF?* look at Streeter standing near the coffeepot.

He shrugged.

"Your hair don't look messy to me," Olivia said.

"Well, that's . . . because your dad did a good job of fixing it."

And that was that.

Bailey shouldered her gym bag and headed for the exit.

Before she opened the door, she turned around and said, "Aren't you forgetting something this morning, Olivia?"

Her eyes lit up. "May I please have my drums back, Sergeant B?"

"Not today, girlie, but I'll let you play them later."

"Yay!"

Bailey blew him a kiss and walked out.

Streeter glanced at the clock, then at his daughter. "After you make your bed and brush your teeth, we've gotta get movin'."

"Where are we goin'?"

"To meet Grandpa Steve." He paused. "At Trampoline World."

The kid was so pumped she bounced all the way to her room.

Streeter wasn't as thrilled, even when he'd called Steve for the meet-up.

Two hours later, Olivia was happily supervised, bouncing on every trampoline and bouncy castle imaginable.

He and Steve grabbed a seat in the parental observation area.

Danica's father had always been a quiet man, but it'd been hard for him to get a word in with his overly chatty wife.

Streeter didn't really know Steve well, despite being married to his daughter for a decade. He had nothing in common with the man; Steve was an accountant at a private firm. He didn't hunt or fish. He golfed. He read. He did lawn care and household repairs. He hadn't seemed particularly close to his daughter, but he was at every family gathering, dinner, holiday and party arranged by his wife.

Within two years of Danica's death, Steve Joyce's life had imploded.

He quit his lucrative job to head up a nonprofit in Rock Springs. He left his wife. He bought a maintenance-free condo. He traded in his new Mercedes for an older-model Jeep. No longer was Steve the clean-cut guy in a suit; he wore jeans and T-shirts. He'd grown out his salt-and-pepper hair. And he looked old, much older than when Streeter had met him twenty years ago.

"I was surprised to hear from you, Streeter. Happy, but surprised."

"I'm sorry for that. I've stayed out of the pass-off between you and Deenie on the weekends."

"I'd stay out of it too, if I could." He picked at the edge of his foam coffee cup. "What's she done now?"

No need to clarify who "she" was. "About a month and a half ago I started seein' a woman. It's been low-key"—such a lie—"so I didn't mention it."

"And to be blunt, why would you?" Steve said. "It's your life. But go on."

"Bailey, the woman I'm seein', and I were out for dinner this week and we ran into Deenie. It was an ugly scene, not as ugly as it could've been, but it ended with Deenie sayin' she was done spendin' weekends with Olivia so I could be with Bailey."

"Goddamn woman."

"Not to be a smart-ass, but it ain't like Olivia's gonna care if Deenie cuts her out."

"Olivia didn't ask why she wasn't going to her grandma's this weekend?"

Streeter shook his head. "I ain't gonna beg her to spend time with her granddaughter. And I won't apologize for livin' my life."

"You shouldn't."

"So what's the best thing to do?"

"Where Deenie is concerned? Who the fuck knows." He paused and rubbed his beard. "Sorry. Uncalled-for."

"No worries."

Steve sighed before he spoke. "Danica left us all in a helluva mess. I loved my daughter, and it pains me to admit I didn't know her. I don't think anyone knew her, and that's where Deenie has always disagreed with me. She couldn't accept that she didn't see the signs for postpartum depression. Or she blamed you for not seeing them. Or she blamed you for hiding them from us. Every week she had a different theory on what 'really happened.' So for the first six months, I didn't get to mourn my daughter. Deenie acted as if, if she could solve the mystery of Danica's suicide, then we'd be allowed to grieve." He sent Streeter a sideways glance. "You know some of this, but not all. She refused to go to counseling. For a while I had to lie to her about where I was going because she didn't want me going either. We were a team with a capital 'T'. And Team 'figure out why our daughter killed herself' did everything together. Bear in mind, we'd had separate interests the whole of our married life.

"I went along with all of it at first, figuring at some point the finality of the loss of our child would kick in. Then we could grieve together. Maybe learn new things about ourselves in the process. Because there are some serious fucking questions that arise about who you are privately and the public face you show to the world when everyone is looking at you like if you would've been a better father, your daughter would still be alive. Like you must've failed her. Like her life had to have been truly awful to end it in such a gruesome manner. A piece of myself will always take part of the blame for her suicide. Isn't that what parents are supposed to do? Absorb the guilt? Was I so self-involved her entire childhood that I'd created that disconnect in her that didn't allow her to bond to *her* child? What could I have done differently? And then the next day I'd be pissed off because I'd been the best father I knew how to be. I'd worked my ass off to give her a decent life. And it hadn't been enough."

Streeter closed his eyes. He'd dealt with all of those questions and issues himself. But while he'd been trying to sort the truth from the lies in his life, he had to take care of a child who didn't want to be touched. Who screamed instead of laughed. It'd been easier for him to hate Danica. Not just for what she'd done to him but for the devastation she'd created for everyone in her life, including her parents. But somewhere along the way, he *had* moved on from his bitterness. He couldn't claim he'd forgiven Danica for her actions, but he had accepted he'd never have an answer to the question of *why* and dwelling on that wouldn't change anything. Now, he felt sorry for her because all she'd seen was despair when she looked at Olivia, and all he'd ever seen in their beautiful baby girl was pure joy.

"The final straw for me was Deenie's insistence, probably nine months after Danica's death, right around the time you and Olivia moved to Muddy Gap, that Danica hadn't meant to kill herself."

His gut churned remembering all of the blood . . . the absolute guarantee she wouldn't survive with the use of a knife and a gun. "Why would she think that?"

"Deenie had gotten on a 'survivors of suicide' website and read testimonials from people who'd tried to kill themselves and lived to tell about it. Of course they were all filled with regret, warning others of the dangers of suicide, which is noble, but not helpful to people like us who were absolutely caught blindsided by it. No suicide note, no tearful final phone calls, no giving away of prized possessions. Deenie read those suicide survivor letters and swore if Danica had known the heartache her death would cause us, she never would've done it.

"That's when I knew, in order for me to heal, I had to leave her, because Deenie didn't want to heal. She was searching for an excuse, or someone to blame. Then she went through that psychic and medium phase, where she honestly believed Danica's spirit was hanging around out of guilt because she hadn't meant to do it." He scrubbed his hands over his face. "The part of me that cared about Deenie wished one of those con artists would tell her, 'Yes, Danica is here, standing right beside you and she's sorry because she didn't mean to end her life and she's begging for your forgiveness so you both can move on.' But even on the off chance that happened, Deenie wouldn't be satisfied because she doesn't want to face a world without our daughter in it."

They were quiet as they watched Olivia having the time of her life being a normal kid.

"I'm glad you've got someone in your life, Street. You're a good man. You deserve it. Olivia has come a long way and it's all due to you. You wouldn't bring a woman into your world if she weren't good for Olivia. You're too damn honest not to bear all the struggles ahead. Olivia has a tough road and the more people who can keep her on the right path, the better. You won't fail her."

"I appreciate you sayin' that, Steve."

"As far as Deenie . . . she'll pout and rant and curse your name, but ultimately she'll contact you because she'll miss Olivia. Despite Deenie's failings, she loves her."

"I know."

"But she will try to manipulate Olivia. She'll try to undermine your new relationship." He sighed. "Christ, she was doing that *before* you started seeing anyone. Deenie didn't bother to be sneaky during our handoff at the beginning of the summer, when she tearfully spewed all that crap about Olivia never needing another mother. She had her grandma, and just knowing that her mother had loved her more than, *blah blah blah*. I was about to let her have it when Olivia called her out on it." He chuckled. "I don't know if calling bullshit on her grandma's bullshit is a good attribute for a five-year-old, but I was damn happy to see it."

Streeter smiled.

"I don't have to tell you that I'll be in Olivia's life as much or as little as you decide. And I'm always here to talk if you need it. I never offered before because we were all just so damn . . . wounded. It's not an open cut anymore. For me it's finally started to scab over and even heal a little bit." Steve stood and clapped Streeter on the shoulder. "Now if you'll excuse me, I'm gonna go bounce on that big trampoline with my granddaughter."

Chapter Nineteen

The knock on her door came at six forty-five a.m.

A little early to be Olivia.

Yawning because Streeter had kept her up way too late last night, she used the hand not holding her oversized coffee mug to unlock and open the door.

Streeter stepped inside. "Mornin', sexy." He tried to kiss her but she turned her cheek.

"I haven't brushed my teeth yet."

He curled his hand below her jaw, holding her in place. "Then you'll still taste like me, so gimme that mouth."

The man scrambled her brain with a wet, hungry kiss that reminded her of how thoroughly he'd kissed her between her legs last night.

"Mmm," he said when he finally shifted to sugar bites. "Kissin' you is one of my favorite things." Then he looked into her eyes. "So damn easy to get sidetracked."

"Why are you here early?"

"I gotta ask a huge favor. Like really huge."

"What?"

"You're off today, right?"

She nodded.

"The babysitter called in sick. Which wouldna been a problem, but the cattle broker is comin' earlier today. He wants to get through Renner's cattle and mine'n Tobin's before the storms start this afternoon. Olivia's got an appointment with her counselor this morning that she can't miss, so could you take her to Casper?"

"And?"

He flashed her that sheepish grin. "And take her to the library? She's in the summer reading program and she wants a new stack of books to mark off."

"Anything else?"

"She's got an eye appointment at two and a dental visit at four."

Bailey's jaw dropped. "Are you kidding me?"

"Yep." Streeter laughed and kissed her. "I thought if I added two more on, then the first two wouldn't seem like a big deal."

But it was a big deal. Streeter entrusting her with the most precious thing in his life. "I'm happy to do this favor for you. Except I have an appointment of my own around noon."

"I'll call the Learning Center and let them know you'll be droppin' her off for a couple of hours."

Her eyes narrowed. "You have drop-in status with them?"

"It's earned. A perk thing. Never used it before." He ran his knuckles across her jaw. "You really okay with doin' this?"

"Meaning . . . can I handle one five-year-old for a day?"

An odd look flitted across his face. "I'm sure it'll be fine."

Bailey couldn't tell if he was trying to convince her or himself.

"You wanna drive my SUV? Or should I move her car seat into yours?"

"I'd rather drive mine." She looked over his shoulder. "Where is Olivia?"

"Bonding over Fruity Pebbles with Ted. I'll switch out the car seat and get her and her stuff."

"Do I have time to take a shower?"

"A fast one." He pressed a kiss to the spot below her ear and whispered, "I didn't shower this morning. I like havin' the scent of you all over me." He trailed an openmouthed kiss down the arch of her neck. "Maybe I'll grow a beard so that sweet musk of yours stays on me longer."

"Stop. You are not getting me all hot and bothered so I have to rub one out in the shower."

"I'll rub one out for you later." He nipped her earlobe. "With my tongue."

Bailey's skin rippled with gooseflesh. "Why did I believe you when you told me you weren't good at dirty talk?"

"Because I wasn't good at it until you. Hands-on experience is the best way to learn." A low sound like a growl rumbled in her ear. "If I had time, I'd bend you over that easy chair. You'd have to brace yourself on the arms because I'd be fucking you so hard." He blew in her ear. "So very hard that you'd have fabric burns on your belly."

Oh, sweet Jesus. She loved it when he let that beautiful sexual beast inside him out; it'd been caged for far too long.

He placed a soft kiss on the edge of her jaw and stepped back. "But I'll save that for another day."

"Go do your stuff."

❧

Bailey let Olivia play her drums as she finished getting ready.

They listened to the radio on the drive to Casper, which kept Olivia's litany of questions contained.

She'd known that her counselor and Olivia's counselor were in the same medical group and shared the same office space, but it was weird sitting in the waiting room for longer than her normal ten minutes.

When Dr. Waverly, Bailey's counselor, came out to talk to the woman manning the appointment desk, she noticed Bailey. She beckoned her over.

"Is everything okay? I saw you were on the schedule for next Thursday, not today."

"I'm helping a friend out, bringing his daughter to her appointment with Dr. Stafford."

She frowned, which wasn't her usual response to anything. Then she caught herself. "I've got ten minutes before my next appointment. Come back and have a cup of coffee with me."

"Are you gonna charge me for an office visit?"

"Of course not."

Bailey followed her into the nicest break room she'd ever been in, with the fanciest coffee machine she'd ever seen.

Dr. Waverly smiled at her. "Mocha latte, if I remember right."

"Yes."

After Dr. Waverly handed Bailey her drink, she said, "The coffee machine was my idea."

"'Free coffee with your session' a slogan that's working for ya?"

Dr. Waverly lifted a brow. "It's not like we have to advertise."

Once they were in the doc's office, Bailey said, "So am I in trouble or something?"

"Not at all. I'm just curious that you indicated you're friends with Olivia Hale's father."

Bailey managed a shrug. "I told you I was running a boot camp at the Split Rock. Since Streeter works there, Olivia is one of my campers. And we're neighbors."

"Is that all?"

Would the good doc know if Bailey lied? As she debated, Dr. Waverly held up her hand.

"You know what? Forget I asked."

"Did you ask because you're Streeter's counselor too?"

She shook her head. "But I am aware of their situation. And this isn't me talking out of turn, that incident was in the news, although I'm sure everyone has forgotten about it now."

Everyone except for Streeter and Olivia.

"I just wondered, in the course of your friendship with Mr. Hale, if you've shared why you're in counseling?"

Bailey drained her coffee and was shocked to see her hand remained steady when she set the cup on the table. Because it felt like an earthquake had erupted inside of her. "No, Dr. Waverly, I haven't told him. There's no reason to. I'm leaving in a few weeks."

"If your friendship with him deepened—"

She stood. "It can't. The man has been through enough that I'd never add the burden of me to the burden he already carries. Never. So there's no need for you to warn me off."

"Bailey. I'm not trying to—"

"Please, let's drop it. And add to your case notes on me that this isn't something I'm willing to discuss when I come in for my appointment next week." She walked to the door and paused. "Thank you for the coffee."

Olivia finished her session more subdued than when she'd started it an hour ago. Was this her normal behavior after a counselor's appointment? Was Bailey supposed to ask what they talked about?

No. Olivia needed standard fun, kid stuff after the mental poking and prodding. So Bailey drove to the park.

"I thought we were goin' to the library," Olivia said after they parked near the playground.

"We are. But it's supposed to rain after lunch, so I figured we could go then." She paused. "Unless you don't *want* to go to this really cool park—"

"I do wanna go!" She unbuckled herself from her car seat. "See? I'm ready."

Before Olivia's foot hit the grass, Bailey crouched down to get her full attention. "Your dad said I'm supposed to remind you to follow the rules even when he isn't here."

"I will," she said absently as she looked longingly over Bailey's shoulder.

"I have a rule too."

Swear to god the kid sighed like a teenager. "What?"

Bailey held up a digital watch without a band. "This is my special military maneuvers watch. I'm letting you borrow it on one condition."

"Really?"

"Yep. No matter how much fun you're having, when you hear the watch beep, you come back to me because it'll be time to go." She held the watch away from Olivia's grabby hand. "Think you can do that?"

"Uh-huh."

After Olivia shoved the watch into the front pocket of her jean shorts, she took off toward the playground.

Bailey chose a park bench in the sunshine where she could keep an eye on Olivia. She purposely left her phone in her car to avoid distractions.

Olivia had no problems making friends. Kids were fascinating at this age, especially the difference between boys and girls. Whenever Gage and Olivia played together, if Olivia got too bossy, Gage would walk away like he did with his older brothers. Here, with girls her age that she didn't know, Olivia was a follower. Made her wonder if Olivia's detachment allowed her to be a go-with-the-flow kid because she didn't always have to be in charge.

Storm clouds had gathered and the wind had picked up. Bailey's Fitbit buzzed. She noticed Olivia had stopped chasing the pack of girls with the ball and dug in her pocket for the watch face.

Without bothering to say good-bye to her play buddies, Olivia skipped toward her and handed over the still-chirping watch. "Now what?"

"A celebration lunch since you followed all the rules."

"Yay! Can we go to Culver's?"

"Because they have ice cream?"

"And mashed potatoes."

During lunch, Bailey asked her, "When you and your dad go to the library, does he help you pick out books?"

"Huh-uh. He tells me if the books I pick are too old for me." She dug her spoon into her ice cream. "Can I get twelve books?"

"Doesn't the library have a limit on how many you can check out at once?"

"Daddy has a limit," she said wrinkling her nose. "He doesn't like bein' in the library for long. Prolly because he doesn't like to read."

Bailey wasn't a huge reader herself unless it was technical manuals.

"Can we go now?" Olivia asked.

She eyed Olivia's tray. She'd eaten one chicken strip, half of her potatoes and half of her ice cream. This was a banner day for her, foodwise. Streeter often lamented how little his kid ate. "Sure. Let's use the bathroom and wash our hands."

Bailey was feeling pretty good about the day right before it went in the toilet.

Literally.

Olivia accidentally knocked an entire roll of toilet paper into the bowl. Then she tried to flush it. Repeatedly. The toilet overflowed, which entailed Bailey making a confession to the manager and receiving odd looks from customers who eavesdropped about the overflowing toilet.

After Bailey dropped Olivia off at the Learning Center, she was flustered when she arrived for her appointment at the VA outreach center. Nothing like being distracted when she had to finalize the biggest decision of her life.

Forty-five minutes after she checked in, her name was finally called.

Chuck, her case manager, ushered her into his office. "Sorry about the wait. We're short-staffed. No matter how many times we try to tell them that our meetings can't be completed in fifteen minutes, the brass doesn't grasp that. Then we get our budget cut because our surveys reflect long wait time for appointments both in scheduling and in-office wait times." He sighed. "Sorry. Not your issue. So how are you, Sergeant Masterson?"

"Mostly good days."

"Still seeing your counselor?"

"I chatted with her briefly today and I have an appointment with her next week."

"Anything new that we need to discuss regarding your brief chat with her?"

Like Bailey needed another person to tell her that she was the worst option for a romantic relationship with a guy like Streeter. "No. But I'm ready to finish the last step in outprocessing."

Chuck tapped his pen on his desk. "Anything in particular you want to discuss about that?"

Bailey shook her head. "Some days I hate not having the routine of knowing exactly what I'll be doing every minute of the day. On active duty I never had to think. There's a huge comfort in the sameness."

"But?"

"But I get a panicked feeling because I don't know what's next. I mean . . . shouldn't I have more than a vague idea of my options?"

"That's the issue for most people leaving military life, Sergeant. You've spent a dozen years following orders. Autonomy takes time to develop, yet nearly all military personnel have to get a paying job within two months of leaving the service. That doesn't leave much time to explore options. And to be perfectly frank with you, the military machine has the distinction of creating jobs to fill specific voids, which require specialized skills, skills that aren't marketable outside the military."

"I'll bet that makes your job particularly frustrating."

"Or it makes it incredibly fulfilling when I can help fit the right person to the right job."

Bailey studied him for a moment, trying to gauge his sincerity. She'd considered her people-judging skills above average, and what she'd heard from this guy seemed genuine. And that allowed her to be equally honest. "Given my recent health history, how much do I have to disclose to potential employers? And to tag on to that question, how much of my military history are they able to access?"

Chuck didn't answer right away. He stared at a spot behind her as he gathered his thoughts. Then his gaze met hers again. "If you apply for a position in the federal government, HR for that division, department, whatever, would have easier access to all records than say . . . a retail or clerical job in the private sector. What you choose to disclose, I can't tell you if complete honesty is preferable to only revealing information pertinent to the position. And that's not me hedging. In your case, Bailey, I'm not sure which route to go."

Groaning, she slumped back in the chair. "So if I'm honest, chances are high that I'll be passed over for jobs in the private sector."

"You mentioned that your oldest sister said she could get you hired where she's working. Is that still a possibility?"

"Getting an interview? Yes. But she works for a security firm. I'd never pass the extensive background check."

Tap-tap-tap went his pen on his desk blotter. "I thought you told me one of your sisters knows about . . . ?"

"Liberty knows about the lupus. Harper doesn't. They both know I'm leaving the military. Neither has a clue about the . . . other thing."

"Bailey, have you discussed with your counselor why you've refused to tell your family—"

"Chuck, you basically just told me it'd be a red flag to employers who don't know me. So how do you think my sisters, who love me, will react to the most selfish, wrong and stupid thing I almost did?"

"That's what I'm saying. You don't know. The longer you wait to talk to them—"

"I'm never going to tell them or anyone else. Never. It's over. I've dealt with it. It won't happen again."

He raised his hands in surrender. "Fair enough. That's your choice."

Goddamned right it was. Bailey stood and went to grab a bottle of water from the tray in the corner of his office. As she drank, she moved to brood out the window.

"Any chance your summer job could become full-time?"

"No. Harper has finally started looking at the whole picture of her life. She has to do what's best for her and her family, and she's decided to close the store." She flashed him a quick grin. "I will miss bullshitting my way through conversations about fashion."

"What are you doing after hours?"

Gorging myself on the hottest sex of my life. "Working on the game app."

"How's that coming?"

She shrugged. "It's challenging, although making weapons accessories for female game characters is fashion related."

When he flipped open a folder, she knew the discussion was over. That caused a pang of melancholy. Chuck had been her sounding board, so who was she supposed to talk to about this life-altering stuff now?

Streeter popped into her head. He would listen with the same open-mindedness as Chuck, be as supportive and positive, but he also wouldn't sugarcoat his responses.

Chuck slid a piece of paper across the desk. "This makes your out-processing official."

Bailey picked up the pen and signed it.

"This will take around three weeks. You'll need to sign a lot of these documents in person, so we'll need to see you once a week until it's done, okay?"

"Sure." She offered her hand. "It doesn't seem like enough to say thanks, but you've really been a huge help to me, Chuck."

"I have every faith that you will be one of my most successful transition examples." He smiled. "Pity I can't share specifics with anyone."

Bailey stopped at the front desk and scheduled her remaining appointments.

It was pouring outside and she was soaked by the time she got to her car.

And she was really drenched when she literally blew into the Learning Center.

Olivia seemed anxious. Bailey wasn't sure if the storm had caused her distress, or her fear that Bailey wouldn't return to pick her up, or if something had happened with one of the other kids during class.

She paused in the entryway, watching out the window as the wind howled and the rain came down in sheets, waiting for a momentary reprieve in the weather so they could make a break for the car. While they waited, she suggested to Olivia that they should head home and skip the library.

Olivia staged a massive fit the likes of which Bailey had never seen. A screaming, crying, throwing-herself-on-the-floor tantrum.

Bailey had no idea how to deal with it.

None.

The other parents in the waiting area glared at her, as if she were the worst parent on the planet. Too bad she couldn't tell them this wasn't her kid. It was really too bad that she couldn't just walk away.

How the fuck did Streeter deal with this? And how often did this happen?

Bailey plopped down on the floor next to her and waited. Olivia would either scream herself hoarse and flail to exhaustion or she'd stop. Bailey was betting on the latter.

The fit lasted almost ten minutes—long enough to chase the judgmental parents into the rain so they were the only ones left in the waiting room.

Bailey didn't say a word about Olivia's behavior. She merely handed Olivia two tissues and said, "Blow your nose and wipe your face."

And then . . . everything was fine.

Getting a kid in and out of a car seat meant Bailey remained soaked while Olivia was somewhat soggy.

However, the library books remained dry.

The librarian added the books Olivia had read to her chart. Then

Olivia asked Bailey to take a picture of her standing next to her chart for her dad because he'd be proud.

There was the glimpse of sweetness Streeter talked about.

Bailey parked herself in a chair in the children's section of the library while Olivia browsed for books.

Other parents in the vicinity sent Bailey "get off your phone and help your kid pick out books" looks, which she ignored. These people had no idea how lucky they were that Olivia was one hundred percent occupied "choosin' her own books by herself" and not in meltdown mode because Bailey insisted on helping her.

So while she checked her results from her blood tests last week, Olivia stacked books by Bailey's chair. She said, "I'm gonna go look at the birds."

Which Bailey took to mean watch the birds in their caged habitat.

Not so.

When a librarian shouted—in the library no less—"Young lady, get out of there right now!" Bailey was on her feet.

She skidded to a stop on the wet tile when she saw Olivia had peeled back a corner of the metal mesh on the outside of the cage and had squeezed inside.

Birds were squawking and flying as Olivia tried to catch them.

The librarian was still yelling. She looked at the assembled crowd and said, "Where is this child's mother?"

"She's dead!" Olivia yelled from inside the cage.

Oh, for fuck's sake.

Bailey marched over and said, "Olivia. Out. Now." Then she crouched down and lifted the mesh.

Olivia scampered out, oblivious to the havoc she'd wreaked.

Or maybe she wasn't so oblivious because she hid behind Bailey when the librarian approached. "Are you her mother?"

"No. She was telling the truth that her mother is dead."

That was probably the only thing that kept them from getting permanently blackballed from the Casper library—not for just two weeks.

Luckily Olivia was allowed to check out her books. Bailey pretended not to notice the *How to Tame Your Bird* book at the top of the stack.

The rain hadn't let up and huge puddles had formed in the parking lot, puddles that Olivia delighted in stomping in.

As much as Bailey hated the idea of sloshing through the rain again, she had to stop at Walmart. At least Olivia could be strapped into the cart for the very brief trip.

In the store Olivia had convinced her to buy umbrellas—matching ones—covered in pink and purple unicorns with glitter-flecked handles.

After standing Olivia next to the car and warning her not to move, Bailey unloaded the bags into the back of her SUV. When she skirted the back end of the car, Olivia wasn't there, but the umbrella was blowing around like a rainbow tumbleweed.

Goddammit.

It was raining cats and dogs out here and if she was running through the parking lot, cars wouldn't see her until it was too late.

Full-blown panic set in and she yelled, "Olivia!"

Something moved over by the cart return—a hand in the air, waving madly.

Jesus, was she hurt?

Bailey raced over and saw Olivia lying in a mud puddle.

"Olivia! What happened?"

"Shh, you'll scare it." She pushed onto her knees and turned with something clutched in her hands. "Look what I found!"

Please don't be a snake.

"Whatever it is, put it down."

"But it's a kitty! Look at her. She's a teeny tiny baby. And she's wet and shaking." Then she rested her cheek on the top of the critter's head and the thing made the most pitiful meow.

"Olivia, you can't—"

"But she's scared! And what if she doesn't have a momma cat to take care of her? We can't just leave her here if she's lost and alone."

And . . . she was done. Maybe Streeter could justify leaving a motherless kitten in the rain, but she couldn't. And if he didn't want Olivia to have it, well, then *he* could take it away from her.

"Okay. We'll take it with us. But on two conditions. One, it has to stay in the box next to your car seat all the way home. Two, it has to have a bath before you can pet it because it might have"—fleas or worms—"germs."

"I promise." Olivia thrust the cat at Bailey and scrambled into her car seat, leaving Bailey to forage in the back of her vehicle one-handed for a box and a towel as the drenched cat clawed and hissed.

The kitten began mewing as soon as Bailey set it in the box.

It cried and cried until about fifteen minutes into the drive, and then it stopped.

She glanced in the rearview mirror and saw Olivia had stretched her arm down until her hand was inside the box. "Olivia. What did I tell you?"

"You said I couldn't pet her. But she's pettin' *me*. I just put my hand over here and she started rubbin' on it. I think she's sad and hungry 'cause she's lickin' my fingers."

Oh, hey, Street, no big deal, but I think your precious daughter might've caught rabies from the feral kitten I let her bring home.

Wait. Did one catch rabies?

No. That's the bubonic plague. Rabies required a bite. Or maybe even just a scratch.

Great. Either way, she might be fucked—and not fucked the way she preferred with her man.

Chapter Twenty

$\mathcal{S}$treeter hadn't heard from Bailey all day.

Not sure if that was a good thing or a bad thing.

He'd told Olivia to be on her best behavior. He might've mentioned something about earning demerits at home if he got a bad report from Sergeant B.

It'd poured all afternoon like he hadn't seen in a couple of years. The cattle broker had been very thorough, which Streeter appreciated since Ted was still fairly new to that aspect of ranching.

Tobin had taken time off work to be there when the broker came to check out their cattle. Theirs was still a fledgling operation. Though they had expanded in the past two years, that meant they hadn't been selling livestock but building their herd. Add in the genetic experimentation Tobin was doing for bucking bulls, and it'd be a couple more years before All Hale Livestock could support two families. But even when they got the business to where they wanted it to be—workwise and financially—he knew his younger brother loved the scientific aspect of his job in Casper.

He still had half an hour before he could leave to head home, so he shot off a quick text to Bailey.

30 min and I'll be OMW. Everything okay?

She immediately answered back.

Purr-fect.

Streeter scratched his head at the cat emoji she tacked on. Weird.

Or maybe it was her veiled way of sexting that her pussy missed him.

He grinned. That had to be it. And he couldn't wait to show her pussy how much he missed it. He scrolled through his emojis, but none seemed to convey that. The tongue emoji? Nah. It'd be his luck if he sent the eggplant emoji next to the spurting liquid emoji that his daughter would demand an explanation.

After he finished, he returned to the Split Rock. If he'd been anywhere near a store today, he would've bought Bailey some flowers for helping him out. He made a mad dash through the rain from his truck to his trailer.

He wiped his feet, kicked off his boots and wiped down his hat before he hung it on the peg. He looked around. No sign of Olivia or Bailey in the living room.

Then Bailey came out of the bathroom and stopped in the hallway. "Hey. You just get here?"

"Yeah. Where's Olivia?"

"In her room." Bailey sauntered forward and stopped in front of him, sliding her palms up his chest. "Kiss me like you missed me, cutie."

His gaze automatically went down the hallway to see if Olivia had exited her room. So far she hadn't caught them doing anything except holding hands.

"Her door is shut." She wrapped her arms around his neck. "Take the shot while you've got it."

Streeter lowered his mouth to hers and her lips yielded to his.

This.

This was what he'd wanted: a woman to greet at home at the end of the day.

Any woman?

No. He wanted *this* woman. Bailey. The taste of her on his tongue, the scent of her in his lungs and the feel of her body twined around his.

He broke the kiss to string soft smooches up her jawline until his lips met her ear. "More of that later."

"Yeah, well, about that." Then Bailey stepped back. Way back.

"What? Am I too wet?"

"That's what *she* said," she joked.

"Bailey."

"You're fine. I had to change clothes too after spending the day in and out of the rain."

"Then why are you so far away?"

"So you can't reach me when you get mad at me."

His eyes narrowed.

Before he could demand answers, Bailey yelled, "Olivia, you can come out now."

The door banged open and Olivia walked carefully—as if she were on a tightrope—toward him, clutching a shoebox to her chest.

First thing he noticed? The huge smile on her face and the light shining from her eyes.

"Daddy! You'll never guess what!"

That was when he heard a high-pitched series of animal noises.

No. No, no, no, no, no, no, no, no.

"We saved this little bitty kitty from dyin'!"

Olivia finally reached him and she held out the box. "See? Isn't she beautiful?"

Streeter peered down at a ball of whitish gray fur with pale blue eyes. While it was cute . . . *beautiful* seemed a stretch.

"This is Wally."

He glanced over at Bailey. "It already has a name?"

She tried—and failed—to hide a smile. "Yep."

"And I love her. So, so much. And she loves me." Olivia walked over to a towel spread out on the floor. She lowered herself to her knees, set the box down and tumbled the kitten out.

"Gentle, remember?" Bailey reminded her.

"Sorry." She flopped on her belly right in front of the kitten. "Sorry, Wally."

Wally meowed.

"See! She already knows her name!" Olivia patted the carpet beside her. "Come on, Daddy. Watch her with me. She's so funny."

"I'll get you a beer," Bailey offered.

"Lemme get dry clothes on first."

In his bedroom, he decided as long as he was stripping down, he might as well shower.

Ten minutes later, he headed down the hallway but paused before entering the living room when he heard Olivia say, "He's mad, huh?"

"I don't know, cupcake."

Bailey had called Olivia . . . *cupcake?*

Talk about melting his heart.

"I love her," Olivia confessed again.

"So you've said," Bailey murmured. "But what does it mean to you to love something?"

"You wanna be around them. You miss them when you can't be with them." She paused. "I love Daddy. And now I love Wally."

Maybe his daughter was only repeating what she'd heard, but that was as accurate an explanation as he'd heard for love. Add in the fact Bailey made her define the term because she knew Olivia's detachment allowed her to repeat things she'd overheard because she didn't feel them, and he realized that Bailey understood his daughter better than he'd imagined.

"But sometimes you have to let go of what you love, Olivia."

"Why?"

"Because it's better for them."

Whoa. Where had that come from? Was Bailey speaking from past experience? Or was this how she was feeling now?

Why don't you know? You've shared every bit of your past with her . . . and what do you know of hers? She's pushed you to open up from the start but she hasn't reciprocated. She's as vague about her past as she is her future.

That reality hit him like a hoof to the gut.

Olivia sighed. "I don't understand."

"I know you don't, and I hope you never do."

His unease turned to frustration. He'd been so focused on the sex and the companionship that soothed his loneliness that he'd done the one thing he'd sworn he'd never do: fallen for a woman on a surface level.

The beer bubbled in his gut, threatening to come back up as he called himself ten kinds of fool. The only person he could blame was himself. Bailey hadn't deviated from her declaration of no strings.

No wonder she understood Olivia so well; she was exactly like her.

Things had to change between them, but he had no fucking experience with how to enact that change.

He needed to distance himself from her so he could get his brain back online and out of the track that'd always led straight to her damn bed, where he couldn't think rationally at all.

Streeter took a moment to gather himself and tuned back into their conversation.

"Do you think she's hungry?" Olivia asked.

Wally mewed pitifully.

"Probably."

"Should we feed her tuna?"

"It's too rich for her. Maybe a little saucer of milk?" Bailey suggested.

"I'll get it!"

Streeter walked in. "You'll get what?"

"Food for my kitty."

"Didn't you buy cat . . . things?" he said to Olivia as he looked at Bailey.

"Nuh-uh," Olivia answered. "Bailey said you'n me had to talk about keepin' the kitty before I got any stuff."

He rested on his haunches. "Tell me how Wally ended up in your care."

"We were at Walmart and Bailey was loading stuff in the car. I saw a box movin'. I went over and Wally stuck her paw up and waved at me. She *waved* at me, Daddy! Like she wanted me to save her. She started tellin' me she's all alone with no mama cat. And I understood her because we're exactly alike. I don't got a mama either, so we belong together. I named her Wally—"

"Because I've always called Walmart Wally World," he said.

"Yes! Then we brought her home and we gave her a bath and now we gotta feed her but we don't got kitty food."

"So there's no litter box either?"

Olivia frowned at him. "What's that?"

Streeter looked to Bailey for help, but she was trying to slip her shoes on and sneak away. He said, "Hold that thought," to his daughter before he stood to intercept the cat co-conspirator before she escaped.

"Where do you think you're goin'?"

"Home. I have a boot camp lesson plan to finish."

"But . . ."

Bailey peered around his arm and then stood on her toes. "Streeter. Don't be afraid of a tiny, motherless kitten that your tiny, motherless daughter rescued. The same tiny, motherless daughter who has a disconnect disorder who instantly bonded with this baby animal." She patted his cheek. "I'm sure it'll be fine. Besides, we both know you have a knack for taming pussies."

"Jesus, woman."

She said, "Good-bye, Olivia. Good-bye, Wally."

Streeter turned to see his daughter holding up the puffball and forcing the kitty to wave its paw at Bailey. "Bye!"

"Oh, two other things you should know. Olivia climbed inside the birdcage today at the library and she's banned from the children's section for two weeks. And she threw an absolute screaming fit today at the Learning Center. So there was no way I could separate her from that kitten. That is your responsibility, Streeter. Not mine."

She vanished into the storm before he could say, "I know."

The almost clinical detachment with which she'd described her day with his daughter reinforced his decision to take a break from her.

That's a little junior high–ish, isn't it? Ignoring her to see if she really likes you? To see if she'll miss you and be the first one to crack and come crawling back?

Maybe. But that was the extent of his relationship experience outside of marriage and it was all he had.

So after Olivia pitched a fit about eating her supper at the table without the cat in her lap, and afterward called him a "big meanie" because he'd refused to allow the kitten in the bathroom during her bath, and she'd sobbed when she learned that Wally would not be sleeping in her bedroom, he struggled with yielding to Olivia's hysteria.

But when the damn cat wouldn't stop meowing in its box in the living room, he told himself it wasn't giving in, letting the kitten snuggle in Olivia's bed.

He told himself it wasn't giving in to his body's demands when he texted Bailey at eleven o'clock and asked her to come over.

He told himself he wouldn't beg her to stay the night after they'd fucked into exhaustion.

He told himself—promised himself—after Bailey rolled out of his bed at three a.m. that he'd be stronger tomorrow.

⟜

Since a veterinary visit had been scheduled for the trail horses at the Split Rock the next morning, Streeter had texted the veterinarian,

August "Fletch" Fletcher, about examining the kitten too. Fletch agreed, which required Olivia to hand over her cat, much to her dismay. His daughter had been under the mistaken impression she could take Wally to boot camp with her.

In hindsight, he should've known she'd try to game the system when she went from despondency to calm acceptance of the day's plans in about one minute.

He'd returned from morning cattle check just shy of noon when his cell phone rang and the caller ID read SERGEANT B.

"Hello?"

"Can you hear this?" The sounds of Olivia's shrieking burned through the earpiece.

"What's wrong with her?"

"I don't know. I've tried everything to calm her and nothing has worked. Come and get her. She's disrupted enough of everyone's day." Bailey hung up.

"Fuck."

"Problems?" Fletch said behind him.

Streeter spun around. "Olivia is throwin' a tantrum. Probably about not havin' that damn cat with her."

Fletch was cuddling the kitten close to his chest. "He is a sweet little thing."

"He?"

"Yep."

"That's a surprise. But the sex won't make a damn difference to Olivia since she's professed her love for Wally."

Fletch stroked the kitten's head. "I know you've gotta go, but can I give you some advice?"

No. "Sure."

"Olivia havin' a pet is a good thing. She'll be starting school, and Tobin mentioned you're building your new house. A lot of changes coming up for her and Wally can be a stabilizing factor in her life."

"You got a PhD as well as a DVM, Dr. Fletcher?"

Fletch laughed. "Nope. I've got two kids and a wife who believes learning to take care of animals—cats, dogs, horses, cows, bunnies, pigs, goats—is necessary to a child's development."

"Christ, Fletch, you've got that many animals at home after you spend your days takin' care of animals?"

"Yeah. But I wouldn't trade it for the world. So how about you let me take Wally back to my clinic in Rawlins. My colleague will check him over, give him shots, prepare the paperwork. And when you and Olivia come by later to pick him up, she can watch a video we have for kids on the responsibility of pet ownership. Believe it or not . . . kids eat that shit up."

"Buddy, I don't know whether to hug you or ask if you can be my new BFF."

Fletch smiled. "Oh, I ain't bein' entirely benevolent. I fully expect you to buy all the kitty accoutrements from the clinic. And it ain't gonna be cheap."

"Deal."

Another fifteen minutes had passed by the time Streeter got to the conference room where the kids were eating lunch.

All the kids but Olivia, who sat with her back in the corner and glared at everyone between hiccuping sobs.

Bailey caught him peering in the window and intercepted him before he entered the room.

But it wasn't the smiling, joking woman he knew. This Bailey was every inch Sergeant Masterson. Hard eyes. Defensive stance.

"I put up with this behavior once. There won't be a repeat or she's out. Are we clear?"

That clipped tone grated on him as much as her impersonal attitude. But it allowed him to follow through with his plan of them taking a break. "I understand, Sergeant. I'm sorry you had to deal with her in that state again today."

She said nothing.

"The good news is you're getting a reprieve from both of us. We'll be back at the Split Rock next week. If I feel Olivia might still be a problem, I'll pull her out of camp myself."

"Streeter—"

He didn't respond. He walked past her, picked up his kid and left without looking back.

Chapter Twenty-One

*B*ailey had her second lupus flare-up in two weeks.

When she woke at three a.m., covered in sweat, with her knees, wrists and shoulders aching, she knew this would be a bad one.

If her brain hadn't been fuzzy, she might've gone into stealth mode like she had the last two times she'd had a flare-up. The first one occurred the weekend after she'd returned to Wyoming. Anxiety had kicked up a toxic cocktail. She'd convinced Harper she had tests at the VA outreach in Casper that required three full days. Nonmilitary personnel never questioned mysterious military requirements, especially during outprocessing. So Bailey had packed a suitcase and checked into a hotel in Casper with room service where she could sleep through the pain and avoid questions from her family on why she'd taken to her bed.

The last flare-up had been the weekend after she and Streeter had run into his former mother-in-law. She'd been lucky the full flare-up happened after the trail ride and after she'd found a hotel in Rawlins. Streeter had thought she was with Harper; Harper had thought she and Streeter had gone away for the weekend.

It was too late for her to escape now. She should've paid attention last night when that last orgasm had left her with a flash of tunnel vision and an instant headache. But no, she attributed that reaction and the tinges of joint pain in the aftermath to the very hard, very thorough and very creative way Streeter had fucked her. She shivered in remembrance of his intensity, his utter dedication to her pleasure and his smugness that he'd given her three orgasms in an hour.

Tears flowed down her face and dampened the pillow she'd curled into. How was she supposed to tell him about her autoimmune disease now? She revisited that list of reasons for keeping her lupus to herself, needing something to distract her from the aching hot spots in her body—even for a little while.

If she hadn't told her sister Harper about her diagnosis, why would she tell him?

Theirs was supposed to be a no-strings, no-emotional-attachment summer fling.

Streeter didn't need the additional weight of her health issues.

She'd taken care of herself for years; she didn't need anyone's help now.

And the biggest reason, the embarrassing, awful and selfish reason that no one knew—no one except her CO, the counselors and army medical staff—would end any relationship they might've had. Bailey cared about Streeter too much to ever burden him with that mistake from her past.

She crawled out of bed and stood. Every step to the bathroom hurt. She popped her medication and took a shower, staying under the spray until she emptied the hot-water tank. Clean clothes on, and a jug of water by her bed, she texted Harper.

I'm so sick today I can't get out of bed. Sorry I can't work. Going to rest. Please don't show up to take care of me. I don't want to infect your family. I'll check in later. XOXO

Hopefully Harper wouldn't be too upset since it was the first time Bailey had missed work this summer.

Bailey didn't send Streeter a text. He and Olivia had plans that would keep them away all day. Maybe by the time he returned she'd be able to lie convincingly about the "forty-eight-hour" flu bug.

God, she hated lying. But telling the truth would lead down paths she wasn't ready to travel with anyone.

Stretching out on top of her covers, she turned on her white-noise machine and succumbed to oblivion.

At some point, she dreamed. Fevered dreams. Ugly dreams. Dreams that crushed her hopes for the future. She rarely remembered more than snippets. But when she awoke it was as if a boulder had settled on her chest, preventing her from escaping. She couldn't breathe. She tried to recall specifics of the dreams so she could understand the sense of futility, the lingering feeling of sadness that clung to her every thought. Her head throbbed, which she took as a sign to stop peering into the dark edges of her mind, expecting them to make sense.

On a better day, Bailey would bounce out of bed and chide herself not to wallow.

Today was not a better day.

She was too exhausted and in physical pain to do anything more than shuffle to the bathroom, refill her water jug, eat a carton of yogurt and return to bed.

Rinse, repeat for day two. Or maybe it was day three.

Day three—or was it four, she'd lost track—persistent shaking dragged Bailey out of slumber. She'd dreamed of bombs and darkness, so it took a moment for her eyes to focus. In the light. On Streeter.

Why was he in her tent in Iraq?

"Bailey. Wake up. Aren't you supposed to open at WWC?"

Her thoughts cleared. She wasn't deployed. She was at the Split Rock. "I can't."

"Why?"

"It hurts."

"Where?"

"Everywhere."

A big hand rested against her forehead. A cool hand. She sighed.

"Baby, you're burnin' up." He pushed her damp hair from her face. "Have you been like this all weekend?"

She nodded.

"Why didn't you tell me?"

"Because there's nothing you can do."

"Bullshit. I can haul your stubborn ass to the damn doctor."

"No one can treat me without my consent." She tried to turn over and give him her back. "Now go away."

His hand on her shoulder held her in place. "Like hell I will."

She kept her eyes closed but the tears leaked past her defenses anyway.

Those rough hands cradled her face so tenderly she had to grit her teeth to keep from sobbing. "I get that you don't want me to help you. So I'm gonna go get Harper."

Bailey opened her eyes. "Don't."

"Tough. Your choices for help are me, your sister or I call an ambulance."

"Streeter."

He got in her face. "Choose."

She managed to raise her hand and touch his cheek. "You should've stayed an aloof asshole with me."

"Bailey."

"Fine. It'll be easier if you call an ambulance."

His beautiful green eyes narrowed. "Easier because they can't legally tell me what's wrong with you."

"If I tell you I'll be fine"—eventually—"would you leave?"

"Nope. I've watched one woman I love hide herself from me. I'll be damned if I'll let it happen with you."

Her heart, her lungs, her brain all froze.

Love.

Streeter turned his head and kissed the inside of her wrist. "Yeah, that's my clumsy way of sayin' I love you."

Oh god. He deserved so much better than her; how could this have happened?

"I love you," he said again, "and I'll sit right here all day until you decide that I'm not blowin' smoke just to get you to talk to me."

"Where's Olivia?"

"With her babysitter." He rubbed his cheek against the base of her hand. "That's just another reason why I love you, by the way. Because you care about my daughter."

I care about you too. More than I should.

"Do you wanna talk here? Or are you feelin' up to sittin' in the living room?"

"Don't you have to work today?"

His quirked eyebrow expressed his annoyance with the question.

"Okay. I'll get up."

"Coffee?"

"Sure."

Streeter bent down and bussed her forehead, then pressed a soft kiss to the spot in front of her ear. "Take your time. I ain't goin' anywhere." He stood and walked to the door, pausing inside the doorway to look at her. "But I will haul your butt outta that bed, babe, if you think you're gonna hide in here. Don't test me on this."

Okay, then.

After she heard him rustling in the kitchen, she shuffled to the bathroom. A shower helped, as did brushing her teeth and donning clean clothes. Tempting to call on her last reserves of energy and sail into the room as if she already felt one hundred percent better, but with the way her knees ached, it took effort just to hobble to the couch. Feeling Streeter's eyes on her, she glanced up at him. She bit back her automatic response of *I'm fine.*

"Do you want food too?"

She shook her head. "Coffee is good."

Streeter filled her favorite *U.S. ARMY* mug and set it on the coffee table. The pushy man didn't plop in the easy chair; he mirrored her position on the other end of the couch. He didn't immediately demand she talk; he lifted her feet onto his lap, stroking the section of skin above her ankle, showing her a simple, loving touch.

Bailey sipped her coffee and tried to order her chaotic thoughts. She finally opted to start at the beginning. "Two and a half years ago, after spending a week outdoors working on a community service project, I developed a rash across my face. It lingered for weeks. Then I discovered white blisterlike bumps in my mouth. I'd also been tired, achy, feeling feverish, and the doc diagnosed me with strep. Antibiotics, bed rest . . . I'd be as good as new and back on duty." She ran her finger around the rim of her coffee cup. "The antibiotics cleared up the rash, but the other issues had worsened. Next treatment was a steroid shot. That helped for a month. But the extreme joint aches, exhaustion, and headaches continued. My hair started to fall out in clumps. At that point my doctor told me my symptoms were likely the result of stress. I didn't disagree and opted to go on antianxiety medication."

"Did that help?"

She glanced up at him. "No. Then I began sleeping through my alarm clock. Showing up late or missing duty days entirely. Sometimes when I reported for duty, I didn't recognize my coworkers or know how to do my job. That was not typical behavior for me. My CO had to write me up, which forced a medical intervention of sorts, because given my erratic behavior, I think she believed I had a substance abuse problem. I spent a week in the hospital, convinced I had cancer or some weird disease I'd picked up overseas that they couldn't find a cure for. But they finally narrowed it down to one condition that's difficult to diagnose anyway. Lupus."

"Lupus," Streeter repeated. "What is that?"

"It's an autoimmune deficiency. It's prevalent among women of color, which is why it took so long to narrow down because I have no idea who my father was. Given my dark hair and skin tone, he could've been Native American or Mexican. Anyway, finally having a medical diagnosis should've been a relief, but that's when all the issues of living with this disease manifested." Bailey drained her coffee.

Without a word, Streeter got up and refilled both of their cups and settled back in. "I'll admit I don't know anything about lupus." The fierce look in his eyes indicated he'd change that ASAP, and Bailey wasn't sure if fear or relief was her stronger reaction.

"I can give you the basics. It's incurable, for one thing. It's not contagious. It can affect your organs, like shutting down your kidneys. Not everyone responds to the medications the same way, so it takes time to get that sorted out. But the medication can stop working entirely for no apparent reason. Then you have to start all over again trying to figure out what will work. So I'll be going along with my life, having lupus mostly under control and then . . . *bam*! The disease reminds me who's really in charge of my body and I have a flare-up."

"What's a flare-up like?"

"It depends. Rashes, blisters, fever, aching joints, headaches, loss of cognitive skills, extreme exhaustion for the major flare-ups. Sometimes it's minor, a twinge here and there. Or I fall asleep in agony and wake up fine. This time I woke up in the middle of the night with fever sweats, excruciating joint pain and the inability to even get out of bed."

"When did that happen?"

"Saturday."

"How often do you have them?"

"It depends."

"Okay. How many have you had since you've been in Wyoming?"

"Three. The first weekend after I got here. I checked into a hotel in Casper when I sensed one coming on."

"Who knew about that?"

"No one."

"And the second one?"

"Two weekends ago. When I said I'd be at the Turner Ranch."

"Where were you?"

"A motel in Rawlins."

"Jesus, Bailey. Why didn't you—"

She held up her hand. "I didn't tell you because there's nothing that you can do. I have to ride it out."

Streeter leveled that hard glare on her. "I get you shutting yourself away and tryin' to survive the flare-ups."

"But?"

"But why didn't you tell me you have lupus? And before you get pissy, baby, I told you the very ugly truth of my past and what I've dealt with. Did you honestly believe I couldn't handle you havin' a medical condition?"

"No, I knew you could handle it. That's why I didn't tell you. We agreed to no strings."

"Which has been a big goddamned lie for both of us since that first night. Yes, we fuck each other stupid at every opportunity, but that's not all we do. That sure as hell isn't all we are to each other, Bailey." He paused. "Is it?"

Lie. Lie and let him move on before he digs any deeper.

But . . . she couldn't. "No."

He visibly relaxed. "We'll circle back to us, but I wanna know how this diagnosis affected your military career."

"Basically, they're kicking me out. Because of the unpredictability of the disease, I've become nondeployable. The new government regulations are weeding out military personnel who are nondeployable. So I failed my last FFD."

"What's FFD?"

"Fit For Duty. The MEB—Medical Evaluation Board—has my case

and will make a ruling any day on my military pay disability rating. I have a dozen years of military service, so my severance package—"

"Hold up. There's no way you can stay on active duty?"

"No. During bad flare-ups I can't keep up with the physical requirements. My judgment is off too, which isn't as big a deal since I'm in supply and requisitions rather than operations. But I don't need my CO babysitting me." *Again* went unsaid. "She has enough shit on her plate without worrying that I can't do my job, which affects how our unit functions as a whole. We're only as strong as our weakest link and when I know that's me, it's time to let someone else step up.

"It sucks because I'd planned on being career military. I don't know what else I'm qualified for—that's part of the reason I'm in Wyoming. I had a ton of leave saved up and I knew the VA placement offices here would be less booked than the ones at my home base."

"So that's the reason for your vague answer about whether you're leavin' the military."

"Technically I've already left. I completed the outprocessing paperwork; I'm just waiting on confirmation of my disability rates and burning my leave."

Streeter drained his coffee and set the cup aside. "Given your reaction to me talkin' to Harper when I thought you were sick, I'm guessing she doesn't know you have lupus."

Bailey shook her head.

"Without bein' a dick . . . Jesus. You've had it for two and a half *years*. Doesn't she have a right to know?"

"I'd planned to talk to Harper about it, but after getting here and seeing her stressing about everything, I refuse to give her another thing to worry about."

"It's her right to worry about you. To be there for you. How do you think she's gonna feel when she finds out you've had this disease and didn't tell her—but you told Liberty?"

"Harper has always been way judgier about me than Liberty has," she retorted. "Harper didn't even know that I had babysitting jobs all through high school. She thought I was lazy and I'd be living off her because that's what Mom told her, and she believed it."

"What has changed?"

She blinked at him. "Excuse me?"

"You're back here and instead of tellin' her that you're here to deal with your career and health issues, you've let her believe all is just fine and fucking dandy with you. You're here to help her. Except, you ain't livin' at the Turner Ranch because then she'd know when you were havin' a flare-up, wouldn't she?"

Her face turned crimson.

"You're keepin' things from her like you've always done." He stood and paced. "I wish Danica would've been honest with me one god-damned time about what she was goin' through. One. Time. Oh, I'm certain she didn't want to worry me either. So I went on thinkin' every-thing was fine. But it wasn't even close to fine."

"Not the same thing at all."

His gaze bored into her. "You're fine with lyin' to your sister about why you missed work for three days?"

"Again, Streeter, what could Harper have done if she knew it was a lupus flare-up?"

"Because she can't fix you, she doesn't get to be there for you in any capacity?"

Bailey told herself he had a right to his anger. "I don't want her pity."

"Before I met you, pity and love were so hopelessly intertwined I never thought I could separate them. But you showed me I was wrong."

How was she supposed to respond to that?

Especially when her head pounded and her body felt battered?

She didn't want to fight with him. So she made the only concession she could. "I'll talk to Harper about it. Not when I'm like this."

"What better time for her to see firsthand how this disease takes a toll on you than when you're incapacitated?" he demanded.

"I'll tell her, but on my time frame—no one else's. Don't push me on this."

Whatever he started to say ended when he snapped his mouth shut. Then he spun on his heel and headed for the door.

Bailey closed her eyes. "Thanks for checking on me. I know you've got to get to work, so don't feel obligated to stay."

"Obligated." He released a mean chuckle. "I've been against spanking Olivia when she gets smart with me, but woman, after that comment, I'm *obligated* to tell you when you're feelin' better I'm gonna paddle your smart ass but good."

Startled, her eyes flew open.

Streeter was taking off his boots, using the bootjack she'd placed for him by the door.

He wasn't leaving?

When he said, "Nope," she realized she'd asked that out loud.

Then he sauntered toward her as he started to unthread his leather belt from his jeans.

"Whoa, wait a minute, cowboy. When you said spanking, I didn't think you meant with your belt."

"I believe I said we'd play a little slap-and-tickle when you're feelin' better, which obviously ain't right now."

"Oh."

"I'm takin' my belt off so the buckle doesn't dig into you when I'm holdin' you. We snuggling up out here or in your bed? You choose."

"Bed."

He said, "Hold on," and the next moment she was airborne.

It felt too good to be close to him to protest his manhandling ways.

After he deposited her on the bed, Streeter stripped down to his boxers and T-shirt before he crawled in next to her.

Despite the fiery feeling of her skin, she snuggled into him. Before she spiraled into that dark hole of exhaustion, she filled her lungs with his clean, comforting scent.

✑

Bailey woke up when her comfy pillow moved.

Soft lips landed on her forehead. "I hate to leave but I gotta get Olivia pretty soon."

She hated losing all track of time during such deep sleep. "You've been in bed with me all day?"

"I got up to eat and check my phone. But you weren't as restless when I laid next to you, so I crawled back in as soon as I could."

"Thank you."

"Are you gonna punch me if I ask how you're feelin'?"

"No punching today. I'm feeling less achy."

"That's good?"

"I hope so. I'll know more after I get up and move around some."

"You too achy for a kiss?" he murmured into her hair.

"Never." Bailey tilted her head back to rest on his biceps.

"God. I've missed you the past three days." He brushed his lips across hers, back and forth, just a sweet glide. A gentle tease. "Kickin' myself that I didn't check on you sooner." His tongue swept in to taste the inside of her bottom lip. "I'm imagining all the ways to punish you for goin' radio silent on me." He sank his teeth into her lower lip and tugged. "Thanks to some of those erotic images I fantasized about, I've spent most of the day tellin' my dick to stand down."

"Poor neglected dick." She licked the seam of his lips, loving that he parted them for her on a deep groan.

The kiss was slow. Thorough. Sweet and gentle and tender. Though they often kissed in this unhurried manner, Bailey couldn't help but wonder if Streeter knowing the truth of her condition would change how he kissed her.

Then Streeter's mouth wandered down her neck and his hand followed the contour of her body, over her hips, stopping between her legs.

"Need a taste of you, baby. Wanna make you ache in a whole new way." He blew in her ear. "But if you're not up for it—"

Her fingers circled his wrist when he tried to pull his hand away and she pressed his palm over her mound.

He chuckled against her throat. "Guess that means you *are* up for it. Take them panties off."

She might've given her ass sheet burns, she whipped her panties onto the floor so fast.

Streeter clutched the backs of her thighs and spread her wide open. "Think you missed me too. This sweet cunt is weeping for me." He licked her from her opening to her clit. "Three days without. No tease, I just fucking need this."

And he dove in, eating her with gusto. Licking, sucking, groaning against her soft wet flesh, making her entire body tingle and shake. And ache in the best possible way.

Parting her folds and lapping up her musky essence, rubbing his whole face against her intimate flesh, marking himself with her scent.

His obsession with making her come with his mouth was way sexier, way hotter than anything she'd ever experienced. He knew when she reached that tipping point and he shoved her over the edge, keeping her pinned so she didn't accidentally squirm away, latching his mouth to her sex as he drank her pleasure down.

After she was spent, he rested his face on the inside of her thigh. His free hand found that spot just below the crease of her leg, the erogenous zone he claimed as his.

When she came back to herself, she slowly opened her eyes to find him staring at her. "Wow."

"I could do that at least a dozen more times today."

"Mmm. I'd love it but I think your dick might feel left out."

He smirked. "He was kind of a needy prick today when you were sleepin' so I'm ignoring him."

"Harsh."

He planted his hands next to her head and kissed her. Lots of tongue, giving her a thorough taste of herself.

"I gotta go," he murmured against her lips.

"I know."

"Feel better, baby." One final smooch and he was on his feet, getting redressed. "Text me later so I know you're okay."

"I will."

Once again Streeter paused in the doorway.

She waited.

"Will you trust me with it someday?"

"Trust you with what?"

"The real reason you hide that you have lupus."

She watched him watching her.

"It's not an uncommon disease," he said softly, "and it's not a self-inflicted condition, so I don't understand why you treat it like an ugly secret. I've lived ugly secrets, and believe me, darlin', this ain't one of them."

Oh, sweet man, you don't know the half of it.

But rather than taking the chance and telling him the truth, she said, "And you know about lupus . . . how?"

Grinning, he held up his phone. "I Googled it."

She threw a pillow at him.

"You're definitely feelin' better."

Chapter Twenty-Two

⤜◆⤏

$\mathcal{S}$treeter's thoughts meandered as he drove back to the Split Rock from Tobin's ranch—or rather the "All Hale" ranch since he'd be living there soon enough.

Holt had been on-site today, and they'd gone over a few things that hadn't been addressed. All in all, he felt really good about the progress being made and the move-in date of mid-November.

He'd brought Bailey out to the site last weekend before they went to Tobin and Jade's for supper. Olivia had been more excited about the equipment on the site than the fact they'd be living there. He'd forced her to hold his hand after she'd raced off and tried to climb on the backhoe. His daughter hadn't minded holding his hand, which was a big step for her.

Bailey hadn't said too much about the place except it would have a great view.

He didn't know what he'd expected.

Maybe he had a fantasy where the first time she saw the space, she admitted it finally felt as if she'd found her home. And after she kissed him and confessed her love for him, he spun her around in a circle as she laughed, and the sun reflected all around them and everything slowed into slow motion.

Bunch of romantic crap. That wasn't him. It definitely wasn't Sergeant Masterson either. Bailey hadn't even told him she loved him. He didn't understand why she withheld those words. It was obvious in the way she acted around him she loved him. It was obvious in the way she treated his daughter she loved her too. Since the discussion about Bailey's lupus two weeks ago, things had changed between them. He, Bailey and Olivia had become a unit. Sharing breakfast at Bailey's every morning when Olivia skipped down to ask Bailey for her drums back. They spent evenings together, the three of them playing games or watching TV. Even splitting up into groups of two—Bailey and Olivia coloring at the kitchen table, or he and Bailey watching TV while Olivia played in her room with her kitten.

Then there was the adult time after Olivia was in bed. When they lost their heads in the passion they created together. Bailey didn't stay over past five a.m., and it frustrated him. Wouldn't it be better for her to have a solid night's sleep rather than getting up and stumbling to her trailer?

But he didn't bring it up because she'd make excuses.

Like when she refused to talk about how she was feeling physically.

Like when she told him to back off if he asked whether she'd brought up her lupus diagnosis with Harper yet.

Like when she closed up when he asked her postmilitary plans.

Then it all spun around in his head and he worried Olivia would knock on her door one morning and they'd find Bailey gone.

What sucked about the thoughts bouncing around in his head was he didn't have anyone to talk to. Wasn't his place to tell anyone about her health and career struggles in the hope it would shine clarity on *his* life. He'd just have to figure this shit out on his own.

Like that's anything new.

Bailey hadn't had a flare-up for two weeks—as far as he could tell.

Even when she'd been working more hours in Wild West Clothiers, helping her sister run the big "Going Out of Business Sale" that had brought in more customers than the shop had had in months.

Since Meghan still had two hours left for Olivia's daycare, Streeter parked at the ranch side of the Split Rock and entered the office.

Renner and Ted were arguing. Shouting at each other as their arms flapped.

"I never would've hired you if I'd known that," Renner snapped.

"You know I'm from Colorado. How could you expect anything different?" Ted retorted.

Damn.

Was this about weed? Streeter had smelled pot smoke late one night when he'd taken the trash out to the Dumpster. There hadn't been anyone lurking around, so he'd forgotten about it. Since the Split Rock didn't have a drug-testing policy, hopefully he'd let Ted off with a warning.

"You are *not* allowed to bring any of that shit in here." Renner leaned forward, slapping his hands on the desk. "Am I clear?"

"What in the devil is goin' on?" Streeter asked as he entered the office.

Renner and Ted glared at each other.

Not good. "Well?"

"Did you have any idea that Ted"—he inhaled and exhaled—"is a goddamned *Broncos* fan?"

"What?"

Renner threw his hands up in the air. "That's exactly what I said!"

"Like you're proud to be a *Chiefs* fan?" Ted scoffed. Then he gestured to the office. "Where's *your* team pride? Oh, that's right, Kansas City ain't got nothin' to be proud of with their football team, so no wonder you don't show it. When was the last time they won—"

"Whoa. Time-out," Streeter said, moving to the edge of the desk. "That's what this is about? Football?"

They both stared at him as if he'd said something stupid.

"What did you think it was about?" Renner asked.

Yeah, not mentioning his initial thought. "No clue. I heard you say he can't bring any of that 'shit' in here—"

"Ted thinks he can decorate his half of the office with Denver Donkeys stuff, which ain't happening."

Ted cocked his head. "Yeah, I can understand that seein' my 'Three-Time Super Bowl Champions' banner every day might make you jealous."

Renner actually growled.

Streeter's gaze winged between these two grown-ass men fighting over . . . football teams? Appeared it'd be up to him to ensure a cooler head prevailed. "As long as I've been here no one has filled their space with sports team knickknacks. Tobin didn't have nothin' like that around here either." Maybe out of self-preservation since his brother was a Broncos fan. "So I suggest you leave the personal stuff at home."

"Fine," Ted said.

"Fine," Renner said.

"But he can't stop me from wearin' my Von Miller jersey on game day," Ted said.

"Of course you pick a defensive player 'cause your offense sucks," Renner shot back. "You'll be seein' me in my Kelce jersey on game day."

"Glad that's settled. Now hug it out. I mean it."

A beat passed and then Ted and Renner both laughed.

"What?"

"You know that ain't happening."

"Fine. At least shake hands to agree to disagree or some damn thing." They bumped fists.

"See? That wasn't so hard." He addressed Renner. "Need anything to go up to the office? I'm headin' up there."

"Yeah." He snagged a manila envelope from an outbox. "Could you take this to Janie?"

"No problem." Streeter crossed the office space, stopping in the open doorway to turn around. "And you're both wrong. The best team in the NFL is the Patriots."

A loud thunk hit the door next to Streeter's head.

Seriously? One of these assholes had thrown a stapler at him?

At least they'd be hatin' on him and not each other.

The sun beat down as he hoofed it up to the lodge. Late summer's brutal heat meant he spent more time checking cattle. Plus, there hadn't been a drop of moisture since the downpour weeks ago. The ground had returned to dry conditions, the constant wind creating red dust devils that ensured dirt coated him by the end of his first hour outside.

He brushed himself off the best he could before he entered the lodge. He walked past a family of five sitting in the main foyer, all of them engrossed in their phones, not talking to one another. He tried not to judge, but if he ever took Olivia on vacation, they sure wouldn't be holed up inside responding to notifications on their phones.

Janie's office door was open but he knocked twice anyway, seeing she was on a call.

"No, that's fine," she said. "I'll discuss it with their father and get back to you tomorrow." She left her earpiece in but moved the microphone in front of her mouth off to the side. "Hey, Street. What's up?"

He passed her the envelope. "This is from Renner."

"Thanks." She leaned back in her chair and folded her arms across her chest. "What have you decided about bus service?"

"Excuse me?"

"For Olivia. To and from school. Are you driving her to the bus stop in Muddy Gap? The bus will stop at the end of our road and that's better for drop-off for us. I have to be here anyway, so I'm considering having the boys picked up in Muddy Gap."

Streeter had wondered when this would come up. "I planned on takin' Olivia in the mornin' and pickin' her up in the afternoon."

"Why?"

"Because she's goin' to school in Casper, not Rawlins."

"Which school are you sending her to?"

"Private Montessori school. They are kindergarten through third grade. Then I'll reassess our options."

"Good thing no one around here was counting on you to contribute to the car pool," Janie said with a huff. Then she added on, "Why is this the first I've heard that Olivia isn't going to local public school with the rest of the kids?"

Hard not to bristle at her tone or to explain that his daughter had different needs. Not special needs, just different. "Well, there's one of the biggest reasons. Location. Once our house is done and I'm workin' on our ranch full-time, we're twenty miles from here. That puts us closer to Casper than Rawlins. Plus this school has fewer students and smaller class size. That'll be better for her. The reason you hadn't known this before now is because no one asked."

"Okay, fine, I didn't ask. But I know that Gage has palled around with Olivia this summer. Does he know that he and Olivia won't be going to school together?"

"I don't know. Maybe if Bailey said something to Harper, he'd know. But I doubt Olivia mentioned it to him. She's in her own little world."

Janie rested her arms on her desk. "I'll miss seeing you at school events. Especially after your time at the Split Rock is done."

"That's kind of you to say, Janie."

She nodded, touching the tiny button on her chest that connected to her earbuds before returning the mike to her mouth. "Thank you for calling the Split Rock Resort. How may I help you?"

Streeter waved good-bye and walked down the hallway until he reached Wild West Clothiers.

The door was open so he meandered in. No one was at the front counter, but the stack of boxes blocked the view to the back room. He cut around a rack of jewelry, about to announce himself, when he heard arguing.

Harper raised her voice. "Really, Bailey? That's how you're gonna play this? *You're* mad? We've been working together all day, heck, all summer, and when you finally muster the guts to tell me something this important, you're shocked that—"

"Our blabbermouth sister Liberty already told you?" Bailey demanded.

Shit. Streeter froze. This was not good.

"For exactly this reason," Harper shot back. "She knew you'd drag your feet telling me about your lupus diagnosis."

"Because it's *my* business. My health, my life, my personal issue to bare to you, not hers! This is also why I don't think I can work for her. She'll treat me like her stupid kid sister who is confused about career options and physically depleted because of her disease, so obviously she needs to explain me."

"Meaning what?"

"I can't trust that she won't tell everyone everything about me, at any time she chooses, not waiting until I'm ready to share some of the most traumatic events of my life! Jesus, Harper, can't you see how I'd be way past upset about this?"

"Can't you see that I'd be even more unhappy with you if I hadn't known the extenuating circumstances around your absences? If Liberty hadn't told me about your condition, I'd be mad and think you were blowing off your responsibilities because the store was closing anyway."

"You were mad at me when I pointed out you needed to make a hard decision."

"It's not the same, Bailey, and you know it."

A pause. "You're right. Liberty broke my trust twice by revealing both of the things I'd told her in confidence. I can't ever trust her again."

"Are you really mad at her or mad at yourself, Bails? Liberty has been exactly where you are in her military career, so she knows what you're feeling—"

"That's where she's wrong. She doesn't have a fucking clue what I've dealt with in the past year. She was injured in the line of duty and

278   LORELEI JAMES

received an honorable medical discharge. My medical discharge isn't duty related, so to be blunt, she's a hero and I'm a zero. I don't have a choice about whether to continue my military career. It's over. Period. And maybe she had to go through months of PT to get back to normal, but at least they knew what was wrong with her. I wasn't diagnosed for six months. And things didn't get better after the diagnosis. It actually got worse for me. Much, much worse, so bad that even know-it-all god-damned Liberty doesn't know the half of what I went through and what I'm still struggling with."

Turn and walk away.

But he couldn't.

"Then tell me," Harper pleaded. "I want to hear from you—not her—why you are so embarrassed about this disease."

"I'm embarrassed because I've not handled having lupus very well." She barked a harsh laugh. "That's putting it mildly."

"Tell me all of it. Walk me through it."

"I can't stomach the idea of you looking at me differently, sis, because you will."

"I won't. And whatever you tell me? Will always and forevermore be between us."

Bailey sniffled. "Promise?"

"I promise."

"Okay."

Leave right goddamned now, man.

"Before the diagnosis I thought I was going crazy. Even the camp shrinks thought it might be a psychological disorder. I was dating Logan at the time and he was as supportive as he knew how to be, which wasn't much. But I never blamed him for his lack of understanding when I understood so little myself. I mean, I was in love with him and thought we could get through anything."

The pause nearly had Streeter shouting for her to get on with it, but he bit the inside of his cheek to stay quiet.

"I'd already gotten pulled from my regular duty station, pending medical results. I suspected my CO thought they wouldn't find anything conclusive, meaning it was all in my head. It should've been a relief to have a diagnosis. But that just forced everything to a head. I believed Logan and I would eventually get married, and he came to a doctor's appointment with me. The doc didn't pull any punches, warning me that my military career was over. Then he addressed the physical issues, the severe depression, the potential for chronic pain, which could cause a dependency on pain meds. He also suggested if we wanted children to look into adoption, because chances were fifty-fifty I'd pass the disease on to a child.

"When I got back home, I holed up and cried about the loss of everything I'd ever wanted, which kicked off my first serious lupus flare-up. Logan saw firsthand what he'd be dealing with if he stayed with me, so he didn't."

"He didn't?" Harper repeated. "Did he break up with you?"

Streeter held his breath.

"Yeah. He said a bunch of stuff, including wanting kids of his own someday, which wouldn't happen if he stayed with me. What sucked was we worked together and I still had to see him every day. While I suffered through the flare-up, he moved on. Maybe if I hadn't had to watch him fall for someone else I would've been okay, instead . . ."

Please don't let it be true. Please don't say what I fear you're about to.

Bailey cleared her throat. Her voice was fairly soft but crystal clear when she said, "Instead I thought I might as well end it."

"End him?" Harper asked.

"No. End myself."

No. No, no, no, no, no, no, no.

Streeter's vision went black and he faced the wall, pressing his forehead into it to keep himself upright since his knees were buckling.

"But you didn't, Bailey," Harper said gently. "You didn't follow through."

"Because my roommate came in and saw me with the gun I wasn't supposed to have in private quarters."

No. No, no, no, no, no, no, no.

"Sweetheart. What happened after that?"

"She turned me in, as she was supposed to. They put me under suicide watch for forty-eight hours and sent me back to Fort Jackson."

"Oh, baby girl, I'm so sorry," Harper said. "How long ago did this happen?"

"A year. Due to the rash of military suicides, they didn't just cut me loose. Might add to their statistics, so I ended up working in a clerical position where my absences due to lupus weren't as big of an issue. I lost my FFD designation and they basically told me once my term of enlistment ended, they'd provide me with medical separation from the military paperwork."

Finally the racing of his blood sent a roar of white noise to his ears and he couldn't hear anything else.

But he'd heard what he needed to.

God, he felt absolutely sick.

He spun around to leave and lost his balance. When he attempted to catch himself on the counter, he knocked a box into the rack of jewelry, which came crashing down.

Harper was the first to see him and she shouted his name but he didn't stop.

Streeter couldn't stop moving—running—until he'd burst out the exit doors and reached the edge of the woods.

That was when Bailey caught him.

He flinched away from her hand on his arm, but he found the guts to face her.

He'd never seen a more haunted look on anyone's face.

Except for the two years following Danica's suicide. He saw that same goddamned look every day in the mirror.

Which was probably how he mustered the guts to say, "How could you keep this from me?"

Tears streamed down her face. "How could I tell you what I'd almost done after what you'd already been through?"

"So you think it was better that I found out from accidentally overhearing a conversation about it with your sister!"

"How much did you hear?"

"From the part where Harper told you she knew about the lupus from Liberty and everything after that."

Bailey shrank back. "So all of it, then."

"No, not even fuckin' close to all of it. This mornin' I told you that I loved you and now as I stand here lookin' at you it seems like I don't even fucking know you."

They stared at each other, breathing hard.

Finally Bailey wiped her face. He watched with a churning in his gut and a tightness in his chest as she regained her composure—military style.

"You're right. You don't know me and I certainly never wanted you to know this about me. I never wanted anyone to know, which is why no one does. Or did, anyway."

"I trusted you. Do you think that was easy for me?"

"No."

"So what do I do with this knowledge now?"

"Nothing. You've known all along I planned to leave at summer's end. That hasn't changed. I hope our time together showed that you deserve more happiness than the little you allowed yourself." She stepped back. "I never meant to hurt you, Streeter."

She walked away from him.

"That's it?" he shouted. "You drop that bombshell and leave the damn thing here for me to defuse? Or is it supposed to level me?"

She stiffened and stopped.

"Who am I supposed to talk to about this when the only person who can give me answers to my questions is you?"

But she didn't turn around and give him a second look.

Still reeling, he managed to get back to the barn, but he didn't remember a single step he took to get there. He climbed into his truck and burned rubber getting back to the employee compound, but when he arrived, Bailey's SUV was already gone.

Fuck.

He closed his eyes, but the phrase *Bailey tried to kill herself* echoed like a death chorus in his brain.

Along with a million questions.

Would she have gone through with it if her roommate hadn't stopped her?

Had she tried again?

Had she *thought* about trying it again?

Was she on antianxiety meds?

Had counseling helped? Back then? What about now?

Jesus. His brain felt like it'd explode. He needed a damn drink.

Inside the trailer he found Meghan gathering her things to leave and Olivia holding Wally.

"Daddy. Guess what? Meghan's friend who is a drummer is playin' with her band in the park! Can we go? Please?"

"Uh. Meghan, what's she talkin' about?"

Meghan petted Wally's head. "My friend scored tonight's 'music in the park series' band gig in Casper so it'll be wicked cool. You two should totally come. There's a hot dog feed beforehand, so one admission gets you into both events."

"People just show up?"

"Yep. Bring your own chairs, blankets and cooler." She looked at Olivia. "Sorry no pets allowed, miss."

"No pets or just no *cats*?" Olivia asked suspiciously.

"No dogs, cats or pet pigs," she said, chucking Olivia under the chin.

Olivia's eyes lit up. "You can actually have a pet pig like Wilbur and Babe?"

Streeter sort of wished Meghan had skipped out before she mentioned that, because now Olivia would beg for a pet pig. She'd seen *Babe* and *Charlotte's Web* far too many times to let it go. Then again, she had stopped asking if she could dye her hair pink.

"You'll like the music," Meghan assured him. "It's not rap."

An open-air concert away from here might be exactly the distraction he needed tonight. "All right, Meghan, you convinced me. We'll see you there."

After Meghan left, Olivia said, "Yay! I'm gonna go down and tell Bailey to get ready."

His hurt squeezed him. He wished he had a disconnect so he could never give Bailey a second thought.

No, you don't. You don't fall out of love with someone in one hour.

"Hold up, Olivia. I saw Bailey earlier and she's busy tonight, so it'll just be us."

"Oh. Okay."

"Let's get snacks packed and hit the happy trail, partner."

Chapter Twenty-Three

$\mathcal{B}$ailey hadn't driven far. Just back up to the main parking lot at the lodge. She wedged her SUV between two RVs, hiding her vehicle so Streeter would think she'd left.

Despite the hollowness that had taken over her thoughts, she couldn't just leave her sister like that. She wasn't surprised to see Harper had turned the sign to Closed, nor was she surprised that she hadn't locked the door.

Harper had moved to the window in the back room that overlooked the sloping hills of the grounds.

"I'm sorry I took off after him like that."

Harper spun around and raced toward Bailey, pulling her into a tight hug. "You had to go. But I'm so glad you came back. I've been sitting here thinking, and that's never good." She squeezed Bailey tighter. "I love you. Period. No 'ifs,' 'ands' or 'buts' about it. And it scares me to the bone that I might not have ever had the chance to tell you that, Bails."

"I know."

"I hate that you were too embarrassed to tell me about what you'd gone through alone—" Her voice caught.

"I know that too, sis," she whispered back.

"So no more of this secretive shit, okay? No more learning important things about you from someone else. No more keeping things from me because you're afraid I can't handle them. I'm stronger than you give me credit for."

Bailey let her tears fall. "That's exactly the wrong thinking, Harper. You are the strongest woman I know, and I never wanted you to see me as a gutless coward who thought about checking out of life rather than dealing with the blows I'd been dealt."

"But you didn't check out," she said fiercely. "You're here and I'm here and we're calling Liberty because you're not keeping this from her either. That way you'll only have to tell it once and we'll put it behind us."

She'd have to tell it again if Streeter demanded answers, but somehow she knew they were done.

She hadn't ever felt this level of despair and she had no idea how she'd get through it.

Harper started to let her go, but Bailey held on. "Please don't let me go. Not yet."

"Of course, sweetheart. For as long as you need." Harper rubbed her back and soothed Bailey as she sobbed, from fear and relief because she knew she wouldn't have to deal with any of this alone ever again.

When Harper's blouse was soaked clear through on the left side and Bailey had no more tears left, Harper released her. She pressed a lingering kiss to her forehead. "Better?"

"Some."

"Good. So I'm hoping that me bringing up Streeter ain't gonna turn those waterworks back on."

"Maybe a little, but I'll try to rein it in."

Harper took her hand and led her to the two conference chairs that faced each other. "What happened?"

"First lemme ask you . . . you know how Streeter's wife died?"

She nodded. "It's too horrific a story to gossip about. I figured if he wanted you to know, he'd tell you. Here he's built a solid community of people that have let him move on from it." She paused. "When did he tell you?"

"The first night after we slept together. The whole time he was telling me, I knew that him finding out I'd considered doing what his wife had done would be the ultimate betrayal and bring back all those bad memories for him."

"But you continued to sleep with him."

"Yes. The sex is outstanding, and I couldn't just do the one-and-done thing because of . . . let's just say his sexual past is complicated and leave it at that. So I swore I'd let my body get involved with him but not my head. Not my heart."

"And how's that going for you?" Harper asked.

"Not worth a damn. I love him. I even have maternal feelings for his daughter. Which given the way things started out is a small miracle."

"How does Olivia feel about you?"

"You mean will she be devastated when I'm not around anymore? No." Not that she could explain the reasons for that either. That was when it occurred to Bailey just how many secrets she'd been keeping—not just her own. No wonder she was mentally exhausted. "The world fell away when it was just us. He'd seen himself as daddy for so long that he'd neglected the sexual side of himself. I helped him reclaim that. And I have zero regrets about it." She swallowed hard, tamping down the sadness that she'd never bask in his passion again. "He'll find someone else eventually. Maybe he'll even be thankful for our short time together. But there's no doubt he saved himself a lot of grief by letting me go."

"Bailey. You're acting like this is a done deal. Like there's no room for understanding or for forgiveness from him."

"From his perspective? There isn't. It's over."

Harper opened her mouth. Closed it. Opened it again and said,

"You're so wrong, honey, but if you wanna live in denial for a while, if it makes it easier for you, then fine. I'm here for you." She pulled out her phone. "And we're calling Liberty so she can be here for you too."

"Do we have to?" God. She sounded like a whiny kid.

"Yes. But I have something that'll make this difficult conversation more palatable."

"What?"

"A bottle of rum."

❧

Two hours later, Bailey didn't feel cleansed, but she did feel lighter. She'd had no idea how heavy that burden had become until she'd shared it with her sisters.

After she and Harper had countered their tipsiness with a pot of strong coffee, they tackled cataloging the remaining merchandise. Throughout the past week of closing the store, they'd talked of options regarding the future of WWC. Even maintaining an updated website with strictly online sales was more effort than Harper wanted to expend at this point.

Bailey understood her sister needed a full break, but keeping a visual record with photos of the existing inventory meant if Harper decided to have a pop-up store a few times a year, half the work would already be done.

She walked down the hill just past dusk, opting to leave her car where it was. It'd be easier all around if Streeter believed she'd moved out.

As she considered the complications for the parents if she canceled the last boot camp on Friday, she decided she'd suck up her reluctance to meet Streeter face-to-face and end the camp as she'd originally intended.

No one sat around the fire pit tonight, not a surprise given that the heat of the day still lingered. She noticed Zack slumped in a chair. Slumped and looking surly. Slumped, looking surly and smoking a joint.

Shit.

Split Rock didn't do drug testing. But such a blatant act would likely get him fired.

"Hey, Zack. Uh, you're not as alone as you might think, so I'm suggesting you ditch the joint before someone else sees you out here getting high."

"Maybe I kinda wished that would happen." He sighed and stubbed out the blunt, and it disappeared from view. "Sorry. Feelin' sorry for myself."

"Sounds familiar."

"Be glad you don't have a roommate." He'd said *roommate* with total sarcasm.

"I get it. Streeter and I had a huge fight today too."

He snorted. "I'm supposed to say it's not the same thing—"

"But it is. From my point of view, it seems trite to call ours a lovers' quarrel when it ended our relationship."

Zack's eyes went wide.

"Are you more surprised that Streeter and I are done? Or that I know you and Ted are more than merely roommates?"

"Both, actually." He studied his hands. "How did you know?"

"I overheard you guys when you had the windows open."

He looked stricken. "Then does Streeter know?"

"If he does, he didn't hear it from me."

"Thank god. That would kill Ted if his beloved boss knew he swung that way. And that circles back to the fight we had." He closed his eyes. "I'm tired of hidin' and pretending we're best friends. Roommates. Coworkers. Buddies from the same town. When we've been together since we were fifteen. I thought we'd leave the secrecy behind once we left behind our asshole families who wouldn't understand, but he still drags that fear with us everywhere we've been. It's exhausting."

"I know what you mean about keeping a secret that in the end . . . no one really gives a damn about because they're so busy keeping their own secrets."

Zack looked at her. "What secret are you keepin', Sergeant?"

She folded her arms over her chest. "I have lupus. It's the main factor in me leaving the military."

"My friend's mom has that. It sucks. It's painful and unpredictable, if I remember right."

"That it is."

"I'm sorry."

"Thanks."

"Have you ever tried cannabis? I remember that helped her."

She shook her head. "Couldn't chance I'd fail a drug test in the army. But now that I'm out, there are a few things I'd like to try if I move someplace where it's legal."

A strange silence stretched between them. Was she supposed to say sorry that his partner was still half in the closet? Before she could say anything, Zack spoke.

"Thanks for bein' cool about this, Bailey."

"Thanks for not scooting your chair away from me like I have a disease." She paused. "Oh, right, I do have a disease. It's just not contagious."

He laughed. "That's where we're alike. Bein' gay ain't contagious either."

"I hope you and Ted kiss and make up."

"We will. That don't mean anything will change." He paused. "Hope you and Streeter get things figured out."

She couldn't even manage a small smile for him when she felt so hollow inside. "Night, Zack."

Inside her trailer, Bailey poured herself a bowl of cereal for supper. Then she took a long, hot shower, which had no effect on drowning out the voices in her head. She feared sleep wouldn't come, given the day she'd had, given the live wire her emotions had become, but she crashed almost as soon as her head hit the pillow.

❧

Olivia didn't show up asking for her drums back the next morning.

Or the morning after that.

Bailey half expected that Olivia wouldn't show up for the final day of boot camp, but she was there in her bossy, pigtailed glory.

She followed the camp rules to the letter. As a matter of fact, all the kids did.

They'd all come so far—such a huge improvement from the first time she'd stumbled into mass chaos at the start of the summer. She wasn't big on speeches, but at the end of the day, these kids deserved something.

She'd ordered pins shaped like combat boots and engraved with the year, a little token for them to remember their accomplishment. Hopefully it'd also remind them to be respectful and disciplined outside of camp.

Olivia was the last to leave, as usual. Since Bran was hanging around with the boys, waiting for Harper, Bailey slipped out the back door. The only thing that kept her tears at bay was the *they're better off without me* mantra she repeated one hundred thirty-seven times as she booked it to her trailer.

She had so few belongings it didn't take long to box them up and set them by the door. She spent her last night at the Split Rock much like the first night she'd arrived: alone, wondering what was next.

After loading her SUV early the next morning, she returned Olivia's drums along with the good-bye gift she'd purchased for her.

She'd given Streeter nothing.

Except her heart.

Scratch that, she'd given him heart*ache*. But he was a strong man.

He'll get through it.

Bailey repeated that mantra over two thousand times on the drive to Harper and Bran's place. She'd screamed it. Sobbed it.

In the aftermath she had no choice but to believe it.

Chapter Twenty-Four

$\mathcal{S}$aturday morning Streeter stumbled over the buckets that comprised Olivia's drums, which had been set directly in front of his door.

The feeling of being utterly lost that he'd suffered through the past five days since he'd last spoken to Bailey intensified by about a million.

She really was gone.

She'd really left, and left it like this between them.

Unresolved.

Goddamn her.

But what had he expected? He hadn't made an effort to talk to her. He could tell himself over and over that he avoided her day after day because he was too hurt, too heartbroken, too blindsided by such a huge omission to speak rationally or without making things worse.

But the real truth was somehow harder. Scarier.

Streeter wanted to understand.

He wanted to forgive her.

She'd healed him and he wanted a chance to help her heal.

What the fuck was wrong with him? How had he let it go on for five fucking days? He should've . . .

Infuriated with himself, he turned around to punch the trailer or some goddamned thing, when Olivia appeared.

"Daddy?"

He dropped his hand to the side. "Hey, punkin."

She spied the drums. But instead of her joyfully saying *Yay!* and asking if she could play them, she peered around him, looking toward Bailey's trailer. "Why'd she just give 'em back?"

He tried to smooth her extreme bedhead. "Probably because she's moved away."

Olivia's reaction . . . not what he'd expected to say the least.

She shoved away from him and ran down the plank walkway until she reached Bailey's trailer. She started beating on the door with both fists. "Sergeant B! Come out right here now!"

No response.

More pounding. "You wouldn't just leave! You said we were friends, and friends don't do that! I mean it! Come out here right now or I'll scream!"

The last thing he needed was an epic Olivia meltdown.

Just then Wally darted out between Streeter's legs and hightailed it down the walkway.

Shit. Wally was a damn house cat. If he took off Olivia would be inconsolable.

Streeter's heart raced a million miles an hour as he slowly stalked the kitten. Wally stopped to sniff and then peered over the edge of the walkway, crouching low, preparing to pounce on something in the grass. In a panic, Streeter said, "Wally, no," which caught Olivia's attention.

She stopped beating on the door, lowered her hands and snapped her fingers. "Wally. Come."

Wally backed up and then happily bounded toward Olivia in that funny way that kittens had. When he reached her, he twined through Olivia's bare calves, meowing.

She reached down and scooped him up. "Good boy."

Not only was Streeter dumbfounded that the cat listened to Olivia, she'd stopped the impending meltdown herself, out of concern for her kitty.

Bringing home that cat was the best thing that had ever happened to her.

Wrong. Bailey *is the best thing that ever happened to her. And to you.*

Olivia cradled Wally in her arms as she walked back.

"Daddy, you gotta remember to close the door. Wally can't be outside if he's not on his leash."

"Sorry. I forgot. But how did he come right to you when you called him?"

"I've been training him. He's a really smart kitty. Smarter than a dog." Then Olivia noticed the four big boxes stacked behind the buckets. "What's that?"

"No idea. Let's take 'em inside and find out."

While Streeter carried the boxes in, Olivia got dressed.

And she didn't immediately demand they open the boxes. She stared at them warily while she ate her cereal. She didn't ask about them again until after she'd fed Wally. She wandered over to where he sat in the easy chair and climbed into his lap.

He kissed the top of her head. "You ready to see what's in there?"

She nodded.

Streeter used his pocketknife to cut the tape on the biggest box, which had OPEN ME FIRST printed on the top.

Inside the box was an envelope, which Olivia immediately plucked up and passed to him. "Read it, Daddy."

"But it's addressed to you."

"You read it," she repeated.

The girlish loops of Bailey's writing threw him off. He'd expected her handwriting to be more military style.

"Daddy. Read it."

"Okay."

Olivia,

Never stop marching to the beat of your own drum.

Love always,
B~

This woman . . .

"I don't get it," Olivia said.

"I know you don't, sweetheart, but you will one day."

They opened the remaining boxes and Olivia didn't say a word.

Finally Streeter said, "This is a really nice drum set. A real one. Aren't you excited?"

She shrugged.

"What's wrong?"

"It's still better to play the old drums for her than the new drums without her."

Oh, baby girl. I know exactly what you mean.

⁓

True to her word, Olivia didn't play her new drum set that night. She didn't play her old drum set either.

She hadn't mentioned she missed Bailey, nor did she ask about her, but her silence spoke volumes.

By Monday morning, Streeter had had enough. As soon as Meghan arrived, he woke Ted up and informed him he'd be on the early cattle check. Then he drove out to the Turner Ranch.

His hopes sank a little when he didn't see Bailey's SUV.

Bran met him on the porch steps, not Harper. "Streeter. I don't gotta ask what you're doin' here."

"Where is she? And please, man, don't say you can't tell me."

"I got no issue tellin' you." He sipped his coffee. "She's in Jackson."

"Jackson Hole?"

"No. Fort Jackson, in Jackson, South Carolina."

All the blood seemed to leave his head. "Why?"

"Final outprocessing paperwork that she had to be there in person for."

"When did she leave?"

"Early Saturday mornin'." Bran held up his hand to stop further questions. "I don't know when she'll be done or if she's comin' back here."

"Bullshit."

"Have you tried getting in touch with her?"

Streeter glared at him.

"Did you march down to her trailer and have it out with her after your big blowup?"

"No."

"Have you called her since then?"

"No."

"Texted her at all?"

"No."

Bran shrugged. "You ain't makin' much of an effort, Hale."

"What do you know about—"

"I'm gonna stop you right there before you really piss me off. I love my sister-in-law. I wouldn't have the life I do if it hadn't been for her makin' a hard choice for both her and Harper years ago. And I know she's struggled since then. I didn't know the extent of it until she told me."

"She told you?"

His jaw tightened. "Yeah. All of it, difficult as that was for her. Believe me when I say there ain't nothin' I wouldn't do for her. So I'm gonna give you some advice. You want her? Go after her with everything you've got. She's fought for her sisters, fought for her place in the world, fought for her country, but she's never had anyone fight for *her*. If you can give her the life she wants, the happiness she deserves—the happiness that you both deserve after the sheer amount of shit that life has dealt you both—then prove to her that she's worth fightin' for. Show her that she belongs with you and that you can handle what it takes to belong to her."

Streeter said, "How do I do that?"

Bran clapped him on the shoulder. "Ah, man. This is the sucky part. You gotta figure it out for yourself."

Streeter walked back to his truck. Before he climbed in, he said, "Once I get there, though, I can call Harper and ask for specifics?"

"I'll do ya one better, buddy. You can call me."

⤳

It took an entire day to arrange the details.

Olivia wasn't nearly as nervous to fly as he was.

Car rented, hotel checked into and then he realized he had no way to get on base. And if he did get on base, the chances were slim he'd be allowed access to the temporary living quarters.

Streeter called Bran in a panic.

Bran pulled out the big guns—aka Liberty clearing the way with a promise of a private Devin McClain show for the base—and here he was. On base. Across from the apartment building where Bailey was staying.

Nervous as fuck.

They waited in the car for an hour before they saw Bailey walking down the sidewalk. Olivia was so excited she almost blew the whole thing. But honestly, he wouldn't have minded. He was just so damn relieved to see her, even if she lacked that confident military stride as she entered the building.

He waited ten minutes and texted his military liaison for the code to get into the building.

Then they waited another ten minutes before going inside and hanging the banner on the wall across from her room.

Thankfully it was a quiet time of day, so only two people passed them in the hallway, both women, both who sent them a thumbs-up and happy grins.

Heart hammering, he sent her a text.

Miss you ☹

The "..." appeared and disappeared twice.

Streeter signaled Olivia.

She began to pound on her snare drum like she was auditioning for *Stomp*.

Within thirty seconds, the door flew open and there Bailey stood. Her hair pulled into a messy bun, wearing his Big Johnson T-shirt and bike shorts, every inch of her five-foot-two frame vibrating with anger.

It—*she*—was the single most beautiful thing he'd ever seen.

Her mouth dropped open. Her gaze went from Olivia, still rat-a-tat-tat-tatting out a drum solo, to the banner between them that proudly exclaimed:

WON'T YOU COME HOME, SERGEANT BAILEY?

"Streeter?"

He couldn't not touch her. He framed her face in his shaking hands. "I love you, Bailey Masterson. Nothin' has changed that. Nothin' you've done, nothin' you've not done, nothin' you *thought* about doin', could ever change that. You are it for me. I know you love me, or you wouldn't have left me for my own good. Sure, we've got some stuff to sort out, but I want us to spend the rest of our lives workin' it out together."

Bailey's eyes searched his. "You're here."

"I am."

"And you brought your own marching band."

"Hey, *you* bought her the damn drum set."

She laughed. Even when tears rolled down her beautiful face. "I love you, Skeeter."

He growled. "I love you too, Barley."

Then she kissed him.

And his heart finally started beating again . . . or maybe he could finally hear it beating since the drumming had stopped.

"I missed you," he whispered against her mouth.

"I can tell." Then she stepped back and faced Olivia. "Hey, little drummer girl. I take it you liked my present?"

His bold daughter acted uncertain before she shook her head. "I like playin' my old drums for you. I told Daddy you're the only one I'd play these new ones for."

"So you haven't practiced?"

"Nope."

"Wow, girlie. You are a natural."

Olivia grinned. "I know."

Bailey laughed. "I can't wait to hear you play the other ones."

"So you *are* comin' back home with us?"

She crouched down. "You'd be okay with me always living with you, your dad and Wally?"

"Yep. And guess what?"

"What?"

"Daddy said if I was good on this trip, he'd let me get a pet pig when we get back!"

Bailey sent him an amused look. "Oh, really?"

"I said I'd *think* about it," Streeter reminded her.

"I'm gonna name him Wilbur. Because then both—"

"Your pet names would start with 'W.' I know how important that is to you."

Olivia said, "So, can I see your dorm?" and walked right inside.

"Maybe we should get out of the hallway."

Streeter crowded her against the wall. "But first, I gotta know if you love me enough to deal with that for the foreseeable future?"

"Yes. I love you, Streeter."

"Say it again," he demanded softly after he kissed her.

"I love you. I love her too. If she ever feels the same way about me . . . I'll just consider that a bonus. So I hope . . ." She hesitated.

"What, baby?"

"Is she enough for you? Because with my health issues I don't think I'd handle pregnancy well, and then there's the chance I'd pass lupus on to our child."

Streeter locked his gaze to hers. "I love *you*. I want *you*. I'd never ask you to jeopardize your health and then watch you live with the guilt if you did pass the condition on to a child. So yes, Olivia is enough. Plus, livin' in Wyoming, we'll have plenty of chances to help out with our siblings' kids."

"True."

He tipped her chin back up. "What else? Although we don't gotta deal with everything right this second."

"I know. It's just . . . I have no idea what I'll end up doing jobwise, postmilitary. I've had a job since I was twelve years old, Street. I don't know how to be idle."

"Maybe it's time you learn." He brushed a tear from the corner of her eye. "Here's where I remind you that we're currently building a house. Olivia is startin' school. I'll be workin' full-time with our cattle company. And you'll still be helpin' Harper as well as finishing that phone app. I don't see that you'll have a lot of downtime. Contributing to a household ain't just throwin' money in the family coffers, hot thing."

"I don't know what I ever did to deserve you, Streeter Hale, but I promise I'll work every day to keep our family happy."

"That's all I ever wanted."

"Hey," Olivia shouted from inside the room, "I think I can see our rental car from here! Does this window open?"

"Yeah, we'll definitely have our hands full with her."

⋙⋘

Later that night, after Olivia had finally fallen asleep midsentence, Streeter took Bailey into the hotel bathroom and showed her just how much he'd loved her and missed her.

Then they'd filled the big hotel bathtub so they could stay naked and twined together longer.

Surrounded by warm water and an even warmer woman, Streeter was so content that he'd started to float away in body and mind.

"Street?"

"Mmm-hmm."

"I know you still have questions about the conversation you overheard between me and Harper."

And . . . he was wide awake again.

"I'll answer them as honestly as I can. To start off, maybe it seems obvious, but my perspective toward an incident that I've tried like hell to forget isn't the same now as it was back then." She paused. "And what I went through isn't meant to help you understand what Danica might've been dealing with. That's not me being self-centered or flip."

"I know. I had to accept I'll never understand what Danica was going through." He pressed his lips to the top of her head. "I've also accepted that *I'm* different now. I'm strong enough for you to lean on. You can show me those dark corners of yourself and I'll help you shine a light on them, deal with them, chase them the fuck away without you havin' to fear that I'll abandon you when you need me the most. Ain't happenin', sweetheart. Ever."

Her silent tears dampened his chest. "Thank you."

"So we'll stay right here all damn night if we have to, if that's what you need."

Several moments passed before she spoke again. "When I don't have my thoughts on lockdown and I actually allow them to return to that night it's like some bizarre nightmare I'm watching happen to someone else. But then I realize I am awake and it happened to me. I chose to smuggle a gun into my quarters with the intent of ending my life." She smoothed her palm across his chest. "To be blunt, the question of why that haunts me has changed from 'what if my roommate hadn't shown up when she did?' to 'what traumatic life event would drive me to consider that as an option again?'"

"Is there an answer?"

"No. But I'm not expecting one. I'm just waiting for the question to change again, because it will." She played with his chest hair. "That's how I can deal with it as a past event. Change, acceptance, growth is crucial to survival. Before I met you, I had no choice but to handle it all on my own—the mental and the physical aspects. So it's really fucking hard for me to say, but from here on out I want to be an open book for you. My counselor here on base has helped me a lot. The counselor I was seeing in Casper, not so much."

"So when you told me seein' a counselor was 'an army thing'?"

"Not entirely untrue. The army required counseling after an 'intent to self-harm' incident. But yeah, I could've been clearer about that." She snorted. "Kind of like how clear my Casper counselor was when she saw me waiting for Olivia that day I took Olivia to her appointment, and took me aside to have a chat about you."

His stomach tied in a knot. "Jesus, were you'n me seein' the same counselor?"

"No. But it's a shared medical practice, Street. They're familiar with each other's cases. She had no issue warning me off a relationship with you. Even a temporary one."

"Baby. I hate that you didn't tell me this because I sure as fuck would've given that woman a piece of my mind the next time *I* took Olivia to her appointment." He squeezed her tighter. "I imagine that run-in just cemented your decision not to tell me about your past."

"Yep. So I'll be looking for a new counselor when we get back." Her hand stilled. "Counseling is a long-term therapy for me. Otherwise, I'd never look inward, and I refuse to let a past mistake dictate fear about how I live my future."

"Have I mentioned that I love you?" he murmured.

Streeter felt her smile against his chest. "A time or two."

A few moments passed where they were each lost in their own thoughts. But the air wasn't thick with tension. Clearing away the half-truths would take time, but for the first time, Streeter felt she trusted him completely. "Thank you for tellin' me."

Bailey tilted her head back and looked at him. "From here on out, Streeter, I promise you'll never have to wonder what I'm feeling because I'll tell you." Her teary-eyed gaze searched his face. "I love you. I won't run away because it's easier for me and better for you. I'll stay. I'll stay and fight with you. For you. For us."

"Same goes."

After that, their conversation lightened. They decided after Bailey finished her final paperwork, they'd surprise Olivia with a trip to the ocean and other touristy family vacation things before they headed back to Wyoming and Olivia started school next week.

They'd drifted back into the not-talking-at-all portion of the discussion, with Streeter on his knees with his head buried between Bailey's thighs, Bailey's whimpers escalating the closer she got to orgasm, when four hard raps sounded on the bathroom door.

They both froze.

Good thing he'd locked the bathroom door because as Streeter had predicted, Olivia tried to get in before she resorted to pounding to be let in.

"Daddy? Is Bailey in there with you?"

"Yeah. Why?"

"I just wanted to make sure she hadn't left again."

Bailey's eyes filled with tears. "I'm here, girlie. I'm not going anywhere ever again. Your dad is just … ah … helping me wash my hair. It's kind of a mess."

Streeter snickered against her thigh and she whapped him on the head.

"Okay," Olivia said with a sigh. "I'll just practice my drumming until you guys come out."

Drumming. In a hotel. At midnight.

Shit.

They both scrambled out of the tub and dried off.

"See? She's definitely gonna be enough for both of us for years to come."

Bailey kissed his chin. "I can't wait."

Chapter Twenty-Five

One month later . . .

FROM THE *MUDDY GAP GAZETTE*—
MISS MAYBELLE'S MUSINGS

Former Sergeant Bailey Masterson was the guest of honor at a surprise retirement party on Sunday night at the Split Rock Ranch and Resort. Co-hosting couples were Harper and Bran Turner of Muddy Gap, and Liberty and Devin Hollister (Devin is best known by his stage name, Devin McClain) of Denver.

Friends and family gathered around the newest returnee to the Muddy Gap area. When asked how she planned to spend her retirement, Bailey answered she'd been too busy helping out her family to look for other work.

Then Sergeant B was treated to a 21–water gun salute from the eleven children who participated in her summer boot camp.

Bailey gave a short speech, thanking her boot camp recruits and her family and friends for surprising her and making her proud to be part of the community once again.

That was when Streeter Hale stole the show, dropping to one knee and proposing to "the love of his life, the woman who chased him from the shadows into the light, the lady who owned his heart" and asking her to keep her combat boots under his bed for eternity.

That really turned on the waterworks—pun intended.

Then the newly engaged couple were serenaded with a drum solo by Streeter's talented daughter, Olivia, accompanied on vocals by Devin McClain and by Jake Turner on harmonica.

No official wedding date has been set, but look to the *Gazette* for exclusive details.

Epilogue

Thirteen years later . . .

"Smile!"

Olivia looked at her father and sighed. "Dad. Make her stop."

"No can do, sweetheart. This is a big day for all of us."

"Hold your drumsticks like a rock star and flash me devil horns," Bailey suggested.

"Mom!"

"Just one time. Then I promise no more."

"Fine." Olivia struck a pose that made both of them laugh.

"Perfect. I'm done."

Bailey lowered her camera and fiddled with the lens cap, trying to delay this moment as long as possible.

Then her daughter was right there, hugging her, not allowing her to hide her emotions. So much like her father.

"Mom. Don't you dare cry."

"Too late," she choked out. "I'm gonna miss you."

"I know. I'll miss you too. But it's not like you're not gonna see me every freakin' weekend during football season." Olivia stepped back and wiped her own tears. "I can't believe you guys bought football season tickets."

Bailey looked at this beautiful young woman they'd raised. It'd been an incredible journey—not an easy one—which was why it made milestones like this, the first day of college, so bittersweet.

"We're allowed to be proud of you and support you," Streeter said. "How many other parents can brag that their kid is in charge of the entire percussion section of the University of Wyoming Western Thunder Marching Band as a *freshman*? Uh. No one but us, sweets."

Olivia flashed them the smile that had only gotten cockier—sweeter, but cockier—over the years. "Hell yeah. Our drumline is gonna make fans scream for *us* instead of the football team."

She and her dad bumped fists. Then Olivia focused those blue eyes on her. "Do you remember after my first day of kindergarten? When I made you promise to be there for every first day of school for me no matter what?"

Bailey felt Streeter move in behind her and kiss the top of her head. "Of course I remember. It seems like yesterday."

"You kept that promise. Every year. I'm not a mushy-gushy girl, but thank you. Thank you for being my mom. Thanks to both of you for being the best parents in the world, especially on the days I wasn't close to the best kid." She smiled through her tears. "So . . . group hug!"

Maybe they clung to one another a little longer than usual, but they all deserved this.

Then Olivia stepped back. "I gotta go. Seriously." She looked at her dad. "And yes, I know the rules."

He raised his eyebrow and expected her to recite them, like he always did. "And what are the rules?"

"No taking drinks from people I don't know."

"And?"

"And never get in a car with someone who's been drinking."

"And?"

"And don't skip class."

"And?"

"And if I feel . . . off, or sad, or mad, or depressed or too stressed, anything that's out of the norm for me, call you guys, or my aunts, or my uncles, or my cousins, or my friends, or my counselor because I have so many people who love me and are willing to help me if I just ask."

Streeter just stared at her.

"What, Dad? Did I miss something?"

He smiled at her. "No, girlie, you hit everything right on. So, I think our work here is done."

Olivia hugged them both one last time and whispered, "I hope not. I still need you. Not every day like I did, but every day in my own way."

Then she waved and hustled away, her mind already on a million new things, like it always had been. Her blond hair swinging across her back, her head held high, her shoulders set as she strode off to begin a new chapter of her life.

Bailey said, "I'm trying not to be sad because there are such remarkable things ahead for our remarkable girl."

"We done good, Mama." Her husband, her love, her life, kissed her temple in the sweet manner she adored and said gruffly, "Come on, let's go home."

Author's Note

If you or a loved one is dealing with depression, please ask for help. For more information, visit or call:

Mental Health America, mentalhealthamerica.net

MotherToBaby, mothertobaby.org (Medications and more during pregnancy and breastfeeding)

National Alliance on Mental Illness, 1-800-950-NAMI (6264)

National Institute of Mental Health, nimh.nih.gov

National Suicide Prevention Lifeline, 1-800-273-TALK (8255)

Don't miss Lorelei James's

I Want You Back

Available now

LUCY

*M*ommy. What time will Daddy get here?"

Whenever the hell he feels like it.

Not an answer I could give my precocious eight-year-old daughter, even when it was the truth. "He said after six. Since it's now six fifteen, he'll be here at any moment."

Mimi sighed heavily. Then she kicked her legs up and hung upside down from the back of the chair, balancing on her hands. It was obvious to everyone she inherited her natural athleticism from her father. Embarrassingly I was one of those people who trip over their own feet . . . and everyone else's.

"You sure that hanging like a monkey in a tree won't upset your stomach?" I asked her. "Or give you a headache? I'd hate for you to miss an overnight with your dad."

"I have to practice so being upside down doesn't make me sick," she replied with another sigh, as if I should've already known that.

"Ah. So what are you practicing for this week?"

"It's between a trapeze artist or an ice skater. If I decide to have a partner I'll have to be used to being upside down."

Last month Mimi wanted to be an astronaut. The month before that a dolphin trainer. While I've always told her that she can be whatever she wants to be when she grows up, it's exhausting finding an activity that holds her attention. After spending money on dance lessons, gymnastics classes, martial arts classes, T-ball, soccer club, fencing, swim team, tennis lessons, golf lessons and horseback riding lessons, I'd put my foot down and said no new organized activities. If none of those worked then she needed to wait until she was older to try others.

Still, I feared she'd play the guilt card and I'd find myself buying tickets to the circus, a Cirque du Soleil show or a Disney on Ice program. Or . . . maybe . . .

"I'm sure your dad would love to take you to a performance." Not really dirty pool—Mimi's father, Jaxson Lund, was a member of the billionaire Lund family as well as a highly paid former pro hockey player, so money had never been an issue for him. And there was nothing he loved more than humoring Mimi's requests, even if it was to alleviate the guilt that he'd missed being a regular presence in her life for most of her life.

The doorbell pealed and Mimi squealed, "I'll get it!" twisting her lithe little body sideways from the chair to land lightly on her feet, agile as a cat.

I heard her disengage the locks and yell, "Daddy! I thought you'd never get here."

He laughed. That sweet indulgent laugh he only had for our daughter. "I missed you too, Mimi."

"I got my stuff all packed. I'm ready to go now."

Without saying good-bye to me? That stung. But I sucked it up and started toward the entryway.

"Sure. Just let me get the all clear from your mom first."

Then Jaxson Lund and I nearly collided as we turned the corner simultaneously.

His big hands circled my upper arms to steady me.

I had to tilt my head back to look at him as he towered over me by almost a foot.

It was unfair that my ex actually looked better now than he did when he and I met a decade ago. His dark hair was shorter—no more long locks befitting the bad-boy defenseman of the NHL. No scruffy beard, just the smooth skin of his outlandishly square jaw and muscled neck. His eyes were clear, not bloodshot as I'd usually seen them, making those turquoise-hued eyes the most striking feature on his face . . . Besides that damn smile. Hockey players were supposed to have teeth missing from taking a puck or two hundred to the face. I knew Jax had a partial, but he'd never removed it when we were together. The lips framing that smile were both soft and hard. Druggingly warm and soft when pressed into a kiss, but cold and hard when twisting into a cruel sneer. A sneer I'd been on the receiving end of many times.

That shook me out of my musings about Jax's amazing physical attributes.

"Hey, Luce."

Jax had called me Luce from the first—a joke between us because I warned him I wasn't loose and wouldn't sleep with him on the first date. An inside joke made me feel special—he made me feel special—until I realized Jaxson Lund used that killer smile and those gorgeous twinkling eyes as a weapon on every woman he wanted to bang the boards with; there wasn't anything special about me.

I forced a smile. "Jaxson. How are you?"

He retreated at my cool demeanor and dropped his hands. "I'm fine. You're looking well."

And people thought we couldn't be civil to each other. "Thanks. You too."

"Anything I should know before Meems and I take off?"

Meems. He'd given our daughter another nickname, even when Mimi was already the shortened version of Milora Michelle. "Nothing worth mentioning. She's been looking forward to this all week."

Those beautiful eyes narrowed. "So don't disappoint her, right?"

"Right."

"Luce. I'm not—"

"Daddy, come *on*. Are we goin' or what?" Mimi demanded.

"We're goin', impatient one." Jaxson hauled her up and cocked her on his hip with seemingly little effort, because his eyes never left mine. "We can do the switch back at the Lund Industries thing on Sunday afternoon?"

"You'll be there?"

"I work there, remember?"

In the past six months since Jax had joined the family business, I'd hardly seen him hustling around the building in a suit and tie, so I had no idea what his actual job title was. As far as I could tell, he didn't "work" there like I did. Sunday's event was a retirement party for a woman I doubted he knew personally. "I'm surprised. I wasn't aware that you knew Lola."

"The poor woman was tasked with getting me up to speed on all departments when I started at LI. I'd still be aimlessly wandering the halls if not for her."

"Lola will be missed, that's for sure. So if you want to bring Mimi's things on Sunday, that'll work. I planned on going for the two hours."

"Sounds like a plan. Speaking of . . . what are your plans for the weekend?"

None of your business. "Oh, this and that. Mimi has more things planned for you two than you could fit into two weeks, say nothing of two days."

His dark eyebrow winged up. "Now I'm taking that as a personal challenge."

Mimi held her arms out for a hug. "Bye, Mommy."

"Bye, wild one. Behave, okay?"

"Okay."

"Promise to call me tomorrow sometime."

She sighed heavily. "I'd call you all the time if I had my own cell phone."

I chuckled. "Nice try. Use Daddy's phone. Or Grandma Edie's."

"But all of my friends have iPhones."

"Eight-year-olds do not need cell phones." I sent Jaxson a stern look as a reminder not to swoop in and buy her one just because he could. Then I kissed her cheek. "Love you, Mimi."

"Love you too."

Jaxson gathered Mimi's stuff with her chattering away at him like she always did. I wondered how much of it he paid attention to.

Not my concern. I'd had to learn to let go of a lot of my issues with Jaxson's parenting style since he'd returned permanently to Minneapolis.

I waved good-bye and locked the door behind them.

⁓

As I readied myself for my first date with Damon, my thoughts scrolled back to the first time I'd met Jaxson Lund a decade ago . . .

I'd left work early to take my mother to the doctor. After I'd dropped her off at her place, I pulled into one of those super fancy deluxe car washes that offered one-hour detailing inside and out. Winter in the Twin Cities meant tons of road salt and freeway grime, and my poor car needed TLC. Not that my Toyota Corolla was anything fancy, but it'd been a major purchase for me after I'd graduated from college. My first new car, and I took good care of it.

With an hour to kill, I grabbed a magazine and a Diet Mountain Dew. The lobby wasn't jam-packed with other customers—which was a total contradiction to the lines of cars outside—but I embraced the quiet for a change and settled in.

My alone time lasted about five minutes. A guy blew in—the wind was blustery, but not nearly as blustering as the man yakking on his cell phone at a thousand decibels.

"Peter. I told you I'm happy to stay at the same salary." Pause. "Why? Because a salary freeze for a year isn't the end of the world for me. Especially if that means they can use that extra money to lure the kind of D-man we need."

I rolled my eyes and wished I'd brought my earbuds.

"No. What it speaks to isn't that I'm not worth more money. It shows that I'm a team player."

I tried to ignore the annoying man. But he paced in front of me, forcing me to listen to him as well as watch his jean-clad legs nearly brush my knees as his hiking boots beat a path in the carpet. From the reflection in the glass that allowed customers to see their cars going through the automated portion of the car wash, I knew he was a big man; tall, at least six foot four, with wide shoulders, long arms and long legs.

And huge lungs, because his voice continued to escalate. His pace increased. He gestured wildly with the hand not holding the phone. He couldn't see me scowling at him, as his head was down and his baseball cap put his face in shadow. Not that he'd looked my way even one time to see if his loud, one-sided conversation might be bothering me.

Look at me, look at me! My job is so crucial that I can't even go to the car wash without dealing with such pressing matters.

Ugh. I hated when people acted inconsiderate and self-important.

He stopped moving. "Fine. It's stupid as shit, but an increase of one dollar if it'll make you happy to have on record that my salary went up again this year. I'll let you keep one hundred percent of that dollar instead of your usual twenty percent commission." Pause. "Do you hear me laughing? Look. I'm done with this convo, Peter. Call me after the trade is over. Bye."

I flipped through a couple of pages.

He sighed and shoved his phone in his back pocket. Then I sensed him taking in his surroundings for the first time. The lack of customers, no car going through the car wash to entertain him.

Please don't assume I'll entertain you. He was definitely that type of guy.

I silently willed him to go away. But I'll be damned if the man didn't plop down on the bench directly across from me. I felt his gaze moving up my legs from my heeled suede boots to where the hem of my wool skirt ended above my knees.

Continuing to ignore him, I thumbed another magazine page and took a swig of my soda.

"Ever have one of those days?" he asked me.

The smart response would've been no response. I'm not sure what compelled me to say, "One of those days where you're enjoying a rare moment of quiet and some rude guy destroys it with an obnoxiously loud phone conversation? Why yes, ironically enough, I *am* having one of those days right now."

Silence.

Then he laughed. A deep rumble of amusement that had me glancing up at him against my better judgment.

Our eyes met.

Holy hell, was this man gorgeous. Like male model gorgeous with amazing bone structure and aquamarine-colored eyes. And his smile. Just wry enough to be compelling and "aw shucks" enough to be charming and wicked enough that I had a hard time not smiling back.

"I'm sorry. I don't normally carry on like that, but he was seriously missing my point."

"So I gathered." Dammit. I'd confessed I'd been listening in.

He leaned in, resting his forearms on his knees. "I'm serious. I'm not that annoying cell phone guy."

"Maybe not normally, but you were today."

"You don't pull any punches, do you?"

"No. Also now you've moved on from being 'annoying cell phone guy' to 'annoying guy determined to convince me that he's not annoying cell phone guy' . . . which is even more annoying."

His grin widened. "I'm supposed to apologize for that too? Okay. Sorry for interrupting your quality time reading"—he snatched the magazine off my lap—"*Redbook* and this article on how to prioritize organization in day-to-day life."

My cheeks flamed even as I scooted forward to snatch back my magazine. "Gimme that."

"After you answer two questions. First, are you married, engaged or currently involved with someone? And if the answer is no, will you go out on a date with me so I can prove that I'm not annoying?"

I laughed. "I actually believed you couldn't get more annoying, but I was wrong."

"Are you single?"

"Annoying and tenacious—there's a winning combo," I retorted.

"And she hedges yet again. Fine. Don't answer. I'll just read this fascinating article that's got you so engrossed you can't even answer a simple question."

"Gimme back my magazine."

He lifted a brow. "I doubt it's your magazine. I'll bet you took it from the stack over there that's for customers to share."

"Fine. Keep it."

"Let's start over." He tossed the magazine aside and offered his hand. "I'm Jaxson. What's your name, beautiful?"

Calling me beautiful threw me off. I automatically answered, "Lucy," and took his hand.

"Lucy. Lovely name. Please put me out of my misery, Lovely Lucy, and tell me that you're single."

"I'm single but I'm not interested in flirting with you because you're bored at the car wash and I'm convenient."

He flashed me a grin that might've made me weak kneed had I been standing. "I'm far from bored. Let me prove it by taking you out for dinner. I promise I'll be on my least-annoying behavior."

That's when I realized he still held my hand. That's also when I realized I was a sucker for his tenacious charm, because I said, "Okay. But if that cell phone comes out even one time I will snatch it from you and grind it under my boot heel as I'm walking away."

"I'd expect nothing less."

I tugged my hand free before he did something else completely charming like kiss my knuckles. "Are you single?"

"Yes, ma'am. And this is the first time I've asked a woman I met at a car wash for a date."

"This is the first time I've agreed to a date with a man I find a—"

"Attractive?" he inserted. "Amusing? Feel free to use any A-word except the one you've repeatedly overused."

"Calling you an asshole is an acceptable A-word?"

"Damn. Opened myself up for that one, didn't I?"

"Yes, in your arrogance."

Another laugh. "I'm definitely not bored with you. Now where am I taking you for our dinner date?"

I smirked. "Pizza Lucé."

"Hilarious, Luce."

"I'm serious. That's where I want to go."

"For real?"

"Why does that surprise you?"

"I figured you'd pick someplace more upscale."

"Sorry to disappoint, but I'm the pizza and beer type."

He leaned in. "I'd ask if this was a setup, with you being a sharp-tongued brunette with those big brown Bambi eyes, because you're exactly my type. But I stopped here on a whim, so I know my friends and family aren't fucking with me."

"Mr. Jaxson, your vehicle is ready," a voice announced via the loudspeaker.

I cocked my head. "You refer to yourself by your last name?"

He shook his head. "Long story that I'll explain over pizza and beer."

"Miz Q, your vehicle is ready," echoed from the loudspeaker.

Jaxson—Mr. Jaxson—whatever his name was—winked. "Lucy Q? What's the 'Q' stand for?"

"Nothing."

We stood simultaneously.

"Come on. Tell me," he urged.

"Maybe, as a single woman in a public venue, I didn't use my real name or initial as a safety precaution."

That declaration—a total lie—was worth it to see his smugness vanish.

Outside, the attendants stood by our cars.

No surprise that Mr. Annoying and Tenacious drove a Porsche.

But my eyes were on how spiffy my beloved blue Corolla looked. I smiled at the attendant and slipped him five bucks. "Thank you."

"My pleasure."

I looked across the roof of my car to see my date staring at me. "I'd say the last one to arrive at Pizza Lucé has to buy the first round, but my Toyota is at a disadvantage in comparison to that beast."

"I planned on following you, in case you decided to make a detour."

"Worried that I might come to my senses and change my mind about this bizarre date?"

"Yep." He grinned at me. "Lead the way, Lucy Q. I'll be right behind you."

The doorbell rang, pulling me out of the memory.

I slicked on a final coat of lip gloss and went to meet my date.

Damon smiled. "Lucy. You look fantastic." He handed me a bouquet of mixed flowers.

"Thanks, Damon, they're lovely." I stepped back to allow him to come inside. "I'll just take a minute to put these in water."

"No rush. Our reservation is at eight. We've got time."

Damon wandered through the main room, looking at the artwork hanging on the walls and the kid stuff that seemed to multiply across every horizontal surface every time I turned around. Points for him that he didn't react to the chaos that was our living space.

Surprisingly I wasn't nervous for this official first date. The potential of a second date would create more nerves, since most men never made it past the first date with me.

I'd met Damon at a business function. We'd hit it off and exchanged emails, then phone numbers. We'd met twice after work, so when he'd asked me out for dinner, I'd said yes without hesitation. I liked him. He was low key, but not so low-key as to have no personality like some of the business-type guys I worked with.

I arranged the blooms and set the vase on the dining table. "Thank you again for the flowers. Great first-date behavior."

"You're welcome." He frowned. "But this is our third date, counting meeting for coffee once and cocktails once."

Jaxson's sexy warning from years ago on our first date echoed in my head . . . *"By our third date you will know how perfectly wicked it'll feel to have my mouth all over you."*

Was that what Damon was hoping for? By assigning this outing a number? So if we made it to date five, then I'd fall into bed with him because it was time?

Wrong.

And here was yet another reminder of why I didn't date. I managed a smile. "Semantics."

Then he looked around. "Your daughter isn't here?"

Here was the awkward part. If I said she was with her father for the weekend, would he take that as the all clear for an adult sleepover? Or did I lie about having a babysitter so if the night sucked I could use Mimi as an excuse to end the date?

After I opted for a simple "No," Damon smiled. "Maybe I'll get to meet her next time."

"Maybe. For now, let's go. I'm starving."

Ready to find
your next great read?

Let us help.

Visit prh.com/nextread

Penguin
Random
House